MARESSA MORTIMER

Beyond The Hills

"But God forbid that I should glory, save in the cross of our Lord Jesus Christ, by whom the world is crucified unto me, and I unto the world."

Galatians 6: 14

Elabi Pronunciation

You might want to know more about the people and places in the Elabi Chronicles. Most of the names were derived from Latin words or names.

Macia –*mat*-sia
    Caecilia –say-*see*-lia
    Gax – Has a g sound like in Loch, so chax
    Ignava – ik -*na* -va
    Tima – *tee*-ma
    Grabus – has a strong guttural G, *gra*-bus
    Inritia – in-*ree*-tsia
    Elabi – e -*laa* - bee
    Mataiox – maa-taa-*yox*

Chapter 1

The first light casts grey shadows as Macia pads to the window, yawning. She sees the snow and thinks the strange light makes it look earlier than it is. She walks to the kitchen, needing something to eat before hitting the gymnasium. The timing of breakfast in relation to her workout is crucial; too late and she will feel sick, too early she will run out of energy. She eats, her eyes looking around the neat, spacious kitchen, devoid of personal touches. A tiny memory creeps in of warm smells, laughter, floured surfaces. She chews down hard, not just on the food, but the memory. She prefers the kitchen this way. Efficient, easy to maintain and straight forward.

Walking back to her room to get ready she passes the doormat. The grey light streams across it highlighting an unexpected cream rectangle. Macia bends over, surprised by the envelope, and even more surprised when she sees her name written across it. *To Macia*, it says in clear handwriting. She picks up the sealed envelope, turning it over in her hand, having recognised the handwriting immediately. It must have been delivered in the night. Macia went to bed late last night to finish a school project she needed to get just right, determined as she was to finish school with good grades to maintain her status. The envelope had not been on the mat last night. It is still very early.

Fear fills her mind, and she almost flings the letter away. Caecilia

1

has been acting strangely lately. Macia almost felt drawn to the newfound peace Caecilia displayed. But no, the joy and warmth that accompanied it smacked too strongly of the sort of erratic emotional response that could get you into trouble. And now a letter delivered in the middle of the night? Macia had been planning to report Caecilia's odd new manner to the council and is anxious she is too late. Would this letter implicate her as well? By far the safest course of action now is to send it to the council unopened.

And yet she hesitates and feels the creamy paper, wondering what is inside. It feels quite thick. It is a letter addressed to her from a classmate who, she must admit, she hesitates to report to the Council and she feels the personal significance of it. Before she can consider the implications of the emotional bond, Macia uses her thumb to slice open the envelope, pulling out the contents whilst slowly walking up the stairs. She can always send it to the council when she knows for sure it is something unhealthy. There is a folded letter, inside of which is a small bundle of thin paper. Macia looks at it briefly, intrigued by the odd thinness of the paper with its minute letters. She looks at the rough brown paper letter, the writing large and sprawling. Sinking on her bed she unfolds the paper, noticing that it's the first use of the sheet. Who would send somebody a letter on new, unused paper? What a waste. She looks at the letter, *"My dearest friend,"* it says and Macia gasps. What? She looks at the words again, her nose wrinkled up, something hard growing inside. *My dearest friend?* Who would say that?

She hesitates, then turns the letter over, reading the name at the bottom; Caecilia. Her friend? Her brain stutters over the word. Macia prides herself that she doesn't have friends. "Having a friend is an emotional connection," she had explained to her sister. "People with friends get themselves attached, they lose their rationale, their judgment gets clouded. I like to keep myself to myself, putting Elabi first, being a good citizen. Imagine the emotional pain you could feel if you found out something negative about a friend? It might put society at risk, as you might hesitate to put national safety first." Her sister had given her an odd look, but Macia didn't care. She likes Caecilia though, and to get a letter from her feels special, even though she tries to push down that feeling. Looking at the heading again, her stomach churns. My dearest friend! What was Caecilia thinking? Had she lost her mind? Macia can picture the dark haired girl's kind eyes and soft mouth, almost always smiling. Lately, Caecilia had been different. Macia was surprised and uncomfortable at the curiosity and warmth towards Caecilia that had bubbled up in her heart at the change. She found herself avoiding Caecilia, and yet was drawn to her. Macia frowns, struggling to move past the greeting.

Macia bites her thumbnail, then takes a deep breath and reads the first sentence of the letter, allowing herself to read Caecilia's words. Her mind feels more confused as the letter goes on. The words sound foreign, as though Caecilia is writing to her in another language. Macia re-reads the first paragraph, her head buzzing with shock. "Please just read...open mind..." Open mind? What is Caecilia talking about? Who speaks of open minds? Macia's stomach flips every time she reads the words, leaving a bitter taste in her mouth. She realises she has made a terrible mistake in opening the letter. People in Elabi don't need an open mind, Macia thinks, her breathing speeding up, her heart jumping simply thinking about what Caecilia is asking her to do. Read this? Clearly something on the forbidden books list. Why would Caecilia give her this and ask her to read, with "an open mind"? Macia's mouth turns down. Her hand holding the little bundle twitches, as if throwing the pages away from her automatically.

Her eyes follow the pencil lines on the brown paper while her mind struggles to focus on the words. "...those words have changed my life, no, the Author of those words has changed my life. I pray..." Pray?

What? What has happened to Caecilia? Where has she learned these words? Pray? Macia stumbles on, her eyes glazing over more with each line. "...for you to come to know God and His forgiveness, His love and salvation..." Macia hesitates. Why is she even reading this? Is she sitting in her bedroom, in Elabi, reading...this? "...I know it won't mean anything to you now, but I hope you will come to understand these words. It must sound like a foreign language to you..." Yeah, no kidding, Macia rolls her eyes, and mutters, "Guessed it in one go, girl." She stops, a thought forming in the back of her mind. Has Caecilia been exposed to Hillixer? That would explain her mood change and this garbage. Macia knows deep down though that this is not Hillixer speaking. Something else has gotten to her friend. Something more serious.

Her eyes travel the last few lines, "...what I am doing will hurt. Please forgive me but I have to go. I will pray for you every day. I'm sorry about leaving you behind, but I can't stay any longer. Goodbye, my friend. Love, Caecilia." Macia sits up with a wild gasp, sucking in air until she thinks her lungs might explode. Leave? Has she left Elabi? Is that what she is saying? Macia stares wildly at the last few lines. Yes, it says she is leaving! But how and where? Macia jumps up, ready to spring into action, then sits down again. What action? She looks at the clock on her wall. If Caecilia is trying to escape Elabi, Macia is duty-bound to report her. Immediately. Her thumbnail bleeds, but Macia doesn't notice. Her eyes are wide open, staring off into the distance. She will need to report Caecilia straight away, but the implications make her cringe.

Until she reminds herself that either way Caecilia is gone. By betraying her, nothing changes for Macia, apart from having scored extra points towards her Amplissimos status. Those points could just secure her application. What should she do? Should she give Caecilia fair warnings? Should she pop in to see her on her way to the gymnasium, and tell her that she will have to pass on the letter to the council? Or should she inform the automated servant of Caecilia's flight plans? Macia fears she is too late. If Caecilia is already gone, Macia will be one of the first people to be investigated. The fact that Caecilia wrote to her is not good news at all. Might she redeem herself a little by reporting the letter? Macia swallows. What if somebody saw Caecilia deliver the letter? If she doesn't report it and the council finds out she's been keeping something from them, the fallout would be disastrous! Macia can feel the anger, fear and resentment growing with each hammering heartbeat. Blow Caecilia! Why did she have to go all weird and drag Macia into it deliberately! What should she do?

Macia finds herself gasping for breath, fury streaming through her until the anger and betrayal seem to have taken over completely. She drops the letter and bundle of thin papers on the bed, clenching her fists, grinding her teeth, fighting against the roar that wants to force its way out of her throat. She manages to lower it to a growl, her jaws aching from the effort. Suddenly she jumps up, breathing hard, still grinding her teeth, grabs the papers and envelope and stuffs it under her stack with jumpers, gets her snow boots on, pulling on the leather with a vengeance. She forces herself to be quiet on the stairs, hands still clenched, her surviving nails digging into the palms of her hands. Grabbing her winter cloak and gymnasium bag, Macia is outside in the cold air, the snow crunching under her feet. She stomps as hard as she can, her feet tingling with the impact, but Macia welcomes the feeling.

She passes Caecilia's house, but all is dark. She hesitates a moment, wondering about going up to the door. Maybe Caecilia was joking? Perhaps it's done to her as a way to check her loyalties and people forced Caecilia to write the letter. Could it be a test designed by the council, to check if she will put Elabi above her friends and acquaintances? Macia looks at the house, turning towards the driveway leading to Caecilia's front door. Her heart knows though, her heart knows that the letter is genuine, that Caecilia is speaking the truth. She has gone, left Elabi behind, and more importantly, left Macia behind. "So much for 'dearest friend'," Macia spits the words out, the cold air steaming up in little puffs of smoke with each syllable. "Not that dear then obviously, happy to just walk out." For a moment she wonders what upset her most, the fact that her friend, her only friend, has just walked out of her life forever or that she showed an involuntary emotional response to that fact. She spins back towards the main road and stamping hard again, makes her way to the gymnasium. The cold air and tiredness are making her eyes itch.

The gymnasium is deserted apart from another young woman running on a treadmill in the corner. Macia grabs a pair of gloves, tugging fiercely to get them on. She turns towards the big bag suspended from a rack. Her eyes still sting and her breathing is odd, and Macia almost feels tempted to allow her body its little reaction, until she remembers the ever-present cameras. They will be watching her, as there's not much else going on in the gymnasium. If they see the daughter of Brutus Durus being emotional and volatile, well, that would create a stir. No, she has to be in control.

She concentrates on the large punch bag, then hits out, punch after punch after punch. Her breathing is becoming harder and louder, the punches precise and deadly. Soon she can feel her hands getting damp inside the gloves, making her wrinkle her nose. Her thumb suddenly hurts where she chewed her nail too much this morning. Her eyes still sting, her head has started throbbing. Soon her arm muscles start to vibrate, telling her they've had enough. But Macia carries on hitting the bag, although now and then a punch begins to almost miss the mark. Once she nearly loses her balance as her hit just scuffs the bag. She recovers herself just in time, furious with her mistake. She snorts with every punch, tears clouding her vision. Not tears, sweat, she corrects, as if arguing with whoever is watching through the cameras. Sweat, because she is doing her best to be a strong, competent young woman, who looks after her body well, to serve her city and its people. Just sweat.

When Macia finally has to give up, she makes her way to the cooling down room. The room is empty, and she tries to look as peaceful as she can, her breath still shuddering with pent up emotions. Caecilia has betrayed her. A tiny voice inside her head reminds her of the plan to check out why Caecilia had changed so much lately by reporting her to the Council. But Macia feels that doesn't count. After all, she hadn't acted upon her suspicions, had she? She had not betrayed Caecilia and she now wonders if she will regret that fact for a very long time to come. If she had reported the change in her friend, Caecilia wouldn't have left Elabi, although, it seems she would have been out of Macia's life either way.

Chapter 2

Macia leaves the gymnasium exhausted but not less angry. Her anger seems to grow the more she thinks it through. Caecilia has dropped her in it. Assuming it isn't a trick, of course, in which case she is in even more trouble. Stomping home her mind is in stark contrast to the peaceful white surroundings. Everything in her is tense and dark. Her mind is spinning in circles, her arms are shaking, her feet hurt from the way she walks, and her thumb is throbbing. All of it is Caecilia's fault. Innocent, sweet smiling Caecilia, she thinks, bitterness filling her mouth and her heart. Always so cheerful and encouraging. Her breath comes faster with each passing thought.

Yes, so sweet, but spiteful enough to destroy Macia's life. Why send her a letter, then disappear? Macia knows she is one of the few people who has spent time regularly with Caecilia and many people would call them friends. Caecilia even does, in her letter. Macia doesn't ever call anybody a friend, but who would believe that? They will look at Caecilia's contacts, people she knows, people she does things with and whose name will be at the top of the list? Hers! Not only that, Macia's older sister Tima is married to Caecilia's brother. So the family connection will be noted too. Macia will be looked at from both perspectives and the council is bound to come up with something in her life. She tries to look back at the last few months of her life, running past days out, meetups, exams…anything that the council will look into, and where she might be pulled up short.

When she was busy last month she missed a few workouts in the gymnasium, choosing to go for a run instead. Would that come up and might they come to the wrong conclusions? Is there camera footage of her running? Will the footage clear her name, as it shows that she never met anybody? Did she ever meet anybody? Macia can feel her heart rate going up, frantically scanning her memory. Did she ever bump into anybody, talking to them? She usually avoids people, not wanting them to form an impression of her. It is so easy to say or do something that people will pass on to others, or that will cause misunderstandings. Like her spending time with Caecilia. That is seen as friendship by most people and Macia is pretty sure that on the enquiry she will be labelled as Caecilia's friend, possibly even 'best friend'. She shudders.

Macia only spent time with Caecilia because a lot of schoolwork needs to be done with a classmate. Most of the people on the course are civil to her because of her father. Classmates like to be seen with her, or even talk to her to boost their status levels. She feels used, although she would probably do the same in their position. Caecilia was different. She was always herself. Macia never saw her behave differently with her. Caecilia treated her the same as she did the others in their class. The last months she even was…Macia searches for the word and an old fashioned expression springs to mind… Caecilia was kind. The word feels strange in her head, in her mouth, and she even whispers the word. "Kind," she breathes, "kind…" Macia's thoughts towards Caecilia are far from kind though.

She hisses, "How could she…" Macia tries to clear her mind. She needs to think. There will be an uproar. Young people don't just disappear. You can't just pack up and leave Elabi, it's not that easy. How did Caecilia get past the borders? Or did she? Macia's heart pounds as she imagines the mess she'll be in if Caecilia was captured by the border guard last night. She will tell them about the letter she sent to her 'dearest friend' Macia, and Macia will find herself beyond the hills in double-quick time. All she can hope for is that Caecilia will have been shot. That would be better for everyone involved. Probably. Although there still will be an enquiry. How did she get out anyway? And why last night? Was she alone? The strange young man's face drifts through her memory for a moment. She can't even remember his name, but she met him when they all went to the beach last summer. He was weird too. An odd smile, like he was happy, grinning at people as if the whole world was his best friend. He most likely started all his letters with 'dearest friend'. That is probably where Caecilia got it from.

Macia comes back to the here and now, as she realises that she will need to make a plan. What should she tell the council? She can't deny her involvement with Caecilia, although she could downplay the friendship. Will they believe her if she tells them that she avoids all friendship? Her record should show her dedication to Elabi, her loyalty. Of course, everyone will know about her mother, her first mother that is. She had been too young to be involved in that though, so hopefully, it will not be held against her. Or will they suspect a family trait? She hasn't spent much time with Caecilia recently, as she was contemplating reporting her friend's change of character. She had been very odd, making strange comments, asking suspicious questions. She had even shown some emotion. Macia remembered she had warned Caecilia. She hadn't threatened her, yet, but she had hinted that she was unhappy with the way Caecilia behaved and that she knew something was up.

Macia sighs. What about the letter? Should she go to the council with it this morning? Tell them what she knew, how she had planned to report her friend and all she was waiting for was clearer evidence?

They might feel she had failed in her duty. She should have put her trust in the council, reported Caecilia and allowed the council to pass judgment. By trying to take matters into her own hands she had given Caecilia a chance to escape, dropping her, her family and Caecilia's family in it. Will the fact that she has a letter in the first place go against her? Her stomach churns as she thinks of the opening sentence, 'My dearest friend'. What council member will ever believe that Macia doesn't do friendship when she gets a letter like that? Then there is the bundle of strange paper in the envelope. How will they know that the bundle is the first one she has ever had? Will they believe her if she tells them that she hasn't even looked at the pages?

Macia can feel the sweat on her back turn to ice. She swallows, fear beating harder than the anger for a moment. What if they don't believe her? What if they are sure that this letter is part of a string of letters, the odd pages part of a large set? Of course, they will search their house, but even if they won't find anything, will that clear her name? Macia's breathing speeds up, she's panting, fear making her knees wobble. What will happen if... She gasps, no, she can't let that happen! She has to convince them of her innocence, she has to distance herself from Caecilia as much as possible. She can imagine what it will look like if she goes running to the council this morning, waving Caecilia's letter. They will assume she only went to them because she knows her game is up. No, there has to be a better way.

By the time Macia spots their large driveway she has made up her mind. The letter stays where it is. She will go to school as always, will feign surprise, but only mild surprise and a total lack of interest when she finds out that Caecilia isn't in school. She might suggest illness or uhm...what other reasons do people give for not making it to school? Family emergency? Well, something probably happened, she will say, practising the disinterested shrug she will put on. Yes, that is the best plan. They will still look into her life, still interview her, interrogate more likely, and they might even look round her room. Would they? Her fists clench and unclench, her mind rushing through options and possibilities. They must not find the letter, of course. Will they search her drawers and cupboards, or just look round? Maybe she should put the letter somewhere safer. Burning it would be the safest, her sensible, reasonable, logical voice tells her. But somehow Macia rebels against logic. Her voice of reason tells her in an ominous voice that she will probably come to regret that emotional decision.

Macia suddenly sniffs, aware that her nose has gone cold. Fury washes over her as she cups her nose. "Caecilia! I hate you!" The whole thing upset her and she forgot to protect her nose. Now it will have turned red at the very tip, the rest of her nose will be white, looking incredibly ugly, obviously a defect in her system, and it's light enough for anybody to see her like this and to find out her fault. Word could get back to her fiancé and he might report her for not declaring it on the Nuptialem List. It's all Caecilia's fault, she thinks, hatred and self-pity making her stumble on the slippery snow.

She cups her nose in her mittened hands, blowing warm air and hoping her nose will look normal by the time she gets into the house. Her stepmother wasn't thrilled that she got attached so quickly and she might see it as an easy way to break up the attachment and put Macia back on the Nuptialem List, defect and all. Macia is relieved to hear voices in the kitchen as she gets into the house and she quickly slips upstairs. She has a shower and gets dressed, checking her nose, thinking about the day ahead, practising surprised, enquiring faces in the mirror. "Who? Oh, Caecilia, that dark-haired girl you mean?" No, that won't do, way too over the top. Everybody knows that they have spent a lot of time together. "Oh? She's not here? Is she not well?" Yes, that could work. She could say that Caecilia's house had been dark this morning on her way to the gymnasium. What about on the way back? She had forgotten to look. Coming out of the bathroom Macia hesitates. Should she hide the letter in a better spot? In her safe spot?

In the end, she decides to play it safe. She listens just outside her door, but all is quiet upstairs. They are still downstairs. She quickly walks to her stack with jumpers and pulls the letter out. For a moment she is tempted to read it again, but no, there isn't time now. She will be expected downstairs very soon, or they might remember during the enquiry that she was upstairs for longer than normal on the day of Caecilia's disappearance. She spins around and quickly walks to her window. She stands on the windowsill, reaches up, the envelope clenched between her lips. Standing on tiptoe she can just reach the board above the windowsill. By pushing on one side, whilst balancing the other side, Macia manages to get the board out of its place. She leans the board against the window, then standing on the very points of her toes, reaches into the dark cavity that is now visible, and pulls out a flat box. She opens the lid briefly enough to get a glimpse of the old dull photograph in there, showing a smiling family. She stuffs the envelope on top of the picture, snaps the lid shut, slides the box back in place and, panting, clicks the board back into its slot.

Macia hops down lightly, her breath faster than usual, feeling her face glow. She presses cold, shaking hands against her burning cheeks, and takes a deep breath. She walks to the door, ready for a proper breakfast, nibbling her thumb on the way downstairs. She is feeling calmer now, relieved to have some sort of plan, knowing the letter is safe. Not even her father is aware of her hiding place, or of the picture hidden in there. She isn't sure what he would do if he knew. Macia gives a tiny shudder, fearing the answer. She walks into the kitchen, her face straight as usual, raising her chin respectfully at the two older people sitting at the kitchen table. They raise their chin in return, her stepmother looking her up and down, the corners of her mouth turned towards the floor as they always seem to be. Her father frowns a little, "You're late," he says, and Macia explains that the snow had slowed her down, her voice sullen, her eyes avoiding looking at him. Just a normal morning, she tells herself, just a normal morning. Her eyes long to look at him, to check if he knows or suspects anything, but her head tells her that he can't know anything yet. Unless there has been a shooting incident at the border, whispers a tiny voice in the back of her head.

She eats her pottage in silence, not tasting any of it. It is only when she rinses her bowl that she realises she had left the garum off. She quickly glances at her parents, but they're talking about their meetings that day and neither seem to have noticed. Macia takes a steadying breath. She will need to be more careful today. People will notice any slight changes and view them in the light of Caecilia's disappearance, and put them together.

Chapter 3

Having left the kitchen worktop immaculate as ever, Macia goes upstairs to pick up her school bag. She hesitates, checking its contents quickly. Is there anything incriminating in there? Should she take something extra to clear her name? Or something to read in case she has to wait before interviews? Will they even track Caecilia's friends and family today, or will that happen tomorrow? She sighs, deciding to leave her bag the way it is. She walks downstairs again, wearing her leather boots. She pops her head around the kitchen door, raises her chin respectfully at her father and stepmother, then she is outside again, tugging at her woollen cloak, shivering in the cold air. She feels tense, her teeth clamped together. It is only her mittens that prevent her from biting her nails. Macia reminds herself that she doesn't care about Caecilia disappearing out of her life, it is merely the inconvenience it will cause. Also, there is a chance that it will be more than inconvenient. All she can do now is play her role well to escape unnecessary scrutiny or sanctions.

The school looks like it does every day. Students hanging around the yard, some of them looking at their books. They tend to be the younger students though, as older students have learned not to look too eager. It is also a sign of bad time management if you are still preparing at this time of day. If seen too often, a note will be made, and that could go against you. Macia sighs. Today she would love to be able to hold a book, get engrossed in something, look busy. She looks at some of the students and wrinkles her nose a little. Some of them are new, recent promotions. Their former Mansit status is very obvious, even though they're doing their best to blend in with the rest of the students. One can always tell though, and some seem too desperate to be promoted for their own good. It never works to come across as too eager. A few even tried to strike up a friendship with Macia once they found out her family connections. She had coldly reminded them of the status gap between them and that had been the end of that.

These students had obviously grown up in a family that didn't take Elabi and its institutions seriously to get their Mansit position in the first place. Once allowed back into society they lost no time to grovel before an Altiorem citizen. How dare they! They seem to have no idea of the sacrifice and effort made to retain that status. It shows their lack of respect, Macia fumes looking away from the other students. However, today her anger is mixed with apprehension for again, thanks to Caecilia, she might have to fight for her status and the pending application for Amplissimos status will probably be put on hold as well. Macia feels her shoulders sag, then shakes herself. How can she allow her emotions to run away? No wonder she hasn't made it to Amplissimos yet! Her counsellor has warned her against that reaction so many times and even made her attend a body language course for a few months. Macia has been very aware of her body language ever since, and straight away recognised her sagging shoulders. She takes a deep breath, reminding herself of who she is, and where she wants to be.

The signal sounds and Macia follows the other students inside. She catches herself looking around for Caecilia, and feels the heat creep into her face. How silly of her! The thing that annoys her most is the disappointment she feels. Macia raises her chin a little, her face tight and hard, her jaws aching from clenching her teeth. She stomps the snow off her boots, relieved to be inside. Another girl comes up to Macia and after raising her chin asks, "Have you seen Caecilia? I have one of her books for her..." her voice trails off when she looks at Macia's face.

"Why would you ask me if it's Caecilia's book?" she snaps at the girl, "If I started taking books for everyone I knew I'd need someone to carry my bags," she adds spitefully. The girl swallows and flushes red, making Macia despise her. The girl mumbles an apology, which infuriates Macia even more. "Why apologise? How about thinking before you ask something next time?" Sarcasm makes her face twist and for a moment the girl opposite her hesitates, a cruel glint appearing in her eyes. Macia pushes past her, recognising the look, knowing that she might go red if the girl says something nasty to her in public. That would never do, so she walks off as haughtily as possible.

Classes start with reciting the Elabi Creed. Macia enjoys the feeling of belonging this gives her and her face glows with pride when she thinks of how far their society has come. It does make her proud of her father, yes, and even of her stepmother. She might not like the cold-blooded woman and she might deep down resent the fact that her father is hardly ever home, but their work for Elabi is outstanding. She herself wants to support Elabi and its citizens to the best of her abilities. Within the school Macia helped set up more counsellor services, offering more hours for children who want to discuss their home life and make the channels of reporting irregularities clearer. But today is not the same. It is tarnished because of the selfishness of Caecilia.

For a moment she wonders if she should change plans and use one of the Reporting Facilitators, to report Caecilia's flight and strange letter. Macia bites a strip of fingernail, thinking about the options. She decides against it, for the same reason she thought of this morning.

It will still look bad, and it still comes with the very real possibility of the council assuming the letter is not the first one. She suddenly realises that the fact that Caecilia used a brand new piece of paper will go against her protests, for it will look as if she was expected to write back to her friend on the same piece of paper. They will assume that letters would have gone back and forth, until the paper got so ragged and grimy, forcing Caecilia to use a new piece. She sighs; everything can be used against her if they want to do so. The best thing to do is to stay clear from the whole mess as much as possible and hope Caecilia hasn't been captured alive by the border guard.

The teacher is taking the register. "I'm missing Caecilia Reizio," she says, looking around the hall, making it sound between a statement and a question. Most students look around, searchingly and Macia hesitates. Should she look or should she pretend not to have heard? When she sees the teacher looking at her she looks around as well, feeling her face warm up. That won't do! She must not look guilty or involved, but unaware and bored, uncaring. After looking around for the appropriate amount of time she shrugs. The teacher is right, Caecilia is not here. When she looks back towards the front the teacher looks at Macia again and says, "I know that you know her well, any ideas?" Macia clenches her fists underneath her desk, trying to look calm and collected. She shakes her head and adds casually, "No idea. She might be unwell. I haven't seen her for a while, so I don't know if she has been feeling ill." She uses her practised shrug then and looks away, feigning a total lack of interest. She is relieved when the teacher merely dips her head in acceptance and starts the lesson. Macia clamps her jaws together, now is not the time to breathe a sigh of relief, or to lean back in her seat.

The school day finally ends and walking home Macia breathes deeply. Nobody can see or hear her now and she is sure that she will not be under surveillance yet. That will take some time, but is bound to happen. The snow crunches underfoot and she would love to stamp her feet as she did early this morning, but she doesn't dare to in daylight. Soon the light will go and she can stomp then. Her anger towards Caecilia has grown during the day. Each lesson had brought the question about her classmate and the fact that every single teacher had looked to her for some kind of explanation both infuriated and frightened her. It confirmed her expectations that the enquiry would most certainly include her. Today has shown her that she will be at the top of the council's list of people to interrogate...interview, she corrects. She believes in Elabi, she believes in the city council wholeheartedly. She trusts them to do what is right, to protect their society and way of living. This feels so unfair though, as she has no idea where Caecilia is. A tiny voice in the back of her head quietly points out that she had noticed the change in Caecilia and that she should have trusted the council to deal with it as soon as she spotted it. How hard it is for her to admit to herself there were two conflicting reasons she hadn't reported Caecilia yet. First, she had wanted more solid proof to present an open and shut case about her classmate to impress the council. And yet she is also aware, although can barely admit it to herself, that there was a second reason. Caecilia is special to her and reporting her had not felt right.

Neither parent is at home yet and Macia is glad. She still needs to work out her response for friends and family. Again the young man's face drifts into her mind with his crew cut hair. Who was he? Macia stares out of her window into the darkness outside, suddenly quite sure he is responsible. She wonders if he has left Elabi too, as she can't imagine sweet, gentle Caecilia walking off by herself through the snow-filled night. Should she mention the young man? If she can convince the council that the man is to blame they might look less closely at her.

She hears the door slam downstairs and gasps. What will she tell her father? Walking to the door she races through the options and possibilities. In the end, she decides the safest way forward would be to casually mention Caecilia's absence at school. If she says nothing, that could seem strange and could raise questions. There will be plenty of questions without her adding to them. She walks down the stairs, her face straight and hard as always. Only her throbbing thumbnail tells of the stress this day has caused her.

Chapter 4

Over the clatter of cutlery on china, Macia casually drops, "Caecilia wasn't in school today." After finishing another mouthful she adds, "As we often work together when we are paired up, the teachers kept looking at me when they realised she wasn't there." She can't help the bitter edge in her voice, but she does manage to pull off her near-professional shrug. Her father stops eating, his mind clearly walking through the consequences of her statement. Her stepmother carries on eating but doesn't look up from her plate. In the end, her father nods. Once.

"Yes, I suppose they will. Caecilia has been to our house, Tima married her brother. Yes, they will look at you. At us," he adds, his voice sounding unhappy. Macia dips her head, yes, she is expecting that. "There will be interviews," he says, and he briefly looks at her. Macia keeps her face as bland and sulky and bored as possible. "Depending on why she was not there, of course," he says, rather quickly. Macia dips her head again and explains that she suggested that Caecilia might have been ill. She hasn't had any contact with her for a few days, so she doesn't know if Caecilia has gone down with something. It is winter, after all. Her father nods and carries on eating.

Macia gets through the meal, helps clear the table and is about to walk out when her stepmother asks, "Do you know if your friend was on the Nuptialem List?"

"I don't think so," Macia shrugs. "Although Caecilia had mentioned doing the test sometime soon."

"And anyway, she's not my friend," she adds, her voice sharp, "I don't do friends. Life stays simpler that way. I have an attachment planned, I have a career in mind, I don't need shallow connections that can derange your life. Like Caecilia not being in school. I couldn't understand why all the teachers looked at me, asking me about her. There are a lot of people Caecilia spent time with but none of those people were looked at or asked. Just me. I hated it. I resented the connection they had made!"

The older woman makes soothing clicking noises with her tongue. Macia glares at the ground, and says, her voice measured, "You see, I wanted my Amplissimos Status application through before leaving school. I want to serve Elabi at the highest level possible, giving it my very best. Caecilia being ill and everyone looking at me is not helpful. If she is ill that is," she says hastily looking at her stepmother's face. "It just made me angry to see other people being careless, and how it affects me without being able to stop them," she adds a bit lamely.

Macia can feel the anger working in her, and she knows she has to be careful. People can blurt out emotional comments when angry. It has taken her many years to channel her anger in such a way that she won't do anything without thinking. She is furious with Caecilia though, and she can just feel her mouth wanting to say things. She looks at Ignava, keeping her face bored, her stomach tight. Did Ignava think her emotional? Something odd shows in the older woman's eyes for a moment, and Macia gives off another shrug. "Hopefully she will be back in school tomorrow," she says, with a sneer, "apologising for the chaos caused." Ignava dips her head. Macia lifts her chin, and leaves the kitchen, trying to make it look casual but purposeful. After all, there are lessons to prepare for, and tomorrow will be another early start if she wants to make it to the gymnasium before school

22

time. Sitting at her desk she thinks about her father and Ignava. Will they believe her innocence? Macia wonders for a moment about that funny look in Ignava's eyes. What had it meant?

Macia sighs over her books. Her mind drifts constantly to the letter hidden in her safe place and the strange man on the beach. She gives a small gasp. The council could hold it against her that she didn't report him last summer.

The guards are waiting for her outside the gymnasium the following morning. Macia spent the session in the gymnasium thinking about the day ahead, expecting to be called into the headteacher's office to answer preliminary questions. She had run through various scenarios, doing more reps than ever as she kept losing count. In the end, she had decided she had trained enough for today, gone to the cooling down room, had her shower at the gymnasium and was looking forward to breakfast. Stepping outside into the cold, she is shocked to see the guards waiting for her. The older one steps forward and says, "Macia Durus." His voice gravelly, a slight smirk on his face, as if he is pleased that he gets to take in an Altiorem. He doesn't ask, just states her name. Macia dips her head, clenching her jaws together, forcing her face to become straight, sullen and bored again. They beckon her between them and set off on the long walk to the city.

The City Hall is quiet, and she feels relieved, as well as the usual sense of awe to be in this place. She slows down as she gazes at the portraits adorning the walls; portraits of those who invented, implemented and defended their laws and way of life. For years she has secretly hoped one day her face will be among them. The younger guard grunts something, and Macia looks at him, the reverie still clearly visible in her eyes. She hesitates a moment, then says, "It's my favourite part about coming to the City Hall," and he dips his head, locking eyes with her for a second. Macia notices that he is looking less proud than before, treating her almost with a level of respect.

They take the large stairs up to the second floor, where the young guard points out a beautifully carved bench for her to sit on. Macia sits down, putting her gymnasium bag on the floor. Sitting up, her stomach protests. She blushes, squeezing her stomach to stop further noises. The older guard looks at her, and says, "We will inform the council that you have not had breakfast. It will be a quick interview anyway." Macia dips her head and thanks the man, her stomach slowly filling up with nerves. Sure enough, when Macia is called in the guard explains that they waited for her outside the gymnasium and that Macia has not been home for breakfast yet. Macia looks at the three council members seated behind the huge, highly polished table. One older man, a younger man and a younger woman. The older man dismisses the guard, then turns his attention on Macia. He points to a chair with his chin, and Macia sits down to face them.

She raises her chin respectfully at them, but only the younger man gives a reaction. The older man starts, "From our information, we see that you are friends with Caecilia." He looks at Macia, who dips her head, and very quietly explains that she doesn't do friendship as such. It clouds people's thinking, she explains when all three council members stare at her. "But you were Caecilia's friend?" The woman asks this time, in a rather tight voice. Macia starts her shrug, then thinks better of it. They might not be impressed to see their question shrugged off.

"I worked on projects with Caecilia," she says, "and I'm sure that she saw me as a friend. I never used the word friend on her though, or on anybody else for that matter. You see, I feel Elabi needs to come first. After all, it is for the good of everybody. In the long run, it will then benefit my family and people I spend time with. I just worried that if I made somebody into a friend, that it could cloud my judgment." The woman dips her head, the younger man pulls a sceptical face and scribbles away on what looks almost new paper, and the older man just looks at her. "I suppose to answer your question," Macia adds, not liking the silence in the large room, and realising she hasn't answered their question. "I suppose people looked on us as friends, and as I said, I'm quite sure Caecilia would see me as a friend. She had a few friends though, as she didn't have the same views on friendship as I do." She hopes that bit gets noted, as it should help her future status. Even from this interview, it should become clear that she will put Elabi first.

The older man leans forward a bit, his face serious. "Caecilia has disappeared," he says, and Macia instantly makes her eyes widen in shock. "We believe she has left Elabi." Macia sits up with a small gasp, looking at each council member in turn. The younger man dips his head, the woman purses her lips, as if the whole idea of somebody leaving Elabi is distasteful. Which it is, Macia agrees. Macia leans forward a little bit as well, and asks with a rather shaky voice if they are sure?

"Of course, she wasn't in school yesterday, but as I hadn't seen her for a few days, I thought she might be ill." The younger man shakes his head and tells Macia in a dark tone that Caecilia's parents had declared her missing late afternoon. "Oh, that's, well…that's," Macia stops, she has no idea what that is, but it's bad, that's for sure. The man nods and explains that of course, they had a look round her usual places and friends. Had Macia seen her? Macia shakes her head, "No, I hadn't seen her much in school lately. It has been busy with exams." The council members nod. "So I have gone straight home each day. As it's cold and snowy, and as I had worked hard, and I assume others too, I simply thought she had been ill yesterday. I didn't usually do much social stuff with Caecilia. We had different interests, and I also don't like to spend time with people outside my family." Not that she liked spending time with people who did belong in her family, but that was another matter.

"Any friends of Caecilia that she was close with?" the younger man asks her, his pencil hovering expectantly above the paper. Macia begins to shake her head, then slowly turns it into a nod; here is the chance she has been waiting for, and she feels a tiny flicker of relief that the interview has gone the way she expected. "No, well, yes, although, you see…" She pauses, not wanting to seem too eager, or too ready to drop somebody in it. She rearranges her woollen dress and looks up again. "Last summer I went with my sister, some other young people and Caecilia to the beach, the further one," she explains. "If I remember correctly, it was Caecilia who invited us. We all went, it was a very hot day. There was this young man, I really cannot recall his name. He was different though, he had a few strange habits, I suppose." The woman leans forward, eyes keen, asking Macia if she reported the young man.

Macia swallows hard, and shakes her head, pulling her most regretful face. "No," she sighs, "no, you see, I didn't know his name or anything. Also, I couldn't quite say in which way he was strange. I mean, he seemed all proper, but there were a few odd things. He picked up the rubbish we left on the sand and stuffed it in his bag." The three council members stare at her in confusion. "Everybody leaves their rubbish on the beach," she explains, "everybody does. In the evening some Mansits clear the beach. So why take your rubbish home with you?" The three members give a nod, why indeed? "But you see, it was something small, something just strange, so I left it, and now I wonder…" her voice drifts off, and she makes her mouth form a hard line. The older man suddenly raises his chin a little, his eyes on the clock just behind her.

"It is time for you to go. Otherwise, you will be late for school. We will speak to you again soon. For now, you have been clear and helpful." Macia dips her head gratefully, then raises her chin respectfully before walking out of the room. Her whole body wants to sigh with relief once outside the room, but she makes herself hold it together. You never know who is watching you, and showing obvious relief after an interview could mean trouble.

Once she is out of the city she breathes in and out heavily though, her knees shaking, her arms struggling with her gymnasium bag. At home, she explains her lateness to her father and stepmother in her usual sullen style. Ignava rolls her eyes and says, "You were lucky you had your shower there this morning then."

Chapter 5

Classes hardly started when the Head Teacher's assistant calls, "Macia Durus." Macia is sure that there is more emphasis than necessary on her surname. She wants to scowl, but manages to force her face to stay sullen and blank. She follows the assistant towards the head teacher's office where the older man from the City Hall is sitting, with three other council members. They point at a chair, and the older man leans forward. "Macia," he starts, and looking down on his papers, says, "The young man you mentioned. We are picking up the conversation where we left off this morning," he briefly explains to the other members. One dips his head, the others simply stare at Macia. She wants to squirm under their stares but merely digs her few surviving fingernails into her hands. "Yes, the young man, the one you mentioned. His name turns out to be Gax." Macia nods, and the older man promptly leans back. He stares at her for a moment, the start of a frown on his forehead. "You knew his name after all?"

Macia shakes her head, "No, I had forgotten, but as soon as you mentioned it I recognised it. Caecilia briefly introduced us, as well as some of the others who were there." The older man doesn't take his eyes off her, and she can see him weighing up her answer. Macia just squeezes her hands tighter and looks back at the man. In the end, he briefly nods and writes something down.

"This young man has been a menace," he says, the frown full grown now. "We have already interviewed his co-worker as well as his shop manager." He is glaring at the paper; the interviews had obviously not improved his day. He looks up at Macia again, "How often did Caecilia mention this man?" Macia thinks about that and shrugs. She can't actually remember Caecilia ever mentioning him at all. Apart from introducing him on the beach, she can't recall having heard his name. The older man glares, scribbling away. One of the younger council members dips his head and mutters something about devious, dangerous people. Macia glances at him, agreeing with the man. "Is that the impression he gave you?" the older man asks, seeing her look. Macia hesitates, it wasn't really the idea he had given her, and in how much trouble will it land her if she says he had?

She half shakes her head, "No, not really. Like I said this morning, he had been a bit strange, but nothing concrete or obvious, to be honest. I...I don't know, after all, his name had never been mentioned before or after. That was last summer, I didn't even realise that they were still friends." She shudders a little at the word friend, relieved to have her own policy on that score! Another one of the council members scrapes her throat and looks at Macia, the corners of her mouth turned down.

"On the papers from this morning there was a comment you had made with regards to friendships," she says, "Care to explain that once more, and tell us why you have come to that way of looking at things? In Elabi we certainly do not forbid friendships." She looks at Macia, and the girl catches her wrinkle her nose in distaste. Macia swallows. Nobody has ever looked at her in distaste. Being on the receiving end...hurts. She dips her head, hesitating. How far back does the woman want her to go? On the other hand, her counsellor reports will be in her file, so being open will be wise. The word open reminds her of Caecilia's plea to have an open mind. She takes a quick breath, feeling the heat crawl into her face.

She looks down, hopefully, they will think she will feel shame on her mother's behalf, and assume the red on her cheeks is because of that. "You see, my mother went when I was very young," she starts and glances up. From the way they look back at her, the way especially the woman now openly crinkles her nose, Macia can tell that they have read her file. "So you see, after that, I learned the importance of belonging, of being a part of Elabi. The city looked after us all, and supported me at that time." She swallows, remembering the forced counselling, endless classes, loyalty tests, and assessments she had to go through... "I learned then that friendships and relationships can easily cloud your judgment, especially when you're young. So I decided then, after I found out, that it was better to have acquaintances rather than friends. I don't avoid my classmates. As I said, I went to the beach with Caecilia and some others from our class. I just don't use the word friend, and I don't make hanging out with people a priority. I want to put back into Elabi after it did so much for me, so I work hard. That takes up a lot of my time. I don't see that as a sacrifice," she says hurriedly, realising it could be taken the wrong way, "I just see it as preparation for a useful life."

Some of the council members nod, one man looks impressed, scribbling away. The woman still stares at her, but at least she is no longer crinkling her nose in distaste. Macia desperately wants to sigh, take deep breaths, but that wouldn't look good. She tries to look a little bored, not with the interview of course, but with friends who don't appreciate the life they have. It's a fine balance though, and she hesitates. Should she show more indignation? The older man leans forward a little and asks her about the change she mentioned in Caecilia. Macia dips her head, her fingers tightening up. This is an awkward one. It could lead to a heap of trouble if she gets it wrong! She starts slowly, racking her brain. "It's been a while, not too long though," she hurries, as she sees frowns deepening. "It just started…mild, you know, where she would be smiling that tiny bit longer. Or the way she offered to do things. Not that it's wrong to help people, of course not!" This is harder than she thought. You have to be careful how you phrase things. That is one of the things she learned in counselling. As long as you said things the right way, it often didn't matter what you said.

"You see, she started helping more, but in a strange way," she says, speaking slowly, thinking back over the last few weeks, Caecilia's sweet face, full lips always smiling. "It wasn't just the helping, but the way she offered help. Too…too helpful, if you see what I mean?" She looks at the council members, who stare back, and one or two dip their heads. Yes, there is a way to be too helpful. "Or the way she apologised. Of course, taking responsibility for one's actions is important, but Caecilia apologised even when it was definitely not her fault." Macia swallows, feeling the tightness in her chest when she thinks about the day where she hadn't been able to go to the gymnasium. She had been bitter about it, and Caecilia had said sorry to her. She sees the woman looking, and explains, "I had this gymnasium session I wanted to join. It was a class for young people that I would have enjoyed. The class was full, as I found out too late about the class. It wasn't a big deal, really, just…" How do you describe that feeling without sounding like you let your emotions run away from you? "Well, disappointing, I suppose. Caecilia was with me when I heard, and she could tell that I was disappointed, and she said sorry!" Macia stares ahead, seeing the two of them, feeling her stunned reaction to the other girl's words. The older man smirks a little, he can tell that Macia is still shocked. Macia continues, imitating Caecilia's voice, "I mean, she said, 'So sorry for you, you must feel so disappointed. I really hope another class comes up soon for you.'" Macia glares at her toes, her breathing speeding up. She is still shocked by it. When she looks up at the council members even the older man dips his head. They see what she means straight away.

Then his face becomes very serious. "You have given us some insights but my big question is, why did you not inform the council of this change?" Macia bites her lips, her fingers itching, but she clenches her fists. She looks at him and rolls her shoulders, tears suddenly stinging her eyes. "I can see I have failed," she whispers, her voice no longer supporting her. "You see, I wanted to serve the council well, by gathering more evidence, by presenting a very clear and well-researched case. Instead, I have left it too long, and now Caecilia has come to harm." She swallows, how could she have been so foolish, trusting her own powers and judgement? "I am truly sorry, as I can see that I have failed in my duties as a citizen. The same goes for the man, I should have reported him that same day, rather than be too keen to help." The older man dips his head, not looking away from her though. It stays very quiet for a long time in the room, the council staring at Macia without speaking. Macia can feel the nerves tingling all over her body, but she grips the palms of her hands tighter and clenches her jaws together. If she starts speaking now she will most definitely be emotion-driven, and that will be even worse. She has to stay quiet, has to prevent words from tumbling out.

In the end, the older man sighs a little, "You are not the only one responsible. After all, you are young, like Caecilia. It is really up to the adults in cases like this." Macia's breath catches in her throat, cases like this? Is he implying that it has happened before? Why would any young person want to leave? His voice drones on, "You made a wrong judgment call, we agree with that as a council. However, we can see that you meant well. As there are at least two instances though, you will be required to attend 'Sharing is Caring' classes for the next few weeks. That will refresh your memory, and help you to be clearer in what type of information needs to be passed on, and what to do next time you feel in doubt." Macia dips her head, wondering if this will be the last interview to do with Caecilia and whether there will be another string with sanctions before the case is closed. Attending one type of class is definitely acceptable, and it's a worthwhile class anyway. It is hard to know what sort of information to pass on, and who to pass it on to.

Just before she goes, one of the younger council members rearranges himself in his seat. "Do you know if Caecilia was a great reader?" He looks at her, then down on his papers. Macia's heart stops for a moment, then speeds up to make up for lost time. Macia shakes her head quickly, then hesitates. What is wise? She can feel her face warming up, will they notice? Is there something she can relate this to that will explain why her face has gone all flushed?

"She was quite a fast reader," she says, "and when we did a project together she would do a lot of the reading." Again she blushes, for Macia would get distracted when reading. Just the way sentences were built together, or the words used. She once even complained about the way something was written, not that long ago, and Caecilia had giggled. She can feel the warmth in her face spreading, "You see, I would often look more at the words, and the sentences, and how they sounded, whereas Caecilia would get the idea behind the words very quickly. It just made sense for her to do most of the reading. I..." she hesitates, then decides to make the point. Hopefully, this one will go down on her records, "I loved writing down what we needed. I saw it as a form of important preparation. My father writes a lot, so does my stepmother." Some of the council members nod, the woman nods, but the corners of her mouth turn down even more; she's obviously not keen on the Durus family! "So you see, I was grateful for the practice it provided me. That way we worked well together, which is why I did spend time with her." There, that explained the reason that Caecilia called her friend at the same time.

The younger man nods again, then says, "You see, a special book was mentioned." He stops and looks at her. Macia tries to look attentive, but disinterested at the same time, her fingers suddenly freezing cold. "This book is very poisonous, dangerous and subversive. It has been on the Forbidden Books List for decades. In fact, I believe it was one of the first books to have been taken out of circulation. It appears from what we learned that Caecilia has been introduced to this book, and in fact been reading it." Macia dips her head, her heart beating faster. "Have you ever seen her with a book like that?" he asks, and Macia shakes her head straight away. She rearranges her dress and swallows. Then in a very quiet voice, as if what she's saying is highly confidential, she tells them about the reason for setting up the Information Lines in the school. The woman turns a page in the information in front of her and nods, then raises a hand to cut off Macia's words.

"Yes, thanks, it's here. I see the point you wish to make." Macia nods at her, relieved. It still hurts in a way, and it's another reason that she doesn't do friendships. It had been excruciating that time, and the reaction of her classmates had lasted for…well, for years, and still lasted till now, she realises. The Information Lines. Macia's set up led to several girls and their entire families undergoing special classes and one sent Beyond the Hills. Oh, they are very subtle about it, and they have to be. After all, what she did was right and proper, just painful. It was for the good of them all, though, and she had felt that she had had no other choice. The man asking her if she had ever seen Caecilia read subversive materials, well, that was easily answered. For one thing, she wouldn't have had a chance. She looks down on her woollen dress, feeling her eyes sting a little, hoping that the council members will assume it's from the incident a few years ago, but all Macia can think of is the feel of the extremely thin paper before slipping it into the hidden box.

Chapter 6

The day crawls by. Every time an adult walks past her classes Macia holds her breath. She is pretty sure that she managed to pass the interview, even though she worries more might be coming. Once they have talked to others, they might call her in again. She forces her thoughts away from the odd paper bundle that Caecilia gave her. Macia isn't planning on reading it, of course, although she might read the letter again. Soon. Not too soon though, as she might be watched. Macia thinks back through the interview. It's hard to answer questions when you know too much. Will they have accepted her words? The woman looked a bit doubtful. She sighs.

In the short break, Macia spots Caecilia's younger sister, Savisia. She is standing by herself, of course. Somehow, all students know to stay clear of the Reizio family. The young girl looks like she is in shock. Part of Macia wants to go up to her to ask her what she knows. Does she know why or where Caecilia is? Macia gives a tiny gasp as she suddenly realises she has no idea where Caecilia went. She presumed that she went Downstream. But did she? Macia thinks about it, and frowns, trying to figure it out. Her own mother went Downstream, years ago, but that was for a reason. Caecilia had no reason to go Downstream.

She looks at the young girl, her feet itching to walk up to her and ask her what she knows. Macia thinks about the interview and realises that they seemed to know that Caecilia had been influenced by that dangerous book. How did they know? She groans. This is more complex than she thought. Macia is also shocked by her emotional response, her curiosity and her drive to find out more. She makes herself look the other way. Slowly, seemingly aimlessly she removes herself to a totally different part of the school grounds. Caecilia's sister will be watched, very closely watched, and so will anyone who speaks to her. Macia hopes she won't be under surveillance that long if she is careful.

Macia decides the interviews were so gruelling because they kept throwing surprises at her. She needed more information if she was going to keep up her story. Her anger against Caecilia flares up again. Caecilia seems to be determined to land Macia in it. Maybe she was jealous and having left Elabi, she still wants to harm Macia. Macia clenches her jaws together, forcing the nail of her smallest finger between her teeth. That must be it, she decides; Caecilia couldn't do anything against Macia whilst here, in Elabi. Not many people can. It has always given Macia a sense of security, knowing that she is heading towards almost untouchable status. Certainly, none of her classmates could harm her. Caecilia however, by running away and implicating Macia, has every chance of harming her. That is why the assistant seemed so pleased when Macia was called into the head teacher's office; the idea that someone from the Durus family, the daughter of Brutus Durus AMP is pulled in for questioning, well, some people find a form of pleasure in that. Macia is relieved when the signal sounds for afternoon classes to commence. Sitting in her own class, simply listening to the teacher, sounds like a haven of rest.

It is hard to concentrate during the lessons, as she keeps wondering how she can gain more information. Her sister Tima might know more. But she will be watched. Macia doodles on her notebook paper, trying to formulate a plan, a way of gaining information without sinking into further trouble. By the time classes are over for the day she still hasn't got a plan. She does feel the urgency growing though, and the need to know more seems clearer.

The house is dark and quiet when she gets back, which suits Macia just fine. She has to make a plan. She gets herself some fruit, then sits at her desk with her schoolwork. She has no idea how much they will be watching her, and whether there are now cameras installed in her room. She cringes, the thought of going against the city council, against her Elabi, well, the thought is too hideous for words! She, Macia Durus, nearly AMP, is deceiving the council! This is an emergency situation though, for Macia is trying to undo her friend's trickery. Which is why she has a personal no-friend policy. To avoid situations like these. She finds an old piece of paper, the gum having rubbed the paper thin and rough. She hides the paper under her school books so that even if there is a camera, they probably won't spot her writing on something not school-related.

At the top, she writes, "People" and underlines it. She writes down Savisia's name and Tima's. She hesitates, should she talk to Caecilia's mum? She decides against that for now. After all, she doesn't know Mollis well, and she isn't Macia's type. She never understood why her sister married into that family. They're more or less the opposite of the Durus family. So those are the two people she will need to speak with. She tries to think about what she needs to find out in order to keep herself safe. So next on the tatty paper she writes, "Info". That list is trickier in a way, for there is need to know, and want to know. Wanting to know is emotional though, and could easily lead to a betrayal of her principles. Where, she writes, then hesitates. Does she really need to know where Caecilia went? She tries to think back to the letter; did Caecilia mention it in there? She doesn't need to know who with, that's clear. But why? Why go with him? She leans back in her chair, realising that some of those points can probably be answered merely by reading the letter.

She hesitates a moment, should she get the secret box down? Silly question, she snorts softly. Getting that box down now is the worst thing she could do. It's tempting though, just to have some answers. On the other hand, if she can speak to Tima or Savisia, all those questions might be answered as well. Hopefully with less risk. Under info she writes, How Long? How long has Caecilia known this Gax, how long has she learned about this book, and been different, rebelling against their laws? She shudders, the idea that you can spend time with someone, be with that person, do things together, and then find out that actually, you never knew them, is frightening. She thinks back to the time spent together, Macia reading out lines that she liked, or making derisive comments about badly rhyming sentences. Times where Caecilia would giggle at something Macia had said. The afternoons spent together filling in their coursework as one. Now it turns out that for many weeks, even moons, Caecilia had already left Elabi in her heart. For that is what it comes down to, Macia thinks.

People don't just leave. Nobody leaves everything behind lightly. Her mother drifts through her mind, and Macia swipes across her forehead as if replacing the image of the beautiful, smiling woman with sheer hatred. Yes, her mother had left everything behind, although not quite everything. People chose though, they chose something else over Elabi. It wasn't done in a hurry though, Macia is convinced about that. So Caecilia must have begun considering leaving a very long time ago, whilst still spending time with Macia, still studying Elabi history, Elabi future plans, knowing she was going to leave her 'dearest friend' behind. Knowing that being caught would be the end of her. Why? And when did that start?

Looking at her meagre list, Macia sighs. This isn't going anywhere, she can see that. It's those two people on her list that she needs, really. The rest of her schoolwork time is spent on thinking of ways to contact

Tima or Savisia. Tima will be relatively easy, but it will raise suspicions if she did so now. Savisia is really out of the question. The girl will be watched too closely. On the other hand, the young girl might be more forthcoming as she might be eager to clear her own name. She might also be furious with Caecilia and want to drop her in it as much as possible. Even though Caecilia is no longer in Elabi. Macia stops her thoughts there and leans back in her chair. Is it possible that Caecilia is still in Elabi? Will the guards have caught her, and the council is trying to find more evidence against her?

Is it even possible that Caecilia is still in Elabi, and hasn't actually left yet? Where would she be though? Macia thinks of the lighthouse, but she is certain that the guards will have searched there. They must have searched around her house as well. Macia wonders again about other letters. Will the parents have had a letter? She is quite sure they must have, for even Macia has had one, explaining her flight. So why did the parents not inform the authorities as soon as they found the letter? Or did they? Macia chews a loose nail, thinking about that one, a grim smirk appearing on her face. "That would have gone down well," she mutters, nearly losing her balance when the metallic voice of the automated servant intones that he doesn't understand the question. "I want the music, but toned down," she says, her fast heartbeat making her sound out of breath. She hopes that if there is a camera installed already, that whoever is watching her will think that this is what she asked for just now.

The evening meal is very quiet. Not that other mealtimes are chatty, but this one is extra quiet. An oppressive sort of quiet, Macia thinks. Ignava looks more sour than ever, and even her father looks down. Macia glances at him over her spoon, the soup too salty as usual, and only the garum makes it palatable to her. Near the end of the meal, her father finally looks at her and says, "I know you have had interviews already. They went well, but not all council members are satisfied. Some feel you might know more about Caecilia and her change of attitude." His eyes flicker for a moment, his cheeks turn a darker shade, and he adds, "I also realise the classes they assigned you are more than necessary. That left me speechless." He glares at her and half opens his mouth to say something else, but snaps his mouth shut. His lips press together into a thin line, and Macia almost thinks how old that makes him look, and how unbecoming, but she makes her eyes look somewhere else. She is quite sure that thinking those thoughts will get her into trouble one day.

Ignava sniffs in the most derogatory manner possible, and hisses, "That family! Why Tima was allowed to make that Attachment I will never know." She glares at Brutus, who flushes for a moment, then he simply says in a very quiet and calm tone that there had been no contra-indication. What was more, the score of those two were a perfect match. He had had his doubts, especially after the Attachment, as Tima seemed to have changed. Now he just wonders if that family didn't have a faulty streak in them after all.

"That reminds me," he says, sounding a little more like his normal self, "tomorrow I will look up their genetics. There might be a fault in their line." Macia stares at her plate, Ignava nods a bit more enthusiastically. Macia can feel her hands go cold, almost as if the icy feeling around her heart has moved to her hands. If Brutus finds a genetic defect, the entire family will be sent beyond the hills. That might or might not include Tima. Macia finds it hard to breathe, and she has to keep reminding herself that she is reacting emotionally. After all, Savisia will be eligible for the Nuptialem List in only a few years. It's just that... Macia isn't sure why she even struggles. After all, Elabi itself is at stake.

Chapter 7

Finally, it is time to go to bed. Macia is relieved. She doesn't know if cameras are installed already, but somehow, lying in the dark feels better than sitting up, knowing someone might be watching your every move. She sighs, disappointed with her performance that day. "How will I ever be ready for my AMP status when I react so emotionally," she mused.

First she pitied Savisia. Then there is her odd reaction after her father said he would look into the Reizio's genetics. Again Macia can feel her throat restricting itself automatically as she thinks of Tima. She swallows to open her throat again, telling her head that she has to be sensible. After all, it's for the good of Elabi. They will all benefit from steady genetics. Just before falling asleep, she remembers that tomorrow is her one session per moon with her counsellor. Great. Just what she needs. For a moment Macia considers cancelling the session. No, not an option. Anyway, she might be reacting in such an emotional way because she hasn't been to counselling for a whole moon.

School is uneventful the next day. Macia keeps herself to herself, relieved not to be pulled from class. After school, she walks to the counsellor's office. She sits in the small waiting room. On the light grey wall opposite her is a framed picture of the brain and another of the City Hall in mute colours. There is a coffee table with a few magazines. She picks up a magazine. It is full of articles about Elabi and its policies and support. She groans inwardly, then remembers the camera. So she pretends to read an article with great interest, her mind wandering off by itself.

The counsellor opens her door, raises her chin at Macia, and invites her into the treatment room. The chairs are not comfortable. "That is to tap into people's logical thinking, rather than make them switch off their brain and allow their feelings to take over," the counsellor had explained. "Macia, much has happened of course, but today is a good day. Explain to me what made today a good day." The counsellor has a paper pad on her knees and looks at Macia expectantly. Macia dips her head, feeling safer than she used to, having had a lot of experience in what ticks the counsellor's boxes. For a minute moment she wonders about this as well, is it another way in which she is deceiving the Elabi authorities?

"Today was a good day in many ways," she says, keeping her face blank, edging on bored, a carefully practised expression. It works well in counselling, for looking keen isn't going to do you any good. Looking bored means more classes. "You see, at school, we learned about snow and how to utilize it. Elabi provides us all with the right footwear, the right clothing for our climate. No more waste or using harmful substances, no using labour forces outside of our own citizens. By doing so the council has shown their trustworthiness again." The counsellor nods, a slight smile on her face.

"Now, as I said, much has happened. I wonder if any of the events brought up similar emotions to what you used to have when I first started supporting you." Macia isn't sure about the word 'support' in this context, but she dips her head anyway. The over-calm voice continues, "It is another person leaving your life abruptly, so I wondered." The counsellor looks at her, her pencil hanging over the paper. The paper has been used a lot already, and Macia has the impression that her words will be important enough to make them the final use of this bit of paper. It will probably go into her file. Will she see it again next time the council members interview her? She digs her remaining nails in the palms of her hands, without showing the counsellor the tightness of her fingers. This one is awkward. She will have to balance her words carefully.

She looks at the counsellor and nods. "At first, when I…" She almost mentioned the letter! "…when I heard about Caecilia having gone, I was in shock. It was hard to process too, as they were asking me questions. I wondered if she had really left, or whether she was simply hiding somewhere." She looks at the counsellor who is writing fast. When the woman looks up Macia shrugs her special way, "You see, even now I wonder if she has actually left, or whether she is hiding somewhere close by. Maybe she went for a walk, tripped and got stuck in the snow." She can even believe it, almost, and it's making her throat go tight! The idea of sweet Caecilia lying in the cold, wet snow, unable to move, unable to be heard by anybody, shouting for help…how awful! She swallows and tries to take a deep breath without making it too obvious that she is having a very emotional reaction to that image.

The counsellor leans forward a bit, her eyes bulging slightly, as if Macia is a very interesting specimen. "You seem to react quite severely to this…image," she says, a little bit breathless herself. "Care to expand on that? Would you call Caecilia a friend, or just a schoolmate, or for example a best friend?" She stares at Macia with large, unblinking eyes, and Macia is still struggling with the picture of Caecilia trapped in the snow, by now dead with hypothermia. She blinks and almost falls into the trap the woman has spread for her.

"No, I mean, well…she was my classmate, and we were friendly to each other," she stutters in the end, shaken by how close she got to being tricked! "You see, a lot of our work has to be done with another

43

classmate. We usually paired up, as we worked along similar lines." The counsellor dips her head; is that disappointment Macia can see in her eyes? "So yes, Caecilia would probably describe me as a friend, but I decided against using that term. You see, after what happened in the past, I wanted to stay clear-headed. I found relationships with people can cloud that judgment I might need. It is harder to be logical and put Elabi first once you allow yourself into relationships with people. Not the Attachment type, but even that is made through logic, not by growing a relationship," she quickly adds, thinking of her fiancé. Again the counsellor nods, and Macia can feel herself relaxing that tiny bit.

"The reason I struggled was that I wondered if there was the possibility of Caecilia having had an accident in the snow. In which case she would be a fellow citizen in need of help. If help had arrived early on then she might have still been able to lead a useful life." Macia doesn't feel she is telling lies. Even if Caecilia was running away, she could still have been overcome by an accident. Mind you, if there was a subversive book involved, the chances of her being successfully re-educated might have been slim.

The counsellor shakes her head, and says, "No, the letter makes it clear that she left. So did the book part she left her parents." Macia looks down, forcing the shivers that go through her to stop. Fortunately, the counsellor is too busy writing down Macia's answer and doesn't see the girl's reaction. When she looks up she asks, "Did you ever see her with a book like that?" Macia shakes her head, and straight away the counsellor narrows her eyes, a triumphant gleam in them. "No..?" Macia shakes her head again, having lost all feeling in her freezing cold fingers.

"It would have been a forbidden book, no doubt," she says, in as steady a voice as she can, pushing all images of the strange thin paper out of her head. "You see, if it was forbidden, it's most likely not on the current type of paper." The counsellor's eyes lose their gleam as she simply stares at Macia. "I'm sure it must have been an old book, or a non-Elabi book, otherwise, why would it be forbidden? So it won't have been on ethical, recycled paper, at least, that's what I think. I only saw her with school books, and once she read a book in the Bibliotheca when we were there after school. It was a book about medical responsibilities, if I remember rightly." The counsellor dips her head, the triumphant gleam having been changed into a disappointed look. Macia looks down and rearranges her dress.

The counsellor sighs and writes away. "You're probably right. I haven't seen the book portion, of course, it is in a sealed envelope. And will be destroyed soon. I did hear it whispered that it was made of unusual material though." She glances at Macia, a little hopeful again. Macia merely dips her head and vaguely mutters that she wonders if they used to make books out of thin disposable plastic as well as paper that couldn't be used again. The counsellor hesitates, wondering if she should make a note of that. In the end, she leaves it.

Instead, she asks Macia if she is still considering the Attachment she applied for. Macia nods, yes, although summer feels far away when there is snow, she knows it will be here soon enough. "You might need to consider more counselling sessions nearer the time," the counsellor says, looking a little smug. "Especially in light of your personal policy toward friendships." Her voice is definitely condescending, making Macia clamp her jaws together more tightly. "It will be a new experience, and we all know that being with another person can cause hormonal instabilities, leading to emotional flare-ups. It would be wise to have some support at that time, and especially just before the Attachment date. To make sure you move into married quarters in the right way. Will you be the heir?" She looks at Macia, who can feel the warmth creeping up again.

The whole thing is still so far away, and although she really can't stand Ignava, her heart seems to somehow react more towards her father. Not that she will tell the counsellor of course, but whenever she tries to envisage Elabi and the house without her father, her heart feels odd. To discuss whether she and her husband will be the heir feels weird, almost as if she is wishing her father away. Of course, it's just to arrange for the right married quarters, but still... Macia nods, "Yes, yes we will be, you see, Tima married Crassus, and he was the heir already. As there were only two of us, father decided I would be the heir for the Durus family, especially as I was, I am, interested in joining him and Ignava in supporting Elabi through writing." The counsellor nods and bends her head over the paper, but Macia saw it!

There was a strange look in the counsellor's eyes. "The woman is jealous? Dislikes me? Why? Simply because of my family?" Macia swallows, of course, she knows there are still little pockets of jealous people left in Elabi, but most people will have had several classes on that topic, and especially professional people would never allow jealousy to impair their judgment or make it alter the way they treat clients. For the counsellor to show open jealousy is shocking. Macia is quite certain that some of the questions posed to her were to get Macia into trouble. Macia is shocked. What should she do? Report the woman? What will the consequences be though? How will she even prove it? After all, the woman is a council appointed counsellor, and at the moment Macia is on their 'persons of interest' list. The counsellor looks up and finds Macia's hard stare aimed at her. This time it's the counsellor whose face grows darker. Macia makes her face go hard without taking her eyes off the woman. The counsellor fumbles a bit for words, then looks at the clock.

"We will have to draw this session to a close," she says briskly, relief swirling in her eyes. Macia dips her head but keeps her face hard, her eyes unblinking. The woman hesitates, and says, "Any other issues you wish to raise before we meet again next moon?" Macia shakes her head and stands up. She raises her chin at the woman, her eyes just that little bit narrowed. From the way the woman raises her chin in return, Macia is satisfied the woman has understood the threat. Of course, trying to prove it might be harder, but Macia is determined to speak to her father about the incident.

After all, there might be other clients, people less discerning perhaps, and this woman could do lasting damage to Elabi this way by allowing her own envious feelings to steer the conversation. It must get looked into, she decides, feeling proud that she is making a very logical decision. After all, the woman has been her counsellor ever since... ever since her mother left, so it would have been easy to feel some form of attachment to the woman. She doesn't, and Macia feels clear in her conscience that she is not doing it out of revenge or other petty, emotional reasons. No, the woman was trying to undermine her, rather than support her, and her only reason was Macia's family line. Her father will know what to do. Macia's heart lightens.

Chapter 8

The grey days merge, and Macia starts to relax when another Enday has gone. There have been no further interviews. Savisia has gone, but Tima is still around. She hasn't visited, of course. That would be causing trouble. A message has been passed on, letting the family know that she and Crassus are fine. Somehow those two managed to distance themselves enough from Caecilia's influence, it seems. Macia wonders about that, for Tima liked Caecilia, and she would call Caecilia her friend as well as her sister in law. So how did Tima manage to get away with that? When another Enday arrives without troubles, Macia decides to pop in on her sister. She might be taking a risk, but she needs to know.

Tima is at home by herself, and she raises her chin cheerfully at Macia. Macia raises her chin back and follows her sister into the house. As soon as they sit down in the kitchen, Macia looks at Tima and says, "So, Caecilia…" Tima rolls her eyes and grunts. She tells Macia about the endless interviews they have had, the search all through their house and the interviews for their managers and colleagues. "I have had a few as well. Plus a counsellor trying to talk me into things," Macia says defensively. Tima isn't the only one having had a hard time. Tima dips her head and explains that as she is almost full term with their firstborn, they allowed her just a little more emotional lee-way. They will watch her connections of course, and she might have to attend classes once the baby is in childcare, but for now, they have written it off as a hormonal imbalance. Crassus has to attend Sharing is Caring classes, but not the same ones as Macia. Macia glares at her sister, "How did you know I had to go?" Tima shrugs and says that Crassus saw her name on the list of the Young Attendees.

Macia sighs, "Such a mess. I never thought Caecilia would be the one to do this to us." Tima dips her head and agrees. She tells Macia that she is tempted to have the same friendship policy as Macia has. Macia shakes her head, "Don't bother," she says, "It made it worse, if anything. They kept on and on about it, telling me that it wasn't against Elabi law to have friends. My counsellor tried to trick me, then hinted at it again later. It was awful. It never helped one bit. When I found out that Caecilia had left, I still felt...awful." She hesitates a moment, should she tell her sister this? After all, Crassus is on the Sharing is Caring course, and if Tima tells him, he might feel obliged to let somebody know that Macia has been emotional about the whole affair. She decides it's safe enough to tell her sister that she felt bad about her friend leaving. Even if Caecilia wasn't technically her friend. Tima nods, and almost says something but then looks away. Macia tenses up, Tima doesn't want to tell her something, because she is on the Sharing course, and might betray Tima! For a brief moment, something goes through her, something she can't name, but it's a strange emotion.

She quickly puts a stop to that, and it works. Macia has been practising controlling her emotions better these last few days. Her reaction to Caecilia leaving has rocked her world. She was amazed by emotions she hadn't felt since her mother left. Just then Tima breaks in, "It...It reminded me so much of when mother left with... left...to go Downstream I mean," she stutters and quickly looks away. Macia dips her head, yes, it reminded her too, but her voice is hard and controlled when she tells Tima that this time she is much better equipped to deal with it. Tima looks at her then, and Macia is confused by Tima's eyes. They are looking...weird, as if she feels something, something she doesn't like. Macia shrugs and they both chat about general things, then Macia leaves the house, feeling relieved. It seems Tima and Crassus are in the clear, apart from extra classes. Macia would have liked to ask Tima about Caecilia's parents and Savisia, but she doesn't. It would look nosey, and Tima might resent it. Anyway, there is nothing Macia can do about them, even if she wanted to.

The days and weeks pass, and soon a moon has passed. Macia walks into the counsellor's office, to be greeted by a younger counsellor. It turns out, her previous counsellor has recently specialised in supporting older people in preparing to go Downstream. Macia smirks to herself. Serves the woman right. She's lucky she hasn't joined any of them yet! She's impressed by her father's influence, and for a very brief moment wonders what he would say if he knew about her secret box. The counsellor is much younger than the previous one, and is less aware of Macia's counselling history, but seemingly more aware of her family's influence. She looks a little nervous, as she should, Macia decides, and starts, "As it's a good day, could you begin with listing those things from today where your emotions might have diverted you from that?" Macia dips her head and thinks.

"The snow," she says in the end, "my boots are getting affected after this time, but I know that as always, new boots will arrive at the right time." The counsellor nods, and very subtly moves her own feet under her chair. Macia had already spotted it though. The boots are very new, unlike Macia's, which are worn and old looking. She wonders about it for a brief moment, then decides that they probably ended up lower on the list because of the events of the past moon. Having to attend classes does put one back on privileges, Macia just hadn't expected it to come out in everyday matters like shoes and clothes assignments. For a moment she wonders what life must be like for a Mansit, and she shudders. The counsellor asks how she is getting on with her special classes, and Macia sits up a little. "It is actually helpful," she says, trying to push down on her enthusiasm. "I had forgotten so much, it's interesting how we can stop noticing smaller threats all around us. I suppose that when we see or hear certain things often enough, we get used to them, and stop seeing them as problems."

The counsellor agrees, and as she is quite young, she tells Macia in a very conversational tone that as counsellors they need to attend classes all the time. "As you say, if you are regularly exposed to certain behaviours, it rubs off. People around you can be struggling with emotions, and before you know it, you allow emotions into your life." Macia dips her head, she totally understands. "Looking back now, with hindsight," the counsellor asks, her eyes focussed on Macia, interest glowing in them, "would you have changed anything you did or didn't do in the case your…" She hesitates, then finishes off, "…your classmate?" Macia nods, even though she feels like smiling for the way the counsellor dealt so delicately with the matter. She explains to the young woman that yes, she would have reported her classmate very early on. There were a few odd moments, where it was clear that Caecilia must have been influenced somehow.

"It seems such an odd word," Macia says, "but almost as if Caecilia was being kind, you know, the way they used to talk about that word?" The counsellor nods, yes, she has heard of the word as well. In the past, of course. Macia dips her head, "Well, that's the way Caecilia turned," she says, giving a little shiver. "It was often…inappropriate, but then, she was a very pleasant person, so I didn't think anything of it. You know, the way things just slip past you, because the change is so subtle." The counsellor nods and Macia says, "I find the classes really helpful, they bring you back down to where we should be at, and how we can support each other without undermining Elabi or our way of life. Yes, if I had done the classes before all this, then I would most certainly have talked to somebody." Betrayed your friend, a tiny voice in her heart mutters, but Macia ignores it. It's like a conscience, but one that wants to rebel against Elabi rules, and therefore is some old evolutionary trick that needs to be controlled.

The counsellor is pleased with the progress made and asks if Macia wants to talk about the Attachment date yet. Macia shakes her head, "No, it's only just the beginning of winter, and the attachment won't happen till the summer is more or less finished." Macia is relieved to think it is so far off and wonders why. "It is good knowing it's coming up," she quickly adds, "and I agree I will need to prepare for it. At the moment my schoolwork has priority though, and after all, a match has been found. I look forward to preparing to move in together and start a harmonious life. My main worry is his status, as I'm preparing to apply for Amplissimos relatively soon, and he is nowhere near the same status. His status hasn't been updated or changed for quite some time, and it worries me a little. Not in an envious way," she quickly adds, "but the question is more about how much he is putting into Elabi." The counsellor nods and Macia is glad to see no sign of envy or other negative emotions. The young woman promises to help her to prepare whenever she feels ready for it, as well as for the Amplissimos application should the need arise. Macia dips her chin, glad that this counsellor cottoned on so quickly.

The session is over. Macia raises her chin, and steps outside. She shivers. Her woollen cloak is warm, but today the cold wind seems to cut straight through the cloth, her long woollen dress flapping against her legs. She walks home through the dark streets, pleased with how the session went, but wriggling her toes in her boot to keep them warm. Macia is satisfied that the older counsellor has been reassigned. Life feels more settled now and no more counselling for another moon. It seems that the interviews have finished as well, so time to get stuck into her studies, as well as her fitness. As AMP there will be more fitness opportunities open to her, more types of sport available as well, and Macia can feel her excitement growing. She wants to be as strong as she can by the end of the winter, to choose her new sports wisely when the time comes.

The days slip by, filled with lessons, her extra classes, as well as exam preparation. The Amplissimos invitation could arrive any day now, and Macia wants to do well. She works hard, feeling tired but in a good way. Life has become clearer as well, thanks to the assigned classes. The group attending the classes isn't very large, and most of them are Mansits. Macia had felt superior at first, looking down on the others. When she realises how useful the course is, she changes her mind a little. Her regular classmates keep well away from her, knowing, sensing that she will report them for anything and everything. Macia can feel the anger rumbling inside her, like a dormant volcano, waiting for an excuse to erupt. The fact that she let Caecilia off the hook, overlooking all warning signs, makes her cringe. There is the letter and small bundle of paper, but that is there, hidden, as a matter of expediency. She would get rid of them, but she isn't sure how. Maybe she should tear them up in tiny little fragments, and flush them. Something holds her back, and she tells herself that the letter and papers are a reminder for her. They warn her to not get complacent again, but to be on her guard against bad influences in Elabi society.

Even the return of Savisia near the end of Macia's Sharing is Caring course doesn't soften her against Caecilia. On the contrary. The girl looks tired and poorly, emaciated almost. She doesn't look at Macia at all and keeps to herself. Her soft face has a grey shade to it, and her hair is very short. Macia only saw her eyes once, and it made her heart leap. They look glassy and empty. Macia can feel her heart shaking in sympathy, but only for a moment. Then she reminds herself that

Savisia had been like her, making excuses for Caecilia's behaviour. As her younger sister, she would have seen and noticed the changes even more, and she had said nothing at all. The fact that she obviously was sent beyond the Hills for a short time shows that she had been found too lax. Macia had only had a few interviews and extra classes, so the difference is obvious.

The cold weather keeps her inside, and a few times she has found her mind feeling lost on a Hexaday or Enday. Once or twice she actually turns to Ignava, takes a breath, and the words, "I'm going to study with Caecilia," had almost slipped out without thinking. Macia is shocked by her deep-seated feelings. She hates to admit it, but she misses Caecilia. After all these weeks, her classmates stay well away, and only a new Mansit or desperate student will do an assignment with her when pressed to do so. Macia doesn't care, in a way their quiet whispers behind her back, the way they avoid eye contact makes her feel better. It's more the way it should be, she thinks, they should be aware of subversive people around them, and be aware that we all need to watch each other, and share irregularities. Even so, the days at the end of the week feel empty.

Chapter 9

The Elabi winter continues, frozen and dark. After the compulsory Sharing is Caring Classes Macia plans to sign up for a class called Logical Minds Think Alike. It was advertised at school. She has seen the poster and as her other classes are about to finish, Macia is keen to attend another. The Sharing class has been very beneficial, and of course, it will look good on her AMP application. She looks at the description, "This class will guide us through friendships and relationships, navigating potential emotional reactions with logic and clarity." Just what she needs. After all, she has to work with her classmates, and soon there will be her Attachment date. Then there is her stepmother, and once Macia is working she might see more of Ignava. Her policy of simply having no friends didn't work well, so there has to be a better way.

Macia almost pulls out of the class on the first day when she realises the council member running the course is the sour woman who had been present at her interview several moons ago. The woman had said then, during the interview, that Elabi does allow friendships. Macia cringes. Will the woman remember her, and make snide remarks? However, she doesn't seem to react when reading through the names of those present. The lesson is dry and factual, but Macia manages to take some useful notes. The course isn't long and takes place right after school. Her father was pleased that she took it, and Ignava had dipped her head, pointing out that looking too keen might not work in her favour when it comes to the Amplissimos application. Macia had dipped her head respectfully, aware that her father was watching her. She sighs. If only the invitation to apply would arrive. She is tired, tired of grey days and freezing walks. Tired of being watched, tired of waiting for things to happen. And tired of being alone, although she wouldn't admit that to anybody.

Macia thinks about it that night as she lies in bed. Why does she have this strange, empty feeling inside? She has managed to keep her emotions hard as ice all winter, but every now and then, she has this stabbing pain in her heart. For her mum, for her little... She gasps a little in the dark, what is she thinking? It's because of Caecilia, she tells herself, her eyes hard and angry. The Logical Minds course might help her to set up safe relationships with some classmates, especially as the weather turns warmer. She sighs hopefully, and wonders if there will be others her age who are applying for AMP status. Maybe they can pal up. At least they will have similar aims and values.

The invitation to apply arrives with the first glimmer of sunshine. Macia senses it in the air walking home that night. It is still dark, of course, but somehow the night air feels different. There is a sweeter edge to it. She breathes in deeply, yes, something is different tonight. When she gets home, the cream envelope is waiting for her on the kitchen table. She gasps when she sees the City Council stamp on the front. Ignava rolls her eyes, muttering something about a great start, but Macia ignores her. She quickly rips open the envelope, her eyes scanning the rough paper inside. Yes! It is the invitation, telling her to apply for Amplissimos Status. Macia feels her heart bouncing inside her, and she suddenly wants to laugh and jump up and down. She manages to suppress the urge. Here she is, with an invitation to apply for the highest level of citizenship in Elabi, and her initial reaction is purely emotional. That is a great start; Ignava is right, she thinks.

The next few weeks are a blur, filling in forms, attending the sanatorium, DNA tests, blood samples and the dreaded fitness test. Macia passes running with flying colours, and even the swimming test goes well. The character interviews are very hard, and Macia has a few moments where she really can't tell whether she has passed or not. "If I fail, I will hate you forever, Caecilia," she hisses on her way home. After all, it will be Caecilia's fault. Not that she will forgive Caecilia anyway. Why did she have to run away? Suddenly Macia can imagine the girl's sweet face, full of excitement for Macia and her application. Caecilia would have rolled her eyes at the fitness tests, and giggled at the idea of Macia swimming so far in one go. Macia swallows, what is she doing, thinking about that girl.

Then, one Fifday afternoon, the rush is over. All the papers are handed in, the tests are done, interviews are completed. Now all she needs to do is wait. It will be at least one moon before she will hear the outcome. Macia shakes the soft slushy snow off her leather boots, feeling dejected all of a sudden. She has been looking forward to this moment for so long, and yet now there seems nothing left.

Macia has lost her goal, has nothing to look forward to and nothing to achieve. In the last counselling session, the young woman had warned her this might happen. Macia had nodded but scorned the idea in her head. It sounded like an emotional reaction, and after all these weeks of carefully training her emotions, Macia couldn't imagine her emotions running away like that. But they have, and she's trying to remember what the woman had said. Something about setting new goals. Macia sighs, easier said than done. There are still three weeks of the special classes left, after that she could look for another class. Maybe she should do a sports course? That catches her interest. She stares out of the window, watching the watery early spring sun reflect off the slushy puddles. Yes, a sports course would be fun. She has had enough of sitting inside. Maybe an Attachment course? She shakes her head to herself. No, next counselling session they will be talking about her attachment date. Hirsut Villios, she rolls the name around her mouth, knowing she'll be using it a lot in the coming moons.

She sighs, feeling listless, restless like the Spring, wanting change, wanting something new. It must be the Spring weather making her feel like this. She can even spot the tiniest green hue on the trees nearby. Yes, the air is definitely changing, and Macia takes a deep breath. Her heart rate suddenly spikes, as she realises properly, for the first time really, that her application to become an Amplissimos is handed in. Again, she wants to do a fist pump or little dance, or a high five like they did in nursery. But she clamps her jaws together. How can she call herself AMP if she goes wild at every achievement?

Macia bites what used to be a very short nail and suddenly remembers the secret box, just over her head. She gives a little gasp. Thinking of new beginnings, maybe she should get rid of old stuff too, make a new start, forget about her mother and Caecilia too. Somehow destroy those funny pages as well. That would be a good start to her Amplissimos life.

The secret box stays in her mind. Macia tests the next nail whilst staring outside again. She can picture the photograph, see the faces in her mind's eye, the background, the colours. Then there is Caecilia's letter. She can only recall snippets from that. There is the weirdest greeting at the top, something about an open mind, and the bit where Caecilia apologises and says she is leaving. Macia swallows, her heart racing and stuttering. It's like a flashback she tells herself, just my body recognising the words and reacting physically. Then there is that thin paper, with the tiniest letters. She wonders what is in…No way! She can't possibly read it, even the guards and council put the bundle they had in a secure envelope. Of course, she is as good as an AMP already, but even so. The council members didn't even look at the words, and she contemplated reading it? "Fine, whatever," she hisses, jumping, hurting the flesh at the corner of her nail as the automated servant intones that he didn't quite get that, would she like to repeat the question? Macia gives a nervous snort and licks the sore spot on her finger. Should she look at the secret box? Nobody is home, she isn't expecting them back till much later, so now would be the ideal time.

She looks up at the loose board above her head, hesitates, then, taking a deep breath she stands up on the window seat, pushes at the board on one side and lifts it down carefully. She leans the board against the window seat. Her hands are shaking as she stands on tiptoe, pulling the secret box towards her, catching it as it slides over the edge, her heartbeat drowning out all other sounds.

Chapter 10

The box is a little dusty, and Macia sneezes when she lifts it down. She wipes the dust off the top, and sits down in the window sill, her heart beating fast. She knows what she is about to do. If found out, it will not only be the end of her Amplissimos application, but she could even lose her current status! She swallows, but still opens the box. First, she pulls the picture out, the edges slightly curled, feeling brittle. She looks at the photograph, and her throat tightens up. It's the picture of a family, her family. Her father, and next to him her mother, looking sweet and beautiful, with two little girls and a chubby little boy. She breathes quickly to release the tightness in her chest and gives a little cough to open her throat. She puts the picture back. She can never forgive her mother, never. The chaos and grief afterwards were terrible, and even now it comes up in her records.

She looks out of the window, the greyness of the dirty slush matching her mood. Last week one of the interviews had brought up family history. It was bound to happen, but it still shook her. Macia bites her nail, staring outside, not seeing anything. After a while, she sighs and turns back to the secret box. She pulls out Caecilia's letter, again feeling shocked at the new paper. Macia looks at the greeting and cringes once more. "My dearest friend." Macia feels resentment and bitterness, but she makes herself focus on the rest of the letter.

She rolls her eyes at the "open mind", breathes and with a loud hiss at the revelation of Caecilia's departure and comes to the main part of the letter. Caecilia mentions the pages but doesn't actually tell Macia they're from a book, let alone from a forbidden book. What if she had gone to her father or the council members about it?

Caecilia writes about God and the need for forgiveness, love and salvation. Macia shudders and feels more angry. Caecilia leaves her behind and has the audacity to tell Macia what she needs in her life. Macia thinks about the recent application, and smirks, not much more she needs now! She is certainly not going to find God. Who is he anyway?

She looks at the lines where Caecilia talks about the funny pages. Actually, from the words, she could have figured out it was part of a book, and clearly on the Forbidden Books list. That does make sense, so Caecilia didn't really need to spell it out, but still... She sighs, what is this bit about the author of those pages? Does she refer to God again, or Gax? Mind you, the paper looks old, much older than Gax. So it must be God then. Was he part of Elabi in the past? She thinks back through her history lessons but comes up blank. And why use capitals? Macia can feel her head starting to ache, her heart banging away against the inside of her skull, knocking for attention, begging for a break. She leans back against the window with a groan, noticing it's starting to get darker already. Even though the days are definitely getting longer, it's not Spring yet. She folds the letter up, wondering again if she should just destroy it. Her hands put the thick paper back into the box, and she shrugs.

She hesitates, her shaking hands hovering over the thin bundle. Should she? She knows it's a forbidden book, but then, nobody is watching her. And she really wants to know what made Caecilia leave Elabi behind. What changed her in the first place, a long time before leaving?

What made Gax so weird? And who is God that is mentioned? Macia swallows, and almost shuts the box. She stops, and her fingers curl around the very thin paper. She drops it, as it's too much of a risk, what if anybody found out? What if it poisons her mind straight away? What if her father can tell later, what if it affects your health instantly as Hillixer can do? Macia's breath is speeding up, so is her heart rate. She bites the soft corner next to her nail until it hurts. Then suddenly, she grabs the thin bundle. She looks at it, quickly, her eyes scanning the paper. It's printed in two thin columns, the letters minute. It has a word at the top, a strange word that she doesn't recognise. The back page has larger words right across the page, and it mentions the word Epistle. That's an old word for letter, she knows that. So is it a collection of letters? How weird! Who would read other people's post? Was it just a literary device, a way of making a book more interesting?

Macia pulls a face, why would she want to read other people's letters? Mind you, maybe they are from God? But no, the letter starts saying the letter is from Paul. What an odd name. Macia sighs, should she even bother? The falling dusk makes reading the tiny print hard anyway, and she knows it's the wrong thing to do. Why would she risk her AMP status to read an old letter? Curiosity bangs away though, and she turns back to the front, the sentence about reading the pages with an open mind flitting through her head. The start of the bundle is clearly in the middle of whatever it is, probably another letter, she thinks. She sits very still for a moment, then brings the paper close to her face and reads the first few lines. It starts with a tiny number. Every few lines there is a tiny number, then a large four, then the tiny numbers start again, from the beginning. She looks at the words, her head making soft whooshing noises with each heartbeat. Macia reads, "For as many are of the works of the law are under the curse; for it is written: "Cursed is every one who continueth not in all things which are written in the book of the law to do them."

Well, who would have guessed that? Macia leans back, stunned. To think that Caecilia left Elabi after studying what is clearly an early book about Elabi rules. Nowadays they don't use the word cursed, of course. It's an outdated concept, as is blessing, she thinks. These words were clearly from a time when people expected bad things to happen to you automatically if you broke the rules. So Caecilia believed that bad stuff would happen to those who didn't hold to Elabi law. Then she left. Macia feels confused. She peers at the words again, '... works of the law are under the curse'. What does that mean? Those that work in Elabi, or who work for Elabi? Like the council members? Macia stuffs the bundle back into the box with a swift movement, slams the lid shut, stands upon the window sill and puts the box back in its secret place. The large board follows, and Macia tells her automated servant to switch the light on. Her head aches, so she pours herself some water from the bathroom. The words from the strange papers stick in her head though, and she shudders. It must be the curse bit, no wonder curses and blessings and other emotion-driven language got banished. It made people superstitious, thinking too much, imagining things. "I'll probably feel unwell tomorrow, seeing that I broke the law," she mutters to herself in a sneering voice, needing to hear her voice in the silent house.

That evening she is glad she is eating by herself. She is sure that guilt must be written all over her face, and her father would probably guess that she had done something wrong. She makes sure she is in bed by the time her father and stepmother return. She is just watching telly, so she calls out to them, trying to sound sleepy. She watches the large screen a little longer, then turns everything off and goes to sleep. Tries to, anyway. After more than an hour of struggling to sleep, she rolls onto her back, burning eyes looking towards the ceiling. It must be the curse, she thinks, I have gotten myself under some curse. The language might be banned, that doesn't mean to say that the curse no longer works! I have broken Elabi law, even though I don't work for the law yet. She is planning to work for Elabi though, so maybe the curse is activated against people who plan to work under the law as well? The words sound as if working for the law means you're put under the curse, or is that just because if you work for the law you are more likely to get cursed, as you could break the law more easily? She sighs, this is complex! No wonder Caecilia changed, trying to work out such difficult obscure language would make anyone lose their head. Macia likes words and it's the one thing she realises about those words. Never mind what it said, the rhythm and flow of them were...special. Special but strange.

Part of her regrets looking at the forbidden pages, but another part feels the urge to look at the words again and to maybe look at even more this time. Warning bells go off in her head. No, she can't possibly look at those words again. The lack of sleep, her fear, the way she felt she had to avoid her father, that is definitely a curse, and it can only have come on her because she disobeyed the law. After all, the council member had made it very clear that the book was a forbidden one, one of the first ones to go on the list in fact. It was so dangerous and subversive, none of the council members got to read it, but it was kept in a special, sealed envelope. And she not only has the book out in the open, holding it in her hands, but she actually looked at the words! She bites her nail, the one with the sharp corner. What is she going to do?

When Macia wakes up, the room is almost light. She takes a deep breath, glad nothing happened during the night. She looks in the mirror as soon as she gets to the bathroom, and her normal face glares back at her. Good, the curse obviously hasn't got any physical manifestations then. Macia wonders if the curse only works for a few hours anyway. Does it get erased after the night? She sighs, better forget about it, she thinks, noting that she looks a little more pale than usual. A brisk walk to the gymnasium will hopefully sort that one out. Macia walks to the gymnasium, forcing her thoughts away from the strange papers. She has to work hard, as she wants to be stronger than ever by the time summer arrives. She should have her Amplissimos status by then, so more sports will open up to her. She hasn't decided what she wants to try yet, but probably something around water.

The gymnasium is quiet; most people work out at the end of the day, but Macia likes the early mornings best. It sets you up for the day, she always says. That reminds her of Caecilia who worked out in the evening if she had to. Caecilia wasn't into sports. She preferred to draw, watch telly, or maybe go for a relaxed walk. She liked mechanical things, so she was often working on her father's lighthouse. Macia shakes her head to clear her thoughts. What is she doing thinking about Caecilia? Must be because she read the letter again. She sighs, she can still picture the girl's face, but it is no longer soft and sweet. Macia is sure that she hates the girl, resenting her tremendously. Of course, hate is an emotion and she would never tell somebody that she hates the girl. The cooling down room is quiet as well, and Macia is glad. She chooses a mat and does her stretches. Maybe I should teach some of the gymnasium classes, she thinks, not for the first time. She does like teaching, although the idea of a group of Mansit children in front of her makes her shudder. Their food is so different, and so are their clothes and cleaning materials, making them carry a strange smell around them. The same smell that lingers in the gymnasium in late Spring, summer and early autumn after the Mansit men have been in. She wrinkles her nose, maybe not then. Although it will allow her extra privileges.

Chapter 11

Endays are usually very quiet in the Durus household. Her father has talks to prepare, or he will meet up socially with other council members. Ignava attends local classes and meets up with other council members' spouses. The balance is a fine one. Nobody wants to be seen as more important within the council, but some people seem to end up with more power by default. The spouses are given the task of arranging speaking assignments as well as recording talks for the wider public. Of course, there are also the warning talks that need to be recorded and uploaded onto the automated servant system. Different problems creep into society all the time, so it is important to keep the talks updated and fresh. Council members' spouses have the task of organising for this, as they all know their other half's strengths. Ignava enjoys those meetings, as she likes delegating and organising. Each Enday, the spouses have a very long planning meeting in one of the members' homes. This week it's not at the Durus home, so Ignava will be out for most of the day.

Macia can feel her excitement growing, knowing full well that the idea of doing something illegal can work like drugs. It's exhilarating, addictive and very wrong. She tries to tell herself that the book can't be that wrong; after all, it's encouraging people to obey the law. It's probably forbidden for its outdated language. She pushes the fact that it was one of the first books to be forbidden to the back of her mind.

After all, she only has a small part, and it's just letters. Letter writing isn't really encouraged, but it's not forbidden, Macia tells herself. She waits till both her father and Ignava have left the house. She tidies her room a little, mainly to make sure they don't return because they have forgotten something. She needs her secret space to stay secret.

When she is sure that the coast is clear, she hops back onto the window seat, lifts the board out and reaches for the secret box. This time she turns straight to the little bundle. She lifts the paper out of the box with shaking hands. After a quick glance round to check that nobody is coming up the driveway, sits down to read. What on earth does it mean? Who are all these people? She also can tell that the letter isn't actually the law after all. In the paragraph numbered 21, written to people called Galatians it even says that if there was a law that could have given life, then we'd be right. Righteous it says, but she assumes that's a poetic way of saying right. No wonder the book is seen as subversive, it's actually criticising Elabi law. It's saying that Elabi rule doesn't bring life, and doesn't make anyone right. It's telling her that faith is the thing to have, not laws or rules.

Macia begins to understand why this book was banned. It totally undermines everything the city stands for; the council's hard work, their support of all citizens, everything. She should destroy this book, really she should. What is stopping her? Macia looks at the funny paper, and she knows it's because she likes words, rhythm, sentences. This type of writing is new to her, and she has to admit that her heart loves it, even though her head is screaming warnings. Her heart revels in the newness and flow of the words. She frowns darkly when the letter writer calls obeying the law living under a yoke of bondage. See, that is where they are wrong, she sighs, they haven't understood how much freer life is when the council supports life through Elabi law. What if everyone did whatever they wanted to do, without proper structures in society?

How can anyone live in joy, peace, goodness and all the other positive things mentioned in the letter without Elabi rule? Slowly she puts the bundle back in the box, and with unseeing eyes slides the box back, then returns the board. The book seems to have misjudged Elabi law. It is an old book, so maybe it was written before the present-day laws were properly installed? She wonders why it constantly opposes law with faith though. Surely it is faith in the law and the council that keeps Elabi safe and strong?

Macia spends most of the day trying to avoid thinking about the words as snippets whirl through her head, leaving her tired and with a headache. After lunch she watches television, to try and rest. Her father will be back quite soon, and she needs to be able to function in a normal way. She has to stop thinking about the words, or he'll sense that something is wrong. Fortunately for Macia, her father has had a good, but busy day, and he is too tired to notice her. Ignava is full of the meeting she has had all day, making a derogatory comment about the house she has just been to. Macia looks shocked, "You're not emotionally involved, are you?" "No." Ignava shakes her head when Macia hints at those thoughts, "You see, it's not about having or not having, that would be emotional, envious. It's about having but not sharing it out." Macia frowns, and Ignava waves her hands around, "When you get the council's spouses round, and you have certain things on display, that afterwards turn out to be simply that, a display, well, that says something. You see, it was simply showing off wealth to us." Macia shrugs, and suggests that Ignava reports it, being bored by the dramatics.

"Oh, I just might," Ignava says, a nasty edge to her voice and Macia looks up sharply. She is seriously going to report that a council member's wife had put food, hard to get food at that, out for display, but never offered anything to any of her visitors?

"She might have forgotten," Macia says, shocking herself, why would she even care, trying to come up with excuses for the woman? She was most likely aiming to be petty and trying to trick the others into being jealous. Ignava stares at her, her face blank, but her eyes are hard. Macia shrugs again, a tiny shiver starting deep in her heart. "The woman needs to clearly train her automated servant better," she tries to joke off the rather frigid atmosphere, making her face look bored with the subject. Ignava dips her head, then slowly admits that it was the woman's first time hosting, as the husband is a new member. Hosting is quite a task, of course, so technically it might have been possible that she forgot. Maybe. Macia nods, "Ask around a little, get a character sheet on her." Ignava narrows her eyes. She dislikes Macia, and getting advice from the grumpy girl is too much. There is the Amplissimos application though, so Ignava dips her head, though unable to hide her spiteful looks. Macia moves around the kitchen, rearranging a few things so that she can leave the kitchen soon after, feeling a little shaken by her stepmother's looks. Walking up the stairs she shudders again, thinking of the little thin pages upstairs. It's influencing her already, it's turning her against Elabi rule, making her forget the way life works. It's turning her soft, rather than logical, just like it did to Caecilia.

Macia is determined to stay away from the book. The book doesn't stay away from her though, and its words keep wandering around her mind like aimless Mansits on Hexaday. They pop up in class, in the gymnasium, at dinner times; they make her lose concentration in the Logical Heads class, distracting her with words like goodness, meekness, kindness when the council member explains that faults in friends need passing on to the authorities, to keep Elabi from sinking into darkness. "It has arisen from the turbulent mess it was decades ago. It has taken many years and different council member's dedicated service to bring Elabi into the light, we want to keep it like that." Her voice sounds grim as if she is making it a threat against anyone who wants to challenge her. Did she really mean to look at Macia at that moment? Macia dips her head in agreement. Do they still suspect that she knew more about Caecilia's disappearance? A line slides into her mind, making her cheeks heat up, as a tiny voice reminds her, "For all the law is fulfilled in one word: "You shall love your neighbour as yourself."

Macia swallows, then sternly reminds her mind that loving other Elabi citizens means reporting them sometimes, whatever the cost. It is for the greater good. Somehow, her inner voice doesn't sound as convinced as it should be. Macia bites her thumbnail, scared that she is changing already, weakening against the rules and regulations, arguing about them in her head, questioning the council member's wisdom. She is determined to leave the book where it is, either that or destroy it. Its influence is clearly dangerous, and again she wonders if the woman suspects anything. Has Macia said or done something recently that might have gotten reported? She thinks back through the week, but she can't think of anything. She has kept herself to herself, interacting only when necessary. Macia swallows, her head feeling tired, fear of being found out always round the corner. "I hate you, Caecilia," she mumbles to herself when putting her books in her cloth bag, wishing again and again that the girl had never written to her.

Macia's resolution holds out all the way to Enday. Hexaday saw a few moments where her fingers simply itched to get the board down, but she had been strong. Today the house is quiet again, and Macia decides to read through her notes, ready to write her final papers for the special class. The words about loving your neighbours, obviously other Elabi citizens, comes to mind again. Macia is sure that it means to report them when necessary and to stay away from people where possible. After all, why force your company onto someone? She had liked

Caecilia coming round, but it was a bit burdensome as well. Making her drinks, finding her something good to eat, listening to her, putting up with some of her plans, going upstairs or downstairs depending on what the girl had wanted… It was actually tiring, and of course, you had to always watch yourself, anything could be misinterpreted. Her mind drifts to the council member's wife and the snacks that had not been offered. She could be in trouble if Ignava and a few others complained, simply because she had forgotten about the snacks. What a burden. Macia's mind comes to a screeching halt.

A burden! The laws, Elabi rules, were a burden, and the book asks you to love people around you as you love yourself, to share burdens. Macia pulls a face. Who would do that, and why? It's hard enough to be civil to some neighbours, let alone loving them. The word 'love' makes her pull a face every time she reads or thinks it. It's not a common word, but textbooks sometimes explain it as wanting what is best, although it very easily can slip into emotionalism, where you really like something. This can then lead to feelings of attachment, entitlement, or longing. Macia shivers, not good. Imagine liking all your neighbours like that! She knows some couples need special counselling as they start to get too close to each other after their Attachment day. It's almost acceptable though, not right of course, but it happens when you live with somebody all the time.

She starts on the essay, determined to get back into a normal, logical mindset. In the middle of a sentence, she abruptly gets up, walks to the window, and soon has her box out. For research purposes only, she tells herself, simply to verify that those words about loving others were really showing how Elabi rule got it right. She gets to the next large number, her eyes scanning the lines for proof. Soon she sits back in the wide window sill, her head spinning. "Do good…bear each other's burdens…serve each other." Macia's swallows, it's worse than she thought. This book is…terrible, calling it subversive is the understatement of the year. Telling its readers to…to do what Caecilia and Gax did. Serve people, as a common Mansit, be nice to people, just because you can, do good things for them.

Macia blinks. There is nothing logical about this book at all, she decides, snapping the lid shut with more force than necessary. Staring at her essay paper, Macia swallows, pushing the words far away from her head. "I'm almost an Amplissimos," she hisses to the paper, glaring at it, "that is the ultimate act of kindness towards all my neighbours, for it means I can help to organise this society to make it free and fair and to keep the darkness away." So why does her throat hurt while writing about how to keep friends and their families safe by being aware of destructive undercurrents? Why does the constant threat of being reported feel like a dark shadow hanging over people's heads?

Chapter 12

Macia is determined to forget the words of the thin pages that week. The weather helps, as Spring is definitely on its way. Her essay is well received by the woman council member running the class.

"I worried about you, seeing your name on the list," she says pointedly to Macia when she goes to the office to collect her essay. "I even wondered if you were there by council request. Finding out that you had applied for the class yourself I realised that you were smart enough to take my comments the right way; you know, when we were talking to you about that friend of yours. You did the right thing, and I know from your participation in class that you have grown from the experience. That is what sets council members apart," she adds.

The woman looks at Macia with a triumphant gleam in her eyes, and Macia digs her fingers into the palms of her hands. She didn't attend the class because of the woman's hint. In fact, she had almost quit when she found out it was the woman teaching it! She can't say that, of course; one does not argue with a council member.

Instead, she dips her head, "Thank you for sharing this class with us. It has made a lot of things clearer. Relationships can be so complex, and I am glad that the council works hard to support young people in this," she adds, knowing it will please the woman. Seeing the woman's cheeks blush makes Macia cringe. Who knew the woman was that weak? Then she clenches her jaws together, for feeling the little power surge simply from watching the woman react emotionally to a compliment is equally weak. Macia almost sighs, then reminds herself that at least she's given the woman some love.

She raises her chin at the council member, and swiftly leaves the room before her own face has darkened into a much deeper blush. Her fingers are aching from clenching her fists so tightly, but what was she thinking? How could she even allow that word into her head, whilst talking to a council member? At this rate she won't need the curse to get in trouble, she can do that all by herself.

Macia spends Hexaday and Enday fighting against the urge to look at the pages. She is relieved when Onesday arrives and with it the lack of opportunities. The way the words of the book spring to her mind frightens her and Macia is determined to be loyal to Elabi. She will be an Amplissimos soon, and with it comes the responsibility to encourage and support citizens to adhere to Elabi rule. The book tells her to have faith, whatever that might be, and to not be bound by law. It tells her to serve others. Well, she will be as an AMP, which is the best way to serve. It tells her to bear other people's burdens, which leaves her confused. What are burdens? What kind of burdens are they talking about? Life is good in Elabi. Maybe teaching classes is meant by that, she suddenly thinks. After all, like she told the council member, the Logical Heads class made relationships clearer. In a way, friendships can be a burden, or not knowing how to deal with relationships. By teaching and training people you take that burden off them.

Macia pushes harder at the rowing machine in her morning gymnasium session. She feels pleased with herself that she has figured it out. That's it, she can serve others, relieve their burdens and show 'love' to them by training and teaching. Maybe she should apply to be a trainer? She looks at the large clock, wondering when exactly she will fit it in. Mind you, soon after the summer is over she will leave school. As an AMP she should get more favourable hours of work, and therefore, teaching classes in her free time should work. It will also make her position as an Amplissimos stronger. Macia can feel herself getting more excited about the idea of teaching youngsters. She could do a running class; she likes running and is good at it. Or a Consuete fitness class for those applying for Umbo status? Her heart rate is going up with each idea, and not because of the rowing machine. She is actually getting excited, so time to stop thinking about this, and return to this topic another time, when she can be rational about it.

The first chance she gets is Hexaday. Macia sits down at her desk and using a very used scrap of paper, starts making a list. First, she makes a list of different types of classes she could run. Next comes a list of pros and cons. For example, teaching Consuete Status students means no Mansits in class. Con of this is that those Mansits ought to be pulled back into society proper, to make Elabi stronger. Is feeling repulsed by someone's food habits or different style of clothing an emotional reaction in itself? As an Amplissimos, she should strive to eradicate emotional responses. In other words, by making herself teach Mansits, she will be working on herself at the same time. Definite pro!

Next Macia works on a list of probable qualifications she might need. Some of these she has already, some of it will be part of her Amplissimos status anyway, and even compulsory, some she might have to apply for. She leans back with a very satisfied sigh, looking at the list with…love. Yes, definitely love, she smirks to herself, then her smile slips. She really shouldn't be using that word, it has such bad connotations.

On Enday, the council members' spouses will meet at the Durus home. Ignava has been fretful all week with preparations and Macia surprises herself when she feels concerned for the older woman.

The approaching meeting dominates their Hexaday evening meal. "Now both of you make sure you don't touch anything on the top two shelves in the fridge," Ignava fusses between spoonfuls of lentil stew. Brutus raises his eyes to her patiently, then carries on with his stew.

"I could help out tomorrow if you like, Ignava. You know, serve food or collect empty glasses." As soon as the words leave Macia's mouth she is aware of her grave error. In the stunned silence that follows she realises this uncharacteristic behaviour; this 'kindness' is exactly what Ignava is looking for to report to the Council.

Macia immediately lowers her eyes to avoid Ignava's triumphant gleam. "Actually, that would be helpful," Ignava replies stiffly and Macia looks up in time to see gratitude in her stepmother's eyes. Apart from a slight rise in his eyebrows, Brutus continues to focus on his food.

Chapter 13

Macia and Ignava rise early to cut up flatbread into squares and open paper packets of the more expensive peppered crackers. Soon jars of fish paste, cream cheese, olives, tomatoes and bunches of fresh herbs cover the kitchen counter as the women create a range of savoury toppings, chatting as they work.

"Am I really enjoying time with Ignava?" Macia almost gasps at the thought. A fragrant smell wafts through the kitchen as Ignava brings her apple, almond and cinnamon slice from the oven and for the first time, Macia acknowledges how she admires her stepmother's hosting skills. But of course, she stops herself from saying so.

When the doorbell starts to ring, Ignava is a picture of calm, welcoming each guest while Macia offers them each a drink. Very few of the spouses even acknowledge her. Macia keeps her face straight while she circulates the room with trays of fingerfood for the buffet lunch. She recognises one of the wives as being attached to an important council member. The tall woman critically scans the proffered tray until, unable to find fault, makes her selection, all the while avoiding Macia's eyes. One of the oldest wives there raises her eyes at her questioningly before scooping up some fish paste crackers.

A few raise their chins, and Macia makes a mental note of their names. Then a thin faced young woman she has never seen before arrives. Ignava greets her coolly and takes her coat. Macia offers her a drink. The woman raises her chin pointedly and delicately, almost appreciatively, and takes one. Macia immediately realises she is the disgraced wife who forgot to serve her fancy snacks. She is obviously working hard to stay out of trouble and Macia almost feels sorry for her. Carrying empty trays and glasses back to the kitchen, Macia can hear muffled animated voices from behind the door. The meeting is in full swing, and her stepmother seems to be having a good time.

Macia's thoughts drift off, back to the forbidden book. Yes, she enjoyed serving these people, but why? Mainly because they are important to Elabi, she has to admit. Also, because it will be remembered and mentioned, so it earns her extra points, which can help her AMP application. Yet looking at the empty trays in the kitchen she feels sad. The food was lovely, she's confident about that. It's the balancing act she dislikes, as it is obvious many of the spouses were looking to find fault to report. Like the poor wife of the new council member, who apparently had to attend several classes during the last few weeks, simply because she forgot to serve the snacks she had prepared.

These meetings in themselves are a burden, she realises. This morning she is helping her stepmother bear that burden, and although Ignava is enjoying herself immensely, Macia had also seen her blushes. She had noticed the slightly wild-eyed look when a spouse asked for something whilst Ignava was trying to do something else. Yes, Ignava had panicked for a moment, overwhelmed, and Macia can't blame her. Having to look after one friend after school is bad enough, having twenty spouses at your place, each more sceptical and critical than the other, is the stuff of nightmares. It's no use pretending, jealousy is still the main factor at these meetings, though nobody would admit it.

Macia remembers the book using the words 'biting and devouring', and can't help smiling. It tells you not to provoke, not to envy others. Whoever banned the book must have missed that bit, for it's as relevant now as it was whenever that letter was written. Again Macia wonders about the book. Why and when the book was banned and how large was it? Has anybody else a part? Of course, Caecilia left a portion for her parents. The council has that part, although it's most likely destroyed by now, without it ever having left the envelope. Macia moves around the kitchen, putting the hot water boiler on for drinks. She needs the distraction, as thinking about the book whilst the council members' spouses are in the next room is probably unwise. She wonders if any of them will be able to help with her idea of teaching classes after leaving school. After her Attachment Day, she thinks, her breath suddenly stuck in her throat.

Ignava looks exhausted at the end of the day, and Macia smirks a little. She wonders if Ignava will say something negative, something emotional. It could be useful if she did, although the tiniest whisper in her heart says that a thought like that isn't loving. Macia swallows, banishing the whisper. "It looked like a busy day," she says to her stepmother, trying to make up for her nasty thoughts. Ignava nods and takes a breath as if she is going to say something. She looks at Macia and stops, simply nods again and agrees that it had been a busy day. "Was that all the spouses complete?" Macia asks, whilst clearing things away. Ignava thinks about this, and half dips her head, thinking out loud, going through the list of people.

"I think so," she says in the end, "Only one woman was missing. She was not very well, and actually went to the Sanatorium on Quarday, so she might be going Downstream. Unless she has recovered already." Macia dips her head, thinking many of the spouses seemed to be old.

"What happens if the council member goes Downstream?" she asks.

Ignava shrugs, "The spouse would no longer attend the meetings of course, as they are no longer with the council member. It does happen, and in fact, one might be heading that way in the next week or two. His wife mentioned it today in passing, trying to say it without saying it," Ignava grins. She loves her own puns, and Macia looks down on the dish she is putting in the cleaning machine. She can't stand Ignava's word games. "Anyway, she had to tell us in the end, as she was expected to host soon. So she could no longer hide it. She told us her husband is trying to hold it off as long as possible, as he is tying up loose ends of the enquiry about that friend of yours, the dark-haired one." Macia dips her head, clenching her jaws together, immensely disliking Ignava at that moment. But she saw the glint in the woman's eyes, and she knows if she rises to the bait now, there could be trouble.

Soon the kitchen looks its usual sterile self, and Macia walks upstairs, missing the book, and strangely enough missing Caecilia. Normally, when the spouses met at the Durus home, Macia went out with Caecilia to escape. This is her first time seeing the spouses together. She might be on their level or even higher than some of them soon, but there is nothing attractive about them.

Chapter 14

Before Macia knows it, another Hexaday has arrived. She wakes up happy, reflecting on the news Ignava told them yesterday evening. The old council member has been served his Downstream letter and will be gone in a few days. Ignava had pursed her lips, muttering, "Well, that will be the end of the loose ends then," looking pleased with her joke. Once her father and Ignava leave, the house is quiet. Macia tidies her room. She is determined to stay away from the book. But as she turns it over in her mind, she reflects that some of it has been useful and maybe she should look at it again, as she is thinking of how to serve the citizens of Elabi if her status comes through. Just as she is about to climb up to lift the board down, she spots movement on the long driveway. She stops, her heart beating wildly. That was close!

It is a postman. She doesn't recognise him, but he's clearly a Mansit. Not much post is sent in Elabi as nobody wants to waste paper and Macia wonders about the envelope the Mansit is holding and thinks about the council member who is about to go Downstream. Is this letter about the enquiry? Or a letter clearing them? Can anyone's name be cleared? Probably not, she decides. There is always something to be said against people, and no Enquiry would ever completely clear somebody's name. Macia walks downstairs and takes the envelope from the Mansit. The man raises his chin respectfully, but Macia ignores him. For a second she hesitates, for she can see his eyes trailing up and down the house, an odd light in them. Is he jealous? Then the man turns and trudges back down the driveway. Macia is left standing on the doorstep, still wondering whether she should report him. He was definitely looking at the house with envious eyes.

She closes the large front door, realising she is stalling, nervous about the envelope. There is a large stamp with the City Council emblem on the front and her name. Her heart thuds as she walks upstairs slowly, ripping at the envelope. By the time she gets to her room the envelope is open, but Macia can't make herself pull the letter out. What will it be? Will it be a rejection of her application? A summons for Caecilia's enquiry, something else that has gone wrong? She lowers herself on the bed, and after taking a very deep breath, pulls the letter out. Her eyes fly across the lines, and she gives a gasp, then a fist pump, and an excited wiggle up and down. She has been accepted into Amplissimos Status. She is now one of the very few citizens who have made it all the way to the top and, unusually, she has done so before leaving school.

Macia reads and re-reads the letter, her eyes almost popping out in excitement. The official Recognition Ceremony will be at the Midsummer festival of course, but this letter will serve as proof of her acceptance. She can now sign up for more classes, more privileges, different sports, and even apply for different kinds of jobs. She may also undo her Nuptialem application. Macia hesitates about that one but decides that today is not the day to think about that. She is excited about the different sports options though, and her eyes light up when she spots the list on the back. She scans the outdoor sports, and her eyes land on Paddleboarding. She blinks, paddleboarding, what is that? It sounds like an interesting thing to do, and she checks the location. It's just beyond the first bridge.

Macia stares out of the window, remembering last summer when they went with a small group to the larger beach. It had been a good day, of course, but yes, that was definitely a good day. Caecilia had invited them, Gax was there and it had been hot. She had felt uneasy for most of the day, sure that people were laughing and talking about her behind her back, and that had made her come out with sharp comments. She had made the others uneasy, she knows that, but it made her feel better. Seeing them tiptoe around her, weighing their words and actions made her feel more in control. Of course, now she is Macia Durus AMP, there is no need to grapple for control. She has it. She looks out of the window, her eyes back to the here and now. The sunlight is soft and warm, and she suddenly decides to see the paddleboarding facility. She wants to know what it is like. Ideally, she wants a water sport that requires you to wear a wetsuit as dirty water on her skin makes her shudder.

It is a long walk, nearly an hour, in her new, uncomfortable boots. The boots arrived eventually, the delay no doubt related to the Enquiry. Hopefully, having just reached Amplissimos status, she will be further up the chain and will receive her allotted clothing and shoes more quickly in future.

Finally, she can see the first bridge, and soon after the bridge, she spots the watersports facilities. She walks through the gate, past stacks of kayaks and odd, boat-shaped planks. There are paddles everywhere, and Macia feels her stomach flutter in excitement. In the small office, an older woman comes to the desk. She isn't a Mansit, but not far off it, Macia judges. Macia raises her chin, and the woman returns the greeting. She stares at Macia, not in a rude way, but as if measuring her up. Macia swallows; this feels awkward. She pushes the letter across to the woman, and explains, "I just received my letter, and it says that there are new sports for me to try. One of the sports mentioned is paddleboarding. I...ah... well, I think I would like to..." She stops;

does she really want to try it now? The snow is gone, but the water will still be freezing, even with a wetsuit.

The woman dips her head and briefly glances at the letter. "We do paddleboarding here, yes. It might still be too cold this week. You will need a very good wetsuit, and they don't always help you to stand up on a board. I can show you a board, the paddle and that sort of thing though," and she looks at Macia. Macia nods, the woman seems friendly, almost kind, she thinks, feeling a little shiver inside her. But of course, there is the Amplissimos letter, that would make a lot of people very helpful. She just has to get used to that. Macia follows the woman out of the little building, towards a larger shed with special racks, filled with the same boat-shaped boards. The woman looks back at Macia and walks across to one particular rack. Macia can see that those boards are smaller and the woman lifts one off the rack and holds it next to Macia. It comes over her head, and Macia wonders if paddleboarding might be a mistake.

The woman grabs a wooden paddle, also quite long, and takes both outside. Macia follows. The woman lays the board down on the short grass and points to the picture near the back of the board, where two bare feet have been painted on. "That is where you stand," she says, "and you use this paddle to move forward. That's all really, apart from it sounds easier than it is, but you look strong and fit. You should find your balance without too much trouble." Macia dips her head, her heart beating fast, her face glowing from the woman's words. She quickly looks away over the water, half turning away, afraid that the woman will see that her words gave Macia so much pleasure.

"You can paddle here, all the way to the bridge along the river. That is the turning point, after that it…well, it's a no-go area of course, or you can go there," and she points towards the open water, "but only in very calm water, we would advise. You can use the board in windy weather; it just needs a lot of experience, and a slightly different board, ideally."

Macia nods. Yes, she can imagine larger waves rolling over the board, washing her off! "Of course, some of the water here and towards the first bridge you just walked past is fine, it can be very smooth some days." Macia nods again and feels the corners of her mouth turning up. The woman sounds as if she really likes the water. Macia nibbles her thumb. Should she advise the woman that liking the water could easily turn into loving the water, and become an emotional passion? She sees the woman looking out over the water, her eyes glowing, pleasure for the dark blue waves clearly reflected in them. Macia stops herself. Why shouldn't the woman love the water? Macia likes running, the feel of the grass under her sandals, the fresh air drifting up from the earth. Macia looks away from the woman, not wanting to see the joy there, not wanting to have to mention her to a council member.

When they are back in the little reception area, the woman pulls a list towards them both. Her pencil follows a line on the paper and rests on the following Hexaday. "It will still be cold, but you could try it out," she tells Macia, the pencil hovering above the little space. "You will need to wear a wetsuit, an insulated one, and maybe not be in the water for too long. At first, it can be hard enough to stand up, but as I said, you look athletic. Just don't try it for too long. There will be plenty of other weeks, warmer weeks." Macia dips her head, excitement making her fingers itch, and she digs them into her hands. She can start paddleboarding next week! The woman looks at her, and Macia gives her name. The woman's hand goes very still for a moment when she hears Macia's surname, then she writes her name down in the square. Macia is sure the woman's eyes have suddenly lost a little light, and the way she raises her chin at Macia is less enthusiastic. Macia is used to it. Many people in Elabi react to her that way when they find out who her father is. She makes sure she raises her chin at the woman with the same level of care as when she first saw the woman.

On her way home, Macia feels like running, even in her new boots. Not only has she attained Amplissimos Status, but she has also booked her very first paddleboard lesson. Why shouldn't she be full of joy? Yet she knows it's forbidden, and as Macia Durus AMP she will need to be careful, and control her emotions better than the average Umbo or Altiorem. Especially by the time she gets home, her emotions need to be well under control. She will have to show her father and Ignava the letter, and she might even tell them about her first paddleboard session. She has to be completely factual and controlled. Ignava will be looking for signs of weakness in Macia, and she will make use of any she can find.

Chapter 15

Both her father and Ignava congratulate her, in a matter of fact way. Macia dips her head, having managed to announce her acceptance into Amplissimos status with a neutral face. That evening over dinner she also tells them about her paddleboarding next Hexaday. Ignava snorts, "Well, that could be a very short-lived Amplissimos status then. You'll be Downstream with pneumonia before you even have attended the official ceremony." Macia can feel a grin growing, but she manages to simply shrug and says that the woman had explained about insulated wetsuits. Her father nods and tells her to make sure to remember her standing in society that day. Macia dips her head. Yes, not to look as if you are enjoying yourself, not chat with the woman as if she was one of us.

Macia stares at her plate. The way the woman had looked at the water with such obvious pleasure had made her uneasy. She swallows, but by the time she is helping Ignava to clear the table after dinner she has smoothed her face out into her usual bored, slightly grumpy look. She struggles to sleep that night. The book recommending joy has somehow influenced her. She must stay away from those pages, especially as an Amplissimos. She stares ahead in the dark, imagining herself as a council member in a few years, moved back into the Durus family home, probably with three children, and there she is, sneaking into this room, to remove the secret box. She sits up in the dark with a shock. That won't do. She can't wait so long to destroy those pages. It will have to be done soon.

The threat of the bundle is making her nervous. It was dreadful enough as Altiorem, but now that she is an Amplissimos it is worse. What if she gets found out? The paper has to go. And Caecilia's letter? Macia lies down again, her throat feeling tight. Caecilia might have landed her in a tonne of trouble, but that letter is all she has of the girl. There is the photograph as well, what is she supposed to do about that? She doesn't want to destroy it, but to keep it is such a risk. Or is it? How will anyone find the box? She smiles in the dark. Even if she leaves it there till she is an adult, it won't really make a difference. She can imagine herself as an adult, her father long gone Downstream, sitting on the soft sofa downstairs with her husband, looking at the picture, reading her school friend's letter. Though of course, she won't be sharing it with her husband, or she'll be beyond the hills by the next morning, and who knows what will happen to him. And to their three children. Again her throat feels tight, her eyes itchy from tiredness, and she has to remind herself that she hasn't had her Attachment Day, let alone had a family, it's just in her head. Which is exactly why emotions are to be controlled, she tells herself sternly, for what sort of person loses sleep simply from imagining things years before they actually happen?

That Onesday she feels a little thrill walking into school, her first day as Macia Durus AMP. Not that she can tell her classmates, but some may have heard and they will all know by lunchtime. Her lunch time space has moved, of course, and she is thrilled to find a few other Amplissimos sitting at the same table, their food brought to them, the service quiet and polite. She keeps her face looking bored. It avoids other problems, such as having to talk to people. The Mansits serving them are polite, and Macia almost says thank you to one of them, and nearly dips her head at another, but she manages to mask her words, and redirect her movement in time. The other Amplissimos would report her for inappropriate behaviour at the lunch table, showing a lack of boundaries. Macia chews on her food with effort as if she is trying to chew over her thoughts as well.

Macia is secretly counting down the days to Hexaday, hoping the weather will cooperate. Hexaday is a lovely Spring day. Macia feels relieved when she looks outside at the light blue sky, little streaks of white here and there, the trees definitely getting a green sheen to them. She eats a good breakfast and puts some flatbread in a glass container for lunch. She has no idea how long she will be, and the bowl with pottage might not see her through. She takes a change of clothing and a soft linen towel. Her heart is racing along, leaving her breathless, excitement making her hands shake. She manages to hide it from Ignava, but as soon as she is out of sight of the house Macia allows her grin to grow, just for a moment. She is going paddleboarding.

The walk gives her time to calm down, the fresh Spring air smelling sweet. In the distance, near the sea, she can see some of the dark fields being worked ready for planting. Macia feels lighter, her feet almost bouncing off the ground and she hums the song they learned last week in school, extolling the beauty of Elabi, and how the land feeds them, nurtures them. She is glad to see the bridge, for although her boots have become more comfortable, it is still a long walk. Macia can't wait till sandals are issued, and as Amplissimos she should be getting them quite soon.

The woman is waiting for her. They raise their chins in greeting, and the woman nods at a wetsuit she had put aside already and shows Macia the changing rooms. There is a special hook for her cloth bag as well. Macia wriggles and shrugs into the wetsuit, its material clinging onto her, making it hard to get in. She finally manages though and flexes her toes against the sock-like ends of the suit. The woman is waiting for her when she comes out and points at the hood. "When you start, put the hood up too," she advises, "for wet hair can turn cold very quickly. Also, the water will be more likely to run into the suit down your neck." Macia shivers and tucks her thick plaits into the suit and drags the hood snugly over her head.

The woman beckons her outside, to the larger shed. She gets a board from the same rack as she did the previous week and a long paddle. Macia blinks as the woman hands them to her. Does the woman expect her to carry her own board to the water? Even after seeing her letter last week? She takes the wooden board and paddle, but hesitates, clenching her jaws together. She swallows and starts taking a breath to let the woman know what she thinks of this practice, but the woman has turned back to the rack already. She pulls out another board, grabs another paddle, and motions at Macia with her head to follow her.

Macia quietly releases the breath she was holding; of course, the woman is going on the water with her, and they will just have to carry their own boards this time. Maybe she can make enquiries for a spare Mansit in the city. She follows the woman, glad that the board isn't heavy, and it has a sturdy handle in the middle. They get to the little beach and the woman lowers her board onto the water, Macia copying her. The woman looks at her, and points with her chin at the water in front of them. "Push the board out onto the water. Then, when it's afloat, climb on it on your knees." She looks at Macia to see if the girl understands the instructions. Macia dips her head, relieved that at least this bit sounds easy enough.

They both push their boards out and walk along with the board for a few steps, Macia gasping at the coldness of the water despite her wetsuit. The woman must have good hearing for she comments, "That is why, if you find yourself coming off a lot, leave it for today. Don't get too cold. It is easy to do, not so easy to fix," she says with a small smile. Macia nods. Yes, she can feel the woman's point. Her feet are like ice blocks already, after mere seconds of walking in the water. She is glad when the woman puts the paddle across the board, and holding on the handle, climbs onto the board on her knees. Macia follows her, making her board wobble. She almost overbalances, but clinging on to the handle, Macia manages to stay on top. A sense of achievement makes her grin, and she looks at the woman. The woman looks at her strangely and Macia manages to squash her grin. She knows that look; it's the look of somebody who feels they have seen you do something that you shouldn't have. It's the way she looked at the woman last week when she saw her pleasure in the water, feeling her enthusiasm. Now the woman has seen her feeling thrilled, and very emotional, just because she managed to climb onto a wooden board on her knees.

The woman picks up the long paddle and begins moving through the water, swapping hands regularly, and Macia tries to copy her. "Do I have to swap hands, arms even, to paddle?" she asks.

The woman shrugs. "It's easier that way. You have to paddle both sides, or you'll just float in circles."

Macia nods, "Yes, I get that. I just wondered if there was another way of doing it, less cumbersome?"

The woman shrugs again. "I prefer it this way," she calls out above the spray. Once they're moving at a reasonable speed the woman suggests that she tries to stand up. Macia takes several tries and suddenly she is standing on the board, long paddle in her hand, smooth wooden board under her feet, riding the water.

She suddenly grins at the woman, and seeing the woman's wary eyes she says, "Now I know why you like the water so much." She can feel the warmth creeping into her face because she almost said 'love' and that could have been interesting. As it is, the woman has gone pale, as she understands the quiet underlying threat. Macia meant the threat to be there, for she wants to enjoy this paddleboarding; she wants to be able to smile, or even laugh if she feels like it. She doesn't want the woman to be a threat. With her comment, she has put the woman into the same position, and it works, the hint is taken. When she turns to Macia she smiles. "I knew you would be good at it," she says to the young girl and dips her head. Macia grins, feeling full of joy, she realises. Not just because of the exhilarating feeling of floating on the water, but because of the connection made with the older woman. The fact that they share this experience, enjoying something together is a new but incredible feeling. Later, when Macia changes back into her woollen dress and boots, she can still feel her cheek muscles, taut from grinning and smiling more than she has ever done in her entire life.

Chapter 16

She knew it had been too good to be true. Macia stares out of the window at the rain and wind, bending the trees. The woman had warned her last week that if the weather was bad, there would be no water sports. She could go to the gymnasium, but she had set her heart on paddleboarding. "That comes from loving something," she mutters to herself. Logic should have warned her to see the sessions as good, but nothing more than that, just another sports activity. It had been very good though, and she can feel a smile returning, simply thinking about it. The smile soon slips as she realises she had set up a trap for herself. If she hadn't been so emotionally involved last week, smiling at the older woman, allowing her heart to be excited; if she hadn't let herself go, then this morning wouldn't be so hard.

Macia turns away from the window, a frown stuck on her face. She will need to have breakfast, and nothing should tell her father or Ignava that she felt disappointed.

Ignava is too busy with her own plans to even remember that Macia was supposed to be somewhere else this morning. "I will be out most of the day. My friends are organising a new section in the Bibliotheca, and some of your father's books will go in that section. We will also deposit some of the teaching videos, probably on special floppy disks that people can then play on their computers at home, or in the

Bibliotheca." She looks pleased, but when Macia looks at her Ignava pulls her face straight, trying to look as if she is only vaguely interested, brought in by her friends, nothing more.

Her father dips his head and tells Ignava that it's a good thing. The Bibliotheca should have had a good audio and video section a long time ago. Even Macia forgets her paddleboarding disaster for a moment, and wonders out loud how many of the videos will be made available, and whether students could access some of these for a distance learning course. Ignava's eyes light up at the idea, but she purses her lips, "It is only a trial. We will need to monitor the usage of those videos closely, as some are classed by Status levels. To have many students of different status levels come and access the videos could pose a safety risk." Her face is a little bit flushed, and Macia wants to smirk. She knows her stepmother well enough to know she loves the idea but hates the fact it was suggested by Macia.

Brutus Durus is out for the day as well. He was supposed to go fishing but his day has been rearranged. He looks out of the kitchen windows, "Fishing would have been good. Apparently, people used to go fishing in the rain; they said the fish used to bite better. The water sports board discredited that, so it's a bit odd to do those kinds of sports in the rain." He looks at Macia and says, "I take it you won't go paddleboarding?" Macia shakes her head. He gets up and leaves the room. Macia glares at her bowl with pottage. So much for bearing each other's burdens. Is it really too hard to say, 'Oh what a shame, never mind, hopefully, you'll be able to go next week'? Is it really illogical to feel disappointed when you miss out on something that you like? Isn't it more logical to have feelings? Of course, she would never advocate feelings dictating to your life, but to simply feel them for a while, within limits and with self-control?

Macia is left by herself very soon, and she walks upstairs with slow steps. What is she going to do all day? Of course, there is her school work and things she could do, but nothing that she wants to do just now. She wants…she sighs, she actually wants her friend, for today would have been the ideal day to spend with a friend, doing something together. Not that she would use the word friend, of course. She wants her mother, for they could have done something today. Macia starts, frightened she has allowed her thoughts to stray this far.

Macia sits down in the window seat, watching the grey scenery outside. She looks around her room, then suddenly she stands up. "Just to check…" she whispers to herself, "That's all." She stands upon the window seat, removes the board, and reaches down the secret box. She sits back down in the seat, and opens the box, pulling out the thin bundle. Her hands shake but she feels this need, and the questions that have started in her head need an answer as well. This book mentioned bearing each other's burdens, and obeying the law as well as having joy and peace. One letter is finished, so today she will be starting another letter. It still feels a little awkward reading somebody else's post, but as it's printed, she supposes they were meant to be read publicly.

She turns the flimsy pages till she gets to the new letter. It is another letter from the person called Paul, to people at some unknown place. It sounds like Elabi, but it isn't, or could it be the ancient name for Elabi? She reads on, the words flowing through her mind and her heart, captivating her. Macia looks up and realises she is actually out of breath, her heart pounding. She shuts the little bundle, puts it back in the secret box, and returns the box to its special place. After returning the larger board, she looks at the window. She is sure that the loose board can't be detected. She has always made sure that she is very careful in lifting it down, so the paint won't get chipped or scratched. If this book is found in her possession… she shivers, the precious words going around her head. Adopted, beloved, family, accepted, glory…it's a foreign language to her. Most of these words sound unfamiliar, but they do make her heart react.

She keeps herself busy the rest of the day, guilt and fear driving her, making her hands move restlessly. In the end, she clears a space in the lounge, asking the automated servant to find a fitness programme. Macia loves the cardio workouts they have on offer, but they are too easy. The woman in the video is quite a bit older than Macia, and she sneers at the woman, for Macia's speed is better, she can squat lower as well as jump higher than the woman. Knowing it's just a recording means that she can smirk and look down on the woman openly, without having to keep her face bland. The workout helps, and soon Macia feels better mentally, as well as physically tired. A hot shower helps too, and soon she is focused on her school work, trying to get ready for Onesday.

Looking at her books, the strange words still creep into her mind, and once or twice she even almost uses some of the new words, making her feel a slight sense of panic. Yet she would like to know what they mean and strains to work it out through the context, or through familiar words that sound the same. Macia looks at her computer, knowing that the Elabi Wide Web has a dictionary on it. As her hand reaches for the keyboard she freezes. What if it is a forbidden word? On the other hand, as an Amplissimos she has more freedom and is allowed access to more information. Getting the wrong word might not have any consequences at all. Her fingers itch, and she can feel the excitement growing.

She starts the computer, waiting for it to load, then goes to the main screen, types in the path to the Elabi Wide Web, EWW/dictionary.elabi and presses enter, her breath coming faster. The dictionary appears and Macia hesitates. Which word? In the end, she types in a word often found in the bundle that seems negative from the context, but important. With shaking fingers she taps out, 'sin' and presses the enter button. The answer comes back straight away without red flashes or screen closure, and Macia releases the huge breath she was holding.

The screen tells her, "Sin, spelled syn, was a point system used under an ancient programme for people trying to lose weight. People dissatisfied with their weight tried to correct it by eating certain foods, leading to emotional struggles. Many unhealthy foods were still around, and some of these were allocated points or syns. One was only allowed certain syns per day to reduce weight. Elabi rule has made this way of living redundant by ensuring healthy lifestyles and foods, and therefore this word is no longer in use. Use of the word is discouraged, as it has very emotional connotations."

Macia leans back in her chair, trying to fit the explanation of the word into the letter she read. Was that talking about weight loss? It doesn't seem to make the letter any clearer, and she rolls her eyes at the computer. Could the computer have it wrong? Should she try again, or do a part sentence? Her hand hovers above her keyboard, but she holds back. No, that would be asking for trouble. The fact that the usage of this word is discouraged means red warning flags will be raised if she pushes it. Macia glares at the words again. She can remember the phrase 'forgiveness of sins, according to the riches of his grace', but she has no idea what grace means either. Should she look it up? Forgiveness about overeating? Then there is the bit about being dead in trespasses and sins, where they used to walk in? Macia groans, and rubs her forehead, "I don't get it," she mutters out loud.

Immediately her automated servant pipes up, "Ask me again, please, and I will help you to get what it is you want." Macia takes a breath, flushes hot red, only to feel her face drain pale white straight away. The knowledge of what could happen to her had she answered her automated servant makes her feel queasy. With shaking hands, she shuts down the computer, relieved it has ended well this time.

Chapter 17

Macia wakes to see the Spring storms still raging outside her window. She dreads another day at home and will need to get out of the house, for she can feel the curse growing against her. She is sure it's the curse mentioned in the earlier pages, poured out on those who do not keep the law. Of course, she could go to the Bibliotheca, and look at books. Is wading through the mud worth it?

Ignava is getting ready to go to her weekly spouse's meeting. The hostess will be travelling Downstream tomorrow, having been released from the Sanatorium to host this last meeting. Ignava had explained to Macia that the only reason she is allowed a last meeting is that she had done a lot of the administrative tasks, and this will need to be handed over. Ignava is hopeless with admin, but Macia picks up that Ignava hopes to be chosen for this task. In which case it will become either her or her father's task, as Ignava will need help. She wants to be out of the house when Ignava gets back so that hopefully her father will be asked to help first.

She hears the front door shut and watches Ignava walk down the driveway, oilcloth cloak around her, head bent against the wind. Not long after her father leaves for a meeting with other council members on parameters that need to be set in place for students in the Bibliotheca. Macia's suggestion of the distance learning course was clearly a brainwave. Not that she will get any of the credit for it, of course. "A thank you would have been nice, or some extra points," she mutters in the silence. Even the automated servant stays quiet. She waits a while, staring blindly at the rain coming down in thick grey sheets. The trees bend and bow, the fresh green leaves clinging on for dear life. When Macia is sure Ignava and Brutus are not coming back for the moment, she goes through the usual routine to retrieve the box. She sits down with the thin pages and reads, just reads, right to the end of that letter. The words leave her breathless.

Carefully she slides the secret box back in its hiding place, slots the board in place, and sits back in the window sill to think. She swallows, realising what she is doing. If somebody caught her there'd likely be a full-scale enquiry. Even sitting in a window seat thinking like this would be an issue. Macia decides she doesn't care, then gasps. Staring out of the window, she sees Savisia's grey face, skulking alone around the school grounds, not making any eye contact, her days full with extra classes. All because her sister let herself be influenced by a man and a book, then did a runner. Macia bites her nail, worried. There is something about this book, and she can see how somebody like Caecilia would fall for it. Of course, Macia is much stronger than Caecilia, but even she can feel the curse against those breaking the law.

Macia leans back against the cold window panes, exhausted. It's almost as though she has become two Macias. One who is totally aware, and in full agreement with Elabi law. The present law that is. And another Macia that revels in this book, which seems to talk about a much older law; a book that promotes an emotional life, appealing to the head as well as the heart. A tiny warning voice tells her that if anyone finds her sitting like this there could be trouble. With a strained voice, she tells the servant to put her music on. The songs calm her down as they reaffirm the strength of Elabi, its goodness and helpfulness and its ability to protect minds and lives. It helps her to know what she stands for and pushes the disturbing thoughts to the background. She doesn't need hope, she has a good head, comes from good genetics, and she is sure about every day being a good day. The city council has worked out the details, there is nothing for her to hope for, or wish for. She is part of a strong community that looks after its city and its citizens.

Feeling more relaxed, she thinks of a way to get out of the house before Ignava returns and pulls her in. Tima! The news that she is home with her new baby came earlier in the week. It's not far to walk to Tima's house. Another tiny Brutus has been born into Elabi and as Macia knocks on her sister's door, she can hear him crying above the steady rain.

Tima's husband opens the door and helps Macia hang up her oilskin cloak. "Tima's through there with Brutus," he almost smiles, ushering her into the lounge.

The moment Macia sees her sister comforting little Brutus on her shoulder, her heart skips a beat. She has never noticed the likeness between her sister and mother before. She clamps her lips together, keeping the words in.

"Macia," Tima exclaims, barely making any effort to wipe the joy from her face. "Come and sit here by me. Meet Brutus, your new nephew."

There is something infectious in her sister's barely controlled display of happiness as Macia is suddenly face to face with the adorable form of baby Brutus, who peers at her fixedly with large blue eyes from his red wrinkled face. Just as Macia's heart is melting, the loss of her mother and baby brother makes it sink like lead and so she balances awkwardly on the edge of her chair, listening politely to Tima. Finally, enough time has elapsed for her to excuse herself and trudge home through the welcome mud and rain.

She arrives in the house to see her father bent over a pile of papers with Ignava. Smiling wryly, she quietly makes her way to her room, pushing the picture of Tima and tiny Brutus away from her mind.

Macia is relieved when Onesday starts, and she is back to her busy schedule. Near the end of Fifday, the Spring storms peter out, and Macia feels excitement growing in her.

Hexaday starts off wonderfully calm, no sign of the storm left, apart from a lot of new green leaves on the ground, and a muddy driveway. Macia looks at the mud and decides to wear her boots. The summer season's brand new sandals have just arrived, but she's not going to ruin them today. She packs her bag, feeling the nervous thrill, forcing herself to move slowly to control the slight tremor in her hands. Breakfast is the same way as usual, with Macia casually announcing she'll be off today, "It's my paddleboarding session. I will be a while, as it's past the first bridge, and the lesson lasts a long time as well." Her father nods, and Ignava just about dips her head, not showing the slightest interest. "It's a good workout, really," she says, hoping her father will rise to the bait, and talk to her. No reaction.

Macia collects the pottage bowls and takes them to the sink. The splashing water hides her fast breathing, and the activity gives her a chance to recover herself. That book is bringing a curse on her, she is sure. Why does she suddenly want her father to love her when it's just genetics and family lines they share? Love is a dangerous concept, it blurs people's thinking. Her father of all people knows that and has given countless lectures on it. Many of those lectures have been listened to, read and edited by Macia. She agrees with his talks, proud of his clear thinking and arguments.

None of those lectures or articles ever moved her though, none of them made her heart burn or glow as the thin pages do. Not once have her father's words been stuck in her head for days, and she can't imagine being desperate for a chance to read his words again and again.

He always explains, "There can be no misunderstanding, as I would not ever want to be the cause of anyone being led astray through their feelings. People who misunderstand how logic works can feel hurt, misunderstood themselves, and that would lead to underlying anger. Trying to suppress that anger could lead to emotional instability. Of course, once people are aware of their anger they will seek counselling, but still, not many Mansits go to regular counselling." Macia had seen that, yes, feeling that you are not heard makes people irrational. Brutus wants to make sure that his entire audience sees the logic and safety of his words. It had always given her that exact sense of safety, made her see how right her father was. Now that feeling of security in her father's logic is gone, replaced with fear, questions and forbidden words filling her mind. Macia dries her hands, trying to ignore the turmoil within, forcing herself to focus on the here and now, to pack lunch, and to pick up her bag.

As she walks, the light breeze strokes Macia's face, making her feel empty inside. It is as if the wind touches her heart, its soft fingers reminding her of the words that call people beloved, precious, a habitation of the Spirit. She doesn't know what it means, but the words fill her with longings that frighten her. Both letters talk about the Spirit. Maybe she should type this into the dictionary? No, she tells herself, she is simply looking forward to being on the water, to paddleboarding, to the physical exertion needed, and maybe even to the tentative connection between her and the older woman. That should be enough risk for one day. But to be called a habitation of the Spirit makes her heart grow and beat stronger than ever, her hands turning to ice.

Chapter 18

The waterfront looks inviting. The older woman is expecting her, raising her chin warmly, and soon Macia has managed to shrug herself into the wetsuit again. She feels like a pro, carrying her board and paddle, no longer wanting a Mansit to carry it for her. Walking into the water is cold as ever, and she allows a tiny giggle to escape her throat. What will the woman think; here she is, out of control like a common Mansit. The woman doesn't seem to mind, but Macia can see her eyes; they look amused, as if she enjoys Macia's little slip-up.

The woman teaches her some more techniques, and soon Macia can turn her board round, and get on and off without getting too wet. She feels physically tired, her core muscles having to work hard to keep her balance. After lunch, the woman suggests Macia goes off by herself, not too far, just to practice what she's learnt. Macia is pleased and soon finds herself following the coastline towards the further bridge. When she can see the bridge clearly, she turns around. She has no desire to go near, knowing that at the other side of the stone structure is the launching point for craft taking people Downstream. Macia does not want to spot the craft or be reminded of this place. She shivers, an aching deep down in her heart. She turns her board around and paddles back, away from wrong longings, anger giving her arms the needed adrenaline. Paddling against the current is harder than she had expected, and she heaves a sigh of relief when the watersports shed comes into view.

The woman has a slight smile on her face as Macia staggers off the board, her legs shaking a little. It was more tiring than she expected, and thinking of the walk home fills her with dread. The woman dips her head, her voice warm as she says, "You did well. I thought you would." Macia suddenly grins, feeling warm inside at the woman's words. Then she swallows, wondering why the woman is kind? She brushes the thought aside, and nods, explaining that she would like to teach some sports classes once she has left school. The woman nods, "It's good to see people learn new skills, it is very rewarding in itself. It is also a way of passing on skills and knowledge to a new generation. It is essential to our society." Macia dips her head, a tiny part of her wondering if the woman put that last bit in as a threat or to prove that she follows Elabi Law, just in case Macia wants to report her for smiling and making unnecessary comments.

The walk home seems longer than this morning's walk. Yet she can't help smiling. Her arms feel like jelly, and every few steps her knees buckle, prompting involuntary giggles. Spotting another citizen in the distance sobers her up, but finds she is questioning Elabi's suppression of feelings all over again. The book she read talked about having joy, peace, kindness, but also temperance and control. The woman's smile comes to mind. "It's so much nicer," Macia muses, "when somebody smiles at you and says something nice. Not a lie, but just a genuine nice compliment."

Neither her father nor Ignava asks her how her day went, and although Macia is itching to tell them, she doesn't say a word. She would love to share the thrill it gave her to turn around, all by herself, and paddle back to the water sports shed. The smile and kind words of the older woman still make her heart glad. "But," she tells herself, "that is exactly why emotions are dangerous. It makes us needy and dependent. Instead of simply having had a good day, now I need to hear other people saying how well I did; I should have stopped the woman immediately." Macia groans. How could she be so weak?

The next morning, Macia's entire body protests when she tries to get up to go to the gymnasium. Macia stares at the ceiling, glad that the mornings are getting lighter every week. She can't help thinking about the bond she is developing with her watersport teacher and how important it is to her. One of the verses in the letter she read last week comes to mind. It said to be kind to one another, tenderhearted, soft-hearted, forgiving one another. Why would you forgive someone? You can't pretend something didn't happen. If you let someone off, that would lead to chaos and lawlessness.

In Elabi, even if somebody has made a huge mistake and is sent beyond the Hills, they can work themselves back into Elabi, starting again as a Mansit. Through work and education, they can climb back up the ladder. Unless someone is beyond hope, too entrenched in their beliefs and attitudes.

That isn't the same as forgiveness though. If someone shows that they have a weakness, a character defect or they have misunderstood the Elabi teachings, that should be sorted out straight away. You don't just say, "Never mind, I forgive you, just carry on, nothing happened." Macia groans, why is she even thinking about all this? When the automated servant tells her it is time to get up, she is relieved, looking forward to having breakfast. Her stomach was protesting already, clearly she used up a lot of energy yesterday. Ignava looks important again, "I'm off soon after breakfast," she tells the other two, "as the meeting today is at the other end of the city." Macia looks at Ignava, feeling nothing but scorn for the woman, although she tries to make sure this doesn't show. "The meeting is going to be important, for we are still looking at the videos and talks placed in the Bibliotheca," Ignava continues, trying to make it sound like common business. Being proud is not a good thing, and people have been reported for less. "The council has made some very good suggestions already," and she dips her head at Brutus, who merely grunts.

He scrapes the bowl with pottage clean, then leans back, and Macia suddenly feels sure that he would have liked to give a big sigh of satisfaction. Food is for physical strength as sustenance, and wise options are strongly encouraged. It is of the utmost importance to look after your body, so you can be a valued citizen for as long as possible. To get overtaken by feelings, simply because you really liked the food is not a good thing, as the past has shown that people could easily end up with nutritional deficits. Macia looks down on her own pottage and suddenly feels sorry for Brutus

Brutus nods towards Ignava, and says, "The council are meeting today as well, to work out a few extra details again for the Bibliotheca. It shows how well our government works together in all of this. Maybe that should be another book or even just a talk? It is important to show the younger generation that the council stands together on matters, and how all higher-level citizens have the same goals in this place, to protect and provide. I think that would be a good topic," he concludes. Ignava looks pleased, and nods, not too eagerly, but Macia can tell from her stepmother's eyes that she loves the idea. She is relieved when they both have gone, for Macia is quite sure that soon some of this resentment must show. It is growing at every turn.

Macia leans back in her chair, smiling. Maybe at a dinner table and she will say, "Thanks Ignava, that was a delicious meal. I don't know how you manage to get that flatbread so light. And the soup was so tasty, thanks for your effort." She snorts, imagining their shocked faces. She clears up the breakfast things, taking her time, fear already making her hands unsteady.

Chapter 19

Her heart is beating fast by the time she gets upstairs, and her arms almost squeak in protest as she reaches above her head to lift down the board. The board slips out of her fingers for the last few inches, but nothing seems to have been damaged. She sits down with her secret box, her legs sore and shaky. Macia turns the thin pages to get to the end of the letter she just read and starts the next. It's written to another group of people, not just by Paul, but this time a co-author is mentioned. The start sounds very similar to the start of the previous letter, and Macia can feel her heart leaning into the words, which are beginning to have a familiar feel.

She drinks in the words, most still unknown, but there is something in them that keeps her wanting more, needing more. Her eyes come to a stuttering halt through one portion. None of it sounds like the status levels they now have in Elabi but in those days they clearly had a ranking system as well. This Paul has the bad taste to list his achievements. Macia pulls a face. She would never do that. Macia doesn't recognise any of the levels Paul lists but it sounds like it's the top, even Amplissimos. He actually says that with regards to the law his life was blameless.

Macia wrinkles her nose at that, for she doubts it very much. For one thing, Paul wrote those letters which are now on the forbidden book list. They might not have been forbidden at his time, but they were one of the first books to go on the list. Macia is pretty sure that these letters were revolutionary for Paul's own day as well. All citizens slip up every now and again, maybe not in big ways, but they do. Even her father.

Maybe Paul is just making a point though, and she reads on, trying to find status similarities or matters that come up during the application process. Then her heart stutters and she can feel her mouth go dry. He didn't care anymore about his top status? Macia shudders. Fancy making it to Amplissimos status and then turn round and say, "Nah, don't really care about it, it's just status, I count something completely unrelated to Elabi as more important than those Amplissimos papers."

Macia stands up anxiously. Looking out at the driveway, the trees are blowing in the Spring gales. She finally sits down again and leaving the thin bundle on her lap, pulls out the thick paper with Caecilia's handwriting. She hasn't looked at the letter for more than a moon and scrunches up her mouth as she can tell the changes in her own heart. No longer does the greeting 'dearest friend' fill her with rage, or even hatred, but it sounds…simply familiar. This time, when reading Caecilia's writing about how the words, or rather the Author of the words, changed Caecilia's life, Macia finds herself giving a sideways grin. No kidding there, the curse is just as strong on her as it obviously was on Caecilia. She wonders how much Caecilia knew about Paul, does she mean him with the author? He did write the words after all, but then Caecilia writes him with a capital. How odd.

Then Caecilia writes that she prays Macia will come to know God and His forgiveness, love and salvation. Macia groans, "Thanks, Caecilia, no wonder I was under the curse so quickly." What does she mean "pray"? This word is in Paul's letters as well. To ask or tell? Caecilia wants her to know God? Paul says he'd happily give up his status in society to know God. Now Caecilia is asking that Macia will come to the same conclusion as Paul. "No thanks," Macia says, "dearest friend," but the sneer with which she meant to give those words doesn't quite work.

On the other hand, Paul seems to have thrown it all out quite happily. He was an adult though, which is different. It will affect her father if she did that, and after all, she is under her father's authority at the moment, so for her to do something like that she would need his permission. Macia snorts, she can imagine her father's face if she asked him for permission to ditch her Amplissimos status to be part of God, to be in Christ. Actually, she can't imagine his face, the idea makes her shudder with dread, and she quickly stops her imagination from going down that route. Anyway, it means that she can't simply reject her status. Of course, Caecilia did; she not only left her status behind, but she also left the whole of Elabi behind. Causing trouble for a lot of people. Even Tima has to attend classes now that baby Brutus is born. Macia smiles a little. He was cute.

She leans back in the window sill, the words from both letters going around her head... "...that I may be found in Him...That you may come to Him..." Even if she wanted to, she can't. It's alright for Caecilia who was a Consuete, although her hard work might have given her Umbo status by the time she left school. To give that up, well, it's only one or almost two levels up from Mansit, and the requirements are less demanding. To attain Amplissimos status, at Macia's age, that really is an incredible achievement. Caecilia is now telling her to throw it all out, and Paul is telling her that he did. "I can't" Macia hisses, a little too loudly, for her automated servant says, "Sorry, did you say you can't do something? How may I help?" Macia feels herself go pale, and stammers that she can't hear the music, could he turn it up. The servant obliges, of course, and Macia wipes her clammy forehead with freezing fingers, realising she can't give everything up for God because she hasn't got a clue who God is.

For one thing, she has only a portion of the book. The council had a portion as well, but Macia feels that there must be more of the book in existence than two small bundles. Paul mentions so many names and places. The other thing is, she has nobody to help her or explain things to her. The one person who could help has left Elabi behind. The book part she has is forbidden, meaning she can't look things up, there are no talks about it, no classes explaining it to her. For Caecilia to ask that she will come to know God is a bit much. Macia can feel the resentment tiptoeing back into her heart, although not as powerfully as before.

She looks at the small bundle on her lap and flicks the pages open to where Paul said he'd given everything up. Then she realises the words talk not about her coming to know God, but about her being found in Him, not being right in herself because of sticking to the law, but being right with God through faith. She stops, forcing her eyes away from the pages. She made it to Amplissimos by sticking to the rules, by ticking the boxes, by accepting the law. Nothing to do with trusting or believing anybody, only the rules set by the Elabi government, the city council. By following the rules people are kept safe so that every day can be a good day, even if you are a Mansit. After many years, she will simply float Downstream in one of the vessels, having been told by the council that her time has come. As soon as the vessel sets off, she will be forgotten in Elabi. The fact that she obeyed all the rules and regulations won't count for anything.

She thinks of the council member who went Downstream recently. He managed to literally stall the Downstream papers by a few days because he was on an important Enquiry. That was it, and then he went, with nobody ever talking about him anymore. He has been forgotten, the Enquiry has been closed, the consequences landed where there should, and that's that. All his effort, his time and energy, gone. The fact that he was clearly right before the law most of his life counted for nothing. Now he is Downstream, and who knows what has happened to him? Paul often seems to talk about eternity, things after he dies, and the fact that he will still be right with God, still be in Christ. Macia swallows, and coughs, for her throat is closed up, realising that maybe Paul wasn't that foolish after all. Reaching Amplissimos status is only worth something in Elabi, but it won't be worth anything once she goes Downstream. Maybe, just maybe, she will need to look into it more, and be given a place in God, rather than in the city council.

Chapter 20

Macia holds the book, her fingers curling the edges of the ultra-thin paper. She really doesn't want to put the book back. She doesn't want to wait till the following week, and getting the box down during weekdays feels too risky. Macia looks around her room, neat and tidy, with not a single thing out of place. To hide the bundle of thin pages shouldn't be hard, but anything different will stick out in her room. Not that anybody ever comes in, but she doesn't want to take unnecessary risks. Having the book is dangerous enough. In the end, she decides on her paper drawer. The thick paper, most of it having been used many times, will hide the thin pages. She pushes the little bundle towards the back, not at the very bottom of the pile, and not completely at the back. Hopefully hiding it in reasonably plain sight will help. She moves as quietly as she can, the music droning out most of the small noises, like opening and shutting her paper drawer. She doesn't trust her automated servant.

She turns to the window to put the large board back, after sliding the little box back into the secret space. Just as the board locks into place, she spots Brutus walking up the driveway. He is looking up at the house, and Macia freezes in place. Has he seen her? It is light outside, and her room is not as light as the blue skies and soft Spring colours outside. He is still some way away from the house, and he seems to just be looking up at the house generally, rather than focusing on her window in particular. Her woollen dress is a soft blue, the colour having faded a little at the end of a long winter. She swallows, what is she going to do? If she jumps down, he will spot the movement. If she stands still he will probably spot her as well. Quickly she makes up her mind. She hops down from the window sill, spins round, tells the automated servant to play her workout music, and Macia gets changed into her workout clothes the fastest she has ever done. Within a few minutes, she is sweating, not just from the energetic workout, but her blood is pumping, and she is doing box jumps using her window sill. It's quite a high jump, and she is glad it's at home and not in the gymnasium with people watching.

Sure enough, she can hear Brutus' footsteps coming up the stairs, followed by a knock on her door. "Come in," she gasps, raising her chin at him, whilst wiping it dry with her sleeve at the same time. Her father looks at her and raises his chin in return. "Pause the workout," she commands the automated servant, and she turns to her father, gasping for breath. Those window jumps are hard work. Her father looks at her, and dips his head, telling her to be careful of the window. If she misjudges her speed, she will go through the window, landing in the garden below. "I know, I like box jumps and wanted to try these before doing them in public in the gymnasium," she explains, hoping that he will assume the blush is from the exertion, rather than her being free with the truth. He dips his head and leaves her room, and Macia releases the breath she didn't even know she was holding. She tells the servant to put the workout back on, and she carries on, this time to work off the stress and fear.

Onesday can't pass fast enough, the pages calling her all day. She looks around the classrooms, taking in the other students. She is in school, would it compare favourably to being in God? She will lose this if she accepts that. At lunchtime, she looks at the Mansits serving their special table, their faces bland, not making eye contact with them. She has never looked at them, at least not like this. Not once has she wondered about their lives or their feelings. Having to serve other students like this, do they accept it happily? Are they made to do this, or are they serving by choice? Macia glances at the other Amplissimos students, and not a single one of them even looks at the Mansits. She never did either, but now she finds herself staring at them, her mind trying to imagine their lives. Some Mansits will not know any different, having been born a Mansit in a Mansit family, but those that were born a higher status, and have fallen down because of relatives' choices, surely they must feel it. She would! She can still feel the anger and hatred towards Caecilia, and the trouble she caused.

As soon as she gets home from school Macia has her usual snack. Nothing should look different about her or her day. Any slight change in habits could get picked up, and make people nosey. Ignava is always watching, her face blank, but her eyes sometimes betray her dislike of Macia. The girl feels that her stepmother would relish the idea of finding a fault and reporting it. Of course, that could potentially harm Brutus as well, but Ignava probably assumes that his status in the community is secure enough to deal with it. So Macia has her snack, and Ignava wanders around the kitchen, preparing dinner. "Will you go to the gymnasium this evening?" She asks suddenly, staring hard at Macia as if missing the gymnasium for a few days is a serious offence. Macia nods and explains that the paddleboarding left her stiff and sore, but she did a workout at home yesterday. "Yes, your father told me," Ignava says, her face hard, clearly disapproving, "and I hope you were aware of the risks? It sounds like a rather impulsive workout and not one that was thought through at all," her voice carries on, her sharp eyes never blinking once. Macia dips her head. She can't explain her reason for the workout.

She is relieved to sit at her desk in her room. "Play my school music," she demands and the soft, orchestral movements she uses when doing her studies starts. Macia gets her books out. Carefully she slips the little bundle of thin paper in between two used sheets. She keeps listening out for any sounds coming from downstairs. Brutus has not returned yet, and Ignava was busy chopping herbs. Carefully she pulls the thin pages to the edge, so she can open the book, read it, and easily cover it with the thick paper should the need arise. Her hands shake a little, making the paper rustle, the sound seemingly louder than her drumming heart. Macia hesitates, should she read on to the end of the bundle, or go back to the start, looking for the right answer?

In the end, she decides to go back. The words feel new to her heart. After a while she leans back in her chair, pushing the pages back a little so they are hidden from view. The main question that she uses to weigh the words is, Would it be worth it? Would it be worth my entire life, my status, my relatives? Would it be worth becoming a Mansit, probably for the rest of my Elabi life? However, the passion and depth of the words keep distracting her.

Every day that week, when doing her homework, Macia reads and scours the pages of the thin bundle, looking for the answer. On Fifday her marks have dropped. The teacher looks at the leaderboard, and then at Macia. "This week looks like a one-off, so I know whatever it is that was distracting you will be overcome by Onesday," he says, making it sound like a command with a hidden threat, rather than the encouragement that would have been nice. Macia swallows and dips her head. The search for the answer has taken up all her headspace, and to study at the same time was too much. She will need to find a balance though, otherwise, she will be in trouble before she has decided if being in God is worth her Elabi life. She walks home deep in thought and looks around at the trees with their soft green foliage, suddenly missing Caecilia. Caecilia would have been able to help her.

When she gets home, she sits down at her desk, slowly pulling out some well-used paper. She needs to think, and there is nobody with whom she can discuss the thin pages. After a quick look over her shoulder, she starts in tiny writing near the top of the page, "Dearest friend." Then leans back in her chair, grinning. There, she will write a letter too, either to an imaginary Caecilia, asking her the difficult questions, or just any friend that knows the answers. It's a chance to write down words that she would never use, a way to unburden herself and clarify her thoughts. "Dearest friend, I'm writing to you, as I'm thinking about..." Macia stops. Should she mention the book? What if the pages are ever found? She shakes her head, no, she will hide her diary papers with the thin pages. If they're found, the thin pages will be found too, so it won't make any difference. "The thin pages confuse me, and I can't decide." When she finally puts her pencil down, she sits back, feeling lighter in her heart. It was almost like discussing the whole matter with Caecilia or another understanding friend. The call for dinner makes her jump, and she hastily stuffs the papers in her bottom drawer, underneath other papers, pulling a face as she realises that her schoolwork will keep her very busy this evening.

Hexaday is another sweet Spring day, and Macia is glad. She needs the time on the water, by herself. Secretly she knows that it is because of the woman and her kindness. Macia wants to test the woman's kindness. Will she say or do something else that is kind? Will she smile at Macia, as if she means it? What if it is a trap? What if the woman does it all the time to unsuspecting newbies, those people who have just achieved their Amplissimos status and then she smiles at them, leading them on. Until they smile back, say something, loosen up... then she reports them for being inappropriate. Would she do that? Macia chews a loose bit of nail and thinks of the woman's warm eyes, the way she had smiled at Macia's enthusiasm, and she feels certain that the woman was genuine. You can never tell though.

The woman raises her chin, a slight smile on her face, her eyes friendly. Macia answers the greeting, feeling the corners of her mouth turn up in response. She finds herself hurrying with the wetsuit, not wanting to lose any time. The woman is waiting for her, and together they go to the shed and pick up their boards and paddles. "This time we will go out a little further towards the open water," the woman says, "as you must know what to do if the water is choppier than you'd hoped." She smiles a little, but Macia has seen the excitement in the woman's eyes. She really loves the water, Macia thinks, and she can understand that. Although Macia loves paddleboarding, she still dreads feeling the freezing water coming through the material. If she loses her balance when waves are rolling across the board, she will be drenched, and water will be everywhere.

Despite her fears, the waves are gentle. Macia soon learns to take a warrior stance with one foot further forward and one nearer the back, facing the waves head-on. Once she loses her balance and gasps, hearing the woman shout, "Drop on your knees, drop down, quick!" Macia drops down, feeling the paddle starting to slip from her hands, but her freezing fingers cling on. Her other hand grips the board, and the thought of falling headlong in the filthy water makes her work hard to stay on top. It works, and soon she has steadied herself enough to get back up, adrenaline making her breathe hard. The woman is laughing. Macia finds herself responding with a giggle, and then suddenly she rides the tidal wave of elation that has been released, her heart soaring higher than ever. She tilts her head back and laughs, doing an excited whoop. Old habits come in and she struggles to get herself back under control. When she looks around, fear making her almost sick, the woman is on her knees on her paddleboard, laughing too much to stand up any longer. As Macia licks the salt from her lips she tastes freedom and life.

Chapter 21

As Macia walks home she feels lighter than she has ever done before. She breathes the fresh air, already with a hint of the heavy summer smells, and smiles. Today was such a good day. Now it's time to come back down though, she knows, for if she walks into the house like this, there will be trouble. Macia pulls a face, suddenly feeling sad and weighed down, her feet dragging along. Her shoulders ache, and her head throbs a little. Probably dehydration, which is easily done with this type of weather. It's not just that, she knows. She felt so free and now she needs to fit back in. Suddenly the rules feel oppressive.

When Macia gets home, Ignava looks at her, and Macia can feel her hands go cold. Has her face changed that much? Ignava says, "I suppose you will use paddleboarding again as an excuse to live an ill-disciplined life for the next few days? It is not setting a good example for other young people, making them think that when doing special, privileged sports, you then can avoid the usual routines the council has recommended." Macia swallows, is that all? She feels like answering back, being sharp with Ignava, simply because of the spike in heart rate the woman caused. She steps on her words though, reminding herself that Ignava doesn't know any better, and after all, it must be painful to see Macia overtake her status-wise. So Macia shrugs, but not disrespectfully, and explains that last week she had gone a long way on the paddleboard, making it hard to get back to the water sports place.

"The woman taught me to ride waves today. I did work hard and I'm tired, but not as much as last week, so I will probably go to the gymnasium. I want to make the most of it as the gymnasium will be men-only soon on Hexaday evenings when the Mansits return to the Hills. Next week more people have booked a paddleboarding session, so the water could be busy, making it harder to go out further." Ignava squeezes her lips tightly shut, not at all pleased with Macia's long answer. She looks at Macia with hard eyes. Has she changed? Why did she even tell Ignava all her thinking? What a weird, emotional thing to do, to ramble on way. Will Ignava figure it out? Will she tell Brutus?

Instead, Ignava seems to be drawn to do the same thing, and she says, "We have done some planning today, and with some of the other spouses we are outlining the talks or books your father was talking about." She looks pleased. Macia dips her head, trying to think back to what her father had recommended or suggested, and she realises it's part of using the Bibliotheca.

Macia walks upstairs to put her things away, thinking about the question again. Is 'it' worth my life? This time in Elabi is short, for some people very short, and then there is eternity. Her heart jumps wildly, and Macia is not sure whether it's jumping in protest or agreement. Once she has showered and changed she sits down with her school books, the thin bundle safely tucked between the two sheets. She re-reads some of the lines, excitement growing. Could it be true? Could going Downstream be gain, and life in Elabi be good with God? After today Macia suddenly wonders if life in Elabi can ever be good. She felt the load and oppression this afternoon, and now she wonders why she has never realised this before. Why would having your thoughts and feelings controlled by other people ever be a good thing? On the other hand, what would a society look like where people said and did what they wanted, when they wanted? Would that be any better, or would that lead to constant anger and sadness? "Dearest friend," her pencil hesitates, then fills several inches of paper as Macia voices her doubts and fears.

She looks at the thick brown paper, next to the very thin white pages and blinks, her eyes blurry. She could simply forget about it, move on with her life, be an AMP, get Attached in the summer, have her three children, work, write, do whatever she can to organise people's lives and make it even smoother. More controlled you mean, a tiny voice comments, and Macia has to agree. Yes, that is just it, it's about control, not temperance, not kindness, meekness, esteeming others higher than yourself, not bearing each other's burdens, not showing love or helping anybody. It's all about society as a whole, not about people. She whispers, very quietly, "You're beloved, you're precious, you're set apart, you are in Christ." The words sound like she is speaking some foreign language, but her heart seems to understand this strange language, for it flutters and jitters inside her chest. Am I, she wonders, am I really? Her heart tells her that, yes, she is if she believes and accepts and trusts. "I have faith," she breathes the words, in God? Is that what it means to pray? To speak, to ask God, but can you tell things in prayer as well?

She remembers some of the things that Paul wrote to those places, where he says that he always mentions them in his prayers, so yes, that must mean that you can tell God things as well. Should she introduce herself? From the letters, she is quite sure that God knows anyway, but still, "I'm Macia, um…Macia Durus AMP, well, does that mean anything?" Paul says he'd happily throw his entire life away to be in Christ, so maybe it's not necessary to tell God that she is an Amplissimos? How does she sign up though, do you need to enrol, or is it just a way of being?

Does she need to apologise for being so set in her ways, and so determined to follow Elabi rule for all this time? Would God still be angry with her for all those times where she has been unkind to others, and where she reported others for the wrong reasons, or where she had nasty thoughts towards her stepmother? What about her hatred and anger towards her mother and Caecilia, to both of them for abandoning her? Would that count against her? Does she start collecting a different kind of life points now, or does God not keep a points list; does He not work with levels or status? Macia groans softly, there is so much she doesn't know! If only Caecilia were still here, she thinks, or that Gax man. Macia suddenly feels very lonely. It reminds her of the days after her mother had gone, and it was just her, her sister Tima and their father. She had felt so empty inside then, but this is a little different. She feels very alone, but her heart is filled up.

Dinner time is a struggle, as Macia finds it hard to stay quiet. She would love to regale her father and Ignava with tales of her paddleboarding session. She can just imagine telling them about almost falling off into the horrible, freezing water, and how the woman had yelled out the instructions. The adrenaline-filled struggle to stay on the board, and the exuberance she had felt afterwards. None of these can be shared with the adults, as they would not see why she was telling them. Of course, she could never tell them about her laughing, or the woman laughing so much she had to sit down on her knees as well. She frowns at her vegetables, feeling squashed inside all of a sudden. None of this has ever bothered her before, but now it makes her feel sad and angry. They are all missing out so much, by only dealing with facts and logical thinking, rather than sharing their hearts as well.

For all the talk about community and togetherness, there is no real connection between people, she realises. People are watching each other all the time to see if they will trip up. Everybody is waiting for somebody to make a mistake, so they can report them, get life points for being a zealous citizen as well as feel good for protecting Elabi. There is no kindness in any of this though, and Macia shivers, thinking back to the times where she has reported people. She had always felt she did it for the right reasons, never out of revenge or other emotional causes, but now she can see that there was no real desire to help or support. It was all about her, done out of selfish desires, thinking herself better than others. Her heart cringes. Will God really want her to be found in Him? Is she really worthy of his love and forgiveness?

She can tell that Ignava is looking at her, but Macia is determined to get through the meal without trouble. She still has so much to learn and remember, and hopes she should be able to live a good life in Elabi as well. Surely she can live by faith, and be a useful citizen at the same time, blessing whoever she meets? Blessing? Interesting concept, but surely supporting citizens is blessing them? She can help people around her to be truly fulfilled, she can start teaching them to connect better. Maybe, in small ways, she can show love to people, and start changing them in tiny measures. Maybe she can bring back an interest in the old laws and writings, and reintroduce Paul's letters. She wrinkles her nose, maybe not, but there must be a way to live her life in Christ, as well as being an exemplary Amplissimos citizen.

Macia is glad that the following day is Enday. She spends most of her day at her desk, either with her school books or drawing up a list with possible projects the Bibliotheca can offer. All of this simply to allow her time to read and think about the thin pages hidden under the larger, cream coloured papers. Brutus and Ignava are both out, but Macia doesn't want to take any chances. Her father's sudden return last week is still fresh in her memory. He might get suspicious if she is doing something unexpected every time he arrives home early. She needs him to think all is well. She hesitates, should she get changed for her home workout, and be ready to start exercising as soon as he comes up the drive again? Will that be better than her sitting at her desk at this time of the day? She gets up reluctantly, she is now almost at the end of another letter. There is only the start of that letter, but she wants to finish reading all the pages just so she knows what she has got to remember and find out. Once Macia is changed, ready for exercise at a moment's notice, she fishes the pages out again and is soon engrossed in the words, her heart singing every time Paul writes, 'beloved' as she is now included.

So deep into the reading of the pages, that Macia forgets to keep checking the driveway. She pulls herself away from the pages at last, knowing that she really needs to keep a better check on her father and Ignava. When she peeks out of the window, she can just see her father's head disappearing out of sight underneath her room, which means he is almost in the house! Macia almost yells at her automated servant, "Workout!" then hesitates, and adds, "Move to ten minutes down," and the obedient metallic voice tells her it's done. The workout music winds forward and Macia hesitates. She will need to do something that makes her look like she has been exercising for a very long time. In the end, she decides on burpees, for they are a great all-round exercise, making her work up a sweat in literally seconds. Just as she decides to do T-jacks, her father knocks on her door, and his head appears around the dark wooden door. He looks at her hot and sweaty face and raises his chin with a smirk. His eyes stay hard as ever, though.

Macia raises her chin too, her eyes itching to look at her desk to triple check that the thin pages are out of sight. She forces her eyes to focus on her father, but it's hard. She knows she should trust her memory, and she is convinced she pushed the thin pages as well as her new diary paper to safety before checking the driveway. Her father doesn't seem happy she is doing a home workout again, and Macia shrugs with one shoulder, "I have some ideas that I would like to think about more. There are some things I need to try out before I mention those ideas, and one of them is doing special exercise classes to help people pass their status tests. The fitness side of the test, I mean" she says quickly, "and I want to see if there are certain workouts I can definitely do, and do faster than some of the videos available at the moment. They are usually for older people or those with very young children who might not make it to the gymnasium often enough. I find them too slow, and I wonder if the same is true for other young people. I'm just trying out to see if I can improve those videos."

Macia feels satisfied that she isn't telling a lie. True, she is working out this very moment because her father was coming home, and he would be suspicious if she was sitting at her desk. She is trying to establish some kind of routine that she can keep up on Enday. This way she can read and think about the book, as well as avoid detection. And it's true, she really would love to teach some high paced exercise videos. Maybe she should get herself a little fitter. So she can call out encouragements and new routines without struggling for oxygen.

Chapter 22

Macia smiles as she looks out of the window at the bright Onesday morning, drinking in the colours. The rich browns and reds of the freshly ploughed and seeded fields, interspersed with the soft green on the trees against the light blue sky at the horizon make her heart soar. Why has she never noticed it before? She is looking forward to today, but it frightens her as well. Now that she is found in God, will anything change? Is she ready for the consequences?

At breakfast, Ignava chatters about the Bibliotheca project. "We want to add more and more over time, but there will need to be special training in place, especially for the staff that work at the Bibliotheca. Their main concern seems to be the Mansits who work Hexaday and Enday. They would end up with access to some of the videos unsuitable for their status," she says, her mouth taking on a sour look. "Some of those Mansits have already tried to access books barred to them, claiming that they have read them before. It's astonishing how entitled some of them feel, seeing that they were sent down for a serious misdemeanour. They still expect the same privileges after they return." Brutus dips his head, his face looking tight. Macia can tell that he feels a little torn. After all, when her mother left Elabi with her little brother, Brutus had to work hard to get his status back.

"People don't realise how serious it is if one family member dishonours Elabi rule," he says after a while. "They think that they have not been influenced at all, and therefore don't understand the need to prove themselves loyal. Some of us have been there, and it's an important subject. Maybe the council should make a new, updated video on this, and make it compulsory viewing for everyone." His wife nods and Macia senses Ignava feeling smug. She does resent Brutus' status and would love to remind him that she became Attached to him despite the cloud of suspicion that was hanging over him. Macia looks down on her bowl still half full with pottage, and sprinkles a little more garum on it, mainly to have something to distract her thoughts. She strongly dislikes Ignava and has done so ever since the woman entered their household. It's her tiny hints that she is morally above Brutus and the others, despite her lower status, that grates on Macia. The usual feelings of resentment start to grow as she stirs her pottage. Then she realises that this feeling of superiority is all Ignava has. She has nothing else to feel good about. She's pretty but not really beautiful. She's not smart or clever. She's a follower, longing to be a leader.

Macia suddenly feels sorry for Ignava. What sort of life is it, where you constantly have to look for a way of making yourself feel better? Ignava is bitter, she realises.

"It's just awful how some people have so little regard for Elabi law, and just want to have their own way, by reading books that they fancy, for example," Ignava continues, making Macia's eyes open wide. That was just what she was thinking! The way Ignava goes on about people doing things she dislikes but bringing in Elabi or Elabi law as if that is her main concern in the matter. Ignava despises Mansits and would love to see them banned from the bibliotheca.

Macia is glad when breakfast is over. It is hard not to say anything in defence of the Mansits. She has always looked down on them, too, but now she wonders why they shouldn't read whatever they want.

Walking up the stairs to her room Macia can feel her cheeks growing warm. She is questioning Elabi rule, questioning the council and their wise decisions, made for the good of Elabi. In her room, she whispers in horror, "I have changed! Something inside me, in my heart, has changed." Getting her bag ready for school, Macia notices her shaking hands and swallows. She needs to get a grip on herself, for if she carries on, people will notice very quickly how she has changed.

The walk to school is lovely and it calms her a little. The warming air carries scents of the fields and Spring. In fact, Macia is feeling so relaxed, that she catches herself starting to smile and raise her chin at random school mates. It is only when one girl looks at her with a tight face that Macia realises what she is doing. Straight away she lowers her eyes to her new sandals, determined to get through the day looking like the old Macia. She forces her facial muscles back to their usual blank, grumpy shape, pulling down the corners of her mouth. By the time she is sitting in class, Macia is confident that her face looks like it always does. Did. She looks down atat her book, feeling tired already. How is she going to keep this up? She can't even remember why she started looking sulky and grumpy, for being grumpy is to allow negative emotions to rule you, something that should not happen in Elabi. That's another worry point, to look sulky enough to be her normal way, but not too grumpy as she might get noticed for her bad emotions. Macia gives off a tiny sigh.

Lunchtime turns out to be the hardest, with Mansits serving them, and other Amplissimos students sitting at the same table. Macia struggles to swallow her food, especially as one of the Amplissimos students sees her dipping her head at the Mansit girl serving her. Macia squeezes her fingers together under the table to stop them from trembling, but her heart beats wildly in her own defence. Surely to say thank you to a person for serving you is a normal thing to do?

How could she have lived like she used to, taking people for granted? On the other hand, surely an organised and ordered society has layers, with people living differently from each other? Those letters she has talk about masters and servants. There were stern warnings in them though. Macia slowly stirs her food, and almost jumps when another Amplissimos student addresses her, "Which classes will you take when regular classes are over?" The girl looks at Macia without showing the slightest interest, and Macia hesitates. Has she missed something? Then the girl pulls out a used scrap of paper, her pencil hovering over it. Macia swallows, she really is getting paranoid, the girl is merely organising classes and the necessary catering for those days.

She manages to make her voice sound the usual way, "I want the Instructor classes, as well as the Movement Instructor one. And the Article Writing one," she adds, feeling her face warm up a little when she thinks of her writing class. Her last project had received a harsh comment at the bottom, leaving Macia fuming. She knew the article was good; she also knew that the teacher was an Altiorem who had not been invited to apply for Amplissimos Status. There was nothing she could do about it, apart from adding the writing course to her summer workload. Without the right grades, her articles would not be accepted. The girl next to her nods and writes the classes down, then looks at Macia again.

"Your name?" she asks, her voice sounding bored, and Macia can tell that the girl feels a little put out by the whole job. She tells the girl her name, almost adding AMP at the end of her name, but remembering just in time that the girl is Amp as well, for their entire lunch table is AMP, which is why they're sitting together served by Mansits. When the girl hears Macia's name her eyes light up the slightest bit. "You are Brutus Durus' daughter then?" She looks at Macia now. First she was a nobody; now, because of her father, she is suddenly a person of interest. Nevertheless, Macia dips her head but presses her lips together when she sees the girl's eyes get brighter. "You must get a lot of support through your father," she says, her voice definitely sounding a little envious.

Macia shrugs and says, "Although my father is supportive, nobody in Elabi will receive preferential treatment, as that would involve jealousy and favouritism." The girl has the grace to blush at least a little and Macia feels satisfied with the result. That put the girl straight. Then Macia feels awkward. She has no idea about the girl's background. Her parents might not be supportive at all or be of a much lower status, so maybe the girl was simply comparing their lives. She softens her voice a little, then explains, "My father and stepmother are working with the council. They're setting up some new options at the Bibliotheca, and that does take up time. Of course, I now have my own interests as well, so it's not like it used to be when we were younger." The girl dips her head this time, and Macia quickly carries on eating the rest of her lunch. Why was she volunteering this information? She doesn't even know the girl's name and now she is chattering about her family as if they are best friends. So between mouthfuls, Macia pulls her sulky, closed face, hoping that the girl gets the message. Hoping also that other people will look at her and see the usual Macia.

The day drags on, and Macia is shocked at the change in herself. Classes that used to feel so important now sound empty and pointless. She even finds herself disagreeing with what the teachers say. The change unsettles her and she knows she will have to be very careful. She thinks back to Caecilia and how she had changed the last few weeks before she left. Caecilia had left Elabi before it was reported, but Macia might not get away that easily. Also, she is an Amplissimos and some of the young people at her lunch table got their AMP status by being very proactive in society. Every day they will watch and observe her. Macia shivers.

The day passes without incident though, and so does the following day. Macia is grateful beyond belief for the Bibliotheca project, as it keeps her stepmother occupied which means she will spend less time looking at Macia, trying to find fault. After dinner each evening Macia goes to do the rest of her homework, and that is when she will hide the thin pages between her brown schoolwork papers, and quietly read a few verses. Macia finds herself trying to memorise some of the verses that move her heart. Going througt her school day, she knows that just thinking the words will help to stay calm, to stop her from worrying about being found out. She carefully copies some of them onto her diary pages. "Beloved," she giggles at that one, "I might not understand it all, but it makes me feel so very alive."

By Fifday Macia feels exhausted, not just from the long days, but mainly from the stress of having to be her old self when everything seems to have changed. Going to the gymnasium in the morning is a lovely quiet time to think and reflect. She also talks to God, very quietly, on her way, asking Him to help her through the day, asking Him not to desert her.

Fifday lunchtime Macia ends up sitting next to the girl who had collected the classes' information. "I have been thinking about what you told me the other day," the girl says after a while. "It got me a little worried, you see. It was the way you said that your parents were very busy and involved with council matters. You made it sound as if you felt their support had slipped, and that you were left more to your own devices. That made me wonder if I should talk to somebody about this."

Macia stares at the girl, then quickly averts her eyes, for she can feel anger and fear bubbling up inside her. When she feels that her eyes are under control she looks at the girl again and dips her head slightly in acknowledgement. "You see, I know your father is Brutus Durus, but even the best Amplissimos could get carried away in a weak moment." The girl sounds very sure of herself and rather sanctimonious about it all. Macia feels anger swirling around, and the fact that she recognises herself in the girl doesn't help. Only a few weeks ago Macia would have done and sounded exactly like this girl! "I might simply mention it to my counsellor," the girl says thoughtfully, looking up at Macia quickly, "just to be on the safe side."

Macia wants to groan, snap at the girl, or stab at her food wildly, for if the girl passes the information on, Macia will have to spend certain supervised hours with her father and Ignava. Will her father come paddleboarding? How will he react to the kind woman there? This girl must be stopped. Macia's brain goes in overdrive, searching for an escape.

Chapter 23

Macia dips her head, then, with an even voice says, "Thank you for your concern. As you said yourself last time, my parents are very supportive and have set an example, not just in our family, but also in Elabi. Yes, they're busy, but so am I. During working hours we all have our part in our society, and especially as Amplissimos, we ought to do what we can for our city. As a family, we do get to spend time together as well, as my parents make sure they are always available to me." The girl's face has started to tighten up, and Macia is sure she can see the disappointment in her eyes. She deliberately takes a bite of her food, chewing it carefully. She looks at the girl and tries to pull a more pleasant face. Not too pleasant of course, she has to keep her reputation in place.

"With my parents, we have been looking at serving our city by adding more videos to the Bibliotheca," she says when her mouth is empty. "I wonder if you have just raised a valid topic for a video message? Or maybe even a class, as I'm quite sure not all families will be as supportive as mine?" She smiles at the girl, knowing the smile doesn't make it to her eyes, but then, it doesn't have to. The girl has been suitably put in her place.

The girl dips her head, her cheeks a bit darker. She hesitates, then says, "My name is Luti, and yes, I agree with you, that would be a helpful addition to the wonderful videos your father has made already."

Macia nods once, then continues eating, wanting to slump in her chair in relief. Nothing is said anymore about raising flags. The girl hasn't made it to Amplissimos status by being too slow though, and she adds, "Maybe an Enquiry could be made, to see how many families would welcome some additional lessons?" Macia thinks about it for a moment, her hands still struggling to hide their shaking. "You see, it would put certain children at a disadvantage, and that could mean our city missing out on talent." Luti's voice sounds a little flat, and again Macia is sure that the girl hasn't had much support from her family. It would have been something to look into if she had found out a week or so ago. Now Macia's heart somehow feels tight thinking about the girl.

Lunchtime passes, and Macia makes her way to the bathrooms, walking as calmly as she can. Once inside the cubicle, she takes very deep, steadying breaths, her hands shaking. She wipes her forehead, and after a few more deep, slow breaths, flushes the toilet and goes to wash her hands. The dark olive soap feels good, its smell familiar and comforting. That was too close, and Macia thinks about the plan she and Luti made. Does that mean she will have to work with the girl? She has seen her in a few of her classes, but the girl looks a little bit younger than Macia. How did she get to her status if her family isn't helpful? Macia's stomach feels heavy. Does that mean the girl is extra keen?

Macia leaves school as soon as the last lesson finishes, afraid to bump into Luti. Suddenly she realises she is walking fast as if she is in a hurry. Rather undignified. She frowns and makes her feet slow down. The slight breeze feels cool on her hot face, and again she wonders when the summer dresses will be given out. As an Amplissimos she will have a larger collection as well as a better choice. She has chosen a light blue one and an olive one. She loves that colour, as it suits her auburn hair and dark green eyes. Blue doesn't really suit her, but light blue reminds her of early morning skies. She has also ticked the boxes for some skirts, a tan one that can be combined easily. If they're too tight she can send them back, but it comes with consequences.

Fortunately, thanks to her active lifestyle, she fits most dresses her size. She's slender, unlike others, and she has heard plenty of people who struggled with the assigned dresses. Macia is glad to get home, and after a snack retreats to her room. She pulls her papers out, her diary and the thin book. After a quick, guilty glance she starts, "Dearest friend," and smiles, then the smile slides. "Today was hard. I had lunch and the girl I mentioned before threatened to tell on our family. She claimed I didn't get enough attention." Macia looks at the paper, worn and rubbed out many times, but her eyes see the girl's hard eyes, the bustle of the dining room, clattering cutlery, and the girl's cool voice. She shudders again, "I was so afraid, as I knew what would happen if she did. How would I manage to write to you, to read, to speak to God, if my parents were with me all the time? How would I hide the change…" Macia stops, confused. Hide the change? Yes, she needs to, doesn't she? If she behaved the way she feels like, she'll be in trouble, and so will her family. But should she hide?

Macia stares ahead, her hands automatically hiding the pages under her school books. That's a hard question. Would Paul hide? Gax did, so did Caecilia. You could tell they were different, but they did hide, sort of. Her hands are shaking at the thought of being found out. What will she say? No, she will have to carry on as best she can. Macia forces herself to look at her books. Another week has gone by, and although her grades have gone up again, it still wasn't at the level she used to be. The teachers couldn't say anything, but there had been plenty of looks. Macia had felt uneasy each time the grades were announced. She will have to improve, so even though it's Fifday, she works on her homework for Onesday. She just hopes the change in routine won't be noticed.

The following morning is another beautiful Spring day, and Macia is soon on her way to the water sports place. Paddleboarding is definitely getting easier each time, but the water still feels cold. The woman's smile is warm though, and Macia finds herself smiling back, her face glowing. In the afternoon, after a hot shower, she sits down at her desk. "Beloved, it was paddleboarding again. I can't tell you how much I enjoyed it." She smiles at the paper, feeling the smooth board under her feet, the gentle rocking motion, the wind in her hair. She hovers her pencil over the paper, as she would love to describe the woman. Like at other times, something holds her back. What if... Of course, she would never let anybody see these papers, but still, she hesitates to mention anybody else. So instead she writes, "The weather was bright, the water still freezing, but so glorious, and I could have done it for longer, but my time slot finished and there were a few other people there. A young man came just after I finished. I..." Again Macia stops.

She feels the same feeling of annoyance as she did at the watersports place. The guy had looked like an Amplissimos, and the fact that he went straight for the boards showed that he had been there before. Macia had felt like she missed out on something. "I would have liked to finish my session properly," she writes down in the end, hoping that she will never forget what she means with those words. Normally, she signs out, and she and the woman share a smile. Today, that had not been an option. Macia remembers the woman's face, all straight and with no expression whatsoever. She had not made eye contact with anybody, and Macia had felt it. "I miss the proper ending that I always have." Maybe she should write it down?

At dinner, Brutus looks at Macia, and says, "There was a note from Luti." Macia's heart stops, then skips on, as she digs her nails into her one free hand, hidden in the folds of her dress. "I was very pleased with the suggestion," he continues, "of course, I recognised your way of thinking straight away, despite the way the note was phrased." Macia relaxes a little and almost rolls her eyes at her father's words. Does he mean Luti tried to pass off the idea of family involvement as her own? Macia shrugs, only just in time to smooth out the smile that had started. Of course, it was a good idea, but she can't show that she is pleased with the compliment. So she shrugs again, her face blank as always.

"Luti just raised the matter, and I felt from her words that she hadn't always felt supported in her work," she says, trying to sound dismissive. Ignava sits up straight away, smelling a chance to cause trouble. "Do you mean her family undermined her?" Her eyes glimmer at the idea of people coming up short. Macia shrugs again, trying to look even more bored, without looking disrespectful. "I'm surprised you didn't recommend some classes for her family, or for the girl herself," Ignava continues, "rather than set up a new plan for other families. After all, you have only recently completed the Sharing is Caring course." Her mouth turned down, she looks at Macia with a cold look. Macia scrunches up her dress in one hand under the table, doing her best to stay calm.

She dips her head, then says, "I didn't mean that her family undermined her, but Luti and I both thought of families who maybe can't really support their children. That way those children miss out, and ultimately Elabi misses out on young talent. We felt that a video or even a class might help." Macia feels the corners of her mouth turn upwards into a soft smile, but seeing Ignava's mouth travel the other way, she stops herself.

"It still doesn't mean the girl shouldn't be looked at," Ignava is not giving up that easily. "It sounds to me that she could have done with more support. Anyway, how did somebody her age get to Amplissimos status without parental support, I wonder." She glances at Brutus, but he shakes his head, explaining that the girl is from another district, and therefore has been under a different team of council members.

"I could have a look," he frowns, sounding reluctant, "for you are right. To reach that status, support is needed, as it is not easy." Ignava nods, looking satisfied. Macia stares at her dinner, eating mechanically, fighting to keep her face straight. Poor Luti! On the other hand, why had the girl decided to write to the council? Also, trying to pass off the idea as her own wasn't a good idea. Elabi had no tolerance for liars, as they caused mistrust. As an Amplissimos, the girl should have known better. Brutus looks at Macia, "Do you know her well, and is she your friend?" Macia shakes her head quickly, too quickly, judging by her father's eyes. She explains that she happened to sit next to her at lunchtime, and how the girl had found out her name as she was sorting classes. The following time together at lunch they had discussed busy parents. "And that is all?" Brutus looks sceptical, then frowns. "When did you have the conversation?" His eyebrows go up when Macia tells him it was Fifday lunchtime.

"Well, she is an ambitious little girl," sneers Ignava, "I wonder why she is like that?" She stacks up the plates in such a way that says that the matter is over. She, Ignava, has given her opinion of the girl, and that's all there is to it. Macia finds both her hands have gripped her dress. She makes herself smooth out the material, and walks over to the kitchen area to help Ignava. Macia is relieved when she can go upstairs. She sits down at her desk and pulls a sheet of paper towards her. She decides to work more on her exercise plans for Elabi, in case somebody comes to check on her. In reality, she stares ahead, wondering if Luti will get in trouble.

She can't remember seeing the girl before, at least not till she turned up with the class list. Maybe a few days before that. The girl is so bland though, she would not be noticed, Macia thinks. She tells the Automated Servant to turn on her music, and after a quick glance pulls her diary out. "Looks like L might be in trouble, dearest friend, and somehow I feel uneasy about her. She has suddenly appeared, who is she?" Macia stares at her diary, where had that come from? Clearly, the girl had only recently been promoted, just like Macia. She hadn't been in any of her Amplissimos classes though, but that didn't mean much. On the other hand, why would a very new Amplissimos be tasked with sorting out class schedules? Maybe she had been ill, or assigned somewhere else? But she looked younger than Macia.

Macia leans back in her chair, feeling...nosey. She knows that curiosity is not something Elabi accepts. It leads to all kinds of problems and is an emotional reaction. Macia shrugs at herself, yes, she is curious, there, she has said it. She simply would love to know who the girl is, and where she is from. Hopefully, Brutus will find out more.

Chapter 24

Enday dinner time brings more news. Macia has trouble keeping her face straight when Brutus tells her that he has looked into Luti's records. "It was actually filed in the wrong place, and something is...odd." He takes a large bite of his fish and looks at Macia. She feels herself cringe inwardly, why that look? She has nothing to do with the girl's files, she doesn't even know her. She only found out her name on Fifday. "How often have you seen her?" His face is hard, and Macia carefully moves her shoulders in her well-practised shrug, wanting to defend, explain...

"I only met her last week," she says, trying to make her voice flat, disinterested, "and then on Fifday we discussed supportive families and their importance, that's all. That's when she told me her name as well." Again she shrugs, almost ending with 'sorry' just like Caecilia! Why should she apologise? She feels that curious feeling though. Who is Luti? "I can't really remember seeing her around many of my classes," she says, "and definitely only recently." Her father nods as if that explains everything. He glares at his dinner and Macia hides her one shaking hand, gripping her fork tightly with her other hand. Ignava's eyes flit from one to the other, a slight tint on her cheeks, she is obviously enjoying this.

Brutus looks up, and putting his fork down carefully, says, "I don't know for sure, but there is something out of order about this girl.

Her records are…sloppy, not really complete. I don't know many people on her Council Member team, so I can't say for sure, but something doesn't add up." He opens his mouth to say more, but snaps his lips together, picks up his fork and eats on, clearly done with the conversation.

Ignava sits up, and pointing her fork at Brutus, says, "You think the girl is not really an Amplissimos?" Her voice is full of excitement, and she realises it. The colour in her cheeks deepens, and she frowns, making her lips form a concerned shape. "You think this girl has lied or is a plant from somewhere? Maybe she has something to do with that other girl," she looks at Macia, her eyes wide, "Caecilia? Macia's friend?" Macia resents the emphasis on friend, knowing Ignava uses it out of spite. Brutus shrugs and frowns at Ignava's flushed face. She gets the hint and stabs at her dinner, and Macia notices the white knuckles and shaking fingers around her step mother's fork. "I wondered if there was a connection, after all, young people leaving Elabi is unheard of, so it might be a large movement that ought to be stopped," Ignava says, but she doesn't look at Brutus anymore.

Macia is glad to get back to her room. She needs to think. There was something wrong about Luti's papers? Is she a plant? She wonders if Ignava was right, and there was a connection with Caecilia. Not in the way her stepmother thought, Macia knows better, but would the council have planted Luti? To spy on the other young people, especially her, after Caecilia's disappearance? She takes a deep breath and quietly pulls her diary papers onto her desk. "Dearest friend, I am afraid." What a way to start an entry. She frowns but leaves it. It is true, she is afraid. "I wonder if L is a plant. Would the council use plants?" She stares at the paper as if hoping the answer will appear on the brown sheet. "I will have to be careful, more than ever as she seems to be targeting me. What do I do?"

Macia chews her thumbnail corner, her pencil balancing on her fingers. She will need to do something. Luti's action wasn't right; there is something odd about her background. Of course, smelly fish produces good garum, but will that apply here? "You see, my beloved," she continues suddenly, "If I don't report her, they will feel I haven't learned my lesson. If I do report her, and it turns out she was innocent, well, that would be awful. How can I be merciful without bringing problems on myself?" That's the question. Should she forgive Luti for trying to take the honour, or should she abide by Elabi rule, passing on Luti's information to the relevant council member?

Onesday, Macia still hasn't made a decision. She spots Luti in the distance when she arrives at school. She tries to look aimless as she drifts through the school grounds, making sure to place several students between her and Luti. When she looks around, she is suddenly faced with Savisia. The girl still looks grey and seems to shake all over. She glances at Macia, then her eyes go to Luti, who is only just visible. She looks at Macia again, and Macia inches closer, making sure to look the other way. Her heart is hammering away, almost drowning out the frail-looking girl's voice. "...careful...who she is. I have seen her..." Then the girl turns away and walks slowly in a different direction. Macia wonders if those shakes are contagious, as her frozen hands are trembling now. What did Savisia mean? Did she know Luti? So her father was right, there was something wrong about Luti.

This new knowledge doesn't help Macia at all. To tell or not to tell, that is still a big question. What should she do? By break time, she has made a decision. She walks to the counsellor's office with calm, casual steps. She mustn't seem too keen, it will be noticed. Not hesitant either, and Macia sighs with relief when she knocks on the door. "You see," she soon finds herself explaining the incident to the counsellor. "You see, there is something that she will need to understand as an

Amplissimos." She straightens her woollen skirt out, trying to look as helpful and concerned as she ought to. "It was the way she mentioned the lack of support she had had, and then the letter…" She doesn't really want to explain how it had been her father who had looked into things, "The letter was not phrased right, you see, and was in fact too eager. I just wanted to check, seeing I have just completed my Sharing is Caring class. I simply wanted to share with you, in case Luti makes another slip-up, just to be sure our city's safety net is in place for her."

The counsellor nods, busily making notes at the same time. "Thank you," she says and dips her head at Macia. "In fact, another Amplissimos has mentioned that she seemed to lack self-control skills, not always being in charge of her facial expressions." She looks at Macia, who does her careful shrug, feeling she has done enough to clear her own name. Yes, she has seen the same lack of control in Luti, but Macia has started to resent the need to control all emotions. The counsellor gives a nod, and Macia leaves the office, feeling like she has just sat an important exam. Maybe she has.

Luti is at the table during lunchtime, but Macia manages to sit next to different students. She avoids eye contact with Luti but studies the girl unnoticed. Something is going on, she is sure. Luti seems to watch the others closely, and Macia feels her hands going cold. Why is Luti staring at the other Amplissimos like that all through lunch? When leaving the table, Luti suddenly appears at her side. "I wrote to the council," she says, coming too close for Macia's liking. "I haven't heard yet, for I wrote to them Fifday evening. They will be meeting about our suggestion. I made sure that the letter made it clear that it had been your idea, as your father is on the council." She dips her head as if Macia has already thanked her. Macia is speechless. The girl has just told her a lie. Unless Brutus Durus AMP lied to her on Hexaday? But he would never do that, and she knows he has seen the letter.

Macia takes a deep breath, and blows it out slowly, ready to correct the girl. Luti seems oblivious, and continues, "I'm sure they will ask for your input, so do let me know when you need me to help you work it all out." Macia's mouth drops and she can feel her cheeks go hot. She stands a little taller, her face hard, but Luti raises her chin and walks off. Just like that! Macia gasps, her anger tripled as she can't put Luti straight. Who does she think she is? Someone whose records are being looked at, talking to her, Macia Durus AMP, daughter of Brutus… Her thoughts grind to a halt, as she can hear the words from the thin pages, "…Hebrew of the Hebrews…as to the righteousness before the law, blameless…I count all things but loss for the excellency of the knowledge of Christ Jesus my Lord…"

Macia makes it to the bathroom without drawing suspicion to herself. Once in the cubicle, she sinks down on the seat, her legs shaking with emotion. How could she? She is in God, but she had treated Luti with anger and contempt because she felt the girl didn't show enough respect. A tiny voice in her head says, "What would Luti say if she knew you'd kept the forbidden book?" Cold sweat on her back makes her shiver. Macia leans forward, taking deep, steadying breaths, then flushes, and goes to wash her hands slowly and thoroughly as if washing away her anger at the same time.

Macia can't wait to get home. She needs to read the thin pages, for the last few days she hasn't, and look what happened! After eating some fruit, and explaining to Ignava that she had seen the school counsellor that morning to let her know about Luti, she goes upstairs. She feels tired, heavy. Even telling Ignava about it had been hard. Part of her wanted Ignava to react the way she knew she would, part of her feels bad for potentially getting Luti into trouble, and all over nothing, really. Macia slumps in her chair, desperate for the thin pages, desperate to read the words again. Telling her automated servant to play her music, she gets her school books out and arranges them carefully. With a quick, guilty look round, she pulls the thin book out of her drawer.

She turns the pages till she gets to the passage that came into her mind after lunch, pleased that she is getting more familiar with the letters. Reading the words all the way to the paragraph numbered 21, she finds her heart rate speeding up. When she gets to number twenty-one she leans back in her chair, carefully pushing the thin pages under her book. So many words to think about. "...our conversation is in Heaven..." Where is Heaven? And vile bodies? Was Paul really old, or did he even have a defect? Is that why this book is forbidden because the writer had a clear defect?

"Dearest friend, I have to write to you. I forgot myself, and the fact that I'm in God, and that I want to win Christ, and therefore I'm prepared to lose all things. Well, I forgot. I can't tell you right now, for I figured something out. I think Paul had a defect. Not like mine, a small, hidden one, but quite an obvious one. That is why this book is forbidden. He says he has a vile body, which in Elabi as things are now isn't an option. I have definitely not got a vile body, although I know that when I reach my father's age, I will have to work a lot harder on my body. So maybe Paul was old?"

Macia pulls her schoolbook closer; she'd better do her homework if she wants to get her grades up by the end of the week. If she doesn't, Luti might not be the only one in trouble. Macia groans when it's time for dinner. She is tired, and she hasn't finished her work yet. Brutus raises his chin at her, and once they're eating he says, "Ignava says you told the counsellor?" Macia dips her head and tells her father what she said. He looks satisfied. "Interesting that others have mentioned her," he notes, looking almost pleased. Macia dips her head, then concentrates on her food. The grain isn't very tasty, it really could have done with more salt, but a generous helping of garum sorts that out. Ignava purses her lips; she dislikes Macia using garum as she feels it's a slight against her cooking.

Seconday lunchtime finds Macia sitting next to Luti. She raises her chin slightly, then quickly studies her sleeve as she finds herself raising her chin at the serving Mansit as well. She peeks at Luti, but the girl is looking at another Amplissimos who nods three or four times at something the student next to him says. Macia swallows, suddenly worried for the nodding student. She finds a surviving nail, and nibbles it, resentment bubbling up inside her again. How can nodding your head more than once lead to trouble? She looks at Luti. The girl's pale face looks a little blotchy. Not in a bad way, of course, just...uneven coloured skin. As if she has been overcome by emotions earlier. Luti looks at her and leans over a little. Macia smells garum and the slightly sour smell associated with Mansits. Macia somehow manages to keep her face straight, not letting the girl see her unease. Luti looks pleased with herself, and says, "I saw a small committee of council members this morning." Macia's eyes widen, does the girl mean there had been an Enquiry?

"They were pleased with our suggestion, and have allocated us both to work out more of the details before handing in the proposal to the council." Macia gasps. Their Supportive Families plan? Then the words sink in. The council wants them to work together? Luti means they have to spend time together? Macia swallows, but somehow forces the corners of her mouth to go up. She dips her head and makes the words come out of her mouth in a calm, collected way.

"That's good news. Hopefully, many families in Elabi will benefit from our plan, and we will see even more talented young people being useful to society." Macia focuses on the plate placed in front of her, the steam from her food flushing her face, allowing her to take deep, steadying breaths. Spending time with Luti!

Chapter 25

Macia is relieved when lunch is over. What is she going to do about Luti spending time with her? Hopefully, they will find a neutral place to look at the plans. After classes are over, Macia slips out of the school gates as quickly as she can without looking as if she is on the run. Walking up the long drive to her home, her heart flips. There are a lot of people in the garden. Wherever she looks, there are workers. Then she relaxes, of course, Spring is definitely here, so teams of Mansits work on the gardens and green spaces. Soon most of them will return to beyond the hills.

When Macia gets to her room, she stops just inside the doorway and looks around critically. What will Luti see? Is there anything out of place, anything that will make the girl look at Macia longer than necessary? Slowly Macia walks to her desk and lowers herself into her chair. The thin pages will need to be hidden, as well as her diary. If Luti gets hold of either of those, the results would be devastating. Macia goes through her usual routine, then, with her music playing in the background, pulls her diary closer.

"Beloved, I had such a shock today. Luti said we were to work on the Family project together. I'm asking God to ensure that we do it somewhere else. I worry, and I know I'm afraid, and feeling emotional about it, rather than rational. Something is different about Luti, and today I smelled a typical Mansit smell on her." Macia suddenly finds her mood lifted a little. Mansit smell, really? It was true though, Luti had an odd smell. Maybe she has a Mansit friend or close family member? Macia frowns, wondering again how the girl made it to Amplissimos status in that case.

"Yes, dearest friend, I'm quite sure that it's all a setup, but why?" She pushes the rough paper back into her drawer. It is hard to concentrate on her schoolwork, and Macia is glad when it's dinner time. She dips her head at Brutus once they're eating. "Luti, the girl, and I have been commissioned to look at what is needed for the Supportive Family project." She feels uncharitably smug when Brutus stares at her, clearly needing time to process that. "So we will be working on it," she says and forces her face to stay blank. Ignava snorts and Macia looks at her.

"Sounds like that girl can give a few examples of how not to get supported. Strange that they allow her to do this after the complaints that have been made. You would think she would need a few classes first?" It seems Ignava is so surprised, she forgets to be spiteful. Macia dips her head, yes, she had been just as surprised.

Brutus frowns, "Have you thought about it more, about something not being right?" He looks at Macia, and she hesitates. Should she share about the strange Mansit smell? After all, it was just a whiff, it might have even been one of the serving Mansits. So Macia does her special shrug, and dinner continues as usual, Ignava telling them about her many projects. Brutus is quiet though, and once Macia finds him studying her. She glances away quickly. Once back in her room, she slowly writes, "Dearest friend, I'm afraid. Too afraid. I know I understood that being in God was worth it, worth all I have and am, but this is," she pauses, "this is frightening me more than I thought it would. Luti, my father, all of it." Writing it down, it doesn't seem that bad. Only two people after all, one at home, one at school, but Macia is starting to dread the pressure.

Luti looks pleased to see Macia, walking up to her as soon as she arrives at school. "I think it is best to work on the project after school today," she starts, looking determined, her eyes staring hard at Macia, "and your home would be best, as mine is not very large, making it less private." Macia feels the temperature in her hands drop instantly, and has to work extremely hard to control her face and eyes. This was exactly what she was worried about, Luti coming to her house. She has hidden the thin pages well, getting up extra early, when still dark, feeling her way around, and putting the book as well as her diary pages in her secret hiding place. She had felt resentment as she did so, for now it will be harder to read the book. With all the stress, she wants to read the book more, not less!

In the end, she dips her head, "My house has a lot of space, you are right. It is further out of the city, but the weather is pleasant." What else can she say? Walking home that afternoon, Luti is gushing about the council members in her area. She asks Macia about her team, and Macia feels her stomach tightening. Surely she can remember her council members? One or two recently went Downstream though and were replaced. "We have a wonderful team," she starts, "even though we have had a few members go Downstream, the team is still working at a high level. It shows the dedication of all council members, don't you think?" Luti dips her head, her dark eyes taking in Macia's face, and Macia is sure that she can see the disappointment in Luti's eyes. Was it another test, a trap? She is mentally exhausted by the time they get to the Durus home.

Luti gives a small gasp when the large house comes into view. Her eyes are wide, and even her mouth is open a little. Macia looks away to hide her own frown. Surely, as an Amplissimos, Luti must have good, comfortable accommodations, even if she hasn't come from a line of Amplissimos? Luti suddenly seems to realise her highly emotional reaction, and Macia has to fight down a giggle as the girl tries to turn her wide-eyed gasp into a sneeze. She looks at the girl, making her face look very concerned, and Luti hastens to explain that something seemed to have tickled her nose. "I hope you don't have an allergic reaction to the freshly done garden?" Macia asks, raising her eyebrows, then almost giggling again as she realises her face is an exact replica of her stepmother's face when she is trying to score points. She manages to keep up the act though, feeling only a little bit sorry for Luti when she sees the girl's reaction.

Luti turns pale, then red, then her face slowly takes on the blotchy look. Macia feels her frown becoming genuine. Luti's facial issues are really a defect. How has that not been noticed before? She will have to report it. Macia feels bad about that though, for it was really her teasing that has brought on this change in Luti's face.

Once inside the house, Macia serves Luti a snack, then the two girls go upstairs to work on the proposal. Macia watches Luti's eyes travel around her room, and she shivers a little. Hopefully, they can work together on this project, then move on. Macia soon finds Luti is no replacement for Caecilia. She might have tried to put Caecilia down a lot, making snide remarks whilst working with her, but they were a good team. Working with Luti is like extracting Garum by hand. Macia pulls an old sheet from her drawer and starts making notes. Luti reads along, mumbling the words softly to herself. Macia's pencil hovers as she notices the girl struggling with a lot of the words. How did she sit for the exams? Just before dinner time, Luti gets up to go. The plan hasn't gotten very far, but a start has been made. Once Luti has left, Macia drags herself upstairs and collapses on her bed, commanding the automated servant to play her music. She needs time to recover before she goes down to face her parents. She misses her diary…

Brutus raises his chin at her, his eyes staying on her face. Macia raises her chin respectfully, struggling not to slump in her chair. Ignava's face looks tight. "The girl didn't have the best of manners," she starts straight away, "not the kind of manners expected from someone of her status." Macia dips her head, she had noticed too. She looks at Brutus, should she tell him about the girl's face? Her lack of reading skills? She swallows her food down with difficulty, although the herbs make for a very tasty dish. The purple carrots somehow contain more flavours than the pale coloured ones they often have in the Spring. "I wonder how much she will be able to advise you? After all, you have been given a lot of opportunities to contribute to society in a meaningful way," says Ignava, looking at Macia as if she wants to check that the girl has understood how much she owes her parents.

Macia flushes a little. Ignava isn't known for sending opportunities Macia's way! She dips her head however and hesitates. Brutus raises his eyebrows, "Are you saying she isn't really leadership material?" Macia swallows a bit of chicken. What can she say?

"She is very dedicated," she says in the end, but it almost sounds like a question. Brutus glares at his food, Ignava snorts, disapproval written all over her. "We didn't get as far as I expected," Macia adds, suddenly wondering if any of this will affect her. If the proposal takes too long or isn't of the expected standard, that could affect her, and her plans for young people in Elabi. When the meal is over, Brutus calls her over.

"Do you have any grounds for reporting her?" He looks at her, and Macia feels the warmth in her cheeks. She dips her head a little and explains that the girl seemed to struggle to read whatever Macia was writing.

"She's also not a fast thinker, and a few times didn't see the consequences of her suggestions," she explains, realising it all sounds rather lame. Should the girl be in trouble, just because she isn't as bright as other young people who have made it to Amplissimos status?

Maybe that is what she meant, that her parents weren't able to support her, simply because they didn't have the capacity. But why were the parents not employed elsewhere? Surely that level of non-ability is a defect in itself? She hasn't heard Brutus' question at all, suddenly aware of his frowning face. "I was just recalling this afternoon," she stammers, and Brutus seems to accept her explanation.

"Her council members are not telling us very much," he says, "so I wondered if you know any more than we do?" Macia shrugs, not the grumpy one this time, and explains that the girl had been adamant about meeting up at Macia's house.

"She told me her house was smaller, and not suitable for us working together in private," she says, "which I don't understand. Surely their living quarters would have been upgraded, even if she was the first one in her family?" Brutus dips his head, telling Macia he will look into it, and for her to simply show to which family she belongs. Macia dips her head too. She is glad that Brutus has turned around, for she feels herself go pale. She belongs here, of course, but really she now belongs to God's family. She is now in Christ Jesus, so how should she treat Luti in that case? How has her new standing in God made a difference to her attitude towards the girl?

Macia is glad to be upstairs by herself. She needs to think. She misses her diary more than ever but doesn't dare to bring the pages down. It seems very likely that they will be working on the proposal again tomorrow, and probably for the rest of the week at the rate they're going. Maybe Luti was simply impressed by the Durus house, but then, that shows her weakness as well. At her level, she should be able to show more restraint, rather than let the newness of it all throw her like that. Macia is still puzzling about it all in the gymnasium the following morning. Her training is going well, she has made herself a schedule, including a reward. The reward is that she will allow herself to contact the team of council members dealing with physical fitness.

She wants to make her own proposal for online classes suitable for younger, fitter people. She doesn't want to do it whilst she still can't catch her breath herself, for she is determined to make the videos of a high standard.

Macia is right, it does take the two girls all of that week to complete the proposal. Macia manages to stop the sigh of relief on Fifday afternoon when they're finally done. The proposal is great, and Macia is sure it will get accepted. However, she merely says stiffly, "I think we made a very beneficial proposal. The council will be pleased, as we have given them a helpful plan to work with." Luti smiles wide, and nods several times, before blurting out how impressed the council will be, and how without this proposal various teams would have really struggled. Macia dips her head, exhausted. She has long given up trying to find all the many ways in which Luti seems to come short of an Amplissimos.

She almost waves at Luti's back when she watches the girl walk down the long drive. Just as she raises her hand, Luti looks back at the house. Even from this distance, her expression is very unpleasant. Macia covers her mouth, and moves back slightly, hoping the olive coloured dress will not show up at this distance.

Luti's face...Macia doesn't think she'll forget that look. She walks to her bed and stares up at the ceiling. "I thought I was cursed, beloved," she whispers softly to her diary, still hidden above the window.

Chapter 26

Hexaday brings more Spring weather, each day the sun seems warmer and brighter. Macia struggles to get into her wetsuit after her long walk. Yet the water doesn't feel any warmer than when she first started. When Macia arrives it is still quiet, and the woman raises her chin, her eyes glowing and warm. Macia smiles at her, wanting to say something, but she can't think of anything that would be appropriate.

Soon she is out on the water. Others are starting to arrive, and Macia suddenly feels her shoulders pull down. This was her special thing, where she laughed out loud with another Elabi citizen. Now she has to keep an eye out, be aware, stay in control of herself at all times. She feels sad as if somehow she is missing out. Her woollen dress clings to her on the way home, so to see the large paper parcel is good news. In the parcel are her summer clothes. Macia takes them upstairs quickly, as she can hear Ignava coming towards the kitchen door. She is aware that her whole face has lit up and she wants to enjoy herself!

The parcel is heavy, and Macia is grateful for the thick paper. That will give a lot more writing paper. She needs it too. Her allocated paper has almost all gone. If she cuts this up, at least most of it, and hides it, it will allow her to write in her diary more freely.

She opens the parcel carefully, undoing the string, rather than cutting it. Inside are her summer dresses, skirts and tops, as well as night dresses. The olive coloured dress is as lovely as she expected, the light blue one the colour of the morning sky. As expected, the gymnasium tops are shapeless. One is sleeveless and pale green while the other is short sleeved in a muted cerise. The gymnasium shorts are both dark brown. Macia gives a little sigh. Surely to design better-fitting shorts can't be that hard?

She strokes some of the pale coloured skirts. The soft, linen materials feel cool. Macia hangs her dresses up, laying her winter clothes on her bed for now. She hesitates, which should she wear today? She'd love to wear the olive one, but worries about Ignava's reaction. The woman will realise that the dress is Macia's favourite, make a remark as well as use it against Macia. In the end, she decides on a dark blue skirt with a soft red top. The sleeves are wide three-quarter ones, giving the top a lovely flowing look. Macia isn't keen on tight-fitting clothes, and this top is the opposite. It has a few buttons, make of wood, with small lines carved into them. It feels a little over the top to have such ornate details, but Macia enjoys it. She is grateful to whatever Mansit went to those lengths.

Soon the parcel contains only the last few items, underwear, a couple of belts, hairbands that suit the outfits. Macia is pleased. She rolls her winter clothes together, ready for them to be collected later. Then she carefully cuts the thick brown paper into rectangles, ready for writing. When she is done she hesitates. She ought to hide a lot of the paper, otherwise, if she uses sheets for her diary, then hides them, people might realise a lot of sheets have gone missing.

Macia takes a handful of sheets and hides them under her mattress for now. She will put them in her secret spot later but doesn't want to risk anybody walking in.

Macia has only just hidden the sheet when there is a brisk knock on her door, and Ignava walks in. Macia only just stops the gasp coming out of her mouth, as she had literally straightened her bedsheets seconds ago. Ignava looks her over, pursing her mouth at the flowing top, but she says nothing. "I hope you had what you asked for," she says, "as it's usually wrapped up by Mansits, and not all of them are good at reading." She almost sneers, then continues, "I feel the council could set up a special committee to deal with that, provide extra support for those who have missed out on education. Nobody should be at a disadvantage." Macia dips her head, not looking at her stepmother's face. She knows full well that Ignava feels Mansits are way beneath her, but it's her pious face, as if she is doing her very best for them out of the goodness of her heart. Macia does agree more support is needed, but she has no idea how to go about it. After all, clothes are made, packed and sent from beyond the hills. She has no idea what facilities they have there for the children. Do they have to work as well, or do children whose parents are sent beyond the hills continue their education as normal? Savisia would know, but Macia doesn't want to ask the girl. Somehow she is quite sure that the children suffer with the adults, judging by Savisia's grey skin and shaking limbs.

Once the house is quiet, Macia slips out of bed, and carefully retrieves the hidden sheets. She would love to write in her diary, as she has missed writing down her thoughts. She decides not to risk it. She tiptoes to her window, and carefully opens her hiding space, places the sheets inside, then, in the light of the moon, pulls her box out. She opens it, and her heart beating faster, lifts the thin pages out. She simply has to read them. Even if it's just a few paragraphs. She has missed her book, missed God. Being in Elabi comes with constant reminders. Being in God means she has to be reminded too, she decides.

She sits down in her windowsill, glad that the moon shines in enough to allow her to see. Her eyes stumble on words talking about Christ living in you by faith, and how it will make you rooted and grounded in love. She still doesn't know what 'saints' means, but apparently, with them, she will comprehend more about the love of Christ, and be filled with all the fullness of God. She smiles, "Beloved," she dictates her diary in her head for now, "I have no idea who the saints are, but I love to have this amazing thing in common with them." She takes a few deep breaths, her heart filled with joy and quietness. Then, reluctantly, she puts the pages back, replaces the large board, and crawls back into bed. She shivers, her summer nightdress isn't made for night time adventures. She will have another chance tomorrow, she hopes, to read those words again, as well as the next few paragraphs. It is worth the risk, and as long as the moon is so bright, it should work.

Onesday morning Macia is glad to wear her summer outfit, even though the walk to the gymnasium is still cold. She has kept her thin cloak and is glad she has done so. School seems quieter, clearly many Mansit families have returned to the hills. Macia finds herself relieved to spot Savisia. She is glad the girl was able to stay in the city. At lunchtime, Luti sits close by, and almost leaning over the student in between, she says, "It seems many of our proposals will be accepted. That is such good news, thank you for helping me with those details." Macia stares, help her? She did all the work, Luti was more hindrance than a help, and now she is turning it around! She swallows her mouthful, wondering what to say.

Luti looks rather pleased and is busy eating. Her way of handling her fork strikes Macia as odd. When she glances at the student in between them, she feels her hands go cold. It is the way he looks at Luti, his nose a little wrinkled like Macia does when she is with a few Mansits. Has he noticed Luti's strange smell? Will he report it? If he does, Macia might be in trouble, as they will check with her as she has spent rather a lot of time with Luti last week. They will wonder why she didn't report it. Macia has to admit she only smelled it once, at lunchtime.

In the afternoon, Macia is horrified to see herself assigned a project with Luti. Just when she thought she had finished with the girl. How will they ever work together? Macia is more advanced, as she is older. Luti looks very pleased, and Macia dips her head at the girl. What else can she do? There is no point asking the teacher to assign her another student. Luti suggests they do the same thing as last week, as it had worked so well. Macia is still sore from Luti's comment at lunchtime but decides to let it slide.

Working on the assignment together is hard work, Macia decides. Caecilia was the one to read things, then they would discuss it, and Macia would write it all down. Luti seems to have no idea how to read the given text. Macia has to explain many of the concepts, and it's not the highest level of reading either. How did the girl pass her status exams?

At dinner time Macia mentions it, struggling to keep the frustration out of her voice. Brutus looks at her, then dips his head. "It is what it is," he says in the end. "Nothing can be done, I'm afraid. The proposal you girls set up was very good, the council is looking at it right now. To stop her from working with you might not be that easy." Macia gives a nod. She had come to the same conclusion. She is also quite sure Luti will claim the assignment was mostly her input! She thinks about the words she read last night, about God being able to give more than we ask or think. Would that apply to assignments with Luti as well? She had shivered reading those words, out of excitement. She was in God, and God could do more than anything she could ask or think, because of his power at work in her.

She is suddenly aware of Ignava's clucking sound, the noise she makes when annoyed. Macia looks up, Brutus is frowning at her, his eyes hard. "I was thinking about today," Macia says, having narrowly missed starting off with the word 'sorry'. "You see, her abilities are… well, not really Amplissimos status, I would think, so with the proposal it was hard to get her to help. Today at lunchtime she thanked me for helping her with some details. As if she had done the proposal, and I had merely helped with a couple of details." Macia grips her fork tight, she really must make sure she controls her emotions, as she can still feel the shock. "I am quite sure she will take all the credit for this assignment too," she says in a calm voice, her face looking a little sullen, "and the problem I have is that she could never do the work by herself. The given text was far above her level."

She takes a few bites, Brutus and Ignava stay quiet, and after a moment Macia asks, "What should I do? Do I report her for not being able to do the work? Do I let the counsellor know that she was taking the credit for the proposal? I don't need the extra Life points, although they would help me, and maybe she is short on points?" Ignava gasps, and Macia feels her heart stop, then stutter on. Showing kindness and forgiveness felt so normal, but that is not how society works. She has also made it sound as if she despises Life points, and sees them as irrelevant. Brutus stares at her.

"Supporting another citizen is important," he says, "and I can see that it would be difficult to report this girl. After all, they might seem minor details. But like they explain in the Sharing is Caring course," his frown grows in intensity as he emphasises the course title. Macia swallows as he continues, "In the course, they explain the importance of trusting counsellors or council members with your information. They know what to do, and what could potentially harm our society. I think mentioning it to the counsellor would be helpful, just in case she no longer speaks the truth. It seems that at lunchtime she overstretched the truth as it was. Life points will help you to reach your usefulness potential," he adds, with a last glare.

Macia dips her head respectfully, her nails digging into her leg through her linen dress. How could she have been so careless with her words! "I will," she says, speaking a little slower, to control her voice, "I will, because of the level of learning support she needs with assignments." Macia collapses on her bed as soon as she manages to leave the kitchen. She looks at her window, to where her diary papers are. She needs to write, needs to express her fright, and more importantly, she wants to thank God for protecting her at dinner time, and ask for His help in the future.

Chapter 27

Macia finishes her homework as quickly as she can, then goes to rest on her bed, taking one of her school books with her, in case somebody walks in. She wants to rest, so she can get up in the night, read the book, write in her diary, and not be too tired tomorrow. She pushes thoughts about Luti to the back of her mind. There is nothing she can do about the girl now, and it might solve itself.

Macia snoozes for a while, then, once the house is quiet, and has been for a while, she goes to the window, taking her pencil with her. She wants to read first, in case something happens. She turns to the pages that she had been reading before, and starts the letter at the large number four. Macia squirms a little bit on the window seat. She knows Luti is not in God, but it is she, Macia, who is called to walk worthy. She reads the words a few times, trying to imprint them on her memory. When working with Luti tomorrow she will need these words. She will need all the patience and kindness she can find, to speak the truth in love. Yes, that's a basic Elabi principle, she smiles. It is important to report people when they go astray, but never for emotional reasons.

After a while, she closes the thin pages and pulls a sheet of thick brown paper towards her. Now for her diary! "Dearest friend," and it feels like that too, "I have missed writing to you. Hexaday was so exciting, not just paddleboarding, but also my summer clothes arrived. That might sound mundane, but I assure you I was thrilled, not least because it was such a hot day. Today was hard," she stops. She won't mention Luti, but it's all about the girl, really. "The assignment we do needs two academically equal people. It is helping me to practise patience and kindness, but this kindness almost got me into trouble this evening. I mentioned my Life points, and how I wasn't as much in need of them as others, but of course, it looked as if I despised Life points. I don't, it's just that after the pages, I feel other things in life seem so much more real. I have dreams for my life in Elabi, like everybody else. I have jobs I would love to have, and I will need Life points for those jobs. Also, the more Life points I have, the better our attached quarters will be at the end of summer."

Macia sits still. How will she read the book once she is attached? Or write in her diary for that matter? "Beloved, I don't know what to do about my attachment. It would be very hard to pull out of the arrangement now without raising suspicion. I don't know what Hirsut will be like. I was worried about his seeming lack of ambition, but maybe that's a positive thing. Will he find out that I'm in God? What will he do about it?" Macia stops. Those questions aren't helping her. It's still moons away. "I just have to be more careful," she ends the diary entry. The day after tomorrow Luti won't come to the house, as Macia has her appointment. Maybe she'll keep the diary sheet out, hiding it as always, so she can write a bit more after her appointment. She wants to think about her upcoming Nuptialem, and what to do about it. She carefully puts the thin pages back in her hiding place, then walks to her drawer and hides the brown paper amidst books and other writing sheets. When everything is put away safely, she slides into bed. Tonight had been very close, and in a few days, she will see the counsellor again. Soon the counsellor will set up special Nuptialem counselling, as well as continue where they left off. The new counsellor is younger and seemed alright, but Macia is worried.

The school counsellor dips his head, taking notes whilst Macia explains about Luti and her struggle to keep up. He doesn't offer any information, unlike the lady counsellor Macia had seen before. It makes her want to say more, to show the man how serious it all is. Should she mention the funny smell? Macia leaves the office feeling dissatisfied, but unsure how to phrase her concerns. After school Macia listens to Luti talking about one of her father's books. "I thought it very good how he explained the balance in daily life," she says, walking along the cypress-lined driveway. Macia dips her head, feeling her patience sink lower with each step. Luti has been on about the book for most of the walk, and for the majority of that time, she has been showing a lack of understanding. Macia bites her thumbnail. Should she point it out to the girl, with grace of course, or would it be kinder to let her chatter on?

The assignment takes ages, and Macia is exhausted by the time dinner is served. Lack of sleep isn't helpful either. Brutus looks pleased, and says, "The council is pleased with the proposals you girls made." Macia dips her head, pleased, yet unhappy about his reference to 'you girls'. "We will be looking at a talk initially, although I might produce a book about it at the same time, as we're gathering the necessary information anyway," Brutus adds. Macia dips her head again, now she knows why he looks pleased. He enjoys writing. For a moment she wonders if he keeps a diary.

That night she sits down in the window sill, noting that the light is not as bright as it was before. She won't be able to read at night much longer. "Beloved, I was pleased to hear the proposal was accepted. It would be good to see more young people supported by their families. It will help them." She thinks about Luti. Something had made her uneasy again. Was it the way Luti had been looking around the room whenever Macia wasn't talking to her? Or the fact that the girl had been standing quite close to her desk when Macia returned from the bathroom? "Dearest friend, it's my counselling tomorrow. Hopefully, she will ask the right questions. So much has happened since my last session, yet I must be as though nothing has changed."

"Beloved, I'm enjoying my morning runs as well, as it gives me time to talk to God. There are so many questions going around in my head. If only there was somebody to answer them and to explain words. Like the word 'fellowship' or 'salvation'. I wished I knew what they meant. I ask God often to send me somebody to explain things, or to help me to find some book with a list of words and their meaning. I wonder if that exists, a bit like the Catalogue of Language that we have. I still fear sometimes whether I have done the right thing. I wonder how I will grow in God or what it will lead to."

Macia sighs softly, she is tired, too tired to think about it all. Being with Luti drains her, and she needs to sleep.

She has to explain to Luti again why they can't work on the assignment today. The girl obviously forgot their conversation about it and looks surprised. Macia can feel her face go tight, the sulky pull of her mouth strangely familiar. She feels like snapping at the girl, telling her how she has seen the school counsellor several times already, and she'd better watch her step. But she doesn't. She remembers that she is supposed to walk worthy of her calling, she is to show grace. So with an effort she dips her head a little, and says patiently, "I did mention it yesterday, a couple of times in fact. Maybe you were distracted. We were working hard on the assignment, so it's possible that you didn't quite register. Anyway, I have my appointment, but we can work on it tomorrow, and as we're almost done, we might even complete the assignment tomorrow." She looks at the girl, trying to feel some kind feelings, but Luti's face is blank, with an odd glint in her eyes. Macia

163

swallows, looking away. Was that really a hate-filled emotion I just saw, she wonders, and why? Just because I'm out this afternoon?

She's still puzzling over this on her way to the counsellor. The same young woman meets her in the waiting room and invites Macia through. This time, Macia notices that her own sandals look older than the young counsellors, so maybe she isn't being pushed down the list any more. They talk about general things, and the counsellor asks how school is and her relationship with other students. "Last time we talked about friendships a little bit, and I believe it has been brought up before as well," she says, trying to look neutral. "How are your responses about that now?" Macia dips her head and explains that she hasn't really changed her internal policy.

"I'm working together with a girl that seems to be new," she explains, feeling it's a good way to cover her own back in case something goes wrong with the assignment. "She is an Amplissimos, although I can't remember seeing her before, really. We discussed supportive families and were asked by the council to write a proposal. It seems whenever we do something, that this girl takes the credit. It's not that I mind so much, as the fact that is very emotional, very needy. After all, the proposal was to benefit all families in Elabi, so why was praise needed?" The counsellor nods once and makes notes rapidly. Macia uses that time to straighten out her light blue dress and slow down her breathing. If she seems too emotional herself, her words will backfire.

"You see, something doesn't quite add up. You know I only recently attained Amplissimos status," the woman dips her head again, "and it wasn't easy. My family supported me, and I worked hard, for I wanted to give my best to the city. Some of the exams were very taxing. Now I find working with this girl really hard, as she doesn't seem to have the academic abilities associated with the Amplissimos status. It puzzles me, and worries me at the same time, as I wonder how she will serve the city. If she ends up in a leadership position, how will she cope with the demands of her role?"

The counsellor nods once and promises to look into it. Then they turn to the upcoming Nuptialem counselling. "It will have to be after your school ends," the woman says, "for you need to have adult status for most of the counselling around the Nuptialem List." Macia dips her head, yes, she was aware of that. "Of course, your father would have explained all this," the woman adds hastily, not wanting Macia to think she didn't believe her parents had done their duty. "There will be at least one more session before that, so we can discuss it then, and set a possible day," she says, looking at her large planner.

Macia is relieved to get out of the office. She is always afraid to say too much, reveal too much. Luti had been quite a safe topic, although she had felt her emotions starting to get involved. The woman had kept a very close eye on Macia, clearly watching out for this. Macia is sure she betrayed nothing. Hopefully, this will be on her records, so if any problems arise over the assignment of Luti's academic level, her name will be in the clear. She has warned, not just the school counsellor, but her own private counsellor as well. Macia enjoys the warm walk home past stately cypress trees and flowers blossoming on the roadside. "This year I'm more alive than ever," she whispers, "thank you, God, for blessing me with all spiritual blessings in heavenly places." She has no idea what heavenly places are, but it sounds a wonderful place, so that's good enough for now.

When Macia walks into her bedroom, she stops. Something isn't right. She doesn't know what it is, but her room feels strangely off. As if somebody is hiding in her bedroom. She walks to her desk, putting her large bag with school books down. She looks at her desk. Yes, something is different. She is sure that things have been moved on her desk. She swallows. Her diary! She opens her large drawer, noting the books and papers. The brown diary paper is still there. Macia can't tell if anybody has touched it or not. It doesn't look like it, but her drawer is neatly stacked as always, so if somebody looked, then put it all back carefully, she'd never know. She shuts the drawer, noticing a faint smell at the same time. It reminds her of Luti, probably from the previous day when they were working on the assignment.

Nothing seems out of place, and in the end, Macia gives up. Dinner is ready, and she is hungry. The smells coming from the kitchen make her stomach grumble in protest. She raises her chin respectfully at Brutus and Ignava. Ignava looks put out, and Macia wonders what has happened. It doesn't take long to find out. "That girl was here, she'd forgotten something, apparently. I'm surprised you hadn't noticed somebody else's belongings in your room," she says, her mouth tight. Macia stares at Ignava. Luti was here? This afternoon? Before she can say anything, Ignava continues, "It took her a while to find it too, she looked all blotchy and hot, wonder if anybody has mentioned her having a defect?" Macia dips her head and explains with difficulty that she had seen it before, but she can't remember mentioning it to the counsellor. In fact, it had been soon after she had seen the counsellor, so she had assumed Luti had been talked to, and that was why her face was blotchy.

Ignava dips her head, and that seems to be the end of the matter. Macia struggles all the way through dinner but manages to explain that her Nuptialem counselling will be after she finishes school, obviously. Brutus nods, "You should always wait till somebody is an adult," he says, in his lecturing voice, and Macia dips her head. "It'll be good for you to finish school, especially as the council is very busy with several new projects coming up, they can use your writing skills. It is helpful to have a young Amplissimos working for our society." Macia is glad when dinner is over, her heart is beating too fast, and she worries that it will show somehow. Luti has been in her room, alone, and came out hot and bothered. Why?

Chapter 28

Macia sinks into her desk chair, looking around at her desk with fresh eyes. So things had moved, it had not been her imagination. What else did Luti look at? Would she have found the diary page? Surely she would have taken it with her in that case? Macia swallows painfully, her hands shaking. She opens the drawer again and studies the content. Nothing tells her that it has been moved. Slowly she shuts the drawer, needing to think, but also needing to do her homework. She has struggled this week, what with the extra assignment taking up time.

She opens her school book but finds her mind drifting off. What will happen if Luti has seen her diary? The girl's reading ability isn't amazing, so maybe she hasn't realised what it is? One thing is sure, she will have to hide the paper tonight! On her way to bed, Ignava pokes her head around Macia's door. "I have no idea what that girl was looking for," she begins, "and as she is an Amplissimos I don't think leaving stuff behind is a good thing. It shows a level of carelessness that I wouldn't expect in an Amplissimos. Also, I'm surprised that you didn't spot something out of place all that time yesterday evening and this morning. I don't know what the girl left behind?" Macia sees the curiosity in Ignava's eyes, but she does her speciality shrug.

"It must have been something small, like a pencil maybe," she says in the end. "Things on my desk have definitely been moved, so maybe

I put her pencil with mine, not realising." Ignava seems satisfied if disappointed, and raises her chin rather half-heartedly.

Macia blows out the air she had been holding. Yes, it might have been a pencil, but she doubts it. She knows her pencils, and it wouldn't take Luti long to find her pencil. Macia had done the writing for the assignment, so Luti never even used her pencil. No, she is pretty sure that Luti did not leave anything behind. So why come back and lie about it?

Once it's dark and quiet, Macia slips out of bed, grabs her diary page and quietly opens her secret place. Despite her fear, she pulls out the thin pages first. Reading the words calms her turmoil. Yes, she can be patient also, she can trust in God, and the words remind her that she has this hope placed by God himself for her in heaven. She has to walk worthy of this, and not be anxious about the details. There is nothing she can do, nothing she can change. She needs to stay grounded and steadfast, not moving away from that hope.

The words soothe her spirit, and she finds herself fast asleep soon after putting her thin book and diary sheet away carefully. The only thing that shows how worried she has been is her thumb which has a sore red spot on one corner of her nail.

Macia keeps a sharp lookout for Luti once she gets to school. Her legs feel tired after her extra fast run this morning. Some of her anxiety had returned with the rising sun, but running and praying to God had calmed her spirit down. Now she wants to see what Luti says about coming to her house yesterday. There is no sign of Luti anywhere. At registration time, she isn't mentioned at all. Macia feels a sinking feeling growing inside of her. What is going on? Why is Luti not even mentioned? All day she hopes for something to be said. The only reason for a student not being mentioned is when they're in the sanatorium and the council is informed, or when somebody is taken for an Enquiry.

Macia isn't sure what to do about the assignment. They had almost finished, and she had been sure that together they would have finished it today. If she has to complete it by herself it would take longer. Also, what about Luti's grade? She hesitates, maybe she should mention it to the teacher, but Macia is reluctant to draw attention to herself. If Luti is in trouble, or even if she *is* trouble, she doesn't want to be noticed. She walks slowly home, her legs still protesting from this morning. She is glad to be alone though, as it gives her time to think and repeat the words from the thin pages to herself. Reminding herself that she can do all things through Christ.

At dinner time Ignava asks about the girl, as she keeps calling Luti. Macia is sure that it's for an emotional reason. She is sure her stepmother resents Luti's status, and in a way, Macia can't blame her. Luti isn't a great model for Amplissimos status. Still, it's an emotional reaction, and therefore has no place in Elabi. "I didn't see the girl today," Ignava starts, her mouth pursed as if she takes it as a personal insult, "I thought you said the assignment wasn't quite finished?" She looks at Macia, her dark eyes hard and cold.

Macia shrugs, trying to look a little bored as if missing classmates is a normal occurrence. "She wasn't in school, nothing was mentioned, so maybe she is in the sanatorium." Both Ignava and Brutus stop eating and stare at Macia. She has to agree deep down that it is quite unusual for a young Amplissimos to suddenly be in the sanatorium. What other explanation is there? Only the one she doesn't want to think about.

Brutus looks very serious, "I did say there was something strange about this girl," he says between slow bites. Macia dips her head, the taste of garum suddenly making her queasy. "There have been various complaints made against her," she hesitates, "I went to the school counsellor a few times, and I know others did too." Brutus dips his head; Ignava looks like she smells excitement.

Macia's heart sinks a little as there is no sign of Luti at school the next day. Her heart rate speeds up as the 'what if' questions build up in her head. She takes a deep breath and tries to focus her mind on the words of last night, which she managed to read, pressed against the window to catch the light of the waning moon. Peace of God... be careful for nothing...rejoice always... By the time she sits down in class her heart rate is more or less normal, and she looks her usual self, slightly sulky, ready to learn and be a useful citizen. She is glad it's Fifday, as not seeing Luti anywhere is easier when she's not in school. Also, there is her paddleboarding, and her parents might be out in the afternoon, leaving her with time to read and write in her diary as well. Macia can feel her mood picking up, struggling to keep her face straight as always.

She hands in her assignment and points out to the teacher that she had started the work with Luti, but had to finish it by herself. The teacher dips her head but gives no explanation as to what has happened to Luti. Macia would love to ask but knows it will be seen as an emotional curiosity, and the last thing she wants is the teacher looking at her too closely. So she leaves it, and walking home, forces her mind away from the missing girl. After all, there is nothing she can do about it. She needs to be logical and collected, not allow her emotions to disturb her life. So instead, she looks at the signs of Spring everywhere, keen to set up the Running Course for Beginners.

She has thought about it a good deal, as she has been enjoying her morning run. It's still cool in the mornings, and even in the summer, it will be quite pleasant when it's early. She would aim the course at those that haven't run before, like young people, or maybe even Mansits returning to society, and needing to be fitter. Being outside will help people, she thinks, especially those who work indoors. Maybe Hexaday afternoon she should work on the workout video proposal as well. It's not likely to happen before she has left school, but that should give her time to plan the workouts, and get practising as well.

Dinner is peaceful, and Macia feels much better. She is glad to have a plan to work on. She mentions it to her parents, "I'm thinking of setting up a running course, specially designed for those not used to running." Brutus dips his head, Ignava frowns and points out that it would probably be Mansits only, as most other citizens would have been to various classes already. Macia gives a nod, "Yes, quite likely. If we can integrate Mansits into society in a good way, that will strengthen our city," she explains. "If they have a sense of belonging they will be more open to logic classes, and that way they will be less emotion-driven, and therefore less likely to be returned beyond the hills. Their children will benefit from the stability this will afford them, and those children might be able to achieve a better status, bringing a stronger mindset to society."

Brutus looks pleased. He agrees, "They will then be the cornerstone of stronger families, having three children, and contributing to society. Many Mansits find their main struggle around family issues, and having logic at the centre of their home." Macia dips her head, but a tiny part deep inside her cringes. She is in God, and what would happen if families were in God, centred on God, rather than on logic? Would it be the end of civilisation? her rational part asks. "It will be a worthwhile class," Brutus says, then frowns a little, "As it will be mainly Mansits, you might have to think about putting safeguards in place. It might have to be combined with lessons in self-discipline and following city guidelines, that kind of thing. Otherwise, you might find yourself running with one Mansit some days, and fifty the following day." Ignava gives a strong nod, verging on emotional.

"It is very hard teaching them, as they don't seem to have the same way of looking at life," Ignava says, in her aloof voice. "Many of the council member's spouses teach classes that have a majority of Mansits, and they all say the same thing. Whether it has anything to do with the geography of the Hills, I don't know." Macia almost snorts in derision. "Also, nutrition is a serious issue," Ignava is on a roll now, "they don't eat nutritious food all the time, and rely on herbs to make their food palatable. You might find their stamina affected by that. One council member had a Mansit die in the gymnasium, and they determined it was lack of proper nutrition." She looks at Macia as if daring her to deny it, but Macia dips her head.

Some of the Mansit students at school seem to have very small portions for lunch, and it often looks like cold pottage. She knows that access to better quality food is restricted, mainly because of their pay. If, however, one of their children manages to raise his or her status, that would benefit the entire family. She wonders out loud if compulsory nutrition classes should be part of their rehabilitation process. Ignava flushes and sits up straighter. Macia smiles into her food, yes, she thought Ignava would like that one!

"That would be very beneficial," Ignava sounds a little breathless, "and even on their payment level, there should be opportunities to feed their children properly." Brutus dips his head, looking less glum, Macia notices. She can feel the excitement growing in herself as well. She is aware that her attitude towards Mansits has changed over the last few moons. She really wishes to see them do well in society, to be blessed...her thoughts stutter to a halt.

She tries to slow down her breathing, hoping it will stop the heat from spreading across her face. Later in the evening, Macia is relieved to sit with her rough paper, close to the window. "Beloved, I am wondering where my feelings came from. That in itself needs thinking about," she smiles at her pencil, "the very idea of being led by feelings isn't a good thing, I know, but there is this warmth in my heart when I think about Mansits. Only a few moons ago they made me feel angry, impatient. They were smelly, lazy, of no value in our society, and a drain on our institutions. Now I see them as people, held down by the system. Their pay is very low, so they have no access to food that we take for granted." She sighs, knowing that isn't her main concern. "It's the attitude they encounter at every turn. People wrinkling their noses, students not wanting to sit with them, looking down at them. I have to confess, I did the same. I would put them in their place when they approached me." She swallows, feeling a pain in her chest when thinking about it. She puts her hand on her heart, why that pain? Is it Christ in her, or his Spirit, like she read in the thin pages? Is it because she has been wrong in the way she dealt with Mansits? Suddenly she thinks about the word 'sin' Maybe that is what it meant, this heaviness, feeling as if your chest, your heart is too large. Wasn't syn or sin to do with weight issues? Is her bad attitude towards Mansit classed as sin?

"Dearest friend, I have been wrong, and I know this sin in me, take it from me. Help me avoid this sin." She stares out into the night, the tall cypress trees lining the driveway like guards. Yes, maybe that is why God let her feel that heaviness just now, so she would avoid it in future. "I'm so glad I was given those pages," she writes, her breathing fast, "I would have lived my life so differently, and I am grateful to be in God. If only Caecilia was here to talk to me…" Her thoughts trail off, and Macia can feel an uncontrollable emotion welling up. The same flood of feelings and reactions she had as a child when her mother had gone with her little brother. She stands up abruptly and carefully puts everything back. Struggling with the large board, she fears for a moment that she'll drop it. Should she risk it and leave it off? No chance, not after what happened with Luti. So taking a very deep breath, she lifts the board into place, then stumbles into bed, asking God to hold her spirit and to calm her heart. Before she knows it, the morning light is brightening up her curtains.

Chapter 29

Macia hesitates in front of her wardrobe. Which dress should she wear? It's going to be a warm walk to the water sports centre. She feels like wearing something special to cheer her up. That would mean her olive coloured dress. On the other hand, as it's a gorgeous day, the light blue one would be lovely. Hearing Ignava's footsteps go past her room, she gives a tiny gasp. What is she doing? She is deciding on a dress, based purely on feelings and emotions! Feeling guilty, she resolutely pulls out the olive dress. It is nicely cut and it will keep her cool. It will also cheer up the woman at the centre, she decides, looking forward to her morning out.

After breakfast Macia sets off, the warmth having dispelled any lingering morning mist. She takes deep breaths, her heart beating faster, feeling so alive. She gives herself a shake and decides to start working on her proposals in her head. First the running club. Her father's words come to mind, and she starts working out what kind of safeguards she would really need. There are preferences, and there are essentials. Some Mansits might not be Mansits by birth, but simply had their childhood interrupted through no fault of their own. They would be new to running but have a Consuete mindset and manners. Savisia, Caecilia's younger sister comes to mind. Of course, the girl was slightly older and has probably done running before, but maybe someone like her could sign up. On the other hand, she could get Mansits who literally grew up beyond the hills, and have only just been rehabilitated into society. Their world view might not be quite along the city lines. She will need to have policies in place to deal with both possibilities.

The woman smiles at her, and Macia smiles back, her lips almost hurting because of the unusual movement, but how good it feels! If only the two of them could go out on the water, and experience that freedom again. Macia feels her happiness slipping away. The woman comes out to help her choose a paddleboard, and she points towards the water further away, as if she had read Macia's thoughts. "It is a quiet day, there are hardly any waves at all. You might want to use that opportunity to get just that little bit further." Macia feels excitement bubbling inside, imagining herself riding off into the ocean. Well, big water. The woman dips her head at Macia's glowing face, her eyes serious for a moment. Then she smiles, "I will come with you for a moment, to show you." She grabs a board, and soon the two of them are out on the water, paddling leisurely.

After a while, the woman shows Macia how to go with the flow, pointing at the currents, and different shades of blue. Macia's eyes reflect the water, and the woman laughs softly. Macia would love to laugh loudly again but has to be content with a soft, modified laugh. It still feels good. The woman chuckles, a sound that warms Macia inside her heart, then after a few last comments, the woman returns to the centre, leaving Macia to explore the open water. The stillness makes her shoulders relax, her hands holding on to the paddle lightly. To glide across the waves like this, Macia feels blessed. She loves the word and would like to know exactly what it means. To enjoy the day, the sun, water, a slight breeze, seagulls and peace; maybe that's what is meant by heavenly places.

Macia is a little reluctant to put the paddleboard back. She knows her session has finished, and her stomach tells her it's lunchtime, but even so, she would love to stay out longer. Maybe she could if she arranged a double session. It would look bad though, as if she was emotionally involved, rather than merely seeing it as exercise. She sighs, what is wrong with loving something, and wanting to do it? It's not as if she is neglecting other things, like school work, for it. Maybe she should sign up for an instructor's course.

She closes the shed door and walks towards the main building to change back out of her wetsuit and swimsuit, into her olive dress. She had seen the woman looking appreciatively at the flowing dress, and Macia had felt her heart glow. As she enters the door, two guards step forward. Macia gives a startled gasp, she hadn't spotted them before. The older one, his eyes narrowed, takes another step, almost making the distance too small. "Macia Durus?" His voice is gravelly and a little slow, clearly enjoying the sound of her name, and his lip goes up a little to show his teeth. Macia dips her head, her thoughts going in all possible directions, whilst trying to hide her disdain for the man. "You will need to come with us. The council has questions for you. You may get changed, you may not leave anything behind." Macia feels herself go pale, especially as she hears the woman in the room gasp, her kind eyes wide, taking in the two guards and the young girl. Macia dips her head again as if it's a daily occurrence to be told to come along with the guards. She can feel her legs beginning to shake though, and her hands are stiff and very cold.

She walks into the room on her way to the changing rooms where her dress and bag awaits. When she is near the curtain, the younger guard sneers, "And do hurry, beloved," making Macia feel faint. Beloved! Her diary...Luti... She hardly registers the woman's gasp, her eyes struggling to focus on the curtain behind which her dress is hanging up. Beloved...beloved... Struggling with the curtain, Macia feels the floor bouncing wilder than the waves ever have underneath her paddleboard. Her stomach churns, and her breath comes in fast, shallow gasps. They have found her diary, or at least, Luti has told them about the diary. Her hiding place? Macia is quite sure it's still safe. What is she going to say though, for her diary page has been hidden again. They must not find the book or her diary pages. Not ever.

Taking a few very deep breaths, leaning over to feel less faint, Macia feels she's got reasonable control over herself again. She must not show them her fear, or any other hints that they have got it right. She takes her bag and opens the curtain, the woman comes forward to take her wetsuit, the guards still at the door. As the woman takes the wet garment, she breathes, "Paddleboard. Lighthouse," locks eyes with Macia for a second, trying to will strength, courage and care across to the young girl. Then she turns to hang the wetsuit out to dry off.

Macia clenches her jaws together, her head spinning, gratefulness for the woman flooding her entire being, momentarily overcoming the nauseating fear.

The two guards take up positions on either side of her, and Macia looks at the long road ahead of them. Normally she enjoys the way back, feeling tired and a little sore, but today everything has changed. The bright blue sky seems low, oppressive, and no bird dares to show its face. She walks on, swallowing against the fear, looking at her sandals and flowing dress. Her stomach rumbles and Macia knows that she will need to eat. She hesitates, then suddenly draws her shoulders back a little. Fine, she might have been collected by guards for an Enquiry, but at the moment she is still Macia Durus AMP. So she slips the bag off her shoulder and gets her glass container out. The flatbread is chewy, but it actually helps to calm her down. She eats slowly, trying to enjoy each bite, savouring the garlic and cheese. The older guard seems to realise what she is doing, and he clicks his tongue,

"Ha! I hope you enjoy that, it might well be the last good tasting meal you have for a while," and snorts. The younger guard grins, and spits at the roadside, making Macia cringe.

At long last, they get to the city, and Macia feels her cheeks warming up. To walk through the large gates, flanked by two guards is humiliating. There is nothing she can do about it, and after all, she hasn't been convicted yet, she is still an Amplissimos, so she straightens herself a little, and glances around as if all is as it should be. During the walk, she has run through various scenarios, with varying questions and accusations. The bit where her thoughts stop is at her answer. "I have no idea what you are talking about," seems to be the most common answer. She is quite sure that they would never find her secret place. All they have is Luti's word, and Luti isn't the best at reading. Macia is glad she has shared that bit of information with her parents, as hopefully her father will support her claims and get her out. She will just have to be very careful.

On the other hand, someone like Luti would not have the ability to make up words like 'beloved' or 'dearest friend' so if she mentions any of the words from her diary, they will know that Macia must have had access to a forbidden book. Would they know which one? Will they know it's the one Caecilia had left for her parents, or at least a similar one? Of course, Macia could always deny everything… The heatwave covers her face. Deny knowing the book? Deny being in God? "No need to volunteer any information," a tiny voice whispers in the back of her mind.

The guards lead her to the Town Hall, and Macia feels a tiny bit of hope growing. It might be that they will lead her to the council members, and she can simply explain. Instead of going up the wide staircase, past all the solemn-looking portraits, the guards take her to a door set underneath the staircase. The older guard enters the door first, the younger guard actually pushes Macia in the back to make her follow. She gasps, wanting to turn round and berate him, but a harder shove makes her change her mind. She grinds her teeth together to stop her lips from trembling, pretending to hold her long dress to stop her from tripping over the material. She is scared, she has to admit it.

At the bottom of the few steps down, the older guard rings a harsh sounding bell set in the stone wall. Another guard opens the large, red door, the noise of its lock making Macia shiver. He looks at Macia and grins. Not a pleasant grin and Macia looks away as if she is slightly bored by it all. The younger guard pushes her again, and she follows the older guard into a cold corridor. There are several doors on either side, and a female guard appears. She sneers at Macia, looking her up and down, then opens a door, motioning for Macia with her head. Nobody says anything, and Macia feels her knees shaking. She feels like saying something, anything. The silence is oppressive, she is sure they're all laughing at her.

The female guard takes another look at Macia, then walks to some shelves, pulls a grey linen bundle off the shelves. She motions towards a curtain that used to be white, and says, "Everything off, this on. Nothing else." She dumps the bundle on a cracked stool behind the curtain, then yanks the cloth past Macia, the wooden rings sounding dull. Macia swallows and tries to catch her breath. She would like to sink on the floor in despair, just for a moment, to catch her thoughts, but she is quite sure there will be a camera. Also, the woman will see, as the curtain doesn't come anywhere near the floor. So, with shaking hands, she undoes her belt and takes her dress off. Her favourite, olive dress. Will they give it back to her at the end? She bites her lip, what end? She unrolls the bundle, and finds that it contains grey rough underwear and a very thin grey gown, like her nightdress, but rough and plain. She changes into them and shivers. She looks at her sandals, but the woman guard has pulled the curtain open already. She points at Macia's feet, "Those!" she barks, and taking the beautiful dress off the stool where Macia had folded it, throws the dress in a corner whilst Macia's frozen fingers fiddle with her sandal straps. That's answered Macia's question as regards her dress.

Macia follows the woman down the corridor, no other guards in sight. Her toes cramp a little, the floor tiles are very cold. She rubs her arms quietly and pushes a stray strand of her auburn hair out of her face. When the guard stops at a door, Macia tries to stand tall and pulls her usual face. No matter, the guard doesn't even look at her. She unlocks the door and points inside the dark room with her chin. Macia hesitates, then steps inside the cell. The door shuts, harder than is necessary Macia thinks.

Then her annoyance disappears, as well as her strength. She makes it to a hard box-like bed. Her breath sounds loud in the small, dark room, and Macia clenches her fists, forcing her breathing to slow down, forcing herself to be calmer. In the end, she manages to regain a sense of control. She looks around, her eyes getting used to the darkness, making the most of the glimmer of light that comes from the barred window in the door. The box she is on is not uncomfortable, just hard. There is a very thin blanket neatly folded up on the foot end of the bed, and a very thin pillow at the other end. Even in the meagre light, Macia can see the circles on the pillow, and she shudders. In a corner is a metal pail, and Macia can feel her stomach protesting even before her brain has fully registered what the bucket is for.

That's it. That is all there is in the little room. Macia can feel panic growing and growing, but she knows she has to stay in control. There will most likely be cameras everywhere, and if she allows her feelings or emotions to show, here, now, as an Amplissimos, she'll be done for. No, she has to take all this with self-control, proving her status, hoping her father will find a way out, and trust in God.

God. Yes, she has to trust, after all, she is in God. Is this the price she has to pay for that fact? She moves the clearly used pillow aside, and lies down, pulling the blanket over her to warm up. She closes her eyes, pretending to be in her comfortable room with its large window, writing in her diary. "Beloved," she can hear the guards voice, and her thoughts stutter for a moment, "Beloved, I'm writing to you from a rather unusual place. It is…" She would like to say awful, but remembers she ought to rejoice. "…it's not quite what I had in mind for this afternoon. I'm well though, I'm healthy, and uhm…" Her mind tries to list all the positives she can come up with. "I have a blanket, not a very thick one, but still. And at least there is a pail in the corner, and a little bit of light shines in from the corridor." That makes her smile, "Dearest friend, do I need that light? No, for I'm in the Kingdom of Light, after all!" Her shoulders relaxed, Macia dozes off, her slight smiles observed by a tight-lipped guard.

Chapter 30

Macia wakes with a start when the heavy door grinds open. The woman guard stands in the door opening, blocking the light. "Macia Durus," her voice sharp, "lunch." With that, she puts a metal plate on the ground, and the door slams shut again. Macia shivers, she is stiff, and reluctantly pushes the blanket off. She staggers over to the plate. It is pottage, not the best-cooked pottage, not the way Ignava makes it. No garum either, but still, it's food, and it's hot. She sits down on her box bed to eat with a cheap tinny spoon. She is right, the food is very tasteless, but she eats fast, just to feel warm inside.

After putting the empty plate back on the doorstep, Macia hesitates. What should she do now? Lie down again? She is cold, so Macia decides that now is a good time to practise her workout videos.

She does her regular stretches, humming her favourite workout video music to herself. Within minutes her door is flung open, and the older guard shouts, "No singing, no noise!" Macia is left frozen in place for a moment. No singing? He means her humming the music to go with her regular workout isn't allowed? She wants to pull a face, scowl at the door but remembers the cameras that are bound to be there. So she takes a breath, calming her shaking limbs. She forces herself to focus on the workout completely, banishing all questions and worries. There is nothing she can do about any of this, so there is no use in being emotional about it.

The workout leaves her hot and sweaty, and she longs for a clean shower, but all she can do is relax on her box bed and dry herself as much as possible with the thin blanket. The cell is cold, and she knows she will cool down quickly. The last thing she needs is a cold.

Macia stares ahead into the dark, her thoughts circling back, wondering what will happen. She isn't even completely sure why she is here, although she is convinced it has to do with her diary page. Luti must have been a plant, just as they suspected. Could she read well, or was that part of the plan? In her mind she sees herself relaxing in her windowsill, her new pencil sharp, and a clean sheet of brown paper. "Dearest friend, actually the only friend," she can feel herself smiling at the imaginary brown paper, "as you know I'm in a bit of a fix. I want to be very angry with Luti for betraying me, but then, she hasn't really, has she?" In her mind, the paper curls one corner in sympathy. "I know, she did what we all have been trained to do, which is to look out for the good of Elabi, for our common protection and welfare."

Macia looks away from her brown paper vision. Yes, she would have done the same. After all, Caecilia was really her friend, despite her non-friend policy, and she was about to tell on her, just because she had changed, and seemed odd. Luti had actually found written proof. She wonders what is going on at her home. Will the guards have come to look for the paper? Will Luti be with them, to show them the way? Macia imagines the pale girl ringing her doorbell, Ignava answering the door. Ignava's eyes would have gone hard, no doubt, as she wasn't keen on the girl. The fact that Macia isn't there would have made Ignava more annoyed. Luti probably would have raised her chin, then casually pointed at the guards, and told Ignava they've come to collect something from Macia's room...

The scene feels so real, Macia is almost convinced that this is the way it would have happened. Another scenario would have seen guards swarming her house, arresting Ignava and Brutus, looking through all their belongings, personal items strewn all over the floor. She shudders. What has she done?

She swallows, her stomach quivering inside her. She leans against the wall, carefully slipping her slightly bored face into place. She must not be seen to panic. She closes her eyes, and forcing her thoughts back to her brown paper she continues her diary, "So I'm in a mess, beloved. Sadly, I have a feeling it is because I wrote to you. I needed you though, so don't feel bad." The top corner of the paper definitely looks sad, she almost giggles. "Don't worry, beloved, it's all in God's hands, isn't it? Like Paul was writing how he felt it an honour to suffer for Christ. Of course, Paul knew more than I did. Should I deny the whole thing, just to protect my family?"

Macia swallows, her breath speeding up at the thought. Should she protest, and lie? Thinking the word in her head makes her face glow with shame. She can't lie, she can't deny God. She might be able to talk her way out of it though, after all, they can't know that she has some pages from the book. Denying the diary will be harder. "I worry about their questions, dearest friend, for they will ask me where the paper is. I can't tell them that. I will have to stay quiet." She shivers and her stomach twists along with her windy thought paths. What will they do if she refuses to tell them anything?

"God," she breathes, "God, it's me, Macia. I need you, for I know they will ask me about You, and I don't know what to say. I don't want to lie, after all, Paul wrote against that too. But God, I know for a fact that they will send me beyond the hills. I am scared, is that wrong?" She sits still, almost as if she is waiting for an answer.

Before she knows it, the door opens again, and Macia turns her head. She clamps her jaws together to keep her face that little bit sulky, but not emotional in a negative way. The older guard sets down a plate, grabs her lunch plate and slams the door shut. Macia winces, what is it with slamming doors?

Her dinner is a goop made of millet. Macia wrinkles her nose, then straightens her face quickly. She takes the plate to her box bed and hesitates before taking the first mouthful. "Thank you God for all food," she thinks, bravely plunging the spoon into the millet, looking overcooked and like thick glue. She shudders. "Beloved," she decides to write whilst eating, something not tolerated in Elabi. It's a sign of being either disorganised or too emotionally involved with the task. "Anyway, it distracts me. So, dearest friend, just to let you know, I recognise the smell of millet anywhere." It's true, she thinks, forcing another mouthful to go down. "So like Paul I'm trying to say that I'm content. Every day is a good day in Elabi, I do love my city, so it's true. Any food is good food, I suppose. There is nothing wrong with millet, I just prefer Ignava's cooking."

Eating her goopy mess is even harder. She fights for control, her hand shaking, making the spoon clatter against the metal plate. "I don't think I will ever eat Ignava's cooking again, dearest friend. Maybe I should dictate to you what it used to be like, so I won't forget." Macia pulls a face, suddenly having to smile at herself. She's dictating merely in her head, there is nothing to be kept from her thoughts.

She sighs and quietly finishes off her meal. After putting the dish back on the doorstep she notices that the cell is getting darker. Time to sleep, she decides. She tugs at her blanket, rolling herself up tight to preserve any bit of warmth that she can, hoping that somehow it will all be resolved, the dark cell and rough nightdress a bad dream.

Macia wakes with a shock as the heavy door opens, the female guard standing in the door opening, hands on hips. Macia sits up with a struggle, all of her body sore. She went to use the pail once in the night, hoping it was after midnight and there would be no watcher.

After that it had taken her a long time to fall asleep again, she was so cold. She is still cold, and her arms and legs are cramped. The guard sniffs and nudges a metal dish. "Clean up. Eat. Enquiry will start soon." Gone is she, the noise of the slamming door reverberating in Macia's head. She stumbles towards the door, glad of the water. She washes carefully, the cold water making her hands feel numb. She is thirsty, so the metal cup with water is very welcome, so is the thin, dry bread. It is dark and tasteless, but it fills her up. She misses having a hot drink; one of Ignava's hot herbal teas.

She thinks about the guard's words, telling her the Enquiry will be soon. Surely they will allow her to get dressed first? She can feel her face heating up thinking about sitting in front of council members in this grey shapeless bit of linen. When the door opens, Macia looks up, expecting the guard to bring her something to wear. It's the older guard, his face an unpleasant grin. He motions with his chin for her to get out. Macia is glad to get out of her small cell, and she finds herself walking down the long corridor again. She looks at the door behind which she got changed when she first arrived. They walk straight past it, and suddenly she is sure that she will be brought before the council members in this nightdress. Her face warms up, seemingly taking all warmth from her hands at the same time. She digs her fingertips into her dress, needing to feel.

The guard takes her through another door which he unlocks with his large bunch of keys. There is a type of waiting room, blissfully warm, and Macia finds herself shivering even more. Through another heavy door, and before Macia knows it they have walked into another room. The room is not very light, its furniture heavy and gloomy and intimidating. Four council members are sitting behind a large dark wooden desk. They stare at her with grim faces. The guard points his chin at the chair where Macia is to sit. It is a rickety-looking contraption, the blue leather seat ripped, and Macia swallows.

It gives her an excuse to look away from the council members for a moment though, and she sits down in as regal a manner as she can, to show them that despite what they think, and even though she is wearing a badly woven nightdress, she is still Macia Durus AMP. Some of those council members might not even have AMP status, she thinks to herself, trying to feel the outrage at being brought in for questioning by a mere Umbo.

She takes a deep, slow breath in and out, then fastens her eyes on the council members, not in a haughty way, but not looking subservient either. No, she is an Amplissimos, she knows how to conduct herself. She doesn't despise anybody, of course, but she doesn't accept people disregarding her status either. She will…

The grating voice interrupts her brave thoughts. "Macia Durus. You were brought here yesterday. We hope that last night gave you a good opportunity to evaluate your conduct?" It sounds like a question, but Macia isn't sure that she is supposed to answer it.

The woman next to the speaker takes over, "We assume you know what has brought you here, and why an Enquiry had to be opened into your life, as well as your family's lives." Macia's hands make an involuntary shuddering movement, and she clenches her fingers together, hiding her white knuckles in the grey material that suddenly feels comfortingly rough.

"This could be a long enquiry, depending on where our questions lead us, and we understand that there is always the possibility that our facts have been wrong, although we did try to check matters out." Macia is sure that the woman's voice has lost a tiny bit of confidence by the end. Is that because her diary papers have not been found? Good, long may it last!

The man with the awful voice starts up again. "We have many questions for you. Some of those you answered several moons ago when your friend went missing." He looks at her, his eyes bulging with pleasure at having to look into such a complex affair.

Macia hesitates a split second, then says in a calm, schooled voice, "As you can see from my records," she assumes they have her records, "as you can see, I do not hold friends. I'm sure you're talking about the girl Caecilia. I have answered many questions about her already. I even attended a Sharing is Caring class, for I realised afterwards that she had, in fact, changed a little before…disappearing." She almost said the word leaving, which would have been telling too much, as she's always claimed to have no knowledge of what happened to the girl.

She takes a breath to carry on, but the man interrupts, and again her hands shake. "Yes, well, save that, we have that. It's not so much about having friends or not. Fact is, there were many outstanding questions after we had spoken to you. Several questions," he gleams, and he taps the papers in front of him. Macia swallows, trying to look calm, but the fact that they used so much paper on her record is not good news.

The woman leans forward, the corners of her mouth turned up, pretending to smile, but she can't quite make her eyes follow suit. "Tell us a little more about your lack of friends or your non-friend policy as you chose to call it to a counsellor. Start with this girl Caecilia."

Macia feels a little more at ease. After all, the Caecilia saga seems far in the past, she has been questioned about the girl before, so it's a safe topic. She talks carefully, and in measured tones, not wanting to show any emotion or involvement. She has to convince them that there is no link between her and Caecilia apart from the odd schoolwork assignment. The woman keeps her mouth turned up, but Macia can see her eyes growing harder and harder.

"Tell me more about your style of working together," the woman suddenly interrupts. Macia feels the warmth in her cheeks. That is the second time they interrupted her. Should she point out to them that she is an Amplissimos? Better not. The question makes her wary as well. Why their style of working? She thinks about the afternoons spent together, Caecilia's kind face, her soft voice reading out loud to Macia… It seems so very long ago, as if it all happened to a different person. And in a way it did, for she is in Christ, who has made all things new. The woman clicks impatiently, and Macia is brought back with a start.

"Well, we only did school assignments together. We were often paired up, and we had found a way to be useful in our team setup," she begins, feeling that she needs to reiterate that they were not friends, just schoolmates. "Caecilia had a good reading voice and was good at grasping the meaning of texts. I normally wrote things down, and we'd formulate the sentences as we went along," she says.

The gravelly voice is back, "So you like writing?"

Chapter 31

Macia almost gasps, as she suddenly understands the question. She will need to be careful. She hesitates, then says, "Yes I do. I have often helped my father when he was working on a new book. I enjoy writing, as I know it will benefit Elabi." She clenches her fists, is she too emphatic in her statement about writing? Then she continues, "In fact, I have worked on a proposal lately, on how to help families to support their children to benefit all of society." Her mind races through those afternoons together. Did she ever say or do anything noteworthy? Would Luti have said something about those afternoons?

"So tell us about your free time," the woman blinks at Macia as if the writing question has been dealt with. Has it? Macia moves a little on the uncomfortable chair. "As an Amplissimos I have taken up paddleboarding," she starts, "and I have found it a great..." She has to dig her fingers into her legs to remind herself not to be too gushy. "It is a great all-round sport, and even though I was generally very fit, the first few weeks I still suffered from muscle ache. I am working on a proposal at the moment, as I have some outlines in mind for new workout videos. To lead those sessions, I will need to be fit, so paddleboarding has been very helpful in this."

One of the younger council members moves a little. Macia looks at him, feeling her heart rate speed up. His voice is quiet, "So, Macia, you seem to function well as an Amplissimos?" He looks at her, his eyes cold and mean. She dips her head, smoothing her face into its normal setting.

"I applied for Amplissimos as I want to serve my city as best I can," she says, trying to find the balance between over keen and willing. "I have seen the work my father and my stepmother have put in, and I love their heart for this city." The man raises his eyebrows in shock at the word 'love', making Macia's heart stutter. "As I said, I have a few proposals that I'm working on at the moment, having had advice from my father. Some will have to wait till the end of the summer, as having adult status would be better."

The man leans forward a bit, his eyes taking her in. She has to dig her fingers into her leg to keep focused. "So you would perhaps write in your spare time as well, especially as you have explained that paddleboarding left you with muscle ache." Macia hesitates, but before she can say something he continues, pulling at a paper in front of the woman, "It shows here on your records that you have been absent from the gymnasium several times, usually on Endays and Onesdays. Would that be to do with paddleboarding?" Macia dips her head again and tells him that yes, paddleboarding is done on Hexaday mornings.

He leans back in his chair, and says, "So maybe, when too tired to exercise, you decided to write instead?" Macia isn't sure what to say. After all, she doesn't write in the day, the risk is too great, but how will she explain... "Not really, you see, the days that I have been too sore for the gymnasium I have spent on schoolwork, or working on proposal ideas." The man dips his head and pulls another paper off the stack. Macia recognises her new brown paper, and her stomach tightens. So they have been to the house.

"You mean like this list here?" He says, looking at the paper.

Macia swallows, then says, "I can't say for certain from this distance, but I did work on various lists, to organise my priorities and time."

191

She swallows again, did that sound too involved, as if she was working on a complete overhaul, changing Elabi in every aspect? Her throat is dry and scratchy, and looking at the drinking glasses in front of the council members isn't helping.

"So you are saying that at the moment not enough is being done for our citizens," the young man says, leaning forward a bit. Macia shudders a little and gives a shake with her head, but before she can defend herself he says, "You tell us that you have a whole raft of proposals for the council, you're working on videos, books, articles. To me, that sounds like you think there are many gaps in our support for the city. You also seem very emotional about how you choose activities. You clearly have very strong likes and dislikes, which makes me wonder how suited you are to be an Amplissimos."

Macia feels her cheeks warm up, and would love to look away, to react to his stinging words in some way, but she has to prove herself. "I assure you that I passed all my tests, and if I have used the wrong words, then I will be very open to correction. It is my aim to serve my city, and to be a useful citizen and family member." Except that Brutus and Ignava are likely locked up as well, thanks to her.

The young man sits back suddenly and nods at the woman. Macia looks at the woman, hoping she will say something to indicate where all this will lead to. The woman looks at the list Macia had written, then at some of the other lists in front of her. She doesn't say anything, merely dips her head at the man with the grating voice. "Tell us about your reading level," he says, looking from Macia to the papers and back. "It says here that you have indicated that some Amplissimos students could have a lower reading level than they ought to. Is that because you were setting yourself up? Was that a feeling you had?" 'Feeling' is said as if it's a disgusting word.

Macia scrapes her throat, making the woman glare at her, then says, "There was one student that I worked with. She had Amplissimos status but misinterpreted and misread books and articles that we discussed. She told me about one of my father's books, for example, having misunderstood his teachings. I did indicate that it worried me, mainly because of her status. She would be able to teach groups once she left school, and could mislead other citizens." Macia is finding it harder and harder to stay calm, she feels the anxiety inside her growing, and it makes it hard to think and speak.

The man leans back too, and the man at the very end, who hasn't said a word so far, rings a loud bell, making Macia jump. The door opens immediately, and the old guard is back. The man at the end of the table points at Macia and motions to the door. The guard dips his head and standing over Macia, motions to the door as well. For a split second, she wonders what would happen if she pretends not to understand the hint, to protest at her treatment. She realises that it wouldn't be wise. All she can hope for and ask God for is that she has handled herself well, that her answers were satisfactory, and that they will let her go soon. She stands up, calmly raises her chin at the council members, then leaves the room, walking as if she has simply been for some kind of business meeting.

Macia struggles to contain her emotions once back in her cell. She sinks down on her box bed, anger towards the innate object making her heart pound. "Hateful bed, hateful room, horrid city..." She stops. She loves Elabi, she loves the view across the blue sea, the rolling hills with the tall cypress trees growing, the tall lighthouse. That reminds her of the kind woman and her whispered words just before she left the watersports centre. Did she mean there is a paddleboard somewhere near the lighthouse? Why? She leans against the wall, wondering why the woman would say and do that. "Beloved, I need to write to you," she moves the pencil in her head across imaginary brown paper, no, white paper, why not?

The paper looks very light, not as thin as the pages from her special book, but still lighter than the brown paper she is used to. "Beloved, I'm exhausted. I think I answered all the questions well, not giving them anything, apart from wanting to change the city." She feels annoyed again, coming up with all sorts of clever answers. "It scares me, dearest friend. They seem to have most of my papers, and many records. I did think my gymnasium absence would be noticed."

Macia thinks back through all the questions, worried that they have arrested Brutus and Ignava as well. Will they question them? "Dearest friend, I feel for them, as none of this is their fault. I have been careful, and I'm quite sure they haven't noticed anything. They are not to blame at all, and I feel bad that this is happening to them." Her emotions are making it hard to breathe, and Macia knows she has to bring herself under control. Just when she is starting to feel a little calmer, the door opens. It is the woman guard bringing her lunch. Macia is glad to see the metal cup with water. She is so thirsty, and thinking about her family has made her throat hurt even more. Lunch is pottage again. Macia eats it, of course, after all, it's warm, and she can feel the cold creeping into her bones already. She misses her garum and her warm room.

After lunch Macia sits back on her box bed, waiting for her lunch to go down. She wants to do her workouts, but not with a full stomach. So, leaning back against the wall, blanket draped over her knees, in her head she tries to recite as many paragraphs from the book as she can remember. She had tried to memorise parts of it, and she longs to have another look at her book.

The day passes with exercise, more writing in her diary, reciting words in her head, napping. Dinner is more millet, not very warm either. Macia is glad when it's time to go to sleep, although she shivers underneath the thin blanket. Hopefully tomorrow they will let her go, with a list of classes to attend no doubt. She isn't looking forward to seeing Brutus and Ignava. They'll not be pleased with her and the trouble she has brought them. A very small voice whispers that if this is about her diary, no amount of classes will fix that. She tries to fall asleep thinking about Paul's words in his letters.

The following day passes by without an Enquiry. Macia shivers and dictates letters in her head. "Beloved, this lunchtime saw my portion of pottage considerably smaller than it has been so far, and breakfast had been a single slice as well. I wonder if I should work out this afternoon, as I need the extra energy to stay warm. I'm repeating Paul's words when he writes that he knows how to abound and to be poor, and how he has learned to be content in it all. I will have to practise that too, so I'm grateful, for the pottage was hot, and I'm grateful for the fact that I had food and drink."

After her dinner plate is empty, Macia hunkers down on her box bed, her chin resting on her knees. She feels overwhelmed, her emotions catching her breath, but she puts a slight sulk on her face, and just a tiny hint of a smile, in case the watchers are staring at her to see how she will react to her dinner. In her head she picks up her beautiful pencil and writes on the crisp, white pages of her diary, "Dearest friend, it was millet again, but a lot less than usual. I actually feel hungry still, and I'm worried. Should I mention to the guard that I am hungry…" Her imaginary pencil hovers about the page, and Macia knows the answer to that question already.

"It is making me worried. Fear is getting at me from every side," and Macia stares into the darkness, repeating to herself that God shall supply all her needs. Then she turns back to her writing. "Beloved, I need to think about those words of Paul where he writes about putting on the armour of God. Tonight, I will do that, piece by piece."

Macia lies down, and she starts with the helmet, putting on each piece in her mind whilst talking to God at the same time. She isn't sure what a sword is, but it seems to be the word of God. Maybe some words you can speak, like a curse? Macia thinks about it for a moment, her frightened mind wandering. "Dearest," she thinks, to arrange her thoughts, "I have no idea what a sword is, but it's the last thing on the list, so I'm passing on for now."

Some doors away an older man is sitting on a similar box bed, his thoughts full of bitterness and anger. All his life he has supported Elabi, and every time somebody else, another family member, spoils it all. How long will it take him to get out of this hole? He has been given several blankets and a substantial meal. He is hopeful that it means the end to this Enquiry as far as it concerns him. He wonders what has happened to his wife. Will she be free to go? She is more prone to allowing feelings to show up, but he hopes she will be able to leave at the same time as him. She is not to blame, neither is he. They both have to move on from this as best as they can. He stares into the dark, taking deep, calming breaths. The shock still making his entire body shake. It had been the last thing he expected in his life.

Macia can feel her fear growing all morning and after lunch, shivering on her box bed. The water meant for washing felt petrifyingly cold, and there had only been one slice of thin, black bread. She had chewed as slowly as she could, to make it last, and hopefully, somehow trick her body into thinking it had had enough to eat. She does some slow exercises, her stomach feeling heavy with fear. After a small portion of pottage at lunchtime, Macia leans against the wall. She pulls the blanket up high and tries to think of something in the letters that will help her. Her special pencil comes out, "Beloved, I'm…I'm struggling. I know I am in God, but I'm also in trouble." She shivers and wipes her nose on her shoulder. The movement makes her freeze in horror. Her nose… She is cold, very cold, and her nose has just started to water a little. That means... She gives a panicky gasp, trying to catch her breath. Her nose. What if they call her now, and see her nose? Can the watcher see her well enough in this dark cell to see her nose? Macia shudders. Never mind secret diaries or forbidden books. One look at her face and her defect will be there for all to see!

"God," she breathes quietly, expecting white puffs in front of her face, "God, I need you to protect me, to shield me, and to provide all my needs. I need my nose warmer, and I need for the Enquiry to wait till I'm warmer, and I need for You to make sure the watcher can't see my nose. I need You to keep me safe and to be my protected and Helper."

Barely have the words floated in the dark cell when a key can be heard turning in the lock. Macia's heart trips. Where is God? Why doesn't He supply all her needs, or at least this one need?

The female guard stands on the doorstep. She motions with her head, and Macia slips off the box bed, moving slowly, her body stiff. The guard shuts the door behind her, then, looking at Macia's face her eyes widen, and she gasps loudly.

Macia turns away, biting her lip, clenching her fists in the folds of her rough dress, clamping her jaws together. Anything to stop the fear and emotions flooding her completely. She hardly registers the guard blowing on a whistle, but a soft moan slips out of her mouth when two other guards appear. They both look at her face, then they smirk at Macia. The woman behind her barks a short laugh, the guards raise their chins at each other, then the woman nudges Macia forward. "God, please, let me be warm enough..."

Chapter 32

All too soon, Macia is pushed into the gloomy room, with the four council members present. The woman isn't there. Another, older woman is sitting in her seat. They all stare at Macia, especially Macia's face. She can feel the heat flooding her cheeks, and her stomach is shaking. She digs her fingertips into her legs, willing the blush to leave her face, as it will make her very white nose and red tip stand out even more.

"Well," says the man with the grating voice, "we obviously have a defect as well as other issues," and he looks almost pleased as Macia stumbles to her chair, not able to look at the council members this time. Her heart beating wildly, she has one thought, she needs to control herself and this situation. She has to get herself back in control. First of all, she must prove to them that she is an Amplissimos, and therefore should receive respect. Once that is straightened out, she might be able to override their views on her defect. Maybe.

She holds her breath, counting in her head, her ears making a whooshing sound, blocking all other noise. After what feels too long she feels she has gotten herself in hand again. She has also warmed up a little, and she can only hope that her nose is looking normal again. Maybe if she manages to distract the members...

She looks up, and the older woman starts off, "So, you like writing, and we know you often write. Some of the words you write are rather odd. Care to explain?" Macia swallows, wondering what they would say if she used the words used in the letters, like meekness, kindness, salvation. Knowing that they haven't found her diary sheets yet, banking on the fact that they would be mentioning the photograph or the thin book first if they had, she dips her head a little at the woman.

"I'm not sure that I understand the question. Are you referring to my assignments I wrote or the list with items for the proposals I was working on?"

Seeing the woman turn a little red feels satisfying, but not for long. Macia realises that angering the council members might not be a smart move. The woman leans forward, "I think you know very well what I meant," she says, her voice like a snake, making Macia shiver. "We will find more papers, of course we will. But until then, explain those words."

She leans back, her sharp eyes never leaving Macia's face. Macia dips her head slowly, what should she say? In the end, she decides that playing ignorant will be best. After all, they have only got Luti's word for it, no further proof.

She swallows quite demonstratively, to try to add to her air of innocence. "I'm still not sure which paper you are referring to? Maybe you could show me an example? I write a lot, as I am very diligent with my schoolwork, and there are extra classes I have taken recently as well." The woman looks furious, and Macia sits back a little, raising one eyebrow at the emotional reaction, and adds, "As I said, please explain which paper you mean," her breath catches for a split second, she'd almost said 'letter' and then says, "as you know I did recently pass my Amplissimos test." She makes her face slide in position: a little bored, a sulky edge, but not too much.

The young man moves in his chair, and Macia slowly moves her head to look at him. "We wonder where you picked up emotional words like 'love' or 'beloved' and used them in your writing and even when speaking to others." Macia feels her hands slightly twitch at the word 'beloved'. And she knows that she used the word 'loved' here at the council as well. It had crept into her vocabulary, as she had known it would. She pulls a deep thinking face, pretending to really dig through her memory.

"I have spent time with a girl that had Amplissimos status, at least she sat at our Amplissimos table, but I don't know when she passed her tests. She had very strange habits, and it was picked up by myself and other students." Macia feels her anger towards Luti growing. The girl landed her in this mess, well, she can deal with her own mess as well. "We had to work on an assignment together, and in fact, I was left to finish off the assignment by myself, as she wasn't in school the last two days. Even before that, it was clear that she wasn't working on the correct level." She can see the woman's eyes, and Macia just knows that she is laughing at Macia. Macia clenches her fists, and carries on, "This girl often used words that seemed a little off, so I wonder if I started taking over words from her? We did spend quite a lot of time together, as we worked on the proposal as well." There, that will teach them to use a badly trained plant.

The woman smirks, and hisses, "She was our agent, Macia Durus, we sent her in especially. We have had our eyes on you ever since that other girl disappeared. We knew there would be more to be found in you. Others denied it, said you were a good little citizen, but I had my doubts." Macia swallows, and only by clenching her jaws together can she keep her face in place. "You see, I just had…" The woman stops, and Macia raises her one eyebrow instantly, aha! "I had a strong suspicion, based on many factors and reports," the woman hastily continues, "and I wanted it looked into. Your previous counsellor, as well as school counsellors, had many question marks. Combined with the regular reports from our plant, I knew we had done the right thing." She leans back, today is clearly a good day.

Macia's stomach feels tight, as well as empty. What can she do? She has no explanation. She can't admit anything. "I did wonder if she was a plant," she says in the end, "mainly because she was in no way fit enough to be an Amplissimos." She almost adds, 'and my father thought so too' but she'll do whatever she can to keep her family out of this mess.

The young man scrapes his throat, "Is it true that you greet and are being inappropriate with Mansits, especially in school? Macia looks surprised, then remembers some instances that might be construed that way, especially by a low-level agent.

"I'm not sure what you are referring to, but as an Amplissimos, I have come to realise that when all citizens work together, our city is strengthened. Maybe not in this generation, but definitely in generations to come. By treating all students the same way across the different status levels I knew the city would be stronger. All levels of students would be working for the good of our city, as none would be outside the team." Macia moves a little in her chair, she is warming to her argument.

The woman interrupts, "You mean you were going against our government policy? You know how this city council works. It was not up to you to try to change the way our council has designed our society. Rules for communication are put in place to protect our city. You as an Amplissimos should have known your responsibility. It was an emotional response, an emotional argument, and you were very wrong." Macia hesitates, wanting to argue her point, wondering if apologising would help. "We know there was something different about you," the woman continues, "you have changed. Your behaviour towards fellow students suddenly changed, without any discussion with anyone around you. That is not a logical thing to happen."

Suddenly the dreadful man at the end of the table speaks up, his voice making Macia shiver inside. "You like writing. So you will write. You will write about how you learned those words. You will tell us. You will write down for us who the letters were for." His dead eyes light up for a second, as Macia jolts a fraction of a second, then the light dies out, and his voice drones on, "You will write it all. There is much you are hiding. You will reveal it to us through your writing." he hesitates for a second, then continues, "You will show us the link between your change and the change in the other girl. You will tell us who you were writing to and how the letters got to that person." He leans back in his chair, the smile on his face makes Macia's hands shake uncontrollably, and she links her fingers together. Suddenly he carries on speaking, making Macia catch her breath. She doesn't know how long she will be able to listen to this horrible man. "There is a defect, so we will give you a room suitable for your defect." His smile is even more malicious this time, making her stomach turn and lurch, and she breathes slow shallow breaths to not be sick. She needs all the food they have given her, as she's hollow inside already. "You will write all the answers, then we will reconvene." He rings the bell, and the guard appears.

"The Writing Room," he smiles at the guard, who barks a short laugh, then the guard pushes Macia towards the door. She forgets to raise her chin at the council members, as she follows the guard in a daze. What can she write?

The guard takes her down the corridor and unlocks a door further along from where her own cell is. He nudges her in. Macia pulls a face, how dare he touch her. Inside the room are a small table and a chair. A bright light shines down from the ceiling. The room is also very cold. Macia gasps as soon as she steps in. The guard cackles, "You better get writing, otherwise, there is no need to write or do anything anymore." He motions with his chin towards the chair, and Macia walks to the chair, her mind rushing through her options. Make a dash for it?

The door slams and locks behind her and Macia is alone. She shivers, goosebumps all over her arms. She rubs her arms vigorously and looks at the blank paper and pencil. She has no idea what to do. "God," she whispers out loud, then she stops. There will be cameras. Will they have heard her already? In that case, she might as well write. She looks down at the paper, and leans over it a little, hoping it will hide her face and the terror all over it. "God," this time she makes sure there is no sound, "I don't know what to do. I don't know what to write." She wonders if she will get away with a lesser sentence if she admits that for a moment she got carried away by the pages Caecilia left behind? Then she remembers the man's comment about her defect, and deep inside her, she knows she's doomed either way. "I know the book was cursed," she suddenly whispers very quietly, her mouth feeling bitter, and her heart as cold as the room. That makes her feel desperately sad, and more lonely than she'd ever been.

In her mind, she sees her brown paper, and she picks up her beautiful new imaginary pencil. "Beloved, I need you, I need you desperately. My feelings and emotions have flooded my life, and I don't know what to do. I hate…" She stops, she was going to say the little book, Paul, God… But she had turned to God, knowingly turned to Him, knowing this day could come. "Not like this, dearest friend, I wasn't thinking of this, not now. I wanted to serve my city first." Her teeth are clattering together, making her jaws ache. A tiny voice tells her that she had to follow God first, serve Him first and that Paul had learned to be content in all sorts of circumstances. "I know, beloved, but I want to live," she breathes, a little puff of air showing up.

It is cold, very cold, and her nose is runny already. She knows her defect is visible, but there is nothing she can do about it. Her hands are cramped, and her toes are numb. How long will she be able to hold out? She knows she will have to write something. The one thing she can say is that she has never written to another person, merely personal lists and plans. So something along those lines might help. They might still wonder where all those pages are, but she could make them think the paper has been reused. What else...It is hard to think. Mention Paul. No. Nor God. Nor Caecilia either, for if they know there is a connection, there might be trouble. She isn't sure why there would be trouble, she simply knows it. The thin pages. There is something about the thin pages. She can't remember whether she ought to mention them.

Her mind is making her hand pick up the pencil, but she's shivering uncontrollably now, and the pencil makes spidery lines on the brown paper. Macia blinks slowly and stares at the lines, wondering if they mean something. Should she be reading those signs? She looks around, her head moving clumsily, but there is nobody there to read to. She is so tired, maybe it's really late and she should go to bed. "I will read tomorrow," her words are odd, slurred together, her tongue moving in slow motion, little clouds accompanying each syllable. At least it's not so cold any more. She smiles a little, but her face won't shape a smile, so she gives up. She slips off her chair onto the floor. She briefly winces at the stinging pain on her face when landing.

The man turns to the guard and shouts an order. Running footsteps sound through the corridor. The man watches the door to the Writing Room open, and two guards grab the girl, shutting the door behind them. He turns away with a frown, where did the girl learn those words? Who was she in contact with? The letter must have left Elabi, but how? Too many questions; the girl is a danger. Maybe sending her away will be too much of a risk. He thinks through the options, knowing the other council members will disagree. After all, the girl is an Amplissimos, and nothing concrete has been found. A quick fix will not be voted through, he knows.

Macia is aware of the warmth. The warmth and the bright light hurting her eyes, her head. Her hands shake, and she struggles to open her eyes. The room is white, the sheets are white, everything is white. A Nurse turns up, a guards' uniform underneath her nurse apron. Her face is hard, and she checks Macia's pulse without saying a word, tugs on one of her eyelids, making Macia wince, then abruptly turns and walks away.

Macia closes her eyes, she is so tired. She vaguely remembers the freezing cold room, and how she had tried to write something down. "What did I write, beloved? Was there anything on that paper?" Suddenly, very clearly she feels deep down inside that she wrote nothing down. The conviction is so strong, it makes her gasp in surprise. "Fine, dearest friend, I take your word for it," she jokes with her beautiful crisp white paper. Maybe she's even writing with a pen, like an official document. That thought makes her smile, her face stinging when she does so. She touches the side of her face, and her breath catches. She has to bite her lip to stop herself from crying out. She touches her face carefully, feeling for blood, but it seems alright, probably just bruised. She'll look a state, she thinks, then shrugs, snuggles underneath the warm sheet and blankets, and is soon fast asleep.

Chapter 33

Rough hands shake Macia awake, and she blinks against the bright lights. The grumpy looking nurse is back, checking her vitals. Macia's stomach complains, and she hesitates, then asks, "Is it nearly time for…" she stops. The woman glares at her but doesn't answer. Macia stares at the closed door, no longer feeling sleepy. She is feeling much better, although her body still gives the occasional shudder. She stares at the ceiling and pulls out a clean sheet of white writing paper, and a real pen. "Dearest friend," she starts, needing someone to talk to, even if just on imaginary paper. "I am in a sanatorium, I think, but it's not the main one. I don't know what will happen next, and beloved, I'm hungry, really, really hungry." She feels her anger growing, how do they expect her to behave well without food?

The nurse returns with a bowl of food, and Macia drags herself into a sitting position. She avoids looking at her, merely takes the bowl, and starts eating straight away. It's pottage, a very small portion, but hot. It helps, she can feel the hot food travel down, warming her up. Macia eats slowly, to make her food last as long as possible. She puts the bowl on her nightstand, and slides under her blankets, shivering again. She manages to fall asleep, waking every now and then, the light bright at all times.

After a bowl with watery pottage, Macia is ordered out of bed. The nurse glares at her, and stands nearby, not saying anything. Macia swallows, what is she supposed to do? Soon footsteps can be heard, and the older guard appears. He smirks at Macia, and motions with his chin towards the door. Macia goes, wondering if he will bring her back to the freezing room again. The guard stops outside her cell door and unlocks the door. Macia is relieved in a way, as the room is familiar and although cold, not as cold as the Writing Room.

Lunch is one small slice of black bread, and Macia's stomach growls loudly when she has eaten the last crumb. She leans against the wall, her chin resting on her knees. The box bed feels hard, but at least it's better than the ground. She thinks about Caecilia. How did she get out of Elabi? She must have gone with Gax, probably the same way he came into Elabi. She misses Cecilia, but thinking about Caecilia makes her vulnerable. She might say something by accident and yet she can't help wondering where the two of them went.

The following morning a younger guard unlocks her door, and motions with his head for her to come out. Macia finds herself out of breath simply from getting up a couple of steps out of her cell. Her legs are a little unsteady, and as they walk along the corridor, she finds herself sweaty, knowing she looks pale. She is so relieved to sink down on the hard chair that she hasn't even looked at the council members. When she finally looks up she shudders to see the dreadful man at the end. The same older woman is there, and the two other men. The man with the dead eyes leans forward a little, his mouth shaping a grin and he says, "Thank you for what you wrote about your friend," he hesitates, and looks at a paper, "your friend Caecilia and the young man. Tell us more."

Macia gasps a little, pressing her lips together, and rearranging her linen dress over her knees to buy herself time. Written about Caecilia? Had she? She can feel panic taking hold of her until she remembers that very strong, clear sensation in the sanatorium that she had not written anything.

She sits up a little, wondering how to proceed, then in as calm a voice as she can she says, "I did not write anything about the girl Caecilia, so maybe you could show me the paper?" She looks at him, and although he makes her stomach churn around, she is determined to outstare him. He looks down first, tapping the paper in front of him.

"You might have forgotten as you seemed very much affected by the room," he says, his smile still there, "and soon after you wrote this the guards removed you from the room. Now, expand." He glares at her this time, and Macia can feel her fear making her hands contract. She looks at him, her vision has gone very blurred, and although her mouth seems to no longer belong to herself, she says, "I know I did not write anything down. I might have made a mistake in trying to include Mansits into the city's society before they were approved, but I am still an Amplissimos. Speaking the truth is the only option for Elabi citizens, as you know. All other options are driven by various emotions, like fear or anger." She stares at where she knows he has to be, wondering how he will punish her.

The woman clicks with her tongue, and Macia moves her head to face the woman council member. Breathing deeply and slowly restores her vision, just in time to see the woman glance at the dreadful man. Good, she has just confirmed what Macia knew to be true. There is no written confession. The woman mentions Macia's writing again, her lack of friends, the way she treated Mansits all of a sudden. Macia leans back in her chair a bit more, her hands no longer digging into her legs, as she answers the same questions over and over. Her face has taken on the familiar slightly sullen, bored look. She makes sure to spend some time explaining her dedication to Elabi has meant she has kept to the no-friends policy, although after the Sharing is Caring course she might have been less determined. "It made things clearer for me, so I did share about Luti a few times, as I knew her attitude and lack of skills would be detrimental to Elabi." There. That will teach them not to use a plant, or at least use a plant that can fit in.

Then there is the awful voice, and Macia can feel herself going empty, totally knocked sideways by the suddenness of the question and its implications. "Do you hate God? Do you deny that you are part of Him? Do you say that Jesus Christ is not in you?" The room is completely quiet, all the oxygen seems to have left the room with the sound of the man's voice, and Macia sees the shock and utter lack of understanding on the faces of the three other council members. They are as taken aback as she is, except she knows what he is talking about.

Looking at the man is a mistake. His eyes no longer dead, the fire in them consuming her, taking all her strength away. Macia hears a loud gasp, then there is just the ceiling above her, and running footsteps. The face of the older woman appears, her eyes wide in shock as she whispers the word 'defect' to herself. Macia feels sick, her head still spinning around, and she closes her eyes, too weak to struggle.

The guard appears, and he yanks her to her feet, pushing her out of the door. Macia is glad to go, even though her legs aren't cooperating at all. She needs to get away from that awful man. She needs to escape those questions. Her head is spinning, and several times the guard has to catch her before she slumps against the cold stone floor. He shoves her into her cell, and Macia trips down the steps, grazing her shins and knees, hardly feeling the pain. She is shaking violently but manages to crawl to her box bed. She leans her head on her arms, her sore knees on the cool floor. "God, can you even hear me in here?" The thought suddenly occurs to her. What if God needs people to be out in the open? After all, her best talks with God had been in the fields, walking to and from school or when out running.

Macia's eyes are stinging, and her beautiful pen writes in very shaky letters on the crisp white paper. "Beloved, am I alone? Do I need to wait till I'm back out in the open?" She thinks about the questions and carries on, "Those questions, I didn't answer them with my words, but that man will know enough. He will also know that I can't deny the words, as I said to him in my pride, lying is not an option in Elabi. Dearest friend, I can't lie about God. I don't have to tell them about you, but everything else, they'll know what to ask me." Macia feels sick, what if they bring her to the Writing Room, to tell them how she learned about God? Will they search the house all over again, determined to find the thin pages? They must have figured out that Caecilia has left her some as well. "Beloved, have I brought more trouble on my family, simply for being in God? Will it help if I…" She stops, even on imaginary paper there is no way she can write down the question. She knows what the answer is anyway, it really wouldn't make a difference, only to her heart it would. She can't deny God. What if He doesn't hear her beyond the hills though, would there be any point in being in Him? In a way it's God who would have deserted her, as He left her behind, unable to follow her in places where she needs Him most. Could that even be true?

This gives her new strength. "Beloved, I need to think for a while, run through the thin pages and the various letters for a while," and Macia can feel her mind working again. She drags herself onto the box bed, and lying on her back, stares into the darkness. She thinks about Paul, writing to the people he called saints, and how he… She sits up with a gasp. He constantly mentioned how he was a prisoner, how he was in bonds, which only happens to the worst kind of Mansits, usually on their way to the Hills. She shivers, pushing away unwanted images. So Paul was a prisoner, but also mentions he was a prisoner in the Lord. So God was still with him, even when he was obviously being transported, and presumably kept in secure confinement.

Her evening meal of millet is cold and lumpy, but somehow Macia doesn't notice. She is glad to have food, any food, and has to force herself to eat slowly. Somehow her cell seems lighter though, as if Paul is sharing the room with her, nodding at his bonds, and shrugging his shoulders, telling her that he counts it an honour to suffer for the Lord. Does she? She blushes a little, thinking of the line she almost wrote on her white paper.

After a surprisingly refreshing night, Macia is glad of the opportunity to wash. Her knees and shins sting when she tries to wipe the dried blood off, but the cold water leaves her feeling cleaner. She touches her hair; if only there was a comb. The woman guard notices and barks a laugh, making Macia frown which she tries to hide. The guard takes the washing water and shuts the cell door, still chuckling and shaking her head. Macia swallows and makes herself focus on her breakfast. Every time she hears a sound in the corridor her heart starts jumping around. She knows hard questions will come soon, and she doesn't know how she will handle them. "God, I know that You can hear me. Thank you for hearing me, even though I'm not really in bonds yet. I know I haven't really shown much joy…"

The dreaded opening of her door happens not long after lunch. Macia can feel her stomach tightening, and she breathes out slowly, mouthing the words, "Rejoice, and again I say rejoice…" For a moment her old crabby self emerges. Rejoicing is easier said than done, but she remembers Paul's bonds. Walking through the corridor, Macia decides to count each step, saying a positive word for each tile. She breathes the word, wishing she was bold like Paul, brave enough to say the word out loud. "Forgiveness, freedom," her mind stutters, why did Paul mention freedom. Those verses start to make more sense now and for the next steps, words come to her more easily, "Joy, kindness, rest, uhm…" It's actually harder than she thought to quickly think of words, as there are so many words that she isn't sure of. "Salvation, redemption, adoption, predestination, deliverance." She doesn't know exactly what they mean, but her heart knows them.

She smiles a little, and whispers, "God knows them, and He knows my heart; He keeps my heart and mind in Christ, so I know them." She almost smiles as they get to the door, pleased with her logic, but smoothes out her face as she sees the nasty grin of the guard. He opens the door to the room after a second's hesitation, then the heavy door opens with more flourish than usual, it seems. Macia shrugs it off and walks past the guard into the room. She walks straight, buoyed up by the different words she thought of. Then her heart drops, and she gasps, her legs almost giving way underneath her. The room has several extra council members, and in front, on hard-backed chairs, wearing simple linen clothes, are her father and stepmother. Macia feels her face starting to light up, she almost calls out their names, but years of practice help her to control herself. Good thing too, for just before her father looks away, she has seen the grief and anguish in his eyes, his clenched jaws shaking slightly.

Macia sits down on her regular chair, fear making her feet numb, her hands shaking. She clenches them together, trying to think of the positive words again.

"We don't need any more questions," the voice which makes Macia shake simply by remembering the man, breaks the silence in the room. "We saw your reaction. For our national security, I will not even mention any of it again." Macia glances at her father but seeing the look of pure hatred he now sends her makes her go cold. "You will be taken to safety, for your own good and for the protection of our society. You may still be a useful citizen, but your poison has to be contained. We will take you where you will do no harm but to yourself."

Macia swallows. The hills. They are sending her beyond the hills, and there is no mention of redemption, return, or rehabilitation. She is going beyond the hills for good. But not alone, and she dips her head slightly, knowing that her heart is in God, and her heart is free in Him. The man's eyes spark for a moment, but he clenches his fists and leans forward a little.

"Ignava?" His voice makes not just Macia shudder; she can see Ignava reacting as well. The woman stands up, her legs clearly shaking, and says, "I denounce her. I don't know her now or ever. Her name is gone from my house." She sits down rather abruptly.

Macia feels her eyes sting, her cheeks glow. She has denounced Macia? She knows it's the only way to escape punishment.

Then Brutus stands up, unasked. Macia looks at her father, who seems a bit older than she last saw him. This must have been so hard on him. She takes a breath to apologise, to say…

His loud voice beats her to it, the venomous emotion taking her breath away. "I denounce her. Her name is gone."

Chapter 34

Macia gasps out loud, half rising out of her chair. She stretches her hand out to her father. Then she drops back onto the hard seat. She is shaking all over, and she finds her face suddenly wet with tears. The dreadful voice sounds in the room, "You have chosen your path. By rejecting the teachings of this council you have brought destruction upon yourself. In your wilfulness, you almost destroyed your parents. Fortunately, they were mature enough to see the wisdom of Elabi's governing council. They have been submitted too much suffering because of you, but have redeemed themselves distancing themselves from you."

The word 'redeemed' makes Macia catch her breath, and she looks at her father and stepmother. No, they're not redeemed. New strength fills her and she says with a clear voice, "I accept, and I forgive, Father and Ignava. I will always love you, and…" Her voice is cut off as the council members cry out, and even Brutus jumps up and roars at her, his face filled with hatred, both his hands clasped over his ears. Macia finds her lips trembling too much to say anything else, and her eyes are too blurred to see her father properly. She vaguely hears the man at the end say something, catches the word 'Hills', then the young guard is at her side and yanks her arm, indicating for her to follow him. She looks back at her parents one more time, but the guard shoves her roughly into the corridor.

She is glad to be back in her cell, overwhelmed. She collapses on her box bed, staring up into the dark. Macia suddenly realises, there is no more reason to hide her faith! She gives a little gasp, and the sun breaks through on her face, and she whispers, "God, I'm so sad, I love my father," she hesitates, she can't honestly say that she loves her stepmother, but the woman had taken care of her. "I definitely feel for her, Lord, and I didn't want either of them to suffer through me." She takes a few deep breaths, feeling a little calmer already, but every time she remembers her father's twisted face, her eyes overflow. "I didn't mean to harm them, and Lord, I miss them. I wish…" yes, she does wish life was back to normal. The usual rhythm of school and weekends had often felt boring and plain, but now it seems wonderful and peaceful.

Her loss seems huge, and a tiny corner of darkness is steadily growing in her heart. Macia closes her eyes, trying to ignore the darkness inside her, and decides to 'write' a little, "Dearest friend, only friend," she gives a sob, then clenches her jaws together. She has to control herself. "I can't begin to describe what I felt when my parents denounced me," she continues, the silver pen wobbling on her white paper. "They were so angry, and I tried to forgive them, for I know why they rejected me. It was the only thing they could do really, and if I were them, I would do the same." She brushes tears away, and heaves another very deep sigh, "The thing is, beloved," she hesitates, the dark corner in her heart no longer just a corner, "I just wonder…" another deep breath, then in very small print she writes on her imaginary paper, "Is it really worth it?"

There. The question is out, and strangely enough, the darkness retreats a little, but not for long. "God," she whispers, "I have lost everything and everybody. My home, my family, all my belongings, my freedom," and her stomach joins in, making her smile a little, "yes, my health too." She shudders, and the shaking returns, her eyes dry with the horrors ahead of her. She knows that people with strong beliefs don't normally live very long beyond the hills. That is even without the risks associated with Hillixer. No, she might be young and she used to be fit, but living beyond the hills will sap her strength. She might not even live long enough to see the next winter. "What have I done," she breathes into the dark, her breathing suddenly laboured, and she has to sit up to catch her breath. Maybe she should have trusted the council, accepted that the book was a forbidden book, and she should have handed it in straight away, together with Caecilia's letter. Surely they would have realised that she was in no way implicated. Yes, she might have had to attend a few classes, they might even have sent Luti anyway. But she would have been innocent, a proper citizen of her beloved Elabi. Now she is an outcast.

"Beloved, I have left everything behind. I went against my teachers, my fellow students, my family." She thinks of her parents, and how she had deceived them, hiding the thin pages, reading the strange words when she knew her parents were out. "Maybe I should give up my pages and my diary and…and God?" She turns her face to the wall, sobbing, her heart shrouded in darkness. The idea of forsaking God is too awful to think about, and Macia weeps quietly, pressing her face against the cold wall. When she is calmer, she thinks about it, but the mere thought makes her feel sick. She has just lost everything and everybody, to be in Christ. Without Him, what would life be? She thinks back to her sunny room, the warm fields, her smooth paddleboard. It looks so sweet and attractive, but when she looks at the pictures again, she sees the coldness underneath, the loneliness and the emptiness. Yes, it looks so attractive and wonderful, but it was really an outward shell.

"Dearest friend, remember the first time I read those words, and how they infuriated me? Remember the first time I read the words on the thin pages…" Macia rolls onto her back, a slight smile returning.

She pictures herself in her windowsill, furtively turning the thin paper, wondering about their quality. She remembers reading the unusual words, and how they had taken over her heart. "God, I remember giving up my life, needing You more than anything, wanting to be in You more than anything. I didn't understand, I couldn't even really count the cost, but I knew what I did was very dangerous. Now I know, and God, could I, would I have taken a different route?" She sighs then, a deep cleansing sigh, releasing the grief, the horror of the last hour.

"Lord, I know that I could not have made a different decision. I'm sad, I'm grieving, I'm hurting and so dreadfully alone. I am very afraid, and desperate, I want to live, to be Attached, to have children, to…to live my life." Macia stops and she thinks of the paddleboard sessions, remembering the sparkling water, the blue sky, the air in her hair, and her loud laugh. Freedom. "Yes, I miss all that," she says softly, having to smile, the memories so sweet, "but Lord, I can't do anything else. I cannot deny You, I cannot turn away from You, I need You more than my old life. I need You to make me whole, to redeem me from the inside." Tears wet her smiling face, and she suddenly chuckles. "I don't know how many more tears my eyes can and will make, but Lord, teach me like Paul to really rejoice in You always, even here, even when I probably will be in bonds too." That makes the smile slink off, and Macia clenches her fists to stop the shaking. She will be brave, she will be at peace, she will rejoice in her bonds. Somehow.

Dinner is cold, lumpy millet, and not very much either. Macia sits on her box bed, eating slowly, shuddering over each mouthful, grateful for food though. She squeezes her stomach at the end, it still feels so hollow. Being hungry makes it hard to sleep, and she shivers under the very thin blanket. She sleeps fitfully and wakes up cold and hungry. The morning pottage is cold too, and the washing water is freezing, making her shake so much, she struggles to eat her breakfast. She walks slowly back to the box bed after finishing her breakfast, rubbing her arms. The day drags past. Macia spends the time talking to God and writing with different exquisite pens on crisp white paper. Every time there is a noise outside her door, her heart rate spikes. Will they come for her? Will the man with the dreadful voice question her some more? She wonders if they will make any efforts to get her to leave her new faith behind. Nobody comes, apart from a guard bringing the thin slice of black bread, and the female guard bringing her millet.

She has just returned her scraped clean bowl to the step and is arranging her thin blanket when the female guard appears. Macia stands motionless. They want to question her now? In the evening? It is dark in the cell, so she can't see the guards face. The woman barks, "Walk!" and stands aside a little. Macia drops the thin blanket on her box bed and slowly walks out of the cell. Her legs feel wobbly, and her hands grip the thin linen dress. Macia is taken to the same room where the dress was handed out at the beginning of her stay. There is a stool, and the woman tells her to sit, loud enough to be heard several cells away. Macia sits down, shivering, as the room is warmer than her cell. She rubs her arms, one of them is itchy as well, something must have bitten her. She looks up to see the guard with scissors in her hand. She gasps, wide awake all of a sudden. "No, what...?"

The woman smirks, "Oh yes, you are one of the special prisoners," she says, grabbing Macia's long braid. With one vicious snip, the braid is off. Macia gives a half gasp, half shriek, and tries to keep the woman at bay with both hands outstretched, shaking.

"Would you like me to call the other guards?" The woman glares at her, lowering the scissors, half turning towards the door. "They would be delighted to help me to get Macia Durus, once-AMP ready for transport," she continues, and Macia groans. A sob escapes, and the woman spins round to stare at Macia, disgusted. "Hadn't expected an

Amplissimos to be the emotional type," she says, her upper lip curled up. She snorts, "Well well, who'd have guessed. Maybe your relatives could write a book about that, 'Unexpected Reactions in Traitors' to help others," and she gives off a loud shrieking laugh. Macia clenches her jaws together, blinking rapidly to try to keep the tears in. She digs her fingers into her dress. They hurt, the nails nibbled away, but somehow the pain helps her. The woman huffs, and taking big clumps of Macia's auburn hair in her hands, snips away vigorously.

When she is finished, she grabs a folded garment off another shelf and hands it to Macia. "Hurry up, the tubular doesn't wait," she says, and putting the scissors back in a drawer, she grabs a broom to sweep the floor. Macia dries her face on her shoulder, then quickly changes into the linen dress the woman has given her. It is another short-sleeved dress, but a better quality one. It's completely shapeless though, like a sack. It is a darker grey than the last one, and on both her shoulders are large yellow rectangles. The woman hands her a thin woollen blanket, and Macia hugs it tight. The blanket is warmer than the one she had so far. Then the woman produces some metal chains, and Macia gasps again. The woman rolls her eyes and clasps the one large ring round Macia's wrist. The other wrist follows. Macia can feel tears splattering on her cheek, but there is nothing she can do. She clutches the blanket in the crook of her elbow and wipes her face on her shoulder.

The woman walks to the door, motioning Macia with her chin to follow her. Along the corridor they go, down more steps, Macia's breath is coming in gasps, and her legs are shaking. She is exhausted by the time they come to a large room. One side is open, showing a strange path. Several others are waiting in the room, all shackled, clutching their blankets. Some have yellow complexions, and Macia shivers at how desperate they all look. Does she look as awful? But she is free, her heart is free, and she can rejoice, can't she?

"Beloved, I'm in bonds, proper bonds, like Paul. Like him, I will rejoice in my bonds. They hurt, dearest friend, and they are heavy, but I suppose they could be even worse. And I have a woollen blanket. It's not very thick, but it's warmer than the one in my cell. My dress is better. I wonder why I have two yellow patches?"

She finds out soon enough. A yellow man points at her patches with his bound hands and cackles. "That's a joke, right, that's a funny joke." He has no teeth it seems, and Macia feels herself recoiling from him, especially as he dribbles a little. He wipes his mouth, then chuckles again. "You know why it's yellow, don't you?" She swallows, and he carries on, "Ha! I thought you wouldn't. Young people know nothing these days. It's yellow, for evil beliefs are learned in secret, see, but they're exposed when the light of our city shines on them. See, I knew that, I listen, I do, I always listen to the talks they give us, and then you find things out. Knowing things helps, see?" Macia dips her head. Evil beliefs?

She tries to breathe calm breaths, but the room smells, making her cough. Her stomach clenches, and she tries to take shallow breaths through her mouth. She can't lose her millet, she is starving as it is! There is a strange rumbling noise, and a strong breeze suddenly fills the room, Macia steps back a little, but there is nowhere to go. The yellow man cackles with glee as he looks at her face. "One can always tell a first-timer," he says, looking pleased with his deductive abilities, "although with those yellow patches, you'd be a one-timer anyway," and he laughs until he coughs. Macia tries to move away from him a little, as a strangely shaped vehicle suddenly glides into the room. It rests on the funny path, like a narrow road. It is grey, with little windows all along its side. With a soft puff large doors slide open, revealing hard wooden benches inside. Guards appear behind the waiting prisoners, herding them into this tube-like vehicle. One guard shouts, "Get into the tubular, now! We don't have all night!" Macia's eyes open wide. So this is the tubular! How exciting; she has heard about it, now she's going inside it. Her dark corner tries to tell her that this isn't something to be proud of. She knows that, but she reminds the darkness that she is rejoicing in everything, even in the fact that she's getting a ride on the tubular. That will give her something for her diary as well. "Rejoice always," she smiles softly, stepping aboard.

Chapter 35

Macia stumbles and sits down hard on the cold metal bench running along the length of the tubular. She swallows when the doors whoosh shut. She's going beyond the Hills. Her stomach clenches tight, and her hands are sweaty. "Beloved," she starts in her head, to distract herself, but that's as far as she gets. Suddenly the tubular shoots forward, making Macia, as well as the other people in transit, lose their balance. She gasps out loud, the fast movement of the tubular making it hard to stay upright on her seat. She digs her toes into the floor and tries to look outside through the tiny window. Just then they enter a tunnel, and everything goes dark.

It's even harder now to stay upright, and Macia's ears hurt because of the pressure. She groans softly, trying to raise her hands with the heavy chains, but she can't quite cover her ears with her hands.

Others moan much louder, with someone near Macia wailing quite loudly, begging to be let Downstream. The tubular shakes and rocks, and each time the cries and shrieks go up in pitch. Macia clenches her jaws together, determined to suffer quietly. She is an Amplissimos after all, even though she's probably a Mansit for now. That distracts her. She has never been told what she has been lowered to, and for how long.

Every now and then the tubular passes a little light in the tunnel, casting an eerie light on the passengers. Macia feels queasy, and watching people's horrified faces, even for a split second, is not helping. She shuts her eyes, wishing she could close her ears the same way. The tubular gives a violent rock, and Macia lunges into the person next to her. Before she can straighten up, she is thrown the other way by the vehicle's movements. She cries a little, gives a little sob, breathing, "God, please help me…" Further away in the carriage, a voice suddenly strikes up. It's a quivery voice and not very loud, but so different from the moans and shrieks, it seems to cut right across them.

"Nearer, my God, to Thee, nearer to Thee…" Macia gasps, the horror and movement suddenly forgotten, the groans fading away. There is only the Voice, unlike anything else Macia has ever heard. "…still all my song shall be," and then the voice stops, cut off as suddenly as it has begun. An angry roaring has taken its place, and Macia can hear the scuffling and clashing, thudding noises further down the carriage, and she sobs out loud. "No, please, don't," her voice unheard, except by her neighbour.

She gasps as a sharp elbow digs into her side, and a low voice hisses, "Don't! Believing types don't live long and get the worst deal. It'll be hard enough as it is without drawing attention to yourself!" Then the voice changes a bit, and cackling adds, "Never guessed a girl like you would be a Hidden One!" It is the obnoxious old man, and Macia shivers. Is that what she's now called? She swallows, her joy gone. In her cell, she'd thought that she was finally free to enjoy her faith, now that it had come out anyway. Seems like she will still have to hide it. What about her yellow patches? Surely they will give her away.

"Is it only…believers who wear the yellow patches," she asks the man, stumbling on the word. Surely everybody believes in something? Her father is a strong believer in the council and Elabi rule.

"Yellow is for believers," the man says, each word accompanied by his fishy breath. "Different beliefs, different relgies…religy, what's it called? Faith, that's it, faith." He sounds pleased, and in the dark

Macia feels the little droplets land on her face. She shudders, her stomach heaves a little, and she tries to dry her face on her shoulder. The edges of her yellow patches scratch her face. She manages to croak out a thank you and the man cackles, making her eyes sting. "Yep, bad enough for everyone, even worse for hidden ones. They thought their thoughts were hidden, but the council will reveal their poisonous thoughts. See, I listen," he adds, clearly glad to be able to show off his knowledge. Macia blinks, glad it's still dark, wondering how much longer it will be. The stench and the movement is making her struggle to keep her cold, lumpy millet inside her stomach, and although she isn't looking forward to the Hills, she is longing for the awful ride to end.

The tubular slows down, its brakes shrieking. People no longer wail and scream, but mumble in despair. Macia tries to breathe through her mouth, as the smell is getting worse. Suddenly the vehicle rocks to a stop, making most of the passengers lose their balance. There are grunts and cries as limbs connect with faces, a scrambling around, then suddenly the lights come on in the carriage. The bright light makes Macia squint; all she can see is bodies trying to get off the floor.

Finally, she is back on her feet, and her throat hurts as the doors slide open. What will it be like?

The heat rolls into the carriage like ocean waves in winter, and Macia is gasping for breath, her nose burning with the hot air. People start pushing their way out of the carriage, and she follows, half pushed by passengers around her. Near the door she looks towards where the singing voice was, "Nearer my God to Thee, yes, how appropriate, God, thank you," she mutters, glad to hear her own voice. Her breath stops when she sees the body on the floor of the carriage, blood on the face and grey metal floor. Macia stares, unable to move or breathe, her legs shaking. Suddenly the sharp elbow is back, and the old man hisses,

"Move! New ones are always the same, move! Don't be involved, it'll be hard enough as it is," and his bound hands suddenly push her, almost making her lose her balance. She staggers out of the tubular, still dazed. The woman…it was a woman… they… did they kill her? Macia is shaking all over now, "God, will that be my lot too in a short while?"

She follows the people in front of her, glancing back to see if she can spot the old man with his yellow skin, just to thank him for helping her. Guards suddenly push her aside, separating her from the other passengers. Macia ends up with about ten others, all looking scared and gasping in the hot air. They must all be new, she realises, looking at them. None of them seem as ill as the other passengers. The guards shout at them to walk along. Macia finds herself struggling to breathe within a few steps. Rocking along in the tubular has disoriented her, and she has no idea what time it is. She is tired, her head hurts, and her throat feels on fire from breathing in the hot, dry air. They are in another large room and are soon made to climb the stairs leading to the outside area. Macia cranes her neck, wanting to glimpse the Hills, but after a while she gives up. Climbing the steps takes up all her energy and more, making her despair of ever making it to the top. Another woman trips and slides down a couple of steps. The guard shouts at her and nudges the woman with his foot to make her get up quicker. Macia looks at the woman for a moment, wanting to help, but knowing full well that she'll need all her strength to make it herself.

At last, she stumbles onto the top step, sweating and trembling. The cooler air brings relief, and Macia breathes deeply. There isn't much of a breeze, but it feels wonderful on her head. She wipes her face on her short sleeve, clutching her woollen blanket. The woman next to her moans softly and Macia tries to smile at her encouragingly. The woman simply glares at her after one look at Macia's yellow patches. Macia looks away.

The guard yells at them to walk again, and they follow a female guard as she marches out into the cool night air. Macia tries to look around, but it's too dark. She can see the pitch-black silhouettes of the Hills, towering above them. To the side, she can see dark outlines of buildings, but she has to concentrate too much to be able to look around.

They are roughly pushed through a door, the sudden brightness inside making her blink. Once inside the building, the guards divide the group with newcomers up by the colour of their shoulder patches. Macia is alone. The guard brings her to a small room and gestures towards a chair with his chin. The large guard lowers himself into a comfortable looking chair behind a small desk. "Macia Durus, former AMP, mmmm, how the mighty have fallen," he smirks, and glances at her. "Oh, no trial, well, that kind of thing makes my day," and he laughs. Macia swallows, wondering if she should protest being here. He has just admitted that she has had no trial, no chance to defend herself, nothing. "You understand the lack of a hearing and trial is not good news," he suddenly asks, looking at her over the paper, as if he had read her thoughts. Macia grips her blanket tighter and decides to give it a try. She shakes her head, but before she can pull her usual face, he snorts. "No, the hidden ones never do," then after wrinkling up his nose in disgust he explains, "No hearing or trial means that you have confirmed by words or actions that you have a faith. Or a belief system that is opposed to Elabi rule. You must have shown that you have followed a faith. Do you deny having a religion?" Macia hesitates, what does he mean? The man rolls his eyes, his jaws clench together, and after taking a deep, noisy breath through his nose he says, "Do you deny that you believe in God?" Macia goes pale like she did when the man with the dreadful voice mentioned the same, and just like him, the guard is satisfied. "Well, got that little point cleared up," he says, looking satisfied.

Macia looks down at her bound hands, her eyes stinging. The man's voice makes her look up, as he explains to her, "You will watch a video. That will explain life in the hills. After that, you will be taken to your sleeping quarters. As an Irredeemable Mansit, you will be in the shared quarters. Tomorrow you will not go to work. You will be assigned a workplace. You will be shown around the shared areas and…" the guard looks at another paper, and smiles, making Macia shudder, her teeth clattering together, "and as you are an Irredeemable Mansit, you will also be privileged to watch the Requipacem of another Irredeemable." When he sees Macia's blank look, he rolls his eyes and says, as if talking to an ignorant child, "It's when an Irredeemable chooses Restfulness, or when their family agrees to their restful departure from beyond the Hills." Macia has no idea what to make of that, so she dips her head, her stomach churning. The man gives a short laugh, making Macia suddenly wonder what she should do if she can't hold on to her dinner any longer.

The guard gets up and switches on a large screen hanging on the plain wall.

Then he leaves the room without a backward look, slamming the door behind him. Macia is alone. She lowers her shoulders a little, then, spotting the camera in the corner, swallows and looks as attentive as she can at the large screen. A woman in guards' uniform has appeared on the screen, staring at Macia. "Welcome to the Hills. As the wearer of yellow patches, you have been sent beyond the hills for belief systems that would poison Elabi. As such, most of you will be irredeemable, unless your papers have specified differently. This means that you will have no chance to return to Elabi City. You may, however, be able to reach a certain age and status that allows you to retire Downstream, rather than request or be handed your Requipacem order. Where possible, Requipacem will be witnessed by new arrivals or Mansits with special status." Macia shudders at the word, she still doesn't know what it means, but as it's opposed to going Downstream, she's sure that it won't be good.

The woman goes on to describe life beyond the Hills. The curfew rules, the workplaces, and food distribution. Macia smoothes out her face as best as she can when she hears that Mansits with yellow patches are the last in line for food. She is exhausted, and most of what the woman says passes by her, too many impressions and new rules to absorb it all. She knows they will be watching her, so she tries to stop herself from nodding off.

Once the video has ended a female guard appears, gesturing towards the door with her chin. Macia stands up, swaying a little, and follows the woman outside. It feels a lot cooler now, and Macia shivers, hugging her blanket close. The woman walks for some time and stops outside a large building. She opens the door, and Macia steps inside. The smell is the first thing she notices, and she smothers a cough. Once her eyes get used to the little light there is, she can see the rows of beds. The guard pushes her forward and takes Macia to an empty bed. She grabs Macia's chains, and moving the numbers around, opens the cuffs. Macia sighs with relief, making the guard's head come up with an angry glare. Macia avoids looking at the guard but rubs her bruised wrists instead. The guard gives a sniff, and Macia raises her chin a little but the guard has gone already. Macia lies down on the hard mattress, rearranges the very thin pillow, drapes the woollen blanket over herself, and stares into the darkness. From around her come sleeping noises. People grunting, moaning, sniffing in the dark room and Macia clenches her jaws to stop the sobs from escaping. She is beyond the Hills.

"Dearest friend," she starts, "I don't know what to even write, it's all too awful for words. I'm called Irredeemable, and all that I can say to that is that I'm redeemed already. I know I'm in Christ, and

I know that He is here, in my bonds. Actually, my bonds have gone, but still…" She thinks through the events of the last hour or so, and tears drop suddenly. "It's the woman in the tubular," she thinks of the soft voice piercing the darkness, "and it seems they thought she was irredeemable, but she is now even nearer to God than I am. I'm very scared, beloved, because of that word they have mentioned. Talking about restfulness and the way he did it, I'm so scared." She thinks of the guard's face, and the shakes return. Then Macia thinks of the verses on the thin pages. "I will have to remind myself, beloved, otherwise I might lose all joy and peace before it's even daytime!" So she rolls onto her back, and pictures herself sitting in the sun, reading the words, turning the thin pages reverently. Soon she is fast asleep.

Chapter 36

Macia wakes up, the loud clanging bell reverberating through her head. She blinks and watches the other women in the room getting up. They all seem to have slept in their dull grey dresses, and Macia slowly slides out of bed. She hangs back a little, not sure what to do. She looks around, and one of the women notices her looking. The woman's eyes immediately travel to Macia's shoulder, and the woman pulls a face. "A Hidden One, well, that's great," she sniffs and after glaring at Macia walks away. Macia straightens her shoulders, and follows the woman through the door, making sure she's last.

It is still cool outside, and she breathes in deeply. Looking around she sees other barracks nearby and across the main dusty street are smaller white houses.

It isn't a very long walk, and Macia can smell the pottage before they reach the large whitewashed building. Inside the room it is dark, and her eyes struggle to adjust. Macia sees long tables with benches on either side, and the long line of women queued up for food. She lines up but one woman, after a quick glance over her shoulder whispers, "Not you, you're yellow. You come after those over there," and she gestures with her chin towards a small group with blue patches. Macia swallows and backs away slowly, ending up behind the people with the blue squares.

Just then she spots two women and a man with yellow patches, and she feels relieved. At least she's not the only one. Maybe they believe too, but as she joins them, they barely raise their chins at her. She glances at them sideways, trying to determine whether those three are in God as well. The man glares at her when he catches her eye and Macia looks away. The other two say nothing, but one has yellow skin, and the other one looks old. Macia nibbles her nail, absent-mindedly. Not much joy here, she thinks, following the slow line filing past the Mansits doling out pottage. She grabs a bowl from the tray when the others do so, and finds herself at the very end of the queue. Just when the yellow-skinned woman holds out her bowl, the Mansit looks in his large cauldron, and says, "Aw, who'd have thought. I have clean run out." Then laughs. The second Mansit looks in his cauldron with an exaggerated look and shakes his head in mock disappointment. "Well," the first one continues, pulling a long face, "looks like you're not served today, but you know, every day is a good day in Elabi, so who knows, you might be back in the city, and have plenty to eat."

The man just in front of Macia takes a snorting breath and pushes forward a little.

"Surely there is at least some left? I work in the factory, I do, and I need to…" But before he has finished a guard appears just behind him. The two Mansits holding the cauldron struggle to stop their grins from showing. They greet the guard extra politely, raising their chins respectfully.

"Is there a problem?" Macia is sure the guard hopes that the answer is yes. The first Mansit dips his head, and explains that the cauldrons are empty. The guard nods, "Extra large tubular last night," he explains to nobody in particular, "that often happens the first morning. Thing to do is work your way up the line," he looks at the yellow-skinned lady and the man in disdain, "and by lunchtime, there should be enough for everybody."

The man opens his mouth again to protest, but the guard suddenly produces a rubbery looking stick and starts tapping it on the palm of his other hand, narrowing his eyes at him. Macia gives a soft gasp, surely he wouldn't hit another person? Judging by the man's reaction, she is quite sure that the guard would, for he slumps back into place, shaking a little. The woman with the yellow skin is crying softly until the guard turns to her. "That's a lot of emotion there, and not much self-control I can see. Maybe you should come with me to a special class?" The woman sucks her lips in, and blinks rapidly, shaking her head, stumbling back a little. Macia purses her lips a little; surely the woman isn't against learning more, attending special courses? Is that why she has yellow patches? Macia is glad that she hasn't cried publicly; imagine going emotional in front of all these people.

She looks back at the Mansits behind the cauldrons, her stomach growling. She follows the other three out of the room again, wondering what to do. Some of the others have eaten already, and the same woman who had helped her before appears at her elbow again. "Back to barracks, wash hands and face," she whispers without looking at Macia. Macia feels grateful for the woman, wondering what the red patches stand for. Washing her hands feels good, the water cold and refreshing. Macia quickly looks around, then drinks several handfuls of water, hoping it will make her feel less hungry. Just as she dries her hands on her dress, a guard shouts out, "Yellow Durus?" Macia feels her face heat up instantly, and she looks up, doing her best to look a little bored as if she's used to be called Yellow. As she walks towards the guard, she tries to walk as tall as she can, and automatically reaches to tuck a loose strand of hair behind her ear, but clenches a fist as her shaking finger encounters the very short stubble that is all that is left of her long auburn hair. She clenches her jaws, fury at the guard, the council, the whole system flaming through her for a moment.

The guard's face is cold, and after a quick glance at Macia, she starts towards the door, clearly expecting Macia to follow. For a second she wonders what would happen if she simply stayed behind. Then she remembers the rubbery looking baton.

The guard takes her to a small building and motions her inside. There is a large hatch inside, and a yellow looking Mansit looks at her with tired eyes. "Yellow?" his voice sounds as tired as he looks, and the guard adds that hated word, Irredeemable. Macia flushes, ready to argue. The guard raises a shocked eyebrow at her and Macia changes her mind. The Mansit grabs a block of soap from a stack to the side and flicks it off the hatch. It lands on the floor, and skids along a little. Macia glares at him, but he merely smirks. The guard clicks impatiently, and Macia decides it's probably better to pick up the soap. As she leans over, the guard suddenly bumps her, making her lose her balance, hurting her knee, still sore from the fall down her steps. Macia cries out in pain as well as anger, but when she turns around, the guard is tapping her hand with her baton, just like the male guard had done in the dining room. Macia clenches her jaws and digs her fingers into the hard soap. When the guard leaves the building Macia rubs her jaws, they are sore and it's giving her a headache. But how is she to stay calm?

The guard takes her back to her barrack, now completely empty. There is one bed with a scrunched up blanket. At Macia's bed, she points at the small cubby hole and tells Macia to put her soap there. Macia does so, her hands shaking a little, afraid the woman will hurt her again. Apparently, the woman has some heart left, for in a not too unkind voice she says, "Wash your dress one night after work, undies the next night. It'll all dry quick enough, you'll be glad about the coolness." Macia dips her head, relaxing a fraction, until the woman continues, "Being Irredeemable, you'll probably not live that long anyway," and laughs. Macia gives a little gasp, but the woman has marched towards the door again. "I will show you around your workplace."

Walking into the cloth factory makes Macia feel dizzy. It's darker inside, and only marginally cooler. Large machines rattle and clang; there is noise and movement everywhere. A quick first glance shows weaving machines, being worked by various Mansits. Others push handcarts around with yarn or huge bales of cloth. The factory has a funny smell, and Macia wrinkles her nose a little, tempted to cover her ears. The guard leans over and shouts, "Follow me, watch your step." Macia follows and soon realises the floor is wet. No puddles can be seen, just general dampness. It's cooling on her sore feet, but it is slippery, and she makes sure to heed the guard's warning.

The guard stops and shows a woman climbing on and off a small platform, handing up yarn to one of the workers. It looks tiring work, and the woman looks hot. Macia notices that it isn't done very quickly, and tries to hold onto that for her tiny speck of joy. Further down the line, two people hand up the yarn to another two Mansits reaching down. Macia wonders what the difference is.

The guard leans over again. "That will be your job. Don't fall into the machine whatever you do," and she smirks, then adds, "as you're yellow, you will be doing the lifting and handing over yourself." Macia dips her head politely, knowing it will hide the anger in her eyes. Saves her from clenching her jaws again. She follows the guard outside, dodging various workers, her head pounding with the noise already. She is relieved to be out, shocked at the brightness of the sun. The hot earth hurts her feet, and she moves carefully from one foot to the other whilst waiting for the guard who is exchanging words with another guard. "Soft feet, have we?" the woman laughs, "you might get used to it, but you'll probably be gone by the time you have hard feet." Macia looks away.

Macia's guard looks at a large tower in the open space between numerous factories and nods. "Time to go," she says, and they're off. Macia is sweating and light-headed by the time they have crossed the open square. She is desperate for food, wondering how much longer till lunchtime, and whether she'll even make it. Maybe the guard is right, she might not live very long. "Beloved, I have learned in whatsoever state I am, therewith to be content," but even her beautiful pen struggles to write the words. So distracted is she by her writing, that she almost bumps into the guard. The woman tuts, and glares at Macia, and Macia shuffles back. Another guard arrives at the same time, bringing two people that Macia recognises from the tubular. It lifts her spirits a little, at least it's familiar faces. The others don't look at her though, clearly distancing themselves from a Hidden One. Macia looks away, pretending to take in her surroundings, blinking against the bright sunlight. Together they walk on, past more barracks, something that looks like a shop, past a gymnasium. "Not for yellow ones," her guard sneers, when she sees Macia's face light up.

Soon they're standing outside a building, a sign with a pestle and mortar on the door. It's the sanatorium, and Macia is surprised to see it beyond the Hills. Of course, Mansits could still get ill, and with those factories around, there will be accidents. She shudders when she thinks of the guard's warning not to fall into the machines.

They go inside, and the building is wonderfully cool. They follow the guards and are soon standing in a small room, with thick glass separating them from another room. In that room is one large chair, and a machine, nothing else. They are told to sit on benches. Macia is glad to sit down, shivering a little at the temperature change, trying to keep her feet slightly off the floor. The other Mansits move away from her. She frowns and purses her lips, but as she sees the guards still hanging around she keeps the sharp words inside. There'll be another time. She looks at the room in front of them, sure this is the

Requipacem the guard talked about last night.

A guard with a white apron walks in, looks around and leaves. More Mansits and guards arrive. Macia feels drowsy. She wonders what would happen if she dozes off for a moment but before she can try, the aproned guard reappears. "This morning," her voice is loud and sharp, making Macia wince a little, "the Mansit you will see was an Irredeemable. Despite that, she had done her work well and attended all appointed classes. As she requested Requipacem herself, she has been given the option to administer it herself. That was a major concession," she glares directly at Macia as if she had disagreed, "as normally Irredeemables are just that, irredeemable. The City council believes in people showing themselves willing to learn, ready to accept the council's guidance, so this Mansit has been rewarded for her attitude."

She walks out, her crisp apron making a sound that makes Macia cringe. The door slams shut, and it goes quiet. Macia glances at the other Mansits, their faces pale. Do they know more about Requipacem? One Mansit looks very tired, and he is shaking all over. Every time he breathes out he makes a low moaning noise, and Macia can feel her irritation growing. It is impossible to block out the noise, and she feels like pointing out to him that they're all in the same way affected, and maybe he should practise more self-control. Before she can say anything, the door opposite their room opens, and an old Mansit shuffles in. Her eyes are wide, and two nurses support her. They bring the woman to the chair. She lowers herself in it, then suddenly tries to stand up again. Immediately both nurses force her down, and soon the old lady is strapped into the chair with a special seatbelt, and a wrist strap on her one hand. One of the nurses says something, and the woman shakes her head vigorously. Macia stares, unable to look away.

The nurses stand to the side and smirk at the frightened faces behind the glass. The woman looks up too, and her eyes widen even more. She tugs at the seatbelt and turns to the nurse who says something to her. All at once, the nurse produces one of the short batons, swinging it loosely by the wrist strap. The old woman holds her hand out as if to protect herself from the baton. The nurse points at the machine with the baton, and after a moment the woman presses the large red button. Within seconds, it looks like the old woman has fallen asleep in the large chair, and it is only the loud moaning of the older Mansit in the room that makes Macia suddenly realise. The woman is gone! Her life has ended. Here, beyond the Hills, in front of all of them. No Downstream, no privacy, but with strangers who have watched her life end. Suddenly her light-headedness overcomes Macia, and she gives a little gasp as she slips off the wooden bench onto the floor with a dull thud, the white walls spiralling into blackness.

Chapter 37

The heat and glaring light hurt her as soon as she opens her eyes. Macia squints against the light, straight into the face of the female guard. The guard doesn't look impressed. "I hadn't taken you for the emotional, weak type," she says, her face hard. Macia licks her dry lips, and feels indignation more than anything else, her head feeling wobbly on her neck. The guard smirks as soon as she sees Macia's face, "Ah well, just a lapse in judgment then," she says and nudges Macia with her foot. "Get up, Yellow," she says, all mirth gone. Macia gets up, swaying a little, her feet hurting as soon as they feel the hot earth. The others are leaving the building, throwing dark looks at Macia. Only the older Mansit who had been moaning looks at her a second longer, his eyes sad. A bell sounds, echoing off the steep hills rising up behind the buildings, their bare slopes reflecting the sunlight. The guard points across the road towards the long building Macia recognises as the dining hall. "Get your lunch, you have classes this afternoon, or did you think leaving Elabi City behind made you into an adult already?"

Macia dips her head and walks off straight away. Classes? Actually, she had forgotten about her education, the last week or so had been strange. She doesn't even know what day of the week it is. She tries not to think of the week just gone, or too much about the days ahead either. Her breath turns into little desperate gasps every time she thinks of what she has just seen. Her body needs food, especially if she has school this afternoon. Do they have Hexaday and Enday off? She enters the dining room and is glad to see it mostly empty. Does that mean she will have to wait her turn until all the Mansits in the Hills have been served? She decides to be bold and walks up to the serving Mansits. She takes a plate from the stack and holds it out, making her face look a little bored, avoiding eye contact. The Mansit lands two slices of flatbread on her plate, dark as always, but with it are a small scoop of olives and a thin slice of meat.

Macia is pleased, then reminds herself of her weeks as Amplissimos and the servings she received in school every day, and her thankfulness disappears. She sits down on one of the benches, looking at her plate, her shoulders down. Her stomach growls, glad to have sustenance coming its way at last. Macia can feel her face warming up, and whilst eating, she decides to write in her head at the same time. She keeps her eyes fixed on her plate, pulls out a crisp sheet, gold pen and starts writing. "Dearest friend, I'm beyond the Hills, but not beyond writing to you. This morning," she stops, her heart racing, palms sweaty. She grabs the rough table tightly, willing her swimming head to stop and her heart to calm down. She takes a few slow, deep breaths, the olives smelling too strong.

"Beloved, I can't tell you how awful it was this morning, I can never talk about it. God knows, and that is all that matters at the moment, as it's too dreadful to think about any more. I ask Him to take care of me all the time, and I need Him to calm my mind. The factory is easier to describe." She remembers the noise and movement, eating slowly, enjoying the meat. She's pretty sure it's goat. It is getting busier, and Macia carries on writing, "Beloved, I will have to eat up, as I'm a yellow, ha. That's all I am for now, not even a Mansit, no, just a yellow, an Irredeemable. Who knows what will happen if I don't eat up. Dearest, I'm scared."

She picks up her empty plate and returns it to the hatch where she has seen others take their plates. The heat outside hits her, and Macia walks to her barrack, not sure where else to go. She decides to wash her hands, more to have something to do than anything else. The guard suddenly appears, her eyes narrowed, and she hisses, "What do you think you're doing? Who gave you permission to waste water in the middle of the day?" Macia stares and the guard lowers the raised baton then points at the door with it. "Get out, and I will let it go this time, Yellow. You are no longer in your precious villa or wherever you used to live. Walk!"

Macia follows the guard once outside, and soon they reach a large building, which turns out to be the education building. Macia is glad to feel the coolness inside, wondering how her education will be combined with working in the factory. "Sit down, do not ask questions." The man has a red face and looks angry, and Macia sits down at the desk appointed to her. The man stomps around the room, grabs a small scrap of paper off his desk, his heavy footsteps making her desk shake as he returns, slamming the paper on her desk. "Your timetable," he says, and looking at her yellow patches, his scowl settles in even more. Macia dips her head, and the man snorts.

Macia is relieved when he walks up to another student who has just walked in. She looks down on the little piece of paper and swallows as she sees her schedule. Work in the factory appears twice each day, in between are classes, and after dinner there are more classes. Time to eat will be minimal, and she suddenly understands the rush in the dining hall this morning. She will be rushing as well. If there is food, that is. No Hexaday off, but at least Enday is free apart from 'training'. She assumes they are extra lectures. Will they be compulsory?

"My name is Grabus," the teacher's harsh guttural voice makes her look up, "I will be your main tutor, although most of the work will be done independently. Soon you will have another tutor, as my stay here is very short term, as I was actually an Umbo." Macia watches the snarl on his face at these last words, and she purses her lips. With that kind of attitude he might find himself beyond the Hills that little bit longer, she thinks. He sees her face, and before she can correct herself, Grabus has made a mark on a large sheet of paper. "Yellow Irredeemable," he sneers, "you have just received a class mark. It won't bring you down much further I would imagine, but no progress upwards has been made, even if you could."

Macia looks down at her desk, her eyes burning. How dare he, he was an Umbo, he must have known that she used to be an Amplissimos. She knows she has seen him before, but where? The paper handed out is a dreadful quality, and the pencil isn't much better. Macia wonders how much paper they will be given each time. Do they need to hand the paper in as well? "That is for calculations and preparation," Grabus says, almost reluctantly handing out a slightly better sheet of paper. "Even though you are a Yellow, you are given the same as other students." He glares at her, and she dips her head, trying to show a hint of gratefulness, balancing her usual school face. "This is for handing in assignments. You will receive new paper each new moon. You might not get that many papers," and he pulls his lips in a smile, his eyes looking mean. "You might be here even shorter term than I am," he adds, and Macia feels her face warm up. She grips her fingers together under her desk to stop them from shaking. They feel cold, but she is determined not to give in to fear.

She will be careful, she will work hard, and on no account will she ever accept Requipacem, so she might just be their longest term Yellow Irredeemable ever. The assignment doesn't sound too difficult, and Macia is relieved when they are given the right study book to look at. "I used to be a bookshop manager," Grabus says, half dropping a thick book on her desk, his greasy hand resting on the cover. "People like you wouldn't even be allowed in my shop, so I hope you will be suitably grateful to the council, and possibly even redeem yourself. There is always Requipacem as well, of course," he looks at her, and Macia bends her head a little, hiding her wet eyes.

"I must not be emotional, beloved, or I will be in more trouble. But that word makes my stomach turn, and I can't forget..." She stops, no, she can't tell her paper what she saw. She desperately misses her journal though, and seeing the rough paper reminds her of the times spent scribbling away, sharing her thoughts. A plan forms, after all, if it's a narrow strip, nobody will realise. She will need to be careful though, too many eyes around here.

Classes end when a loud clanging bell announces work time. Macia is relieved, her head hurts, and it is hard to concentrate. Now what? Does she need to go to the factory? The female guard is waiting for her at the door, and instead of going outside, she points with her chin at the corridor. "Training classes as well, as you're new, yellow and irredeemable." Her voice sounds mean, but her eyes look at Macia without spite for a change. Macia dips her head and follows the guard. The room is large, and several Mansits are sitting down already. She recognises people from the tubular, including the toothless man. He ignores her, and Macia sits down by herself, a little bit away from the others.

Soon the large screen is lowered, and the video appears. It is the same person as last night, which now seems a very long time ago. Macia listens carefully, making sure her face shows her attentiveness without looking eager. She has to redeem herself a little, and most importantly, she has to blend in, as she needs paper and a quiet corner to write, to talk to God and to think about the paragraphs on the very thin paper.

The lecture carries on for quite some time. After a short break, in which they are escorted to bathrooms, then brought back to the same room, the second lecture starts. Macia suppresses a yawn, turning it into a cough, and is relieved when the second lecture finishes just as the loud bell starts up again. Dinner time. She knows she will need to hurry this time. One, she will need to be in line with all the yellows, and two, she has classes afterwards, and she can't be late for those. Finding the way to the dining room is easy, and Macia sighs with relief to be inside. Her feet hurt, and she is sure she's got blisters all over them. If she could, she would have run from the school, to stop the hot dusty street from burning her. She blinks away tears of pain, missing her beautiful soft sandals. Dinner is millet, of course, but it comes with some purple carrot and small pieces of meat. The long benches are full, and Macia hesitates. Does she sit down? She spots the other yellow woman from this morning, standing near the wall, eating rapidly. The man is standing too, but leaning over to grab a bottle from the table to sprinkle something on his food. Garum! Macia's heart does a merry jig; garum will make everything so much better. She steps forward, trying to move quietly, unobtrusive and smooth so as not to draw attention to herself. When she gets the bottle and sprinkles a little on her millet she pulls a face. Allec. Of course, why would they feed garum to Mansits? They're the lowest of the low here, and so is their sauce. Well, at least it's better than nothing.

She eats quickly, hungry after the long afternoon, then returns the bowl to the hatch, and leaves the dining hall. She hesitates on the doorstep, reluctant to put her feet on the scorching hot road. However, with no choice she walks back to the school building, trying to tread lightly, taking quick steps without making it look rushed. She gives small gasps with each step, her eyes watering by the time she gets to the building. Inside the floor is lovely and cool, and Macia takes even smaller steps, rolling the soles of her feet against the floor in turn.

The assignments carry on, a video shows them more of the numeric assignment and classes finish with a video about the need for assignments to be handed in correctly and at the right time. "There will be a record of each student's assignment and its standard," the video concludes, "and it is important to remember this. Beyond the Hills is a unique area designed to foment growth, instil values and give each citizen a chance to redeem themselves up to a certain extent. Failure to embrace this opportunity is a very grave matter for all concerned." The voice lacks all emotion, and Macia shudders a little. She has heard warnings like this before. It sounds positive, but she is sure after all she has been through that there is another side to it.

Walking back to her barrack after class she whispers softly, "God, I feel so alone. And Lord, I suddenly realised something while watching that last video. I'm seen as Irredeemable, and to Elabi I am, I suppose. There is nothing I can do to change myself or my state. But God, I was like that before I was found in You, as well. I knew nothing about You, but unlike the video, it wasn't a threat that made me listen, it was You pouring Your grace in my heart."

She smiles a little as she walks to her bed, putting her papers away, too exhausted to try to rip a narrow strip off the paper for now. Also, they'll be more likely to watch her as she is new. She will have to do it sometime when she manages to be alone. She watches some of the other women return from the washroom with wet dresses, which reminds her, so retrieving her block of soap, Macia makes her way to the washroom. The cold water feels good, and soon she is in bed, the barrack dark, staring up at the ceiling, thinking about the day, but not for long. It's making her heart cringe, and instead, Macia pictures herself in her windowsill at home, reading the very thin pages, the words making her smile in the dark, drying her wet cheeks on her damp shoulder.

Chapter 38

The clanging bell wakes Macia and she groans. Several times during the night she found herself sitting up in bed, sweating, her heart drumming away wildly. She slips out of bed, trying to straighten her dress. Maybe going to sleep in a wet dress wasn't the best thing. Macia follows the other women to the dining hall, hoping there will be enough pottage this morning. There is, and she helps herself to the allec as well. The pottage is thick and warm, almost hot. She eats quickly, her stomach tight. What will the factory be like?

She walks to the barracks to wash afterwards, glad with the cool water. At least she can wash her hair and face easily with her hair cropped, she smiles, her eyes stinging. She liked her long hair. Macia swallows, no point thinking about the past now, she needs to focus on surviving. She walks to the door, and just outside, in the shade, is the female guard. Macia raises her chin at the woman, which earns her a glare. She follows the woman down the dusty road to the factory. Once inside the guard takes her to a thin woman with dark eyes. The woman glares at Macia's yellow patches. Macia looks away, trying to make her face look bland.

The guard leaves and Macia follows the bony woman to a trolley filled with large spools, and a big step towards the weaving loom. The noise is as deafening as it was the day before, and the woman motions to Macia. "Yarn. Up. Give. Down. Next." She looks at Macia to see if the girl understands. She does. Macia dips her head, and don't fall in the machine, she reminds herself, giving a little shudder. The woman nods towards the trolley and walks away. Macia takes a deep breath, her first working day. She grabs one of the spools which is heavier than she expected. She struggles to get a good grip on the damp yarn and turns to the platform. With the spool in her hands, she climbs onto the little platform. She's gasping by the time she stands up, handing the heavy spool to the thin, yellowed man. He grabs it without even looking at her, and Macia slips down the platform, trying to catch her breath. The air in the factory is hot and very humid, and she flexes her arms a few times. She can do this, she is fit, after all. With a steadying breath, she grabs hold of the next spool, wishing she had someone to do it with her

The morning turns into a tiring blur. Her arms and shoulders ache and her breath comes in gasps. She keeps wiping the sweat off her face and has a few sudden landings when trying to get off the platform. Every surface is slippery, and so are her hands and feet. Macia casts anxious looks at the large loom, forcing her eyes back to the spool in her arms. When getting off the platform, she looks over at the next loom, noting the way the woman carries the spool up onto the step. Macia lugs the next spool into her arms as the woman did, and finds it easier to get up the platform that way.

The loud clanging bell makes her almost lose her footing, but she wobbles straight. The old man comes off the platform too and walks past her to the exit. Macia decides to follow him, after hesitating for a second. Does she leave the trolley with spools? A look towards the other platforms confirms this. Outside, she blinks against the glaring sun as well as the pain on her feet from the hot sandy road. Macia makes her way to the dining hall. Approaching it from this side, she sees the rows of taps, and the other factory workers quickly washing their hands. She is relieved, for her hands are sweaty and dirty, the

246

damp linen thread on the spools making her hands feel sticky. The water is cold, and although she is aching all over, Macia is satisfied with her first morning. Waiting in the queue, she decides to write in her head, making sure to stare at her feet.

"Dearest friend, I have just had my first morning working. It's not the dream job I had looked forward to, no teaching or helping role, but rather hard, sweaty work. I managed though, and there have been no accidents either." Macia thinks about the morning, wondering if she'll get used to it enough to be able to think about the thin pages or even her own diary whilst working. "Beloved, it's hot in the factory, and the spools were heavy. My arms ache and so does my back, but hopefully, I will get used to it soon."

Macia is glad to be in school that afternoon. Sitting down is wonderful despite the hardback desk chair. She struggles to stay awake for some of the videos and has to rub her eyes to keep them open. The clanging noise means she has to return to the factory. The factory is hot, hotter than it was in the morning, and still humid. Macia struggles to breathe, having difficulty lifting the heavy spools. Her legs and arms tremble with the effort, and she finds herself wobbling a few times when turning to step off the platform. It scares her and she slows her movements. It helps, and she can still get the spool to the old man before he is waiting for her. Macia can tell that he is moving slower as well. A few times he struggles to take the spool from her. She tries to smile at him to encourage him, but he looks at her yellow patches and gives her a hateful look. Macia sighs. She frowns, wipes her face again, steadying herself and picks up the next spool. One of the small paragraphs comes to mind, telling her to be tenderhearted, forgiving and kind. So when she hands the man the next spool, she forces herself to smile the same little smile at him, trying to find it in her to forgive him, to think kindly of him. The man narrows his eyes a little, but no longer glares. When the loud clanging tells them it is dinner time, Macia slowly slides off the platform, her body shaking. She is exhausted.

She staggers to the dining hall, not really feeling the burning pain from her tired feet. She washes her hands with the cold water, splattering a bit to get it on her arms and her face as well.

The millet is hot, and the allec makes the pieces of meat and cabbage taste even better. She is hungry, and Macia doesn't care that she has no seat. She scrapes the bowl empty, tempted for a second to clean it out with her finger, but stops herself. She feels her face heat up. Where are her manners? What an emotional reaction to food.

Sitting down in school feels good, but her body aches all over. Trying to concentrate is almost impossible, and a few times she finds her eyes turning into a squint at her efforts to keep them open. Fortunately, Grabus' loud voice and stomping footsteps help to keep her on track in the lesson, but she is nearly crying with relief when the day is over. She stumbles back to the barrack, craving sleep, knowing she will need to do some washing first. If she doesn't, she might be told on, and who knows what will happen. She is half nodding off by the time she gets to her bed, and asleep before her head hits the pillow.

The morning bells sound too soon, and Macia groans out loud when she tries to sit up. The woman next to her whispers on the way out, "It will get better," and Macia smiles at her, glad about the kind words. She struggles to eat her pottage, her arms stiff and shaking with the effort. After climbing up and down the platform for a while, her muscles loosen up, and Macia finds she's feeling a little better. Nevertheless, the morning drags on, and she is sobbing by the time the lunch bell sounds. She keeps her head down on her way to the dining hall, not wanting anybody to notice her wet eyes. She washes her face as well as her hands, using the opportunity to dry her eyes. The thin slices of bread have some hard cheese with it today as well as some radishes. The strong flavour does her good, and Macia feels herself recovering a little, looking forward to the cool education building, and the chance to sit down. Her feet feel sore and bruised all over, and Macia stretches her legs under her desk. She realises she will need to use her time and energy wisely if she wants to survive. She has given up on scoring points and doing well. Her aim is to live, and preferably get out of the Hills alive.

Suddenly, staring wide-eyed at her school book, she remembers the water sports woman's words about the paddleboard. She has a way to get out. But where would she go? Not along the coast, that would simply bring her to the Downstream landing place. No, she would have to go the other way, out of Elabi altogether. She is so taken up with it that she doesn't hear the heavy footsteps coming close until Grabus' angry face appears close to hers. She sucks in her breath, trying to keep a straight face. "I said," Grabus' face is red, "you will need to take your book back and get ready for the next assignment. That is another class mark for you, maybe even two, seeing that you're irredeemable anyway," and he nods, stomping back to his desk. Macia swallows and carries the book back to the shelf. She doesn't even know what the marks are for, and her stomach clenches tight. Then she remembers that her aim is to survive, to stay out of trouble, and to get to the lighthouse.

In the factory, Macia works to reach this aim. "Beloved," she mumbles to herself, a tiny smile forming as she realises that the noise is so deafening, she could talk to God out loud, and nobody would hear! "Beloved, I will need to concentrate, but it feels more familiar already. I'm so very sore and so tired, I could sleep whilst walking." Her eyes sting and she wipes the sweat off her face. "I have to try and keep my mind on heavenly places, I think, otherwise I might just lose my mind completely." She patiently holds the spool for the old man as he struggles again to take the spool. That is definitely the third time he has almost dropped it, she thinks. He looks at her, briefly, and Macia forms a slight smile, willing him on. He shuffles off with the spool, and Macia returns to her cart, trying to move slowly without too much time lost. "Dearest friend, I need a friend here. Do you think God will hear me in here? Can He see me here in this dark, noisy, busy place? We all look the same, apart from our shoulder patches. Will He still know me?"

Macia can feel her shoulders weighing down, worry making it even harder to lift the spools. She straightens her shoulders. "Beloved, I will need to think of the different letters that Paul wrote. I might not be in bonds as such, but in a way I still am. So I need to rejoice, and my joy plan has gone. I will start again."

She climbs up, and half loud says, "God, I have joy, because of the woman's kindness this morning, telling me it would get better. I am grateful for food, especially the radishes." The old man stares at her, and she smiles a little. "And God, I'm asking for this man here," she can feel excitement flowing through her, making her walk faster. She is pulled up short as she slips, and her heart drops down the platform before her feet touch the ground. That was close, Macia thinks, her face rigid, her breath struggling to catch up. "God, I just know You are here, You can see and hear me, and I am glad. I'm trying to find joy, and the main thing is that I can speak to You without anybody hearing me."

Grabus glares at the slight girl with the white face. His eyes are constantly drawn to her yellow patches. Yellow. She is a Hidden One, but the council found her out. He hates her already, especially as she pretends to listen, or when she dips her head oh so politely. Just like that helper in the shop. The one who turned up, then just vanished again. The weird one. The one that landed him here. He grinds his teeth, his breath coming in little gasps. He glances at the corner where he knows the camera is. He needs to be careful. It wasn't really his fault that he got here, but showing his emotions would easily keep him here. No way will this girl be the cause of a prolonged stay. He switches the video on, telling the students what to expect. Grabus' thoughts drift off, back to Elabi. When will his term be over? Will he be able to return as a Consuete? Surely they won't keep him, an Umbo, as a Mansit on his return. He bites his lip. Hatred for the weird young lad burning in him. Always smiling, always raising his chin at all the customers, scrubbing the shelves as if his life depended on it. No thought for Grabus though. And now he is here, beyond the Hills, teaching young Mansits, and especially that Yellow Girl. It gives Grabus great pleasure to elbow Macia hard when he sees her nodding off. "Two marks," he smirks and all the way back to his desk he struggles to keep the smile off his face. He doesn't want revenge as such, but those weird people need to know the damage they do to good citizens. The pleased feeling is still there as he watches the students leave the building, the slight girl last, limping a little.

Macia shivers in the dark, her dress half wet, her hands too sore and tired to wring the material out properly. At least she's not too hot. Her thoughts drift off to sleep, and she wants to try to fall asleep whilst thinking about some of Paul's letters. She needs all the energy she can get. Maybe thinking about God and the words of Paul will help her to sleep well.

Chapter 39

Macia blinks when the clanging bell wakes her in the morning. She shivers, then gets up and rubbing her arms, follows the other women to the dining hall. She rubs her stomach which seems to be too empty all the time, gnawing away. The queue moves slower, and it doesn't look as rushed as it was the day before. Macia looks around and the older woman with the yellow skin leans over a bit. "It's Enday," she says, her voice hoarse, "you will be in the Lowest Set lectures." The relief makes Macia choke on her mouthful of pottage, but she manages to cough and nod at the same time. She eats the last few mouthfuls a little slower, savouring the hot food, wondering what the lectures will be like. Will they be given a choice? It doesn't sound like it, and Macia glares at her empty bowl. Surely an Amplissimos, or even an ex-Amplissimos, should get to hear different lectures than someone who has been a Mansit all their lives?

The lectures are similar to the courses she attended in Elabi. The only difference is the people around her. Mansits only, obviously, and most of them look worn out. Macia is glad the chairs are comfortable, and she enjoys what feels like a day off. She doesn't mind the lectures, and the fact that she can sit down for them is enough for now. The voices on the screen drone on and on, the lectures simpler than she is used to and less…encouraging. Macia only hears half of it. She needs to think, a plan has to be made. She has to live long enough to escape.

How does one escape though?

The second lecture follows straight after a short bathroom break. Macia stretches and flexes as long as she dares in the cubicle, trying to make the most of the free moment. She has to work hard to keep a straight face during this talk, as it goes on and on about the area beyond the Hills. It tells them how fortunate they are to have this opportunity. The council has given them this chance to either redeem themselves or to pay restitution for the damage they have done. Macia tries to keep her breathing calm, taking slow breaths, feeling anger growing inside. All her life she has believed in Elabi. Maybe when her mother left there was a slip, and she was a little emotional, but now, here she is, beyond the Hills and irredeemable. They still try to tell her the council has her best interests at heart?

Her stomach growls a little as if disagreeing with the video as well, and she squeezes her arms across her body. She needs to get out, and probably soon as well. The little rations they are given, the heavy work, the long hours; it will all take its toll on her and soon she will be too weak to get out. The lecture passes soon enough, and the lunch bell sounds. Macia follows the others out and finds herself waiting near the woman with the yellow patches. She whispers, "My name is Macia, who are you?" The woman looks up for a second, glances around quickly, then whilst avoiding looking at Macia's face tells her that her name is Crassia. "So, what do we do this afternoon?" Macia wonders if there will be more lectures, but Crassia informs her that the afternoon is free. Macia dips her head, relieved.

"We need to clean and tidy our bed space and barrack, and then we are free to do what we want," Crassia tells her. Macia hesitates, then asks if there is somewhere to go by yourself, just for a while to have some quiet. Crassia glances at her then looks away. "You are new," she says softly, "and you will be watched more carefully than later. If you disappear they will find you, and you might get extra lectures, or have your rations cut down." Macia's eyes widen. Less food? Crassia dips her head, "Yes, so you need to be careful. The best place is the foothills. Many herbs are growing there, and sometimes even some fruit trees or berries. You can go there, be busy doing something useful, but you'll be alone, nobody sees you." Macia can feel her heart beat faster and Crassia explains how to get to the area. "Don't go too far into the hills as the men will be there, making Hillixer." Macia dips her head and shudders as the woman gives her another hard stare. Is Hillixer forbidden here? She'd always thought everybody beyond the hills drank it.

After lunch, Macia tidies her bed area, looking at the other women. Whilst tidying and sweeping around her bed, she rips the bottom half off her paper and hides the paper and her pencil under her dress. Her hands are shaking, and she keeps her face under her bed until she is sure that her face is no longer red. When she is done, she sets off the way Crassia told her. It is hot, but Macia is determined to be by herself. She has taken the cleaning rag they were given after lunch, hoping to find extra food.

The air is still, and Macia finally gets to look around. She had noticed already that to call this area beyond the hills isn't actually very accurate. The other side of the barracks and factories has more Hills, steeper ones than the one dividing them from Elabi City. The hills are a red rusty colour, barren apart from the foothills. The rest of the hills are interspersed with sharp, narrow gullies, and nearer the built-up area, some of those gullies are green, water cascading down the steep slopes. One or two hills have plateaus that are covered in green as well, but most of the hills are barren. Nothing moves on the slopes, and only a few large birds float in the air above the greener areas.

The built-up part of the Hills area is extensive, with long barracks, a few smaller houses and several factories. There are the sanatorium, the education building and some smaller offices and workhouses. Towards the foothills beyond the area are olive groves, vineyards and orchards. In the hot, still air she can hear the bleating of goats. It all seems so peaceful and quiet, but Macia shivers.

Soon she reaches the foothills standing between her and home. These hills are more covered in shrubs and small trees although the ground is very rocky, with some of the hills simply covered in spree. Macia's eyes devour the scene, looking for a pass, a road, a path. The sunlight reflecting off the rocks makes her head swim, and her feet hurt from the rocky path. Her eyes burn and she keeps looking up towards the summits as if longing to scale them and run back to where she belongs. Except she doesn't belong there anymore. The only reason to go back would be to get the thin papers. She misses the words by Paul, struggling sometimes to recall them correctly. Maybe she should use her spare bit of paper to copy some of Paul's words, rather than write her diary. After all, her diary can be written in her head, but Macia is afraid of forgetting more and more of the letters. Those promises, telling her that she is in God, and how He has chosen her, adopted her, made her to be a partaker of His heavenly blessings… what if she forgets?

Macia slows down looking at the small green plants. She stoops down to pick a few herbs that she recognises, glad about the cookery course she attended last winter. Ignava had enrolled her, which had made Macia angry, as she had another course in mind. "God, maybe You knew already what I needed," she smiles, smelling another little bush. Macia makes sure she starts drifting off the path, slowly of course, and moving from one bush or tree to the next, to make sure it looks natural. There might be guards watching her, and they need to be convinced that she is merely collecting herbs and food. After a while she sinks down under a large tree, her back leaning against the rough bark. It's so quiet up here. It reminds her of her long walks to the water sports centre.

Macia is exhausted, her body trembling. She eats the berries she has picked as well as two peaches. They're only just ripe, but it will have to do. It does help her to feel better, and Macia leans her head back against the tree, whispering softly. "Thank You, God, for helping me so far. I didn't mean to complain, I know You give me spiritual blessings, but the fear inside me seems to take over. I want to live, Lord, and I know that being with You is gain, but there is so much I still want to do. I will accept the end of my life, of course, for I know You do all things well for me." She stares ahead for a moment, does she? Can she actually say those words? Yes, she decides, she has to accept those words, even when her feelings aren't quite there yet.

Macia eats the last of her berries, then tries to sing the song the old woman had sung on the tubular. Macia liked it very much and wonders where the old woman learned it. But the words and tune have been half-forgotten already. After a quick look round she pulls the paper and pencil out and writes down the words. She can't remember all of them, but it's a good start, and she could always make up the words for the gaps. It's wonderful to be able to sing about God, and Macia laughs softly with pleasure. Next she writes, in small letters to save her precious paper, "For unto you it is given...in Christ." She hesitates, was it in Christ? "...not only to believe in Him, but also to suffer for His name." Name? She isn't sure, but it was something like that. It was just before Paul wrote that one day everybody would bow down before Jesus, kneel before Him and acknowledge Him. She looks at the buildings shimmering in the heat, their white walls glaring in the bright light, and tries to imagine the guards, Grabus, the Mansits handing out food, as well as all the people living in those barracks all bowing down before Jesus.

Soon it is time to return to the barrack, and Macia struggles off the ground. She drinks a bit more from the little stream nearby, then slowly walks back. Her legs are shaking by the time she gets to the barrack. She wonders what to do with the herbs, but just as she stands near the door, looking at the herbs in her cloth, the woman who has been friendly before appears. "This way," she says and looks around quickly. Macia clenches her jaws; the woman obviously doesn't want to be seen with a Yellow. The woman takes her to the washing area, and hands Macia a chipped bowl from a shelf. Macia puts the herbs in the bowl with some water. "You can keep your bowl there," the woman points and Macia puts her bowl with the other two that are there already. She turns round to thank the woman, but she has gone already. Macia turns back to her herbs, pushing them down into the water a little, then goes inside as well. She lies down on her bed exhausted, even though the walk was not nearly as long as the walk to the paddleboard sessions.

Macia closes her eyes, to make people think she's dozing off. "Beloved," she writes, her pen smooth on the white paper. "I went for a walk to the foothills, collecting fruit and herbs. I'm so tired, but it was lovely to go out and to be by myself for a while. I talked to God." She smiles a little, growing more serious when thinking about her conversation with God, then continues, "I wonder when to eat my herbs. I might take some of them with me to the dining hall to mix into my millet. Dearest friend, I need to get out of here, I'm so exhausted, my legs are shaking, just from my walk. I don't know if there is a way out through the hills? Do I climb them? Surely somebody would see me in the daytime, and to climb those rocky hills at night doesn't sound like a good idea. I wonder what happens if they catch you trying to escape."

Crassia tells her after dinner when Macia asks her. She looks at Macia, her eyes narrowed. "The hills have no escape," she says, her words sharp. Macia dips her head, she'd figured that. "People have tried. Fools always try," Crassia continues, looking at Macia as if trying to figure out whether she is a potential fool or not. "It's too hard, they will always see you. Or you fall in the dark." Just as she had thought, and Macia feels her shoulders go down a little. Crassia glares at her as if she has made up her mind that Macia is a fool after all. "When they get you, you will receive your Requipacem straight away, as you have despised the correction of the council, you have deserted all of Elabi, including its correction and guidance. By trying to avoid their lessons, you are no longer worthy to be part of the council's benevolent gifts of food and drink." Macia is quite sure the woman has that bit from one of the lectures. She shudders, so escaping isn't really an option, then?

On the other hand, she is irredeemable, and when she is completely worn out, which at this rate isn't going to be long, she will be faced with Requipacem anyway. What difference would it make? And if she succeeds... But where would she go? She dips her head a little.

"How long have you been here," she asks the woman, needing to change the subject. The woman shrugs and Macia thinks she'll say several years, but Crassia says she has been here about five moons. Macia stares, and swallows. Crassia looks old enough to be sent Downstream. Crassia looks at Macia again and asks if Macia is Irredeemable by any chance. Macia gives a nod, still hating the word. Crassia's eyes open wide, and after a very quick chin raise, walks off. Macia swallows, her eyes stinging. Crassia has simply walked off, not wanting to be seen with an Irredeemable, even though Macia has yellow patches on her shoulders just like herself.

She walks back to her barrack slowly, deciding on an early night, to recover some of her strength for tomorrow.

That night Macia dreams of paddleboarding up the little stream, eating peaches along the way and bathing grazed knees after slipping down the hills on her way to freedom. She dreams of angry guards, a yellow-skinned Crassia looking at her with narrowed eyes as Macia sits in the large chair, guards pointing their batons at the red button for her to press. Behind the glass is Grabus scowling at her, but also sweet Caecilia shaking her arm to persuade her to come. She wakes up to the woman shaking her, hissing at her to be quiet. Macia nods and whispers a thank you, then turns over on her other side, her face wet, smothering her sobs in her thin blanket.

Chapter 40

Onesday morning comes and goes. Macia feels refreshed after Enday, but by lunchtime, that feeling has gone. "Dearest friend," she writes, while eating her flatbread, "I'm tired already, and my arms ache. Surely they should be getting used to the weight of the spools? I need to find a way to get out as well." She stares at her plate, brooding. She walks to the education centre, glad that she'll be able to sit down, but not looking forward to her lessons. She is so used to always giving her best, working hard for the good of Elabi, and to improve her grades, that it feels wrong to use school as a break, a rest to recover her strength.

Grabus is stomping around, scowling at Macia whenever he sees her. Macia ignores him, her thoughts going to the Hills, and wondering if there is a way out somehow. Not over the top, that is for sure. What about the stream? It's not a big stream, but would some of the waterfalls or streams come from within the hills, making a way through? She has heard about that happening, so surely it could be an option? Or is there a way of hiding on the tubular when it returns to Elabi? She rejects that one straight away; after all, the cameras and guards would soon spot her.

The week passes in a heavy blur, Macia only looking forward to Enday and her free time. It will also give her more food, which she desperately needs. By Fifday, Macia is exhausted, and she lies awake on her bed, staring at the ceiling. "Lord, I can't do this much longer," she breathes, "I can feel myself getting weaker already, and I haven't even been here two weeks. What will I be like after one moon? I won't even have the strength to escape, let alone make it all the way to the lighthouse and get on the paddleboard." Her thoughts drift off; will the paddleboard still be there? Will the woman remove it when she thinks Macia has had a good chance?

Hexaday feels like a normal day, and Macia tries not to think back to her usual Hexaday routine. "Beloved, I realise that living in the past is not helping me. It weighs me down. It's an emotional thing to do, I suppose, and I should accept today as a good day, regardless of my circumstances. The council is right on that one." She longs for more rest, more food. After lunch, the classes start with a video about the need for doing one's best. Macia clenches her fists, she has always done her best, even made it Amplissimos, and now she's here! She leans back in her chair a little, the monotone voice on the screen drones on about the reasons for serving the city and all its citizens. The room fades, and Macia only jolts back to reality when Grabus elbows her sharply. She blinks against the lights, and swallows at his red, angry face, his lips curled up in a sneer. "That's another two points for you, bringing you up to a total of ten class marks," he says, looking pleased for a second. Then he pulls his face straight, looking very grave.

"The council has given you this wonderful opportunity to redeem yourself and to still be a useful citizen even after your appalling conduct," he says, walking back to his desk, pencil at the ready. "You have not taken up their offer of kindness, instead you have shown nothing but contempt for all of us who live here beyond the Hills." His voice goes a little hoarse, and he looks at her for a second, his eyes filled with hate. "You have rejected their goodness and this video," and he gestures towards the screen with what feels like an emotional level of force, "this lecture was to help you to understand how important it is to use your efforts." He ticks off some boxes on the paper and walks over to Macia with something in his hand. It turns out to be a rather large pin, and he clips it onto her yellow patch on her right shoulder. His breath near her face makes her wrinkle up her nose, but seeing the other students watching her, Macia smoothes out her face, trying to look a little bored as usual. It has gone very quiet in the class, the video has finished and the other students stare at her, their eyes wide open. All Macia can see is contempt and anger, and she knows that not that long ago she would have been equally horrified to be in the same room with a student who showed such a lack of compliance with Elabi rule.

"You will have half rations until you show yourself a better citizen, more determined to serve Elabi than you have so far. It will teach you how good the council has been to you, and it might give you a greater appreciation." Macia stares, half rations? She can feel her face heating up and she glares at Grabus, ready to tell him what she thinks. She never gets there, for he suddenly leans into her face, both his fists on her desk. "Don't even argue. You are very fortunate that I merely halved your rations. Disagreeing with me will see me calling the guards, and they will lock you up in the thinking chamber on water only. By the end, you'll wish you had chosen Requipacem." He looks at her with narrowed eyes, as if daring her to carry on arguing. Macia swallows, should she risk it? She needs to get out, she needs free time as well as time to think, talk to God and plan her exit. By drawing attention to herself, getting out will be harder. All this takes a few seconds to weigh up, and she lowers her eyes to her desk. Grabus' face shows his satisfaction as he stomps back to his desk, ready to put the next lesson on the screen. Macia tries to stop her body from shaking, but it isn't till she walks out of the room that she feels she is in control of her body once more. At the door, she looks back, just in time to see Grabus' happy smirk, which he wipes off as soon as she looks at him.

Outside in the heat, Macia wonders whether she should appeal the sentence, or whether that would make matters a lot worse. She decides against it, knowing it would be her word, as a Yellow Irredeemable, against Grabus, who is about to be sent back to Elabi. The cameras might have picked up on it too, but she can't be sure. Slowly Macia walks to the factory, a frown on her face. Her feet don't feel the heat and in her head, she writes with wobbly letters, "Beloved, I think I'm in trouble. My food has been halved, and I feel weak already. I don't know what to do…" She groans softly, where is her joy now? How can she be expected to be joyful anyway? It was unfair, it was done simply out of spite. A tiny voice in the back of her head whispers, "Why didn't God protect you?"

The work is hard as always, and Macia is relieved when it's dinner time. She walks back, washes up, then queues with the other yellows. Some of them look at her shoulder pin and turn away quickly. The woman with the yellow skin looks at her pin, her eyes widen and she moves away from Macia, making it clear that she wants nothing to do with her. Macia glares at her. Surely they're all in the same garum tub, why not stand by each other? They're all citizens together, and it's as a people that they form Elabi. The woman doesn't look at Macia anymore, and in the end, Macia looks away, unable to keep up her furious look. She feels pain inside, the same kind of pain when her mother left, as well as Caecilia. An empty, hollowness inside her. She feels very alone, and staring at her dusty feet, she tries to think of bits from Paul's letters. It's harder and harder each time to remember some of the words, and her heart rate picks up. God might see her, be with her and help her, but what will happen if she forgets about

Him and His promises? What if she is the one to leave God, not on purpose, but simply by drifting away.

She is stirred out of her worrying thoughts by the woman clicking her tongue at her. She glances up and sees the gap in front. Macia grabs a bowl and holds it out to the Mansit serving the queue. He looks at her shoulder, grins, and gives her one small scoop of millet. The next Mansit gives her only a few pieces of meat and a couple of beans. She stares, surely they're not expecting her to be satisfied with that? That isn't even half ration, that's more like a quarter! She takes a breath to point it out, but the last Mansit drops his grin, quickly replacing it with a menacing scowl. "Move it, Yellow," he says, "otherwise I'll take the lot off you!" He moves a little towards her, and Macia turns away fast, her eyes stinging from anger and despair.

Sitting in the relatively cool classroom, she still hovers between fury and despair. Surely as an ex-Amplissimos, they will listen to her? Her stomach growls, and Grabus, who is nearby, handing out books, looks at her and smirks. "Seems you're educating yourself on life," he says, his lips pursed as if he wasn't laughing at her. Macia glares at her desk, afraid to look up and be in trouble for being emotional. The time drags on, and Macia is glad when it's bedtime. She drinks extra water when washing her dress, hoping that it will fill her stomach so she can sleep.

Once it's dark, she rolls onto her back, shivering a little in her damp dress, but glad for the coolness at the same time. "Dearest friend, only friend," her cheeks are wet already, "I am even more scared than I was already. I could feel myself getting weaker these last few days, and now that I have even less food, I don't know what will happen." She squeezes her eyes shut, trying to keep the sobs in. Last week there had been an accident in the factory, and she knows it could easily happen. "When I get too weak, I could have an accident. I can't stay awake in class, so when will my punishment be lifted? Or will I get even more class marks, and end up in more trouble?" She has to stop her thoughts from going there, as it's not helping. In the dark, in her head, only her mouth shaping the words she tries to sing "Nearer my God to Thee," and before she knows it she has drifted off to sleep.

Enday is a relief, for although she will have to attend the special lectures, it means sitting down. Her bowl with pottage is not even half full, but Macia decides to not bother arguing over it. She eats slowly, leaning against the wall. She is glad to sit in the lecture room, trying to look attentive, rather than simply collapsed in her seat. It's hard to stay awake, but she knows she'll have to be seen to listen, otherwise she'll be in trouble. During the bathroom break, she gulps down as much water as she can, to stop the pain and endless growling noises coming from her stomach. Standing in the queue for lunch, Macia is shocked how weak she feels already. "Beloved, hopefully it's just my imagination. It's the shock of having such small rations. I know I'm stronger than this, and I will just have to imagine myself fit and well," she tries to cheer herself up.

After lunch, she tidies the space around her bed. She does the same thing as last week, hiding the paper and pencil under her dress. Going out in the midday heat makes her gasp a little. She looks at the foothills in the distance and feels her heart sink. How is she going to get there? "God, I want to talk to You, and I want to go to the same place, but I need more strength." She blinks, takes a deep breath, and reminds herself it's just a matter of taking steps. So Macia sets off, slowly, trying to walk in the shade wherever possible. She follows the same path, picking herbs, greedily devouring the peaches she picks. She forces herself to wait between each fruit, worried that the warm fruits will upset her stomach, something she can't afford just now!

In the shade of the large tree, she sits down again and leans her head against the trunk. She wipes her face dry impatiently, how has she become this emotional in just a few days? "God, please help me to get out," she whispers, then, after a quick look round to make sure nobody is around, she says a little louder, "I need food, Lord, and I need to get out. Last week saw me lose strength, and this week I will have even less food. Soon I will be too weak to get out, let alone make it all the way to the lighthouse."

She tries to remember the lighthouse, run by Caecilia's dad. At least it used to be. She looks at the white buildings in the distance and allows her mind to go back home. Her sister Tima, holding the little baby. Caecilia's parents. The woman at the water sports centre. Macia sniffs and wipes her face, her mind walking past all the familiar faces, missing them. Even Brutus and Ignava. Macia remembers Ignava's cooking, and her stomach rumbles loudly as if blaming Macia for missing the good food her stepmother used to serve up. She thinks of the photograph hidden in her secret place, the picture with her sweet looking mother and Macia's small brother. In the end, she gives up and simply lets the tears run down.

Macia can't remember crying like this before, apart from when her mother left. Even then, she had to cry at night and quietly. The sobs have worn her out, but part of her feels lighter, as if her heart has been cleaned. She dries her face and continues talking to God. "I will try to rejoice, I know You do all things well, and that it's for being in You that I'm here. I should be happy about that, it should remind me of You and how You redeemed me. I know I'm in Christ, and I know that should be enough. Is it wrong that I want to live in Elabi as well? I miss all those people, even though they're probably glad I'm gone."

Macia scowls at that, part of her blaming the people. After all, she had to push them away as they would tell on her, or make her life harder if she had allowed them close. Look what happened with Caecilia. They were almost friends, and then Caecilia disappears. It caused Macia to know God, and she will always be grateful to Caecilia for that, but it also led to Macia being sent beyond the Hills. It could now cost Macia her life. She stops, "I'm being too emotional, Beloved," she says, her voice determined, "for I'm still alive, and who knows how I will cope. After all, I'm quite fit; at least I was, so I should be able to cope with less food for a while. Dearest friend, I have still lots to be thankful for. Please Lord, help me to stay close to You in all this! Oh, and please, send Grabus back to Elabi within the next few days!"

Chapter 41

When Macia has eaten a couple more peaches, she pulls out her paper and pencil. Chewing on some mint, she wonders what to write. The strip isn't very large, so she will have to choose carefully. She stares into nothingness, letting her mind walk through the thin pages. She carefully writes down the words about walking in love, to be tenderhearted, kind to others, to be forgiving towards others, just as God for Christ's sake has forgiven her. She thinks about that for a while slowly putting pencil and paper away. She can feel her anger flaring up every time she thinks about her tutor. Grabus had picked on her out of spite. Macia feels her hatred growing, then she draws in a breath. Not only would that be against Elabi rule, but it's also against God's rule.

Elabi rule would punish her for her emotion-driven response, and she can see what they mean. It is very destructive and distracting, clouding her judgment. It's physically affecting her too, making her heart race and her face flushed. She knows the words just before the ones she wrote down tell her to put away bitterness, wrath and anger. So God doesn't want her to go around hating Grabus either.

Of course, he is just doing his job, and if she had been in his position, she would have done the same thing. She is seen as Irredeemable for a reason.

"Dearest friend, as I told you some moons ago, by reading the thin pages, and by writing to you, I was putting myself at risk. I knew what I was doing. I might not have known what it was like beyond the Hills, but I knew I would end up here if I was ever caught." She wonders if she would have changed anything had she known beforehand. She might. "Beloved, I would have handed in the pages, I think, but I am glad that I didn't. I wouldn't change back to not knowing God."

Soon after, she decides it's time to go back. She picks a few more herbs, and drinks from the stream. She washes her hands and face, glad to feel the short stubble is growing a little. Macia gets up, looks around one more time, then slowly walks down to her barrack. She restocks her bowl, pushing the herbs down carefully. She would have loved to bring back some of the fruit, but she doesn't know where to store them. She knows some of her herbs went missing, so she assumes the fruit would do too. Thinking about the week ahead with her halved rations makes her stomach tighten up. "...tenderhearted... be kind...forgiving..." Muttering she walks into the dark barracks, the lack of windows making the place hot and stuffy. Tomorrow is the longest day, she knows, as she overheard the guards talking about it.

Macia lies down on her bed for a while, waiting for dinner time. "Dearest friend, I'm quite surprised how quickly things feel normal. There are guards everywhere, often tapping their hands with their awful sticks," and she shudders. "I am used to standing at the back of the queue, I'm used to people treating me in a dreadful way. It's such a different life than I had before!" Macia thinks about the Mansit children who live here with their families. She has seen them when they return to the education building after lunch, pushing each other. The first time she had simply stood there and stared. Two boys were actually touching each other, using their fists to push each others' shoulders!

"Yes, life is different, but being in Christ, I will just need to move ahead one day at a time," she decides, just like on her walk this afternoon. The foothills had seemed so far, but by taking one step at the time, she had made it there and back. Granted, she was exhausted, but she did it. Soon Grabus will be gone, or he will take the pin off and she will be back to normal rations. A tiny voice reminds her how hungry and faint she had been the last week, but Macia ignores it. She will be fine, her body will adjust.

She eats her dinner slowly, adding some of her fresh herbs. Macia is looking forward to an early night, it will conserve energy and she needs the rest. It's still light and very hot outside, but the barrack is dark, so she soon falls asleep, the long walk in the foothills has worn her out.

Onesday morning, she queues up with the others, and silently accepts her small portion. She eats slowly; with only half a bowl full, it won't take her long to eat it. The food doesn't seem to make a difference to her stomach, she still feels empty. After washing her hands and face, and having another long drink, Macia walks to the factory. She still isn't used to the humid air or the noise. She takes up her position, the trolley with spools in place already. She takes the first spool, surprised as always by its weight. Soon she is too exhausted and out of breath to write on her imaginary paper, and Macia hasn't got the breath left to speak to God. She plods on, eyes wide open, fixed on the step right in front of her, not seeing or hearing anything or anybody. The old man is no longer there, and Macia can't ask about him either. She has a feeling she wouldn't like the answer. She shivers every time she thinks about him, sure that he has gone for good.

Just as Macia thinks she can't do this anymore, the lunch bell sounds. She lets go of the spool that she had just started to pick up and slowly staggers to the exit of the factory. She is jostled by a few workers in a hurry, but she doesn't even notice. Queuing for food, she sways and has to take quick shallow breaths to stay vertical. "I have to make it to the serving Mansits," she breathes, determined not to faint. She is given one thin slice and a very thin slither of meat. She leans against the wall, her head swimming in the heat. She struggles to eat the slice, not having enough energy to chew the dry bread. Rinsing it down with water, she looks at the hatch. It seems too much effort to have to go and hand in her plate and glass. In the end, she manages to muster up the energy to do so, then slowly walks to the school building. At least it will be cooler in there. It is the longest day of the year. She has no idea why that feels important, but somehow it is.

Macia leans back in her chair. She has to look alert, watch the video, do the assignment. Grabus looks marginally happier, maybe he has been told he will be returning to Elabi soon? Macia is glad of the rest the cool room provides, and when the bell goes, she stands up, wishing she could delay a little. She makes her way to the factory and is soon sweating, lugging heavy spools up the step, slipping down the step to get the next spool. Her breathing is loud, but there is nothing she can do. She is way past caring, so with her mouth half open, gasping for air, Macia struggles on all afternoon. Near the end, the dark little voice returns, "Why not accept Requipacem? Why struggle like this? You're a disgrace to your family, who have denounced you, you're unwanted here with everybody stepping back in horror when they see you. Nobody likes you, nobody wants you. Why not go out of this life?"

Macia's eyes go blurry, and she blinks violently, as she needs to see. She has to stay calm, she tells herself sternly, and tugging at the next spool, she slips her arms underneath the wet yarn and staggers to the little platform. The man at the top is a bit younger than the previous man and just as sullen. He had looked at her for a second, then his eyes had landed on her yellow patches, especially the one with the pin, his eyes had hardened and he had turned away rather abruptly. Since then he had not looked at her again. Macia hovers between angry and sad, self-pity repeating the bit about being unloved. *Irredeemable, unlovable,* the voice hisses. That makes Macia stand up straighter, if only a little. "Loved by God, chosen by Him, delivered from the power of darkness and translated into the kingdom of His dear Son," she remembers the bits of paragraphs, which sometimes almost read like poetry. The words give her more energy and strength, and Macia smiles a little. The words came from a part of Paul's letter that she loved, and she tries to remember the words, knowing it will keep the soft voice at bay. Her favourite part is the bit about powers and dominions having been created by God, and how they exist by Him. Even the council?

She makes it through the afternoon and slowly follows the other Mansits to the dining hall. The water is cool, and she is glad to wash her hands and face, drinking some as well. Her portion of millet is small, but at least it has some meat and cabbage to go with it. Leaning against the wall she eats slowly, watching the others. The dining hall is not as full as it was the previous week, and she wonders what has happened to those Mansits. Maybe some of them have returned to the city?

Curiosity wins, and she asks the other woman with the yellow patches, "Where are the others? Normally there are more people here?" The woman glances up, then looks away, but leaning over a little explains it's the summer solstice. Macia frowns a little, "The longest day?" She has heard of it, of course, but what has it to do with missing people?

"Some…people will go and celebrate," the woman says, and Macia is sure she was going to say 'Mansits', so the woman has clearly been sent here for punishment. Correction, she says quickly in her head, feeling her face warm up as she realises how her entire view of the council has changed in these last few weeks. "When they are caught celebrating at sunrise, they are in a lot of trouble. Some of them will probably choose

Requipacem," the woman continues, and Macia dips her head, hiding the shock in her eyes. People celebrate the sunrise? The woman gives a nod and wrinkles her nose. "Some people like to get very emotional, even over certain days of the year." She hesitates, as if to add more, then after a quick look at Macia's pin says, "Some people have beliefs, and their beliefs come with special days." Macia opens her eyes wide and stares at the woman. God has special celebration dates?

"Do all...uhm...beliefs have special days?" She looks at the woman, and almost holds her breath. "What kind of days do they have?" The woman shrugs, and licking her lips looks around quickly. She leans a little closer and tells Macia that some beliefs had, in fact, special days every week. Then she walks over to the hatch, handing in her plate and drinking glass. Macia has to think about that. Fancy having a special day to do with God every week. What would they do on that special day though? Would they get together, like the Mansits at sunrise this morning?

Macia's head is full of it in school, and too busy thinking about it to feel hungry. Grabus still looks rather pleased and confirms her thoughts about his return to Elabi. "Next Onesday I will be returning to Elabi. I have learned a lot from being here, beyond the Hills, and I have gained new skills," he sounds important, and Macia can imagine him as an Umbo. She grins to herself, he is clearly making sure that the cameras are picking up his little speech. "I won't be returning to my previous job, of course, or my previous status," and she can see his face going more red than usual, "but I will be contributing to society once more in a direct way." He looks pleased, and Macia finds herself wishing him the best in her heart. She dips her head a little bit at him, and his pleased expression changes. "I have also been made more aware of people who hold odd views, and the tremendous danger they pose to our society," he snarls, looking at her directly. "Instead of those people being simply weird or even a nuisance, they

273

are a great danger and are able to destroy Elabi in a very underhand manner. It happens before good citizens are even aware, which is why informing the council is so important. I'm horrified by the fact that I didn't sound the alarm, and had to pay for that grave lapse of judgment. I was in a position of trust," and he sticks his chest out a little, "and with that comes responsibility. Never will I take that for granted again."

Macia looks down at her desk, knowing it's best to avoid eye contact with him. She wants to roll her eyes like she has seen some of the girls in school do. It used to make her cringe, now she understands the gesture. She feels for Grabus even though she can't stand the man's overbearing manner, for had she not made the same mistake with Caecilia? Grabus puts the next video on, and Macia manages to sit through the entire session without falling asleep. Walking back to her barrack she mumbles, "Well, that certainly felt like the longest day!" That makes her think again about beliefs and their special days. Maybe Enday should be her special day?

Chapter 42

Not long now, she thinks, stroking her baby bump absent-mindedly. Just a week, and she'll be back in Elabi. She bites her lip, her cat-like teeth showing. Her husband had been furious as well as worried. He knew what it was like beyond the Hills, and he wasn't sure she'd survive. She had done quite well, really, as the job in the sanatorium had come with a private room. The hours were long, and it could be busy, but they had taken her situation into consideration. Just another week, and she'd be home. Inritia sighs, a week seems such a long time. It's all Gax's fault, she thinks, knowing that she ought to have told on him. Mind you, she had, about the animal books that he'd mentioned. At least that had worked in her favour. Nobody knew about the very thin pages though, with the weird title, psalm...psalem...something like that. She shudders, what would have happened if she'd admitted to that? Her husband had been annoyed enough as it was.

Macia leans against the wall for her meagre dinner, her hands shaking. She is so tired and weak, how will she manage? "Dearest friend," she writes with a golden pen this time, although her mind is so tired, even the golden pen keeps slipping off the crisp white paper every now and then. "Dearest friend, I'm so tired, I want to go home," and her eyes sting all of a sudden. She bends her head over her bowl a little, imagine someone seeing her emotional! She tries to breathe, and after a while finds her vision has cleared. "I didn't think I'd make it till the end of the day, but somehow I did. I can do this, I can do all things through Christ, even the factory work, as well as staying awake in class. It's hard though, and God will need to help me if I am to survive this." She wrinkles her nose at herself, ashamed at being emotionally overwhelmed.

She looks around, then takes her bowl back to the hatch. One more session in the education building. Soon this day will be over, and she will have made it one more day. The bright light outside makes her flinch a little, even though it's quite late in the day. The education building is lovely and cool, and Macia is grateful for small mercies. She wipes the sweat off her face and sits down at her desk. None of the other students look at her, and Macia clenches her jaws.

Grabus is still looking pleased, and when he passes Macia's desk he stops for a moment. "I have arranged for your full rations to be restored on Onesday," he says, looking generous, "if you're still around of course. People in your position and with your background would be better off choosing Requipacem, doing the right thing. It would be a sign of accepting responsibilities as well as relieving Elabi resources." He looks at her, his eyes hard, and Macia blinks. He is still angry and bitter about it all. She actually takes a breath to tell him that he is the one missing out, that she has forgiven him for what he has done to her.

Grabus has moved on, however, and Macia releases her breath, shocked at what she'd almost done. That would have been a disaster, she realises, but on the other hand, what does she have to lose? It will be incredible if she makes it till Onesday. Gloomily she stares at her desk. Five more days till Onesday, and will the half portions be lifted for breakfast, or will it be after her school session? What if the new tutor hasn't been told? She does her best to stay alert, but her body is shaking with the exertion. Simply sitting on a chair is sapping her strength.

It takes all Macia's willpower to get through Thirday, and she dreads Quarday coming up. She looks at the foothills, slightly hazy in the evening sunlight. Maybe she should go there, and pick some fruit? Her herbs have all gone. Just looking makes her knees buckle, and she knows that she's unable to walk to the foothills at the end of a long day.

Quarday morning, as soon as the breakfast bell clangs, Macia sits up. She ignores the noises around her, thinking about her options. She could skip the little bit of pottage this morning, and instead walk to the hills, pick enough fruit to last her a day? If she hurries, she might make it before it's time to be in the factory. She bites her nail. It's the hurrying bit that she isn't sure about. Just walking from her bed to the dining hall leaves her out of breath. How is she going to walk fast all the way to the foothills? Will the guards even let her? "Lord, I don't know what to do. I can't go on with the little bit of food I have, and I can't walk fast enough to get peaches." She sits a moment longer, longing to hear from God. If only there was something in the writing, or another person telling her what to do. She needs more food.

In the end, Macia gives up and gets up to go to the dining hall. She looks longingly at the foothills, but she knows they're too far away. The noise of clattering bowls, scraping spoons, benches moving around in the enclosed space makes Macia's head spin. The heat inside is stuffy, and her legs are not as obedient as they ought to be. She is glad about the pottage serving though, for the Mansit serving her got distracted. He looks away, just when ladling the pottage into her bowl, and Macia turns away quickly, in case he realises his mistake and insists on taking some of it back.

Macia moves as slowly as she dares in the factory. A few times the man who takes the spool off her is waiting, glaring at her and making an impatient clicking noise. Macia licks her dry lips, hoping he won't alarm any of the guards to get her to move on. She staggers back to the trolley, and tugs at the next spool, tears blurring her sight. She can't move any faster. In fact, it's hard to move at all. She collapses in a heap on the little platform when the lunch bell clangs away, the noise making her head spin. Macia is gasping for breath, then drags herself off the platform, and staggers to the exit. She is shocked by how weak she is. Just a few weeks ago she was healthy and fit, how can she have gone downhill so quickly? Just a few more days, she tells herself, and then she will have more food. She'll do better then.

The cool classroom helps, and Macia tries to relax in her chair as much as possible. This is her one chance to recover a little, ready for her afternoon time in the factory. She struggles to take her book back and has to hold on to the bookshelf to recover enough to leave the classroom. They are given a new paper for their assignments, meaning she will have to walk to her barrack before going to the factory. Macia blinks away tears, feeling anger at the injustice and resentment towards Grabus for putting her in this position. She has to keep her face straight though, for she knows he has given her several class marks already. He had smirked at the last one, "Well, you obviously enjoy your half rations. In a way that is a positive thing. Maybe it shows that you understand how undeserving you are and that as a Yellow Irredeemable you are taking more off the council than you could ever repay."

Macia wipes the sweat off her face when she walks into the factory, the dust of the road making her eyes sting. The humidity and noise make her feel dizzy, and she walks slowly to her position. The man who normally takes the spools off her is helping himself to one of the damp spools from the trolley. "You're late," he snarls, panting a little.

Good, Macia thinks, narrowing her eyes at him, that will teach him how hard my job is and how fortunate he is that I bring him the spools. She smoothes out her face and explains that the new paper had to be put back first. The man shrugs, "Well, get the next one ready, and don't make me wait each time, or I will let the guards know it's you who is upsetting the whole line."

Macia glares at the spool, tugging at it ferociously, muttering hateful words towards the man, Grabus, the guards, and whoever else works down the line, making her rush. She climbs onto the little platform, staggering to her feet, taking the few steps across to where the man is waiting. She scowls back at him, then turns around. She blinks, trying to think of the words on her precious paper strip, being kind, tenderhearted… "This doesn't count, dearest friend," she writes in quick, angry letters, "it's nothing against him as a person, it's people's awful attitudes, surely I'm right to make a stand against those?" Her paper stares back at her quietly, and Macia flicks her ornate pen off her hand-carved bureau.

Staggering back after the next spool, she realises that she has just upset her one and only friend. She has been unkind and snappy to her one quiet, patient listener, defending herself and her own unkindness. She gasps a little, and the grief makes Macia lose her footing. She slips off the little platform, and lands with a thud, followed by a scream, as her wrist bone snaps. She moves her right hand to support her wrist, but blackness overtakes her before she gets there.

Macia opens her eyes, her forehead on the damp floor, running footsteps coming closer. The man at the top of the platform is making angry clicking noises, but Macia is in too much pain to hear him. One of the guards tells him to cut it out and to get on with work. Then he glares at Macia. "What did you do? Shirking work? Falling asleep on the job?" Macia shakes her head, but the movement makes her

279

feel sick, and she lowers her head back onto the floor, taking fast, shallow breaths. The guard kneels down and nudges her with his foot, making Macia gasp. She lifts her head up and tries to focus her eyes on the man's face. He finally looks at her wrist and a frown appears. "Broken," he says, matter of factly, and looking over her head at another guard, "She needs the sanatorium. Get up," he continues to Macia, and she stares at him. The guard rolls his eyes, and motioning at the other guard, grabs her elbow. The two guards pull her onto her feet, and Macia gives a shriek ending in a loud groan, her knees buckling, everything going black again. The two men hold her upright and after a while, the noise from the factory comes back and she takes a few big, loud breaths. Macia manages to remain standing up, her teeth chattering.

The guards push her towards the exit, and Macia sobs with pain by the time they get to the large doors. Other guards grin, but she doesn't even see them. Slowly they walk down the dusty road, Macia stumbling and crying. The older guard leans over a little, his fishy breath making her stomach churn even more. "You will need to be stronger than this if you want to live," his voice not unkind. Macia tries her best to stop crying and manages to bring it down to the odd sob. The guard dips his head at her, and as the other guard looks the other way, whispers, "Better. They will end you if they think the pain is too much. Give yourself a chance." Macia gulps down a new sob but manages to give him a quick nod. Requipacem. They will insist on her choosing Requipacem!

The sanatorium is cool, and the guards bring her through various doors, into a quiet room. They lower Macia into a chair and the older guard briefly raises his chin at her, the other guard leaves the room in a hurry. At the door, the older guard looks back for a moment, and Macia is sure he is feeling sorry for her. That makes her heartbeat do overtime, for the only reason can be that he knows she will be forced into Requipacem. Well, she isn't going to.

She clenches her jaws so tightly together that they hurt, and she digs her toes into the cool floor. She has to be calm, she has to be strong and she has to prove to them that she is fine, that her broken arm can be healed. She can still be a useful citizen. Maybe she should explain that she used to be an Amplissimos, and therefore able to support the council here, beyond the Hills. She could help them by writing proposals or by doing light work. She simply has to prove to them how much she could benefit everybody by staying alive. The alternative is too awful for words.

A woman in a white apron enters the room. Macia looks at her, noticing the extended shape under her apron, as well as the strange cat-like teeth as the nurse smirks at her, seeing Macia's red eyes, and the way her hand supports her wrist. Looking at Macia's wrist once she gets a little closer, the woman raises her eyebrows, "Oh dear," she says, "and a Yellow as well. I hope you didn't have any expectations for your life?"

Chapter 43

Macia clenches her jaws, angry words struggling to get out. Meekness…kindness…forgiveness. She swallows, then decides she has nothing to lose after all. "My life is not my own," she says, her voice soft, her eyes suddenly stinging again, this time with feeling overwhelmed by the fact that she, Macia Durus, previously AMP, might not have plans for her life any more, but her plans are held by God.

The nurse's eyes open wide, then narrow; they glare at Macia, only for the glare to be replaced with a softer look. It makes Macia smile a little in spite of everything, then the nurse steps closer, and leans over Macia, peering at her hurt wrist.

"Oh, that doesn't look great," she says out loud, and taking Macia's shoulder pulls her across a little. Macia gasps, then her eyes open wide as the nurse removes her special badge from her shoulder. "It'll be bad enough without needing a lack of food," the woman hisses and continues out loud, "I will get a special strap ready for your arm, and then I will show you your bed." She stands up, her hand dropping the badge into her large apron pocket before turning away from Macia. Macia merely dips her head, trying to conceal her startled look.

The nurse soon returns, accompanied by a pale looking doctor. The doctor takes one look at her arm, clicks his tongue, and walks out again, after dipping his head at the nurse. The nurse turns a little pale and turns away quickly to get things ready to stabilize Macia's wrist. Macia has to clench her jaws again, grinding her teeth, unable to stop the occasional whimper from escaping. Near the end, she tries to say between gasps, "I thought it would need plaster?" The nurse looks at her, her eyes soft, and after a half glance behind her at the camera Macia only now spots, she shakes her head.

"Normally the wrist will swell, and we don't want to put permanent plaster on for a while. Normally," she adds and looks hard at Macia. Macia dips her head a little, looking at her feet to hide her confusion. Normally? But not now? Then she gasps as the realisation hits her. She looks at the nurse, her ears making a loud whooshing sound. They will give her...they will make her... Macia struggles to breathe, tears suddenly making her face wet. The nurse glares at her, and hisses, "Don't! You get emotional, it will make it worse, just don't!" Macia digs her toes into the cool floor, pressing hard, her sore fingertips digging into the palm of her hand, forcing herself to take deep, deep breaths in and out. By the time the nurse has finished the wrapping up of her wrist, Macia has herself back under control, and only her hand is still shaking.

"I will now walk you to your room," the nurse says out loud and takes Macia by her good arm. As soon as they through the door, walking into the corridor, the nurse hisses, "Tonight. At midnight. Lights out. Turn left out of your room. Follow the corridor." She stops as they turn a corner, then continues. "There is a door at the end, go through, then down the steps to the basement. At the end is another door to the special tubular." Macia feels the shiver the nurse gives at that moment and looks at her face briefly. The nurse smirks at her, cat-like teeth making Macia swallow. "If you don't go tonight, you will be going the same route tomorrow evening," she says, maliciously.

Once they're past the next camera she continues, "There is a small, hidden opening opposite the tubular entrance. It's another tunnel. It leaves the Hills, I have heard." Macia stares at her. A way out? The nurse shrugs. "It might not. Who knows? Nothing to lose though, have you?"

They walk in silence, then Macia whispers, "Why?" The nurse digs her odd-looking teeth into her bottom lip, not improving her looks, and shrugs.

"For the sake of an odd guy I once worked with. He gave me a few pages of some ancient book," she suddenly states, and Macia gasps, and stares at her, forgetting to walk. The nurse tugs her on, "I didn't really look at it, gave it back the next day. Sometimes I wonder though..." Macia opens her mouth to ask more questions, but they have arrived at her room. The nurse doesn't look down the hallway, and Macia forces her eyes to stay away as well.

The room is cool, with a simple bed and nightstand. The pale grey walls are depressing, and the thin grey blanket makes Macia shiver. It reminds her of her first issued blanket after her arrest. The nurse helps Macia onto the bed. Macia lies down, grateful for the rest, her head spinning, her wrist throbbing in sync with her heartbeat.

Will she really be escaping the Hills tonight? How long will it take her? She knows the cameras aren't manned in Elabi till four in the morning, will it be the same here? That will give her four hours to walk to... Whereto? Where will the other tunnel lead? What if she ends up in the middle of Elabi? The lighthouse is her aim, praying that the paddleboard will still be there. She looks at her bandaged wrist. Will she be able to handle a paddleboard with one hand?

She closes her eyes. "Dearly beloved," for a moment she smiles, as it's her left arm that is broken, which means she can still write in her imaginary diary, "Today has been awful." She shudders, not wanting to think about the accident. "Tonight I will need all my strength and courage, I think. I will be leaving the Hills. As the nurse said, I have nothing to lose, but my earthly life to gain." She wonders whether she is taking the easy way out, and should face her Requipacem with more courage. In the end, she decides that she should try to escape. Escape! Her heart beats wildly, making her right hand feel cold and sweaty. Is she really going to leave Elabi behind? Where will she go?

She feels sick, her stomach churning, and Macia can feel the shakes in all her limbs. She has to calm down, has to rest and recover as much as she can. She has to be rational about this all. There will be time to reflect and think later. She must rest… So Macia slows down her breathing as much as she can, forcing her body to relax into the rather hard mattress, ignoring the odd smell coming off her thin blanket.

She manages to doze off and only wakes up when the nurse comes in to check her blood pressure and temperature. It's hard to fall asleep after that, so Macia simply stares at the ceiling, her stomach tight at the thought of running away in the dark. It might be summer, but midnight will be dark and chilly. She will have to walk through a tunnel, who knows for how long. She tries to think through words of her thin pages, digging through the corners of her heart to find some excitement at the idea of getting out of Elabi. But all she can find is fear and grief at leaving Elabi behind. She does love her city with its terracotta houses, tall cypress trees and blue water. To leave it all behind is hard, even though technically, she has left already. She knows, even if her arm was allowed to heal, she would not be living very long. There would be another accident, another fall. She shudders, grateful to God that it's her wrist that was broken, nothing more. Macia feels resentment towards the doctor, "It's unfair, beloved, for he didn't even ask anything, I had no way of defending myself. Surely they could give me another task?"

The nurse brings her tea and spends some time tugging a small table across Macia's bed, from her good side. Whilst leaning over to adjust the table, she drops something in the crook of Macia's bandaged arm. Macia blinks, and carefully moves her arm a little to conceal the small package. The nurse points out that as it's her Requipacem tomorrow, her food will be upgraded this evening and tomorrow morning. Macia dips her head, "Thank you, that is very generous of the council," she says, trying to make her voice sound warm, rather than sarcastic.

"I will come later to switch your light off," the nurse says at the door, then disappears. Macia enjoys her dinner. It's millet of course, but there is a tiny china jug with allec as well as meat and beans. The water contains a little wine, and Macia sighs with contentment when she is done. She feels overfull, even though she has eaten as slowly as she could, determined to eat it all, as she will need the energy later that night.

Macia closes her eyes again, still feeling weary, and prays, "God, I don't know what to expect, I don't even know if I will get through this and whether my escape will be successful. Please give me the strength I need." She thinks of the people she has met beyond the Hills. There is Crassia, the woman who had been kind to her. And Grabus, the mentor who was partly responsible for the plight she is in now, she thinks, trying to keep her face smooth. Yet thanks to the injury, she now has a chance to make it out.

She thinks of the nurse, and about the words the woman spoke to her. Suddenly Macia opens her eyes wide, of course, the woman used to work with Gax! She must have done, as she mentioned the ancient papers! Macia closes her eyes again, not wanting the watchers to see her excitement. So the woman had seen the ancient pages? But not for long, obviously. Macia wonders if they were the same pages. She is sure that there must be a larger collection, and her heart longs to see more of the words that have come to mean so much. And that has left her life in pieces.

She wonders why the woman was sent beyond the hills, sure that it has something to do with Gax. He was clearly different, and if she worked with him, she would have noticed. It wouldn't look good if she hadn't alerted the authorities.

The nurse comes in, looking tired and pale. She checks Macia's blood pressure and temperature once more, then mouths, "Good trip!" to her, with a smile that is probably meant to be kind. Macia swallows and quickly dips her head at the woman. The nurse puts two pillows on Macia's bed, half blocking the view to the camera. "This will help you to sleep," she says and slides one under Macia's arm. The other one is half tucked in, then she leaves. She doesn't look round at the door, simply walks out of the grey room. Macia swallows, feeling very alone, so she pretends to settle in, and closes her eyes, in her mind pulling out her gold pen.

"Dearest friend, tonight I'm going on an adventure," she starts and pulls a face. Lying to your own diary isn't good. "I will make a run for freedom, without the running bit," she writes on the perfectly white paper. "I have no idea where I will get to, how long it will take me, and even if there is a destination at the end." She nibbles the corner of her thumbnail. What if the tunnel simply ends? She would have to walk all the way back. Should she take the tubular tunnel, try to get in there and follow that?

Time crawls, and Macia forces herself to rest, looking at the lights in the corridor, knowing they will be dimmed at midnight. As soon as they will go out, Macia will get up, check the package the nurse dropped on her bed, and rearrange the pillows to look like her in the dark. She thinks about the blanket. She might need it in the cold night air, but Macia wants to use it to buy herself more time. Hopefully, the watchers won't see the difference, and nobody will check up on her till the morning. It might buy her another two hours.

Finally, the lights in the corridor are suddenly turned down, leaving one small light to throw ghostly shadows. Macia waits a few more seconds, slips out of bed, hugging the little package under her arm. She staggers to the small bathroom, her knees shaking. It's time! In the little bathroom, she switches on the light and gives a surprised gasp as she sees that the package contains several slices of thin, black bread. She is still full, but by morning, this food will be very welcome.

She quietly returns to the room, rearranges the pillows, pats the blanket after a last hesitation, and walks to the door, shivering, her feet silent on the cold floor.

Chapter 44

Macia can feel the fear growing in the vein on the side of her head, drumming on her temple. She swallows, in cadence with her pulse reciting in her head, "...by Him were all things created that are in heaven and that are on earth, visible and invisible." She shuffles back, noiselessly, her feet never leaving the ground, millimetre by millimetre, her right hand slightly extended behind her, anticipating the rough stone walls. "Yes, visible and invisible, whether they be thrones or dominions or principalities or powers." She can sense the wall just behind her, her eyes desperately trying to pierce the darkness, and the tiniest whisper in her head says, "What if it's all of those together? These dominions, powers, principalities, the lot? What if the whole world is against you?"

She stops moving backwards and draws herself up that little bit taller. Not that it makes much difference, 1 metre 65 never reaches more than 1 metre 65 after all, but inside, in her innermost being, she stands tall. "It is true, all of it is, He is before all things, and by Him all things consist, I live in Him, I exist!" The nasty voice sniggers at that, and reminds her that she might exist, for now, but only just.

She fights the downward sag of her shoulders, and resumes her extremely careful movements, pressing her lips together to stop them from trembling, to stop herself from breaking down into tears. She has to trust the words, she believes them after all, now she has to live it!

"Dearest friend," she breathes, "I'm scared. This must be the other tunnel, at least the start of it. But where will it end?" Finally, her hand touches the stones, and she takes a deep breath. The stones feel cold but solid. When Macia looks back, she can see the dim light where the entrance to the tunnel was, opposite the entrance door to the tubular.

She looks back ahead, into the pitch darkness. Will this tunnel have a track too? Is there space for her to walk? Macia decides to walk carefully, keeping close to the wall. She stands still, listening, staring. Should she cross the tunnel to the other side? She tried that, but gave up, afraid to get lost in the dark, but it would be easier, as she could use her right hand to steady herself on the wall. She hesitates, then takes resolute steps straight ahead into the darkness, her eyes as wide as she can get them, trying to catch any bit of light in the tunnel. Sooner than she expected the opposite wall looms up, and Macia releases the breath she'd been holding.

She pulls her shoulders back, resettles the sling holding her left arm, puts a shaking hand on the wall, and walks into the dark.

The wall seems endless and once Macia starts walking, she feels the relief growing along with the excitement. She is getting away from the Hills! Every step she takes, however small and careful, is taking her towards freedom. After a while she stops for a moment, just to catch her breath. Her legs are shaking, and Macia tugs her dress a little tighter around herself, regretting the loss of the thin blanket. After a short break, she shuffles on again, her feet a little numb already, and she worries that she might hurt herself. The ground is reasonably smooth, but every now and then there is some debris or grit.

On and on she paces, the grey entrance long out of sight, and no other light anywhere. Then the wall disappears under her touch and Macia half shrieks at the suddenness. She stops, blinking in the hope that her eyes will somehow adjust to the pitch darkness, but nothing changes. Is this the end of the tunnel? Is there a sharp bend? She feels around in the dark, eyes stinging with disappointment. What will she do if the tunnel simply ends here?

Macia steps forward, her toes testing every inch ahead. Progress is slow, and Macia can feel the start of panic sprouting in her heart. Four hours. The cameras will be off for four hours, that's all the time she has. In her growing haste, she stumps her toe, and gasps, her knees almost giving way. She rubs the sore spot with her other foot, then on again. Just as her fingertips touch the wall ahead of her, she hears a noise.

Macia freezes. Then, holding her breath, moves her feet towards the wall she just reached. Her fingers dig into the rough stone, her new lifeline. It must have been a gap in the tunnel, maybe an emergency exit? Or another tunnel?

The noise is repeated, and Macia stands still, pressing herself into the wall, breathing as quietly as she can, listening with her eyes shut. There, the scraping noise, somewhere behind her. She pushes herself further into the wall, her heartbeat drowning out all other sounds. She takes a deep breath, this won't do, she needs to hear. The noise sounds closer, this time there is heavy breathing as well, making Macia feel queasy. A footstep? Other loud breathing, grunting noises, and she pushes her forehead into the cold wall, trying to stop the panic from flooding all her systems. The grunting noise comes closer with each wild heartbeat, and Macia is dimly aware that the breathing noise seems close to the ground. Is the other person crawling? The footsteps come closer, a tapping sound, and Macia clenches her jaws to prevent herself from whimpering again. They might not know she is here, she has to be quiet.

The panting noise is now right under her, and suddenly, something hot and wet covers her foot, and Macia shrieks, in vain trying to quell

291

the noise. She sobs in horror, trying to shuffle along the wall, but her legs refuse to obey her. She gives up, her face pressed into the wall. Then a voice, in the darkness. "Is alright, is alright. Is simply Jericho. He's just a dog, he won't do nothing to you, don't be afraid. Jericho, see? Jericho, like in Joshua." The voice is wheezy and slow and somehow manages to rumble through the panic. Macia stops crying but doesn't move, just listens to the words floating down the track. "It's my dog, my Jericho, you see? Jericho. Be strong and of a good courage; be not afraid, neither be thou dismayed, for the Lord thy God is with thee withersoever thou goest, see? Jericho. He will lead you, Jericho will, just be not dismayed or afraid but strong and filled with courage. Just follow Jericho…Jericho…hmmm," and the deep voice mumbles on and on, "Jericho…" The dog, whatever that is, pushes against Macia's legs, in the direction of the tunnel. She hesitates. The…thing, should she go with it? The voice in the dark chuckles, then starts singing, "Joshua fit the battle of Jericho, Jericho… hmmm, Jerichooo," to end in humming and more laughter, and Macia shivers.

The reference to the Lord her God gave her a shock, suddenly making the tunnel feel lighter, the darkness less heavy. Now she doesn't know what to do, for the grunting, slobbering dog at her feet fills her with dread, but the man sounded like the pages, her thin, ancient pages. Was it God, answering her prayers, sending her a guide in the darkness? Resolutely she faces the tunnel, her hand on the cold wall, hissing the nurse's words to herself, "Not much to lose, have you?" No, and everything to gain. "Right, Jericho, lead the way," she whispers, and gasps as the dog makes a whining sound, echoed by the tunnel walls. She shuffles off after the grunting, breathing sounds just in front of her, half looking back towards where the man should be. Is he coming? No, she can hear him singing still, but fainter and fainter, "…fell tumbling down, dooownnnn."

With the animal called 'dog' in front of her, Macia makes slightly better progress, muscle memory helping her to move faster. She's not running, of course, but her legs pick up a steady rhythm like they used to. She still is wary of sharp stones or uneven ground, but at least she knows there will be no other obstacles. A few times she nearly loses her balance as the wall suddenly ends, but she can hear Jericho's nails ticking on the ground, his grunting breath, and his tail touches her knees every now and then. He seems to be swinging it a lot. Macia is exhausted and struggles to stay alert, trusting Jericho to get her out of the tunnel. Her head is heavy, and she finds it harder and harder to keep her eyes open, thinking that in this darkness it doesn't make any difference anyway. She is worried about walking off the track, though, so she blinks, and rubs her eyes on her shoulders.

After a while, her legs are starting to shake, and Macia knows she will need a break. "Jericho, wait," she says to the dog, and she stops. Jericho stops as well, and when she crouches down, he whines and tries to lick her face. Macia manages to stop him in time, "Don't, dog, that's gross," she says, cringing as her voice echoes off the walls around her. What time is it?

She carefully pulls a thin slice out of the package the nurse gave her. Leaning her head against the wall she closes her eyes, savouring each little bite. "Beloved," she writes with her mouth full, "I'm on my way to freedom properly. With me is an animal called a dog. Its name is Jericho. The man that came with him talked about God, and somebody called Joshua. There was a song too," and she smiles at the memory. "Jericho is helping me through this tunnel, and I think I'm making good progress."

Soon she gets up, and Jericho seems happy about this. He makes a funny coughing sound, not loud, but it does spike Macia's heart rate. Will there be guards? She walks on and on, the tunnel feeling endless. She reminds herself that there must be an exit, otherwise the man who was with Jericho would have told her. She walks a bit faster for a few moments as she thinks about that. Still the darkness continues. Macia has to slow down eventually, her legs wobbling more and more, and her head almost too heavy to keep upright. Then Jericho is there, between her and the wall. She feels his rough hairs, and every now and then Jericho nudges her with its nose as if to encourage her. "Thank You, Lord, for my strange companion," she whispers, and Jericho gives another deep coughing sound. It makes her smile, and she leans on the sturdy animal, glad of the warmth that comes from his hairy coat.

In the far distance, Macia is sure there is grey to be seen. She blinks and looks at the little spot again. Yes, it's still there! She walks a little faster, drawn by the hope growing in the distance. Her breath is as noisy as Jericho's and holding up her hand against the wall is suddenly too much. She lowers her hand onto Jericho's soft, velvety head. Her hand is numb from the cold stones, but the dog's head warms her fingers quickly. She absent-mindedly wriggles her fingers into the soft fur, her eyes never leaving the growing grey spot.

The grey spot becomes clearer, and Macia can see the drop quite close to the track they're walking on. It must be the old rail, she realises and shudders. It would be a nasty fall if she misstepped! She walks on, her eyes stinging, but too worn out to cry. Her wrist throbs, her knees buckle every now and then, but the lighter spot is growing with each step. At last, the greyness lights the path she is on, and Macia sighs with relief to see that there is an opening for her to go through. After a few more minutes, she is standing at the exit, one hand on Jericho's head, taking in the nightly scene before her. Where is she? It's still night, but not for long, she can tell. She must have walked for hours. Both are quiet, and the only sound is Jericho's quick panting breaths.

Macia straight away notices the lighthouse. She's at the lighthouse. "Thank You, God," she whispers, her eyes stinging with happiness. It's between her and Elabi, she can tell. She will have to go back a little along the coastline to get to it. Will the paddleboard be there? "Dearest friend, I'm out. I can see our dear lighthouse," and she smiles, fancy getting emotional just from seeing a lighthouse. Macia has to keep blinking tears away, and even though she tries to tell her diary they're purely in her eyes because of exhaustion, she knows better. "Well, beloved, why should I not feel something at seeing the lighthouse? It's far from the Hills, I'm no longer beyond them, and freedom is no longer beyond me either," she giggles, and Jericho makes his cough sound. She pats his head, "You've been a really good help, Jericho, thanks," she says, and dips her head at the dog as he coughs again. "Now, let's get closer to the lighthouse and find that paddleboard, shall we?"

She is tempted to sit down for another short rest, her feet tripping over themselves a few times, but the light sky worries her. She needs to get out of sight as soon as possible. With Jericho's help, she gets close to the lighthouse and looks around, staying hidden from the bright beam flashing across the landscape every few moments. "Now, dog, where would you hide a paddleboard, if you were a nice woman?" she whispers, looking at Jericho. He really is an odd creature, large baleful eyes, brown coat, white face with a rather horrid looking mouth, black and wet. The eyes are sad but sweet, she decides. He tries to lick her as she looks at him, and she dodges aside quickly. "No, yuk, why would you do that, you odd animal," she says, frowning. He merely pants and breathes in her face, making her shudder. "No idea what you ate last," she says, then looks around again. After a while, Jericho clearly is bored with sitting still. He walks around, sniffing at every bush, then, as he disappears around another bush, he does his coughing sound, but louder. Macia's eyes open wide, she will need to stop him, quick, before they are heard! "Jericho, shhh," she hisses desperately and waiting for the right moment, dashes to where she saw him last. There, under a large bush, half-hidden in a gully is a paddleboard,

Jericho standing next to it looking at her sideways.

Chapter 45

Macia tugs at the paddleboard with one hand, grunting and muttering. The smooth board slides out of the gully, and she pulls it along the grass towards the cliff's edges. There must be a path down somewhere. Underneath where the board was she spots the paddle but decides to come back for it. When she looks over her shoulder to see what Jericho is up to, she is happily surprised to see the dog dragging the paddle with its mouth. "Ah, thanks, Jericho," she says, shuddering a little to think of the paddle handle in the dog's slobbery mouth.

Macia finds the narrow path zigzagging down to a little cove, perfect for launching. Her stomach feels tight at the idea of paddling down the river with one arm. Will she be able to balance?

Swaying on her feet, Macia makes it down to the tiny beach. The sand slopes gently to the water; perfect for getting onto the paddleboard. "Thank You, God," she whispers again, and Jericho does his cough. Macia looks at him with a smile, which disappears fast as she sees he no longer carries the paddle! "Jericho! The paddle! You dropped it. How could you be so irresponsible!" The dog merely coughs, and pants at her, sticking its tongue out as if he is laughing, his tail wagging. Macia rolls her eyes, and starts back up the slope, struggling with just one arm. She clenches her jaws, afraid that she will slip and bash her broken wrist. Jericho bounces past her and soon appears with the paddle. Macia frowns, why can't the animal just carry the paddle down without her having to risk climbing up the steep path?

The water is smooth, dark and cool. Macia gasps as she steps into the water, and shudders. Without a wetsuit, she can feel the water touching her skin. She tries not to imagine what could be in the water and forces herself to merely focus on the trip ahead. She can't go towards Elabi and the water sports centre. Soon after the bridges and the centre is the Downstream landing place, and there will be guards all over the place. No, she will have to go the other way. She has no idea where the water will take her. She does know that soon it will turn into a river, going south. Who knows what she will find though? A tiny voice in her heart suggests that she might find Caecilia and more of the Book, but she stops the voice, not wanting to be disappointed at the end of her journey.

She puts the paddle across the board with some difficulty, trying to clamp the board between her knees. Then she looks at the dog, standing on the sandy patch just behind her. "Bye dear Jericho, and thank you very much. You've been a blessing," and she giggles, the odd words sounding funny in the still night air. Macia has wanted to say those words out loud to someone for ages, and here is her chance! Jericho coughs his funny noise, loud but happy.

She turns back to the water, intent now, for if she messes this up, Macia doesn't know what she will do. Slowly she slides her knee onto the board, holding her breath. Shaking and shivering, she finally leans back on her heels, a grin on her face. She is on! Once the board is steady, and her heart rate is back to normal, Macia reaches for the paddle. She decides to stay sitting down on the board, and after a few hair-raising wobbles, she manages to get the paddle in a comfortable grip and starts paddling. Going along with the current, Macia begins to enjoy herself, the Hills feeling very far away. She is still exhausted, but being out on the water is as invigorating as it has always been.

Macia paddles on, conserving energy, as she has no idea how long she will be paddling for. Once the sun is up, she looks around, vaguely wondering about guards. The river is broad and doesn't flow fast, but helps her make good progress. Macia rests the paddle across the board, knowing it will be hard to pick it up again, but she needs to eat. Nibbling her thin slices, she looks around, glad about the light breeze in her very short hair, making her grey dress ripple a little. "I'm free, beloved, free and on my way to wherever the river takes me!" She smiles, and then her eyes open wide. If she makes it to freedom, she might be able to keep a diary properly. How fun that will be! And what about getting the complete Book? Does it exist as one whole book?

The stream goes on and on, and Macia paddles leisurely, resting every now and then. By the time the sun is high in the skies, Macia knows she will have to stop and sleep or risk falling into the water. She soon spots a sheltered bit of beach and slides off the paddleboard without incident. When she wakes up, the sun is further down than she had hoped. "Dearest friend, I had a rest," she mutters, because everything is so very quiet around here, "and now I will need to get back on board, and I will carry on." Macia is sweating by the time she is back on her board and splashes cool river water on her face and arms.

As the sun trails down the sky, Macia feels herself relaxing, excitement growing inside her. The river cuts deep through a gorge, and Macia drinks in the sights. Until there is a shout, high above her head. The paddleboard rocks dangerously as she swings her head from side to side, she shrieks as something hits the water some way behind her. Then she sees them. Guards. Several of them, and one is aiming something at her, and there is a whistling sound as a projectile hits the water just beyond her. Macia grabs the paddle tighter, and paddles for all she is worth. The paddleboard zigzags through the water, as she can only use one arm, but she feels she is doing something at least. The whizzing and pinging sounds come closer, until one chips a tiny chunk out of her board. Macia gives a desperate shriek, then gasps, "Lord, please help me!" The shooting stops, and soon a sharp bend cuts the men off, and Macia sobs with relief. She carries on paddling a bit longer, looking at the cliffs differently. No longer simply beautiful and imposing, they now also are a source of danger.

Darkness slowly swims along the river, overtaking Macia bit by bit. She looks at both sides, hoping to find a safe place to spend the night. She spots a crack in the rocks just in time and manoeuvring against the current, she manages to get the board into the crack, hopefully out of sight. The water is deeper here, and Macia makes sure the board is wedged in, using the paddle as a rudimentary anchor. Slowly she stretches herself out on the smooth board, shivering in the cool air. She'd love to have the thin grey blanket. She dozes off after a while but sleep isn't very deep, hindered by dreams of guards pointing their gun at her, of bullets sinking her board, and slobbery dogs making her foot wet. Macia blinks, as her foot does feel cold and wet. Sitting up carefully she pulls a face as she lifts her foot from the cold river. The sun isn't awake yet, but the sky is light enough to see by, so Macia decides she might as well get up and start off again. She is so thirsty, and once she is out in the middle of the river, she scoops some water in her hand. Should she look at the water, or is it better to simply drink and pray for God's protection? In the end, she greedily drinks the water with her eyes shut, rubbing some over her face to freshen up.

On and on the river goes, and Macia is sure it's cooler as she glides along. Not that she minds, her arms and neck are just that little bit tight after yesterday's time on the water. The cliffs get lower, topped with sweet greenery. She feels anxious at seeing the occasional hut, den or other signs of people. Will they be friendly? Is this still part of Elabi? She's quite sure that Elabi isn't this big, and she wonders if the guards with guns were the border guards.

The river widens out again, and Macia has to paddle with more effort to keep up her speed. Rounding another bend makes her gasp. There are odd, high buildings in the distance, hazy and unclear as yet. Macia stares, her stomach tight. Part of her wants to turn round and go...back? There isn't a way back. It's this unknown place or the Hills and death. Resolutely she picks up the paddle and goes on.

"So, this is Boxing Day?" The dark-haired girl smiles, her sweet voice lilting, and the young man grins at her. "I have enjoyed it, I have, and it's been lovely to go to the Meeting House as well. It makes the day extra special." Caecilia wriggles her toes deeper into the soft sand; she loves the beach, even if it is a river beach. Mataiox is noisy with its vehicles clogging the streets, people talking and general noise. The beach isn't quiet, but sitting on their own towels quickly gives a sense of calm. She smiles at Gax again, and he smiles back.

"Your first Christmas, I hope you have enjoyed it?" He looks a little anxious, for he knows these last few months haven't been easy at all. Escaping from Elabi was the easy part, although he still shudders as he thinks of the long night and day in the freezing weather. They'd both been sore and ended up with nasty colds for a few days. All that seems long ago, but Caecilia hasn't found her new life easy. He is glad to see her smiling though. He opens his mouth to say something, then frowns, staring across the water. Caecilia follows his look and grabs his arm.

"It's someone coming, look! Do you think it could be someone from Elabi?" Gax looks at her for a moment, then frowns back across the water.

The figure is coming closer, and Gax and Caecilia stand up at the same time and run towards the water's edge. They shield their eyes against the lights sparkling on the smooth water and watch. It's a paddleboard with a huddled figure on it. Other people have noticed as well, and a few people get up to watch. Gax looks at Caecilia, "It must be someone from Elabi. Come on, let's get in!" Caecilia nods, and together they wade into the river. Caecilia gasps, the water is cold on her hot skin. They swim to the paddleboard, and the figure with short, uneven hair looks at them. Caecilia gasps, chokes on a mouthful of river water, "Macia?" The huddled figure's eyes open wide, and the tired face lights up.

"Caecilia!"

Gax and Caecilia reach Macia, who suddenly looks too exhausted to care anymore. As they help her off in shallower water, she smiles at them.

"Do you have the Book? The whole Book? Praise God..." Then everything turns black, whilst Gax and Caecilia stare at each other, speechless, eyes shining.

Acknowledgements

Thank you for reading Beyond the Hills. I enjoyed living vicariously through Macia, and seeing the change in her as well as her struggle when she has to choose. I loved seeing the power of the Word of God at work, and I'm so grateful for the freedoms we have and take for granted.

I'd like to say thank you to my editor, Beverley Haagensen, for helping me to make the story so much better. Thank you, Beverley, for your encouragement, prayers and friendship, I really appreciate it! Thank you for your endless patience as well…

I want to thank Richard, my wonderful husband, for supporting me and for being there for me when I need more coffee and time! I'm grateful for many friends who have been such a wonderful support and source of entertainment and joy.

I'm thankful especially to God, *"who at sundry times and in divers manners spoke in times past unto the fathers by the prophets, hath in these last days spoken unto us by His Son,"* and who gave us His Word and Spirit. Seeing Macia and her struggles has given me a greater appreciation of the Bible, and I would love to hear from you if and how Beyond the Hills has encouraged you, too.

Do visit my website, **www.vicarioushome.com** or follow me on Instagram at vicarioush.ome. I love to hear from my readers!

You can buy my other books, *Sapphire Beach*, *Viking Ferry* as well as the first book in the Elabi Chronicles, *Walled City*, from my website or other bookshops.